John Updike was born in 1932 in Shillington, Pennsylvania. He attended Shillington High School, Harvard College and the Ruskin School of Drawing and Fine Art at Oxford, where he spent a year on a Knox Fellowship. From 1955 to 1957 he was a member of the staff of the *New Yorker*, to which he has contributed numerous poems, short stories, essays and book reviews.

John Updike's first novel, *The Poorhouse Fair*, was published in 1959. It was followed by *Rabbit, Run*, the first volume of a series that has since become known as the *Rabbit* books, which John Banville described as 'one of the finest literary achievements to have come out of the US since the war'. *Rabbit is Rich* (1981) and *Rabbit at Rest* (1990) were awarded the Pulitzer Prize for Fiction. Other novels by John Updike include *Marry Me*, *The Witches of Eastwick*, which was made into a major feature film, *In the Beauty of the Lilies*, *Toward the End of Time*, *Gertrude and Claudius* and *Seek My Face*. He wrote a number of volumes of short stories, including the highly acclaimed *The Afterlife and Other Stories* and *Licks of Love*, which includes 'Rabbit Remembered'. *The Early Stories* gathers together almost all his short fiction from the years 1953 to 1975. His essays and criticism which first appeared in magazines such as the *New Yorker* and the *New York Review of Books* have been collected into six volumes, the most recent of which is *More Matter: Essays and Criticism* (1999). *Collected Poems 1953–1993* brings together almost all of his verse, whilst his most recent book of poems is entitled *Americana*. Most of his titles are published by Penguin. John Updike died in 2009.

Charles Shearer was born in Kirkwall, Orkney in 1956. He studied art and design at Gray's School of Art, Aberdeen and Illustration at the Royal College of Art, London. He is a part-time teacher, illustrator, artist and printmaker. His creative workspace will always be a print-room but he finds inspiration in abandoned wastelands, spoil heaps and drowned quarries as well as tumbled mansions where time and weather have worked gloriously in neglect.

Villages

JOHN UPDIKE

PENGUIN BOOKS

PENGUIN BOOKS

UK | USA | Canada | Ireland | Australia
India | New Zealand | South Africa

Penguin Books is part of the Penguin Random House group of companies
whose addresses can be found at global.penguinrandomhouse.com.

Penguin
Random House
UK

First published in the United States of America by Random House, Inc 2004
First published in Great Britain by Hamish Hamilton 2004
Published in Penguin Books 2006
This Penguin Essentials edition published 2018
001

David Updike walked me through MIT, and Charles Gardiner and Ken
Schneider kindly scanned the computer parts of this novel. But errors
and missteps are all my own. — J. U.

Portions of the first four chapters were previously published in the *New
Yorker* magazine under the titles "Sin: Early Impressions,"
"Elsie by Starlight" and "Village Sex—II"

Printed in Great Britain by Clays Ltd, St Ives plc

A CIP catalogue record for this book is available from the British Library

ISBN: 978–0–241–98379–9

www.greenpenguin.co.uk

Ah, love, let us be true
To one another! for the world, which seems
To lie before us like a land of dreams,
So various, so beautiful, so new,
Hath really neither joy, nor love, nor light,
Nor certitude, nor peace, nor help for pain. . . .

—MATTHEW ARNOLD, "Dover Beach"

Chapters

VILLAGES

i. *Dream On, Dear Owen*

FOR A LONG TIME, his wife has awoken early, at five or five-thirty. By the rhythms of her chemistry, sometimes discordant with Owen's, Julia wakes full of affection for him, her companion on the bed's motionless voyage through that night of imperfect sleep. She hugs him and, above his protests that he is still sleeping, declares in a soft but relentless voice how much she loves him, how pleased she is by their marriage. "I'm just so happy with *you*."

This after twenty-five years of life together. He is seventy, she sixty-five; her announcement, newsworthy to her, slightly insults him: how could it be otherwise? After all their trials, and the pain they gave others. They waded through; here they are, on the other side. She tugs at him; she twists his head in order to kiss his mouth. But his lips are puffy and numb with sleep, and in his anesthetized state, his nerves misaligned, it feels like an attempt to suffocate him; it rubs him, as people used to say, the wrong way. After a few minutes more of lovestricken fidgeting, while he stubbornly fails to respond, protecting the possibility of returning to his precious dreams, Julia relents and rises from the bed, and Owen, gratefully stretching himself into her vacated side, falls asleep for another hour or two.

One morning in this last, stolen hour he dreams that, in a house he does not know (it has a shabby, public air to it, as of a boarding-house or a hospital), faceless official presences guide him into a room where, on a bed like theirs, two single beds yoked together to make a king-size, a man—rather young, to judge from the smoothness of his blond body, with its plump buttocks—lies upon his wife's body as if attempting resuscitation or (not at all the same thing) concealment. When, under silent direction from the accompanying, officiating presences, this stranger removes himself, Owen's wife's body, also naked, is revealed, supine: the white relaxed belly, the breasts flattened by gravity, her dear known sex in its gauzy beard of fur. She is dead, a suicide. She has found the way out of her pain. Owen thinks, *If I had not interfered with her life, she would be still alive.* He yearns to embrace her and breathe her back to life and suck back into himself the poison that his existence has worked upon hers.

Then, slowly, reluctantly, as one lifts one's attention from a still-unsolved puzzle, he wakes up, and of course she is not dead; she is downstairs generating the smell of coffee and the rumble of an early news show: several bantering voices, male and female. Traffic and weather, Julia loves them both, they never cease to interest her, these chronic daily contingencies, though she quit commuting to Boston three years ago. He can hear the blue rubber flip-flops she insists on wearing, as if forever young and dressed for a beach, slap back and forth in the kitchen, refrigerator to countertop to breakfast table, and then to sink and trashmasher and dishwasher and on into the dining room, watering her plants.

She loves her plants with the same emotional organ, perhaps, with which she loves the weather. The noise the flip-flops make, and the hazard they represent to her footing—she keeps slipping on the stairs—irritate him, but he does like the sight of her bare toes, spread slightly apart, as on hardworking Asian feet, their little joints whitened by the tension of keeping her flip-flops on. She is a small, densebodied brunette; unlike his first wife, she takes a good smooth tan.

Some days, half-roused, he finds the way back to sleep only by remembering one of the women, Alissa or Vanessa or Karen or Faye, who shared with him the town of Middle Falls, Connecticut, in the 'sixties and 'seventies. His hand gripping his drowsy prick, he relives having one of them beneath him, beside him, above him, brushing back her hair as she bends her face to his swollen core, its every nerve crying out for moist, knowing contact; but today is not one of those days. The strengthening white sun of spring glares brutally beneath the window shade. The real world, a tiger unwounded by his dream, awaits. It is time to get up and shoulder a day much like yesterday, a day that his animal optimism assumes to be the first of a sequence stretching endlessly into the future but that his cerebrum—hypertrophied in the species *Homo sapiens*—knows to be one more of a diminishing finite supply.

The village, so-called, of Haskells Crossing awakens around their private hill; the steady dull whir of traffic presses through the pine and plaster house walls and the insulating woods beyond. The newspapers—the *Boston Globe* for him, the *New York Times* for her—have already been delivered. Birds long have been astir, the robins picking after worms, the crows boring into the lawn for chinchbug grubs, the swallows snatching mosquitoes from midair, kind calling to kind in their jubilant pea-brained codes. He shouts down the stairs on his way to the bathroom, "Good morning, Julia!"

Her cry returns: "Owen! You're up!"

"Sweetie, of course I'm up; my goodness, it's after seven o'clock."

The older they get, the more they talk like children. Her voice comes up the stairs, lightly arguing, semi-teasing: "You always sleep to eight, now that you have no train to catch."

"Darling, what a liar you are! I *never* sleep past seven; I wish I could," he goes on, though uncertain if she has moved away from the stairs and can't hear him, "but that's one of the things of old age, you're up with the birds. Wait until it hits *you*."

This is connubial nonsense: talk about pea-brained codes. If the day were a computer, he thinks, this is how it boots up, reloading main memory. Julia in fact sleeps less than he (as did his first wife, Phyllis), but her being five years younger has always been for him a source of pride and sexual stimulus, like the sight of her toes at the front of her blue flip-flops. He also likes to see, below her bathrobe, her pink heels as they retreat, the vertical strokes of her Achilles tendons alternating, one quick firm step after the other, her feet splayed outward in the female way.

They hold this conversation while he waits, his bladder aching, outside the door to his bathroom, beside the stairs that descend to the kitchen. The image of his beloved Julia lying naked and dead in his dream, and the dream sensation of guilt that made her suicide in reality a murder committed by him, are still more vivid than the daily waking facts—the wallpaper with its sepia roses and muted metallic gloss, the new hall carpet with its fresh beige nap and thick, springy undercarpet, the day ahead with its hours to climb like rungs on an ancient, dangerous, splintering ladder.

While Owen shaves at the mirror mounted by the window, where his pouchy and sun-damaged old face, cruelly magnified, frontally accepts the pitiless light, he hears the mockingbird, mounted on its favorite perch at the tip of the tallest cedar, deliver a thrilling long scolding about something or other, some minor, chronic procedural matter. All these local levels of Nature—the birds, the insects, the flowers, the furtive fauna of chipmunks and woodchucks scuttling in and out of their holes as if a shotgun might blast them the next instant—have their own network of concerns and communications; the human world to them is merely a marginal flurry, an inscrutable static, an intermittent interference rarely lethal and bearing no perceived relation to the organic bounty (the garbage, the gardens) that the human species brings to Nature's table. *They snub us*, Owen thinks. We should be gods to them, but they lack our capacity for worship—for foresight and the terrors and convoluted mental grovelling that foresight brings with it, including the invention of an afterlife. Animals do not distinguish between us and the other beasts, or between us and the rocks and trees, each with its pungence and relevance to the struggle for existence. The earth offers haven to scorpions and woodchucks and quintillions of ants; the stars guide the Canada geese and arctic terns, the barn swallows and monarch butterflies in their immense annual migrations. We are mere dots beneath their wings, our cities foul and barren interruptions in the discourse of predator and prey. No, not interruptions, for many species accept our cities as habitats, not just the rats in the cellar and the bats in the attic but the hawks and pigeons on the skyscraper ledges and now the deer brazenly, helplessly stalking through sub- urban back yards, both pets and pests.

Owen stiffens his lower lip to take the razor's ticklish sideways scrape. He tries to shave without seeing his face, which has never been exactly the face he wanted—too much nose, not enough chin. An inviting weakness, and yet a sharp-eyed wariness. Lately, creases drag at the corners of his mouth, and the eyelids are wrinkled like a desert rep- tile's, so that their folds snag and weigh on his lashes in the morning. He hates that familiar feeling of something in his eye, elusive but bothersome. Pollen. An eyelash. A burst capillary. Behind him, through the insulating woods, the sounds of engines, of backfiring, and of backing trucks' warning beep, make felt the skimpy commercial section, a block or two long, of Haskells Crossing; it is audible but not visible from his house in its leafy hilltop concealment. Though he can see the lights of the town clearly from his upstairs windows, he has never found a spot in town from which his house is visible. That pleases him; it is like his consciousness, invisible but central.

As a child he assumed that somehow the world was set in motion by his awaking. What happened before he awoke was like the time before he was born, a void he could not contemplate. It always surprises him how early, in villages as well as cities, morning activity begins, not just among fabled worm-catching birds but among men—the com- muter hastening to catch the 6:11 train, the owner of the fruit store in town already back with his truck from the open market near the Callahan Tunnel, the jogging young mothers having done their miles before standing with their children at the bus stop, the village idlers already stationed on their bench by the war memorial, there next to the old brick fire station, across the main street from the bakery. The baker, an ill-shaved French Canadian with a chest sunken from too many cigarettes, has been up since four, tinging the cold air with the fragrance of baking croissants, cinnamon rolls, and blueberry muffins.

Owen can see it all in his mind's eye as he scrapes at the last of the shaving soap, thrusting his insufficient chin forward to smooth the slack creases underneath. The fire station, if you want to know, is an ornate nineteenth-century structure almost too narrow for the modern fire truck recently purchased by the aldermen in Cabot City, of which Haskells Crossing is an outlying ward; after each call, usually a false alarm, the truck backs into its berth, excitedly beeping, with only a few inches to spare on either side. The war memorial is an expandable list of names, movable white letters on a black, slotted surface behind glass, the dead from Haskells Crossing listed back to the French and Indian War. The largest group fell in the Civil War, the next largest in World War II. Below the Korean conflict (two names) and the Vietnam intervention (four) and the 1991 Iraqi action (a single name, an enlisted man accidentally crushed while helping unload a sixty-seven-ton M1A1 Abrams heavy-armor battle tank from the belly of a C-5 Galaxy cargo plane at Saudi Arabia's Jabayl Airfield), a considerable space has been left for future casualties, in future conflicts. Sensible New England thrift: Owen likes it. He has found his final village here.

The first was in Pennsylvania: the borough of Willow, population four thousand, a "string town" grown, as the nineteenth century became the twentieth, from a wayside inn along the road, surrounded by fields growing corn and tobacco. The road, following a southeasterly river for forty-five miles, eventually reached Philadelphia but was here called Mifflin Avenue, after the quarrelsome first governor of the Keystone State. Three miles in another direction lay a medium-sized city, Alton—Alton, with its factories of blackened brick set right in amid the row houses, its railroad tracks cutting the downtown in two, its red-light district called Pussy Alley, its corner bars faced in Permastone, its movie palaces of pseudo-Islamic grandeur, and its noisy, porky restaurants. "Rip-off joints," his father called the restaurants. His father hated eating out; he hated being waited on, especially by men, who he felt were more expensive and bullying than waitresses; he hated rich restaurant food, which he sometimes vomited later, as a sign of contempt; he hated dessert, the sales tax, and the tip. Owen's mother, overweight in all but her son's earliest memories of her, loved eating well, and would sit there cowed and fuming while her husband methodically ruined her pleasure. Or so it seemed to their only child, who read the marital drama from a limited point of view: though his hair was the dull, safe brown of his father's—hair so fine it lifted from their heads when they removed their hats or sat near an electric fan—his sympathies lay with his auburn-haired mother. Yet his father's fear of running out of money sank into his stomach, and gnawed there. Perhaps by no accident did his life's migration take him northeast, to a region of rocky, shallow soil and reluctant expenditure.

In Pennsylvania, the sandstone inns—seeds of villages some of which thrived and expanded while others became a decaying huddle—were spaced every three miles or so, the distance a man could walk in an hour or a team of horses could pull a farm wagon on a summer day without needing to be watered. Farm life still controlled time. Old people dozed in the middle of the day. Neighbors on the street peddled asparagus, beans, and tomatoes grown in their back yards to one another, and Mifflin Avenue, with its high crown that made rainwater rush in the gutters, resounded in the morning to the languid hoofbeats of horses drawing wagons to the farmers' market a half-mile away, on the far side of the central thoroughfare, the Alton Pike, which had trolley tracks in its center. By the time Owen was born, in 1933, and was brought home for lack of another home to his grandfather's house in Willow, Roosevelt was newly in office, and the village, named for a huge old tree hard by the inn, its roots watered by the creek that meandered toward Philadelphia, had been incorporated as a borough. It had grown secondary streets parallel to Mifflin Avenue— Second Street, and then Third and Fourth, climbing a hill where children sledded in winter, down the packed snow, bouncing through the barricaded intersections, until the ride ended with a spurt of sparks on a bed of cinders the borough crew had shovelled from a truck. The sparks, the packed snow, the Christmas trees in the front parlors all along the walk to school—these lasted for only a few days, spotted through a drab, damp winter, but made memories that lasted all year and tugged time forward in a child's virtual eternity.

Warm weather lasted from March to October. A haze settled over Willow. Owen's little bedroom, with its wainscoted walls and single bookshelf, overlooked a vacant lot where he often played with the other children of the neighborhood, for an hour after supper in summer, in a milky twilight, the long grass scratchy, going to seed. Fungo, kick-the-can, touch football: girls played them all, since the neighborhood held more girls than boys. Once, in the lot's matted grasses, flattened and wet with dew—for it was fall and school had begun again—Owen came upon his glasses in the brown snap case that had vanished some days before.

Found! He had looked everywhere in the house, and his mother had confided what a grief it would be for his poor father to have to pay for a replacement pair. It was a miracle, it seemed to the child as he bent down and took the case, damp with its nights and days of patiently waiting for him to find it, into his hand. Inside, yes, were the gold-rimmed disks that sharpened his sight, the little bean-shapes that left dents in his nose, the curved metal handles that hurt his ears. When he had been told, in second grade, that he must wear glasses for reading and the movies, he had cried. Some day, he consoled himself, he would outgrow them. Perhaps his finding them was less than a miracle, for he took this diagonal path through the weeds every day to meet Buddy Rourke, his friend from the class above his, so they could walk to school together, away from the pack of girls from Second Street. Buddy had no father, which made him strange and slightly frightening. He was moody, with hairs between his eyebrows. He had straight coarse hair that bristled forward and a mouth that never smiled, because of braces, shiny metal bands with a silver square in the middle of each tooth. Owen wanted to run back to tell his mother that he had found his glasses and his father wouldn't have to pay for new ones, but he didn't want to be late for Buddy, and hurried on, the recovered case making the pocket of his knickers damp, so the skin of his thigh tingled.

From this same side of the house, beyond the lot, early on another morning, Owen heard the sound of a shot. He had been sleeping. He seemed to awake in the moment *before* hearing, as if in a dream, the noise that had awoken him. He had seen enough gangster movies to know the sound of gunpowder under percussion, but in the movies it came in machine-gun waves, whereas this was a single, lonely sound.

His parents heard it, too, for they stirred in their bedroom, beyond his closed door, and the two voices, male and female, intertwined and then fell silent again. It was not quite dark outside; the trees in the side yard had silhouettes, their masses welling into that wash of gray light, with a faint tan tinge to the sky, before birds began to twitter. The street was silent, devoid of traffic, even a farm wagon. Later, he heard a siren, and later still the news, reported at breakfast by his father, who had been up the street news-gathering, that a young man in the Hoffmans' household, two doors up from the house next to the vacant lot, had shot himself, with a service revolver, a Colt .38, that Wes Hoffman had kept from his time in the Great War. Danny Hoffman was not yet twenty, but a child under his supervision at a summer camp had dived into shallow water and broken his neck, and his responsibility had haunted him, though it had happened a summer ago. Danny had never been the same; he had stayed in the house listening to the radio serials and had stopped looking for a job.

That explained that. In a dozen years of Depression and World War II, from 1933 to 1945, it was the most dramatic event in Owen's neighborhood. The woman across the street, Mrs. Yost, had a five-star flag in her front window, but all five soldier-sons came back in fine fettle. Skip Potteiger got Mary Lou Brumbach next door pregnant when she was only seventeen but then he married her so it was all right—by D-Day the baby was in a carriage that Mary Lou pushed back and forth on her way to the Acme, over the shallow troughs that carried roof water out to the gutter and the sidewalk squares that the roots of the horse-chestnut

trees were tilting up, tripping you if you were on roller
skates. On hot summer evenings the sounds of family quar-
rels would come across the street from the screened windows of the crowded row houses on the other side, the high
side, up cement steps in the retaining walls that leaned outward precariously. But there were no divorces, as Owen
remembered things. Voices were raised and shouts and
door-slams cut through the neighborhood, but divorces
happened elsewhere, in Hollywood and New York, and
were tragic scandals, producing what nobody and certainly
no child wanted: a broken home. The very phrase had a sinful, terrible sound and the ashen taste of disaster, like the
bombed and smoking houses that filled the Fox Movietone
newsreels at the Scheherazade, the local movie theatre. The
world was full of destruction and evil, and only the United
States, it seemed, could put it right. The country was at
war, and in Owen's fantasy the vacant lot in view of his
bedroom was a bomb crater, overgrown with weeds.

The original willow tree still lived, coddled like an old
dignitary with injections of pesticide and fertilizer thrust
into its roots by making holes with a crowbar; it survived
from the time when there had been a paper mill with a
water wheel, and a pond stocked with trout, and a dirt race-
track, with harness races, before a grid of streets was laid
out on the level low land north of the Pike. Owen's house—
not his house, really, and not even his parents'; it belonged
to his mother's parents, Isaac and Anna Rausch—was one
of the older and bigger along Mifflin Avenue, bought by his
grandfather when he felt rich from growing leaf tobacco in
the First World War. He sold his farm and moved ten miles
to this newly fashionable borough of Willow. Then, with
the Depression, his savings melted away and his daughter
and her husband and child moved in. One couple had a

house, the other had some earning ability. Owen's father was an accountant for one of the knitting mills in Alton. Owen's auburn-haired, then-slender mother sold draperies in an Alton department store until her little boy pricked her conscience by running after her down Mifflin Avenue, sobbing, as she was on her way to catch the trolley car; she quit the job to spend more time with him. His father, Floyd Mackenzie, came from Maryland. Owen had been named after a sickly grandfather who had died before he was born, but who, by the family's legendary accounts, had had a twinkle, a sprightliness and inventiveness of mind, they thought of as Scots. He owned a hardware store in Mt. Airy, this original Owen, and in his spare time had invented things, improvements on the implements he sold—a weed-extractor a person could operate without bending over, a hedge-trimmer geared to make the crank turn much easier—but no company had ever taken up their manufacture and made him rich. He died bankrupt and tubercular. Yet a glimmer of his hopes of outwitting the hard world descended to his grandson. The Mackenzies were not rich but were clever, canny. Owen's father told him, "You take after my old man. You have his intellectual curiosity. He liked to sit and figure out how things worked. Me, I never wondered about anything except where my next dollar was coming from." Daddy said this somewhat mournfully, as if the Mackenzie heritage was a mixed blessing—a hopeful imagination mixed with a certain frailty of constitution and essential ignorance of the way the world worked as it ground away day by day and picked your pockets.

His other grandfather, whom Owen lived with, had also a touch of the dreamer, selling his farm and investing in stocks that became worthless. He was a Pennsylvania German, but of an adaptable strain, speaking English perfectly, reading the afternoon newspaper faithfully, ornamenting his idleness with large thoughts and stately pronouncements. Owen recognized in the old man, with his yellowish mustache and white hair and gracefully gesturing hands, the wistfulness of the partial outsider, who had not quite found his way to the sources of power, the decisive secrets, in the only environment he knew.

"Pop should have been a politician, he has the gift of gab," his son-in-law would say; but even Owen could see that his grandfather was too fastidious for politics, too passive-minded as he moved through his day, from the back yard, where he hoed and weeded a vegetable garden and could smoke a cigar, to his upstairs bedroom, where he took a nap, to the caneback sofa in the living room, where he sat waiting for Grammy to prepare the evening meal. His house was in Willow but, except for its lone child and Grammy, not quite of it. Grammy was a Yoder, the youngest of ten siblings, a member of a populous clan spread throughout the county. Willow was full of her relatives, cousins and nieces and nephews; sometimes she earned spare money by helping one of them with a big spring housecleaning, or helping prepare and serve a meal for a large gathering. These relatives had money: they owned small businesses or had good positions in the hosiery mills, wore nice clothes, and took vacations in the Poconos or along the Jersey Shore. When Owen heard them speak fondly of "Aunt Annie," in that slow-spoken sentimental vein that country people once so easily slipped into, he at first had trouble realizing that they meant Grammy. We are different people, he realized, to different people.

After Owen had left it behind, his original village seemed an innocent, precious place, but it did not strike him as that while he lived there. It was the world, with a fathomless past and boundaries that were over the horizon. There were snakes in the grass and in piles of rocks warmed by the sun. Sex and religion had distinct, ancient odors; families perched like shaky nests on tangled twigs of previous history; and death could pounce in the middle of the night. In the period of young Danny Hoffman's suicide, when Owen was still a child sleeping beneath a shelf holding two dozen Big Little Books, a one-eyed teddy bear called Bruno, and a rubber Mickey Mouse with a bare black chest and yellow shoes, a big horse-barn on the edge of Willow—the Blake farm, the property of absentee rich people from Delaware—burned down, and his father, who chased after disasters like a boy, reported how the horses, led to safety outside, in their terror bolted back inside, and how terrible the stench of their burning flesh and horsehair was. In the sky from Owen's window that night, an orange glow silhouetted the roof and chimneys of the house next to the vacant lot, and the tallest spruces and hemlocks in people's back yards beyond. The town fire sirens blasted again and again, enormous angry cries to which no answer came. As on the morning of the gunshot, Owen had rolled over and gone back to sleep, letting the world's torrents of pain wash over him.

ii. *Village Sex—I*

KILLING YOURSELF was the ultimate sin, the Bible said, according to Owen's Sunday-school teachers; especially strict on this and other scores was pale-faced, iron-haired Mr. Dickinson, who managed the bank. Killing yourself was worse than killing a man in self-defense, which was what the Yost boys were doing overseas. It was as if, on quiet Mifflin Avenue, where the milk wagons still made the early morning ring with the lazy sound of horseshoes on asphalt, a crater had opened up next to Owen's bedroom, a crater of dreadful possibility, a denial of everything, of trees and birds and blue sky and the blessed rest of Nature. Buddy Rourke's father had fallen into that crater, but he hadn't intended to, or perhaps— it wasn't clear, and Buddy didn't want to talk about it—the father was still alive, but living somewhere else, with another family. He had, the word was, "strayed."

There was another kind of sin, also dizzying. On the back wall of the Willow playground-equipment shed, a child's red crayon had scribbled two penises (the proper word was), their tips touching. Close by, an older, more knowing hand had incised in a pencil that gouged its lines deep into the yellow-painted wood what looked like a swollen letter M but, on examination, was a naked woman, legs bent at the knee and spread to reveal between them a slit, a pumpkin-seed shape, curls of hair around and above it, and below it a dot that Owen could not name even to himself, in the silence of his head, it was so shameful. Refining his idea, the artist showed between the thighs two breasts with blackened, erect nipples and, between *them*, what Owen deciphered as the underside of a nose with its two nostrils. The woman was opening herself to be (as older boys said) fucked: that was clear. Why would she do this? That was not clear. Yet it was certain that a woman somewhere had allowed herself to be viewed this way and drawn so that this image could be reproduced here. She had no arms or head and her ankles trailed off without feet; the artist felt that these were inessential. The essential parts of her were depicted, and something stirred below Owen's belly in acknowledgment that this was true: what mattered most was shown. The slit, the hair, the little dot, and nipples aimed upward like stubby anti-aircraft guns.

Yet the girls all around him seemed remote from these essentials. They had brown legs from being at the playground all summer, and could run as fast as he. They liked to win at all the games—roof ball and box hockey and Chinese checkers. Ginger Bitting, a girl in his class from Second Street, would hang upside down from the jungle gym, hanging on with only her bent legs while her arms, thin and freckled and with a whitish fuzz, reached down toward the dust, and her long hair, clay-red and fine like the dust, hung down between her arms. If her legs let go she would drop and might break her neck, as did the boy at camp under poor Danny Hoffman's care. But she never did. Ginger, with her freckles, and her eyes like green glass a light was shining through, was the most daring, the most wiry girl in his class at grade school, the fastest on her feet, the best singer, and the captain of the girls' team when the boys played them at soccer at recess. If she stole his cap or plaid book bag on the way home from school he could never catch her until she let him. On the playground swing she would kick out and soar; the swing chains would snap and tug and shake the pipe frame, pulling her back from falling as she reached horizontal; still she kicked higher, her brown legs stiff. He watched her feet reach for the sky, in their creased and scuffed leather shoes. Back then, he could wear ankle-high sneakers in summer but girls wore real shoes, with laces and smooth soles.

The playground was approached from the alley behind Owen's house, on a path between two cornfields, and then along a kind of grassy road between the baseball bleachers and a row of cherry trees gone wild. Ginger would climb these trees in her slippery shoes, higher than Owen would ever dare. He would watch her as she ascended, but he never saw up her shorts anything like the complicated business drawn on the back of the equipment shed. In the quiet, long-shadowed hour after the playground supervisor and the other children had gone home, and the equipment—the hockey sticks and Ping-Pong paddles and checkerboards— was all locked up, Owen would experiment on the jungle gym, hanging by his arms and bent knees and daring himself to let go with his hands. But he never could. If he fell and broke his neck he would lie there all night, darkness and dew covering him, and be found only in the morning, when the supervisor, bossy, fussy Miss Mull, arrived at nine o'clock to run up the flag on the pole and lead the assembled children in the Pledge of Allegiance.

Ginger had satellites, though the girls around her perhaps did not think of themselves that way. Each person probably thought of herself, though it was hard to believe, as the center of the universe, just as Owen did. There were a lot of Barbaras—Barbara Emerich, Barbara Jane Gross, Barbara Dolinski—and Alice Stottlemeyer and Georgene King and Carolyn McManus and Grace Bickta, all from Owen's street or the streets above, who collected on the sidewalks and walked together to elementary school and back. It was Alice Stottlemeyer, shorter than the others and, like Owen, saddled with glasses on her nose, who first kissed him with a secret meaning, a sort of push with her mouth, tight but soft, at a game of spin-the-bottle they were playing at somebody's birthday party, not Owen's. His own birthday parties, when his mother gave them, were usually disasters that sent him up the stairs to his room crying, because his guests were having more fun than he, the birthday boy, who had not received exactly the presents he had hoped for. His mother would never allow the game of spin-the-bottle. Their glasses clicked, his and Alice's, in the little kiss while the other children crowed and jeered and then fell silent, seeing they were kissing seriously, all in a second. Then the bottle spun on, in the center of the ring they made, on the linoleum floor or painted concrete floor of the basement they were in, converted to a den or rumpus room.

That was one of the many social distinctions that criss-crossed Willow, the one between people who had basements converted into recreation rooms, with panelling and carpeting and easy chairs, and those who, like Owen's family, the Rausch-Mackenzies, still had cellars, with a sinister bin of filthy coal and cobwebbed shelves of preserves in Mason jars and a spatter-painted old washing machine, tub-shaped and fitted with a wringer of rubber. The wet clothes would emerge from between the two cylinders of white rubber like giant wrinkled tongues and slowly spill into the wicker clothes basket. Owen, when younger even than when Alice Stottlemeyer kissed him, and not yet envious of families with easy chairs and dartboards and electric-train tracks set up on plywood tables in their basements, was enchanted by the plugged-in washing machine's powerful, rhythmic back-and-forth beating action, stirring up a mass of bubbles, and by the smell of soap flakes, so strong it seemed to scour clean his head and sinuses, and by the woody, springy scent of the wicker basket, with its handles so far apart he could not at first reach both at once. It was inevitable that some day he stick his fingers in the wringer. In a quick rush he felt the relentless pressure climbing toward his wrist, and screamed in terror. It was one of those moments when the hungry chasm beneath the sunny daily surface of things rises up, like the gunshot before dawn, but not as bad; a safety device popped the wringers apart even before his mother could dart around him and reach the release lever. In the way of childhood confusions her alarm, and the look of horror that distended her face there in the bare-bulbed cellar light, and the scolding she gave him afterwards got lumped with his moment of pain, as if she had caused it. Still, he remained an admirer of the process, the wash travelling through the wringer into the basket and up the cellar stairs through the bulkhead door into the back yard, where the white bedsheets hung about him like the billowing walls of a fragile castle, a jungle palace he was exploring all by himself. A shift of breeze would cause the clothes pole to lean in a different direction, so that his face was brought into abrupt contact with the towering, damp, light-flooded cotton.

Handing up clothespins to Momma or Grammy was one of his first ways of being useful. The little clothespin basket had no fresh wicker smell, it was dark from being handled, by women's hands, year after year, dating back to before Grammy, who had inherited it, a coil of fiber bound into a bowl hard as clay, made of "sweetwater grasses" by slaves or Indians, he didn't know which. The basket had the musky darkness of the ancient time before cars and movies, radios and light bulbs, long before Owen was born. It was a little heavier and stonier than expected when you touched it, whereas the clothespins were a little lighter. With their two legs and flat knobs at the other end like sailor hats, they were smooth in his hand and could be turned with colored pencils into staring, smiling little men, wearing sailor hats and blue coats. They could be made to do tricks, stuck together like acrobats.

It was too bad Alice wasn't prettier and taller, and that, like Owen, she got good marks at school. She was bright, which made her boring. He was drawn to the tough, dare-devil girls from families his own looked down on, because of some whispered ancestral taint or scandal or because the father drank or did manual labor or was not nice to the mother. Did this not-niceness take the form of hitting her, or calling her names, or something else, furtive and dirty, that happened? Even in Willow, let alone Alton, there were places, bars and pool halls and bowling alleys, that smelled of misbehavior, of sinful transaction. In the nameless gravel alley that ran beside the hedge of Owen's yard and then at a right angle behind the asbestos-shingled chicken house his grandfather had built when he first moved to Willow, and then past several garages and small barns at the bottom of people's yards and a tarpaper shack called a gun shop where a one-eyed man named Smokey Frye noisily pounded and ground metal at odd hours, there was a windowless cinder-block building that a sign above the door identified in hand-painted letters as the Gifford Pinchot Wildlife Society, from which drifted the sounds of men drinking and playing cards. The grown-ups of Willow needed their fun, and for young people there was a recreation hall, the "Rec Hall," opposite the elementary school, where kids older than Owen danced and played pinball and smoked outside the doors. It was said that a girl two classes ahead of his, Carol Wisniewski, had let herself be fucked by Marty Naftzinger standing up, there in the shadowy, gritty space between the Rec Hall and the factory building beside it, where they made hosiery and then, during the war, parachutes.

Willow during the war, as Owen went from eight to twelve, was like a prairie village brushed by black clouds that sweep low overhead but do not discharge their tornado, though at the Scheherazade there were newsreels of airplanes turning cities into fields of fire and of GIs storming sandy island beaches strafed by fanatical Japanese who had to be burned out of their caves with flamethrowers like nests of insects. While the great Eurasian continent from end to end seethed with moving masses and vast death and the oceans drank torpedoed ships, North America held its breath, a land of women and children and old men and price controls and rationing tokens and war stamps and Hollywood comedians on the radio. Yet the tingle of global gambles filled the air and enthralled their island of peace: there was a speeding-up, a sense of stakes higher than the old proprieties. Carol Wisniewski let herself be fucked by Marty Naftzinger standing up, and Momma took a job at the parachute factory and did plane-spotting on the roof of the fire station, playing solitaire with a special deck of cards, and Grampy came out of his retirement to work on the borough highway crew, and Daddy put on a warden's helmet in air-raid drills looking for light leaks from the windows along Mifflin Avenue. Owen took the paper off of tin cans and jumped on them, flattening them on the cement floor of the chicken house for the war effort, while the chickens rustled and cackled on their crusty rungs, or in the cubbyholes where glass eggs lured them into laying more. The eggs—brown, speckled, dabbled with dung—Grammy sold in reused paper egg cartons to her many relatives, and the flattened tin cans piled up on the school grounds, making a shining mountain which only Chub Kroninger, the three-star general of fifth-grade scrap collection, was allowed to climb. Promotion was achieved by weighing the metal turned in, and Owen's family was too small and poor to furnish enough scrap metal to raise him in the ranks. Daddy had taken to rolling his own cigarettes on a clever little machine; the store-bought packs had been a main source of tinfoil, along with sticks of chewing gum.

When Owen suggested to Buddy Rourke that he donate his braces to the scrap drive, Buddy didn't think it was funny. Buddy was a serious boy, headed for a career in engineering or construction or electricity. He could fix lamps, knowing how to insert and screw down hook-shapes of copper wire into the terminals of a switch and how to splice the wires of Christmas lights when a bad socket made the whole string dark. He taught Owen how to tame a current which would flow one way with magical, instant results but which with contacts reversed would balk and melt the wires. Buddy subscribed to *Popular Mechanics* and had sent away for a make-it-yourself radio kit that he had assembled to the point where you could hear static and a faint voice pulsing in and out. Though the two boys could achieve great rapport working on projects in Buddy's cellar—not quite a rumpus room but better-lit than Owen's, with a well-stocked workbench that had been created and abandoned by Buddy's absent father—there was a potential awkwardness in the relationship because of Buddy's being a year and a half older. Once, anticipating Buddy's coming to his house one afternoon to play Monopoly—a game the boys for a season were passionate about, between their passions for gin rummy and chess—Owen had set up the board on the living-room rug with a loving elaboration, arranging the Chance and Community Chest cards in a spiral, like the staircases in Hollywood musicals, and setting out the red hotels and green wooden houses in a formal pattern, a perfect Christmas-colored village as if seen from an airplane.

Buddy, coming into the room, said with limpid disgust, "Oh, Owen!" and scrabbled the cards into the usual rough stack and dumped the hotels and houses back into the box. Owen was stung, and tried for the rest of his life not to risk showing how much he cared for somebody and then looking foolish. Make sure the circuits are established before plugging anything in: otherwise, meltdown.

After a fight over something soon forgotten, leaving the basement in tears, Owen heard himself yelling at Buddy, the crowning insult: "At least I have a father!"

To taunt his friend with this, his lack of a father—he was appalled at himself. Shame bubbled up like mucky black water when his foot went through thin ice in the swamp beyond the high-school grounds. Though he tried to apologize the next day, he was not sure the easy trust between him and Buddy was ever quite restored. Besides wiring things and gluing airplane models together, they used to spend hours making childish artifacts of no clear utility—

plywood cutouts of Disney characters, for example. Owen would hold his breath as he delicately steered the thin blade of his coping saw around some fragile protuberance like Goofy's muzzle or Mickey's ears. Creatures from all the animated Disney cartoons, plus green-skinned gremlins invented to illustrate wartime slang, populated hundreds of armed-forces insignia; it almost seemed that Disney and Hollywood were running the war, with its cast of millions. Buddy wanted to be in the Corps of Engineers, making bridges for armies to cross on; Owen wanted to be a test pilot, pulling out of dives at the last second. He had met Buddy, in fact, while playing with a rubber-tracked toy M-4 tank in the playground sandbox, and this taller boy had come over and offered to show him his collection of model airplanes—P-51s and Zeros and Spitfires and Messerschmitts, some lead models and some he had carved himself out of balsa wood—in his basement, which was just up beyond the cornfield, a mere six odd house numbers from Owen's house, and three beyond the ill-fated Hoffmans'. The Rourkes—Buddy and his mild-mannered mother and twerpy younger sister—lived not exactly in a house but in the first floor and basement of a double house, of yellow brick, fairly new. It held four families all told, people who couldn't afford a house of their own, and this was a little like living on Second Street, or having a father who was not nice to your mother.

Owen was grateful he did not live in an apartment, just as he was glad not to be a girl or left-handed. Imagine having to write in that contorted position to avoid rubbing your hand in wet ink! He was a lucky person, he decided early. He was certainly lucky compared with the children of London or Leningrad or, later on, Berlin and Tokyo. When his family turned out all the lights and crouched on the stair landing to be away from flying glass, it was a mock air raid, a pretense, and when a plane droned overhead, and he waited with his heart pounding for the bomb to fall, it was of course one of our planes, and no bomb fell. But, then, why would Tojo and Hitler want to bomb Willow? Because of one little parachute factory?

His parents took walks on Sunday afternoons; decades would pass before Owen could see this custom as their way of asserting themselves as a young couple, escaping from a house that wasn't theirs. But he, their child, was theirs, and they dragged him along, though the very prospect made his legs heavy, and he would lag behind more and more until his father would eventually double back and lift him up onto his shoulders. It felt weirdly high up there, and his father's head seemed so strangely large and hairy that after a while he was happy to return to the earth on his own legs.

There were several routes the walk could take. One way was to turn left down the nameless alley beyond their hedge and walk across Alton Avenue and through the newer section of Willow to Shale Hill and climb it. There were Victory Gardens along the base, but at the summit paths wandered between pines and flat rocks that reminded him of sliding stacks of newspapers getting dark and wrinkled in the rain. From up here the whole town was open to view: the newest section was closest, composed of curved streets planted with buttonwoods and poplars, and then an older, rectilinear section in darker-leafed, denser Norway maples, and, beyond the Alton Pike, the oldest, southernmost part. Mifflin Avenue was conspicuous, lined on both sides with tall horse chestnuts. He saw his own house—his grandfather's house—the bricks painted custard-yellow and the wood trim parsley-green, and Mifflin Avenue becoming in the haze a road winding through the Blake farm and heading toward Philadelphia as the river ran and glinted beside it. The view always interested his mother, but for Owen it was worth about two seconds of looking. What could you do with a view? He would rather find a dead stick and try to hit pebbles like a baseball.

Or, emerging from under the grape arbor by the side porch and walking out the brick walk, past the pansy bed, to the gap in the hedge, they could turn the other way, right, and walk up Mifflin Avenue, past the spooky Hoffman house and Buddy Rourke's sad apartment building, past where the Bakers' barn had burned down, past the smelly pigpens and the fenced pastures for cows, past the creek, in slow spots solid green with watercress that Grammy sometimes gathered, to a road that led up to Cedar Top, opposite Shale Hill, across the valley that held Willow.

Beyond the town bounds, the road climbed. Unpainted houses held rusting cars in their slanted yards, and mangy dogs barked and barked as the three Mackenzies trudged past. Then came a stretch of pure woods, and a hilltop intersection where a Dairy Queen ice-cream stand had been abandoned. He never learned where the other two roads, the one straight ahead and the one to the left, went. His parents would turn right and head back downhill, through more woods, past the spiky sandstone wall of the Pomeroy estate. Once or twice Owen heard the sound of tennis balls back and forth, and the splashing of a swimming pool, but usually nobody seemed to be home. The lives of the rich were hard to imagine; they involved a lot of not being home. On the other side of the road, on the upper edge of Willow, the cemetery appeared, its granite stones, pale pink and pale gray, sharp-cornered and bald in the sunlight.

The road, heading farther downward, became Washington Street, a street of houses with narrow side yards and terraced front lawns, which after three blocks gave way to the commerce at the center of Willow: the movie theatre, the savings bank, a bicycle shop, and, at the five corners where the street met the Alton Pike, Eberly's Drug Store, the Lutheran church, the Hess Funeral Home, Borough Hall with its little park, and Leinbach's Oyster House, a restaurant on the first floor of the old sandstone building that had once been the inn called The Willow. Owen's heart always lifted, and the weight fell off his legs, when he and his parents would come into this downtown, which he walked through every school day, and which he could reconstruct store by store, house by house, in his mind's eye sixty years afterwards.

It was on this Cedar Top walk, one day, just after the forsaken ice-cream stand, that Owen had noticed in the grit at the side of the road a milky-white thing like a collapsed balloon; it had the glossy look of a toy. He bent down to look closer and his mother, behind and above him, said, in the voice she reserved for extreme urgency, *"Don't touch it!"*

What could be the danger? It was not alive but her voice suggested it somehow was. "What is it?" he asked.

"Something batsy," she said.

"Batsy" was a pretend word, a private word, which Owen had coined when he could not yet pronounce everything and made words up without meaning to, like "odduce" for "orange juice" and "nana" for "banana." "Batsy" had to do with food that he didn't like, that he thought too runny or mixed-up or too much like guts to eat. He must have meant "bad" mixed with "nasty"; the word had stuck, as if describing a reality that couldn't be touched by the tongue with an actual word. Fresh bird doo-doo on the rim of the stone birdbath and earthworms that had dried out crossing the hot sidewalk were also batsy.

"What was it for?" he asked, his past tense showing an awareness of something discarded, of something whose mysterious moment of use was past.

Both his parents were silent as the three of them walked onward, leaving the fascinating rubbery thing behind in the roadside grit. They were the kind of parents, unlike some, who thought it wrong not to answer a child's questions. He could feel guilt nagging at them.

"It was for tidiness' sake, Owen," his father at last said. "Like a Kleenex."

"It was a stork-stopper," his mother added, her voice better-humored now, laced with a girlish complicity. He could feel his parents, behind him, drawn closer in their secret knowledge. Usually it was he and his mother who had the secrets, in all those hours when his father was absent at work. Her unhappiness was the main secret, though what exactly she was unhappy about he could not quite guess. Being a daughter, wife, and mother all in the same house was stressful, she let him know, though he wasn't sure why it would be. He was himself a son and grandson, a classmate and playmate, all at once, and could easily have been some-body's brother. It was as if just being a woman by itself was enough to cause unhappiness. There were days when his mother went to bed with her eyes shut; it frightened him when she was like this, and he stayed away from her. There were days when her whole being said, *Don't touch me*.

Owen's little room was next to his parents', and their exchanges unignorably seeped into his ears—the brisk thrusts and counterthrusts of a quarrel, the sighs and groans of weariness in the evening, the playful chatter that began the day. He was happy to have her love him more than she did his father, but he wanted things to be friendly and cozy between the two grown-ups, so that after one of his nightmares they could comfort him by letting him into the warm space between them in their bed.

As he grew, he discovered more places in Willow where sin cast its shadow, which did not slide away like most shadows but had a sticky, pungent quality. On top of the equipment shed at the playground there was a triangular space, under the pavilion roof, that you could boost yourself into only by jumping and grabbing a crossbeam and swinging your feet up, dangerously hanging in midair for a second, and then leveraging your body onto the top of the shed. As Owen's eyes adjusted, he saw there were more drawings, never painted over, and written messages and allegations involving girls and boys too old for him to have known. Ginger Bitting sometimes scrambled up here after playground hours, and it was pleasant to stretch out imagining her beside him—her wiry, energetic, fearless body—and to look down the perspective of beaded boards to the macadam pavilion floor, where a stray lost jack or red checker could be seen like a secret beside a leg of one of the heavy trestle tables.

In the seventh grade, Owen left the elementary school and went to the high-school building half a mile down the Pike toward Alton. Though girls and boys could enter any of the doors and use the grounds without the sexual division enforced on the elementary-school playground, a whiff of scandal clung to the lower windows on the side of the high school toward Alton, under the corner classroom. They were the windows of the girls' locker room, reinforced with chicken wire and painted black on the inside. Yet cracks in the aging paint appeared, and small holes were mysteriously scratched in it, from the inside. Though there was no written prohibition, teachers shooed boys away from these windows, and the space here, with its mowed grass and narrow sidewalk, gathered such a thick patina of rumored glimpse and determined spying that Owen emerged into adult life with a memory, as luminous as an Ingres seraglio, of naked girls seen at an angle, past fore-grounded asbestos-coated pipes and the dusty green tops of metal lockers—girls with shining shoulders and shower-wet flanks, Barbara Emerich and Alice Stottlemeyer and Babs Dolinski and Grace Bickta but somehow not Ginger Bitting, girls he had grown up with, moving slowly in their budding nudity, oblivious, as if underwater.

Though his mother, a great believer in Nature, often walked around naked on her way to and from the bath-room, and when he was a toddler shared the bathtub with him, Owen had curiously little idea of what a woman's body looked like, as if, she being his mother, a thick veil inter-vened. It was only females of his own generation he could see, and who could guide him. Once, wrestling on the baked late-summer playground grass, after Miss Mull had gone home, with Doris Shanahan, a square-faced tomboy from the B-section of the eighth grade who whistled riding her bike and liked to hang around shooting baskets with boys, Owen looked up her shorts as she stood triumphant over him, straddling his face, and he saw, thanks to her under-pants hanging loose, a few curly black hairs: it was as if he had never seen pubic hair before. He himself still had none. His seeing Doris's was a sin, he knew, but it made him happy, and was real. It was knowledge, and knowledge, all the elders of Willow agreed, was good to have.

iii. *The Husband*

WHEN OWEN AWAKES and discovers that Julia is out of bed, he goes forth in search of her, the two of them enacting semi-comic routines in which they consciously—as if this will placate its advance—flirt with senility.

"Where *are* you, sweetness?" he calls.

"*Here*, darling," she answers, from some far-off room; but the deteriorating quality of his hearing is such that he cannot tell if she is upstairs or downstairs.

"Where's here?" he shouts, growing irritated.

Her hearing too is not what it had once been, nor her need to respond to him. She falls silent, like a car radio in a tunnel. *What a child she still is,* he thinks to himself, *to believe that "here" explained everything, as if she is the center of the universe. How amazingly selfish!*

Still, without being selfish she could not have given him what he so much desired at the time they met: a new center for his life. Spotting self-love in the other had been their *point de départ.* His first wife had been relatively selfless, as if her self were something she had absent-mindedly left in another room, like a pair of reading glasses.

Julia may have wandered outdoors, in her flip-flops. She loves the outdoors, site of weather and of traffic. In summer she wanders into her garden, beginning to pull weeds, in her nightie; its hem becomes soaked with dew, her flip-flops get muddy. He has to go downstairs in his pajamas to win a response. He even paddles out in his bare feet onto the asphalt driveway, not hot enough to burn in the early morning. During two decades of residence here, in this or that small emergency (a car door left ajar and the inner lights devouring battery juice, or a newspaper carelessly thrown into bushes as the delivery man careened around the circle in the pre-dawn dark, or a watering hose absent-mindedly left running when they went to bed, its sound audible in their bedroom like a murmuring heart), Owen has trod barefoot on the macadam in a range of weathers, even in some fresh inches of snow, and found that for a few steps almost anything could be borne, snow and heat imparting to dulled, shoe-bound nerves an invigorating elemental shock.

He wants to share a dream with her. He often wakes with such a desire, though Julia long ago established a considerable lack of interest in his nocturnal brain activity. It is important to strike in the first waking minutes, before the dream's delicate structure is crushed under humdrum reality's weight.

Last night he dreamed that, standing on the lawn on the sea side of their white house, he saw her go off, in her black BMW, on one of her innumerable errands or escapes to Boston. He saw her car, as shiny as patent leather, rush by and, immediately after it, his shabby maroon Mitsubishi follow, driven not by him but by Julia again, her pale profile preoccupied. His first wife, Phyllis, had also held her head in this tense, eye-catching way when behind the wheel—tipped slightly back as if in anticipation of the engine's exploding.

In his dream he saw nothing peculiar in the duplicated Julias, but felt something headlong and dangerous in her speed. *Slow down, darling, slow down.* Now several cars were coming *up* the driveway, which is too narrow for automobiles to pass. To cope with this difficulty, the men driving the cars conducted unprecedented maneuvers—one Volkswagen Bug, that fabled, notoriously unsafe 'sixties vehicle of counterculture rebellion and conspicuous thrift, backed right down off the driveway onto a grassy ramp that Owen had never noticed before. Another vehicle pulled a clattering trailer; he realized that these men were his weekly lawn crew. But it wasn't as simple as that; when he came back into the house, a family of three Chinese, identically blobby, like inflated dolls or swollen gray ticks, were sitting in his living room, silent but expectant. They, and the lawn crew—morbidly tan men who smoke cigarettes while they noisily ride their mowers around and around, missing many corners and scalping many a high spot—appeared to assume, wrongly, that in Julia's absence (she has gone to Boston, in duplicate) he will know what to do, what courtesies to extend, what orders to give. He was the owner, the host, the proprietor, the boss—a role he has never quite grown into. Born young, he has stayed young: a charmed life has kept him so. Nonplussed, he woke up.

He wants to describe all this to Julia, to make her laugh. He wants to discuss with her the dream's possible connections to real life. A few years ago, they visited China for three weeks—another senility-fending maneuver. All the couples they know in Haskells Crossing take trips, in the quick-closing window between retirement and death. Like children trading bubble-gum cards they swap the names of restaurants and hotels, museums, and temples that must not be missed, local guides who must be sought out and consulted. The whole globe has been colonized by Haskells Crossing and its companion community, Haven-by-the-Sea, sending out pilgrims who tread the same paths, in one another's footsteps, eating in the same restaurants, using the same guides, even encountering the same memorably persistent souvenir-saleswomen in the shadow of the Great Wall. Also, Owen's career in computers has given him many Asian-American colleagues, some of them as opaquely expectant and uncoöperative as the figures in his dream. Come to think of it, on a business trip to Chicago last winter he and Julia saw, in the Art Institute, an enigmatic installation of identically smiling, gray spray-painted, pajama-clad artificial Chinamen standing around the marble railings of the majestic central staircase.

Owen imagines Julia laughing with him as he tests these possible connections to the imaginary Oriental visitors, who had been so self-contained, so non-nonplussably *pleased* in the Mackenzies' living room, which had been reconfigured into a largely empty room with a sloping floor. Was the slope an oneiric reference to slant eyes, or to the slanting floor of the Scheherazade back in Willow, where he had watched many a Charlie Chan movie?

He wants to share this dream especially because it was, under its discontinuities, somehow all about Julia. His desire that she not come to ruin in the driveway; his heart leaping in fear that she might slip on wet leaves and fatally crash. So many of his dreams are *not* about her, drawing heavily, as on the raft of the mattress they drift together through their private universes, upon a fraught territory left behind twenty-five years ago—the domestic confusions and commensurate griefs in the town of Middle Falls, Connecticut, where Phyllis had played, with a dramatically understated affect, the role of his wife. Often in his dreams the wife-figure is ambiguous, misty-faced, and could be either woman. Phyllis, a stately dirty-blonde, had been taller, retaining from her student days a certain bohemian insouciance, and Julia, a compact, long-lashed brunette, with controlled passages of frosting in her sleek coiffure, is snappier in her dress and in her way of moving: but both acquire in his dreams a recessive, generic wifeliness.

Falls. Fragility. If an intruding stranger or psychiatrist asked him why he loved Julia so, Owen might have dredged up an erotic memory generated, a few years ago, in the convalescent aftermath of her breaking her leg—one bone in her ankle and another in her foot—while hurrying to pass him on the back stairs. He had felt her, like a pursuing predator, breathing impatiently behind him; then he heard the sharp monosyllable *"Oh!"* as she flipped into the air, having slipped on the narrowest part of the triangular, carpeted treads in her new, smooth-soled Belgians. She flew through the air for a second, hurtling past him in the foreshortened manner of an angel plunging earthward with its announcement, and then she landed on the hall carpet, lying there motionless. He hurried to her with a thudding chest. A sudden disaster on life's stage: what was his role? Julia softly pronounced, while her second husband knelt anxiously above her, "I heard two breaks. *Pop-pop.*" This strict accountancy in the very pit of emergency was just like her: efficient, no-nonsense. As she lay there, showing her hushed profile, and he knelt helpless beside her, swallowing the sudden enormity of this domestic event, she asked,

"Could you take off my sweater? Gently." She added, "I'm hot. I think I might faint."

"What shall we do?" he asked her.

She was silent, as if she had fainted.

In charge by default, he told her, "We've got to get you to the hospital. Can you hop, holding on to my shoulder?" They made it to the car, to the emergency room of the local hospital, where a crude cast was fashioned, and the next day to Massachusetts General Hospital, an hour away in Boston.

For the month afterwards, they did not make love, though he demonstrated love, in his own eyes, by bringing her meals he prepared, by learning to do the laundry and the cooking, and by playing backgammon and watching public television with her at night. After the month, they agreed they should try sex again, though she would have to lie safely still beneath him, and he must be careful of her mending bones. At Mass. General she had been prescribed not a plaster cast but, in the latest therapeutic fashion, a plastic boot—space-tech in feeling, overlapping blue and gray with a ridged sole curved like a chair rocker. It could be briefly removed but had to stay on during something as strenuous as fucking. He tried to hover above her, on his elbows and knees, sparing her as much of his weight as he could, and to his grateful amazement felt her rise to him, in her excitement, quicker than usual; she ground her pubic bone against his decisively and they came together— gemlike dragonflies coupling in air. Breathless afterwards, Julia stared up at him from the pillow with that cloudy face of satisfied desire which puts a man, briefly, right with the universe, all debts honored, all worries unmasked as negligible.

It might have been the boot. In their first winters in this

underheated wooden house, built a century ago as a summer home, it excited them both if she left on her woolly socks. They made her somehow more naked and not less. Husband and wife disagreed politically and suffered a frequent misalignment of prejudices, but an alignment in their nervous systems made up for it. She came from coastal Connecticut and had had "advantages." She used to drive an MG convertible to private day school, through a succession of leafy villages, across a succession of iron bridges. Her school had no basketball or football team; the main sports were tennis, golf, and equestrian competition, including polo. Julia pretended to disbelieve that these had not been offered at Willow High, and that his idea of a happy, fulfilled summer had been walking down through his back yard, past the grape arbor with its buzzing Japanese-beetle traps, past his grandfather's asbestos-shingled chicken house, and cutting across a cornfield to a playground, where it sat on a kind of artificial mesa beside the town baseball field, and killing time all day with a pack of other brown-legged waifs. Summer camp had lain beyond the family financial horizon, and the thought, for squeamish, timid, hydrophobic Owen, of living in a cabin with other boys and canoeing in a deadly black cold lake was in any case terrifying. The whole rugged, self-testing world of the rich, born to command and rule, was fortunately beyond him.

He was afraid of the water, of heights, of spiders, of the dark, of choking, of tough boys, of batsy things. At a travelling fair he had once been placed, rather roughly, by an overworked young attendant, on a smelly spotted pony and had felt impossibly high off the ground, worse than when mounted on his father's shoulders, because the animal under him felt less intelligent and more skittish—as scared, almost, as Owen himself. When Julia, at their local golf,

tennis, and equestrian club, swings herself up on the stirrup
and becomes, in her scarlet coat and round black riding helmet, a horsewoman ten feet high, he is moved to more sin-
cere awe than when, sixty years before, he had looked up,
hand on his heart, at the flag Miss Mull each morning
raised at the Willow playground. On its creaking pulley
it would be hauled up through the nine o'clock sun and
couldn't be long looked at, since the the fiery body left a
pulsing purple spot on his retina that he feared would some
day blind him. Computer screens often leave a similar pulsing afterimage, but he still sees. Seventy, he still sees, walks
on his own legs, and, except when Julia calls to him from
too distant a room, hears well enough. More reckless males
his age have been deafened by gunfire, lamed by contact
sports. His natural caution, overriding the desire to be a
test pilot, has paid off.

Considering his many qualms and the cloistered household his four guardians struggled to maintain around him,
the wonder is that he has managed in life as well as he has.
His only-child capacity for self-amusement, his patience
in solving problems that he set for himself, or that he and
Buddy Rourke devised together, stood him in good stead in
the burgeoning computer industry; but even on the social
level he is not quite inept. His manner is shy but seductive.
The villages he has lived in have been sites of instruction.

In Willow, by the inarguable providence of the state, he
had daily escaped his house to attend the schools, whose
grades up to junior high were taught almost entirely by
motherly, mildly challenging women, and to walk the sidewalks with the twittering, teasing pack of girls, who could
tell (not just Ginger Bitting but Barbara Emerich, with her
cornsilk braids and one gray front tooth which showed
when she smiled, and lithe, dark, grave-eyed Grace Bickta)

that he adored them. Little Owen was malleable, gull-ible. He believed everything he was told and took comfort, abnormally much, from the town's presiding public presences—the schoolteachers, and the highway crew, who from their tarry truck threw down cinders in winter and smoking gravel in the summer, and the three town cops, one short, one fat, and one with a rumored drinking problem. He took comfort from the little old lady, her glasses on a cord around her goitrous neck, who accepted their monthly electric bill at her barred window in Borough Hall, and the mailman, Mr. Bingham, who with the heroism of the well-publicized postal-service slogan heroically plodded his way up and down Mifflin Avenue twice a day, leaning at an angle away from the weight of his leather pouch, in which Mickey Mouse comic books and secret decoding rings and signed photographs of movie stars would sometimes come to Owen. If his diffuse childhood happiness could be distilled into one moment, it would be the day of a snowstorm, in the vicinity of Christmas—mid-afternoon, the outdoors already darkened under the cloud cover, tinsel and dried needles falling off the holiday evergreen in the front parlor onto the miniature landscape below, which he and his mother had concocted: cotton and flakes of Lux for snow, toothpicks stuck into bits of green-painted sponge for trees, and for habitations fragile store-bought papier-mâché houses gathered around the speckled mirror of a pond. Around the oval three-rail track ran his little blue Lionel train with its obedient speed shifts and translucent smell of lubricating oil. Suddenly—a noise that electrified Owen—the clacking letter slot announced that Mr. Bingham had trudged through the blizzard and, for the second time that day, delivered the mail. That mailmen walked and trolley cars clanged through the storm seemed to confirm the Hollywood, comic-strip version of American reality: we were as safe, and as lovingly regarded from on high, as the tiny, unaging figures in a shaken snow globe.

Just slightly above the administrators of local order were the national celebrities. They were, indeed, more accessible and familiar: Jack Benny and Fibber McGee cracking their jokes and suffering their embarrassments in the little Philco right in the piano room, next to the greasy-armed easy chair where Owen ate peanut-butter crackers in a double rapture of laughter and mastication; Tyrone Power, his black eyebrows knitted in a troubled frown, and Joan Crawford, her huge dark lips bravely tremulous and her enlarged eyes each harboring a tear that would fill a bucket, on the screen at the Scheherazade; and the tweedy, pipe-sucking writers and bespectacled lab-coated inventors and slick-haired café-society people present in the shiny magazines, *Life* and *Liberty* and *Collier's* and *The Saturday Evening Post*, on the upright wooden rack at Eberly's Drug Store, buyable by any local person with a dime. There was a friendliness, a closeness, in the way this firmament curved over Willow in its valley. The voices of Bing Crosby and Lowell Thomas and Kate Smith carried none of the abrasive demands of real voices—his mother's, his teachers', the teasing girls'—and yet these celebrities, to judge from the scripts of the radio comedies, lived lives much like ours, visiting the bank and the dentist. Jack Benny even went next door to borrow a cup of sugar from Ronald Colman. At their continental distance these stars partook of the life lived in Owen's neighborhood, with its spindly porches and buckling retaining walls. There was no better way to live, no grander, more virtuous country than America, and no homier state than Pennsylvania. God figured at the top, the unthinkable keystone, but at a mercifully great distance, farther away than even Hollywood and Beverly Hills.

"There you are," he tells his wife, when he has deciphered "Here" and found her in the flesh—her frosted hair, her blue flip-flops—out on the veranda, reading the *New York Times*.

He insists on reading the *Boston Globe*—another misalignment. "I had the weirdest dream," he begins. "You were in it twice."

"Please, baby," she says, not turning her head. "Couldn't you tell me later? I'm trying to understand Enron—the way they did it, siphoning off these fortunes for themselves."

"I'll have forgotten it later, but never mind," he says, feeling the splash of imagery in his mind evaporate, sparkling though it was with an elixir of her, of their life together. "Never mind. Tell me what's on for today." Today was Saturday, his favorite day as a child, but threateningly formless in his retirement.

Julia, her eyelashes fluttering in irritation as she stared into the *Times* version of breathtaking corporate corruption, says, "Nothing until cocktails at the Achesons'."

"Oh, God. Do we have to go?"

"Of course, dear. Miriam is one of my best friends. As Brad is yours."

"They'll be having everybody; we won't be missed."

"Oh yes we will. Why do you put me through this every time? You always enjoy yourself once you're there. You're charming, in fact, in that ah-shucks way you have."

"I pretend to enjoy myself. I have nothing to say to those people. Nothing."

Owen's lifework has been the creation and vetting of computer software, and now that he has closed his last little office in Boston, a four-man (three-man-and-a-woman) consultancy, he has little to say to anybody. The technology has, by geometric leaps and bounds, left him behind; his dashing algorithms and circuitry-saving forked commands, his IF . . . THEN . . . ELSEs and WHILE-loops, have become as homely as patchwork quilts. The chip-power of a thousand-dollar desktop IBM clone dizzies and disgusts him. All those bells and whistles: realistically three-dimensional computer games animated in real time; hard-wired programs for storing and cropping and shading digital photos, for editing digital home videos, for printing in a hundred type fonts; programs for playing music broken into ten thousand digitized tones, for drawing upon the Internet's endlessly enlarging Library of Babel; programs for fending off viruses and worms and spam and unwanted e-mail correspondence. The dot-com bust has made the whole industry seem disreputable, including those who, like him, got out near the top. Correctly judging the Clinton bubble to be unsustainable, Owen reversed the course of his grandfather's investments, bought during the 'twenties bubble and wiped out by the Crash of 1929. He has avenged the old man, whom he loved most purely of those he early loved.

Unlike his mother, Grandpa Rausch had not been too present, nor had he been, like Owen's father, too absent. He had been just right, sitting quiet in the center of the cane-back sofa while Owen played on the living-room carpet with his Tinker Toys and lead warplanes, or made the Lionel train go around and around, backwards and forwards, the little black transformer box overheating to emit a slight, cozy stink of burning, like his mother when she ironed. She also emitted this smell when, sitting at her dresser, she used the long-nosed curling iron on her auburn hair. His mother was hot, hot like the top of the coal-burning kitchen stove, dangerous to touch, though she warmed the kitchen, and the whole house for that matter. She had a redhead's temper, what his father called "a short fuse"; her hand would flash out and slap Owen's face quicker than he could duck. All his life Owen wanted women to be cool and calm except when he (more and more rarely) desired them otherwise.

"Talk about the news, the economy," Julia advises him. "Whether or not we should go to war with Iraq again."

"Another thing that happens at seventy—thank God, darling, you're too young to have it happen to you—is you cease to care about the news. It isn't new. Didn't we do Iraq a Bush or so ago?"

"Talk about golf. You love golf."

"But not golfers necessarily. It's pathetic, it's all we can talk about, you can see the wives start to fidget and move away. The wives didn't use to get so bored in Middle Falls, I wonder what we talked about."

"You talked about how you wanted to fuck them, without exactly saying so."

"Oh, surely not."

"I was there."

"Bless you for that. Right there, playing the game with the best of them." She doesn't like to be reminded of that. To mollify his stab, he asks, in a child's whine, "What am I going to do between now and the Achesons?" Owen used to work in every spare minute; he developed his first marketable program, DigitEyes, using a clumsy mix of machine code and the early version of FORTRAN he had learned at IBM, in a garage behind the clapboarded semi-detached he and Phyllis had rented on Common Lane for their first year and a half in Middle Falls. In Haskells Crossing, his garage, much larger than that historic one, is taken up with three cars and with lawn equipment he never touches, as well as cartons and cartons of prep-school and college texts abandoned by their combined children by previous marriages.

"Go to the club and play golf," Julia suggests. "Or help me weed the hosta and cut back the ivy. It all looks like shit." She has a genteel manner but a salty tongue.

Owen misses the old Willow playground, its plateau long bulldozed out of existence. Time hung heavy there, but the weight was delicious, as he moved the marbles of Chinese checkers from one triangle to another, and braided rickrack lanyards for whistles though only Miss Mull had any need to wear one, and retrieved the roof ball from the cornfields when it went over the pavilion's tarpaper roof, and watched Ginger dangle from the monkey bars or kick high, higher on the creaking swing. He realizes that to the children of Haskells Crossing the country club is their playground, with its pool and snack bar and tetherball and clay tennis courts, and probably with dirty drawings scratched somewhere where grown-ups never think to look, but for Owen this recreational space wears a stupefying glaze of propriety, of that hopeless boringness special to the rich. The poor know boredom but always hope that things will change for the better, whereas the rich simply want things to go on just as they are, which is even less likely to happen. Their problems—the constant crisis state of their golf games, the huge new house some *nouveau riche* from out of state was putting up right in their ocean view, the impossibility of finding dependable help in the house and garden (even the Brazilians and Albanians are overcharging and learning how to loaf), the unshakable slump in the stock market, the rising real-estate taxes, the adult children who are getting divorces and having disappointing, quixotic careers in the arts or bleeding-heart social work—strike Owen as trivial, compared with the do-or-die problems that afflicted his childhood household and from which he had been sheltered.

As the slate roof of the house on Mifflin Avenue withstood rain and the hurricane of '38, so his guardians had shielded him from a pelting hail of worries: poverty with no federal safety net, ill health with no post-war medical miracles, loss of social face with no forgiveness in the social system. The child gathered ominous bits of conversation from other rooms in the house: his father's job was none too secure, the local hosiery industry was a lost cause, his mother's health was uncertain. She had high blood pressure and female complaints. Beyond the drawing on the playground shed, Owen knew nothing about the female sexual organs, but from what he overheard he gathered they were a one-way street to medical disaster. And Grandpa and Grammy were far from young; they rustled in their room, with its wet-paper smell of old bodies, on the edge of oblivion, and beat the odds by appearing each morning for breakfast. Owen made his way through the days, rising steadily through the grades at school, grateful that his world on Mifflin Avenue stayed intact.

Then, when he was thirteen, it didn't. The mill where his father worked closed down. Its war work had been its last gasp. His father walked the baking summer streets of Alton looking for an accountant's job. The humiliation of it wore his face thin and tinted it yellow. He became obsessed—absurdly, thought Owen, who never saw the bills—with the expense of the Mifflin Avenue house; the heating, the maintenance, the need for fresh paint. It had become in his mind another "rip-off joint." He called it "Pop's folly"; he had to get out from under it. The house, the only house Owen had ever lived in, was sold, for the very same amount, eight thousand five hundred dollars, for which Owen's grandfather had bought it twenty-five years ago, in the wake of another world war. For half that amount they bought a house in the country, miles from anywhere, surrounded by eroding fields and the buzz of crickets and the scolding of birds. The little stone house had stood empty for a year. Swifts had built nests in the chimney; flying squirrels lived in the attic; feral cats hid in the old bales of hay in the unpainted barn. There was no electricity, no telephone, no plumbing, and putting in these things took much of their leftover four thousand dollars. Also, they had to have a car; in Willow they could walk everywhere, the five of them in five different directions if they wanted, and for seven cents the trolley car took them right into Alton, with its department stores and movie palaces. Daddy could not find a job in Alton. The entire city was slowly dying, and he, over forty, was too old to retrain. A college classmate in Norristown, toward Philadelphia, finally took him on, as an associate in his accounting firm, for less money than the hosiery mill had paid, and this took the car away from eight in the morning to six at night. Owen was left with his grandparents, his mother, a barnful of cats with runny eyes, and two fluffy collie puppies. The nearest neighbors were Mennonites, whose children had no time for play; they all worked on their farm. A mile away was an old tavern and a grocery store in a cluster of six houses along the road, but this was no kind of village. Owen stayed in the house and read science fiction and mystery novels set in English villages and dreamed of far-fetched inventions that would make him rich. His retrospective image of his life tended to delete those years; they had no place on his résumé, the six rural years before he went away to MIT and New England.

The village he now lives in, his last village most likely save for the Bide-a-Wee Terminal Care Complex, has no government of its own; it is a precinct of a city of forty thousand, Cabot City. Haskells Crossing is the old summer-estate section, where the acreages of Pittsburgh and Chicago millionaires—billionaires in today's money—have been broken into smaller holdings but are still remembered, still felt as a foundation layer of comfort and spaciousness. The great plutocrats, with their yachts and private docks and miles of granite wall and flaring stone staircases leading up to long swimming pools and neo-classic changing rooms and red-clay tennis courts and fanciful gazebos, left a certain aura as well as children who, themselves now nearing extinction, remember coming east from Chicago or Cleveland every June in Daddy's private railroad car. A century before, as the B & M tracks came out from Boston along the North Shore, the crossing took its name from a local salt-water farmer, Enoch Haskell, who had been bought out; his weathered wooden buildings were knocked down and burned and his struggling fields turned into emerald lawns, but his name has outlasted those of those who ousted him. The South Shore lost its commuter lines after the war, but in this direction they hung on, and once an hour a passing train makes the granite bedrock underlying Owen and Julia's house slightly but perceptibly tremble. He likes this elemental touch, this tangible connection between transport and geology.

There is a small downtown—the fire station, the war memorial, the French baker, a branch bank, a 7-Eleven, a fruit store, a health-food store, a drugstore eventually driven out of business by competition from the mall CVSs and

Walgreens, a bookstore always on the verge of being extinguished by the Borders and the Barnes & Noble in the mall ten miles distant, a pizza parlor, a dry cleaner's, two competing hairdressers both from the tropics (Costa Rica, the Philippines), a failing florist beside a vacant office that had housed a travel agency fatally undermined by the World Trade Center disaster and subsequent airline economics, a family restaurant, and a twice-as-expensive restaurant for courting couples and the local well-to-do when they have guests to impress. There is even a Haskells Crossing post office, from the days when the estate owners were deemed as deserving of one, at least, as a Nebraska whistle-stop.

But the ghostly center of power, which in Willow had been gathered at the five-cornered intersection, here hovers three miles and many railroad crossings away, at the city hall and adjoining police station, in the center of Cabot City. Once a riverside hamlet named Colchester after the home town of the early Puritan settlers, it was renamed in honor of the creator of the river-polluting leatherworks that, with its sister factories, populated the close-packed streets of triple-deckers with Polish, Greek, Irish, and even Turkish millworkers. The mills have folded, but the descendants of the workers continue to support city administrations notorious, in the precinct of Haskells Crossing, for high assessments and corruptible zoning regulations. Haskells Crossing in 1880 attempted to secede and join the adjacent summer colony, Haven-by-the-Sea, but the move was thwarted on Beacon Hill, not by the Irish legislature but by the veto of the Boston Brahmin governor, who according to some had been influenced by an undeclared donation of leather money and according to others by a high-minded conservative resistance, in the wake of the Civil War, to revolts and remappings of any kind.

Owen, like his neighbors, likes Haskells Crossing the way it is. Self-governed Haven-by-the-Sea, with its town meetings and hotly debated tax overrides, seems a village too pleased with itself, too busily inturned. The distant Cabot City officialdom leaves him, save financially, untouched. Water, rusty but drinkable, pushes up his hill from a city reservoir; trash is collected at the foot of his driveway once a week. A policeman, the one time he and Julia reported a robbery, appeared the same day, looking baffled but sympathetic, with glistening oval eyes. He looked like a big squirrel without a bushy tail, hunched over his notebook nearsightedly nibbling at every acorn of a clue. The thief was never found.

Owen, raised in a village idyllically becalmed by hard times, in a nation steadfastly abjuring the quick fixes of fascism and communism, holds a mixed bag of socio-economic attitudes: he votes Democrat, because his parents and grandparents had voted for Roosevelt, but at the same time he expects so little from government that all social services and signs of public order pleasantly surprise him. When Bradley Acheson bemoans to him, on the broad sunlit lawn of the day's cocktail party, the latest attempt to subdivide and develop the old Judson estate's sixty-five acres, Owen's tongue is tied, undecided between agreeing, for the sake of the green spaces that old wealth once kept open and that only government intervention can sustain, and pointing out that the North American continent's history has been one of development. "Housing starts," he finally, haltingly says, "are a leading economic indicator, and isn't crying 'Nimby' somewhat anti-democratic, even anti-patriotic under your great guy Bush Two?"

"Nimby?"

"Not in My Back Yard."

Brad has evidently not heard the acronym before, and his bark of laughter hurls a bit of devilled egg at the lapel of Owen's blazer. Owen doesn't flinch, and courteously waits while his host's large, square face—itself a space that invites development—chews through the uncongenial complexity, the sterile conflictedness, of his guest's reply. "The developer," Brad complains, "isn't even from Massachusetts—it's some California megafirm that comes in and knocks down every tree and puts up this horrendous spread of McMansions, jammed in as tight as the zoning allows. We'll wind up looking like Watertown."

"Sounds horrible, Brad, but, hey, it creates jobs, jobs in one of the few American industries they can't take overseas. Listen: every town in this country was once a farm or a forest. If you right-wing tree-huggers had been in charge, nothing would ever have been built. Cabot City would still be a river full of fish. Haven-by-the-Sea would be Nothing-by-the-Sea. It would be a heap of clamshells beside some rotting wigwams."

Brad presses his lips together and looks as if he might sputter; he squints over Owen's shoulder to see what other of his guests need attending, what pleasanter conversations he might join. "There has to be a balance," he finally decides.

"Exactly," Owen agrees. He loves Brad, as a golfer. When he looks at him he sees not his soul, as God is said to, nor the statistics of his income and net worth, as the tax authorities hope to discern, but a certain swing, a kind of twirling motion with the fingers held too near the end of the grip, a dainty yet determined swing which, on good days, delivers drives down the middle, sometimes sneaky long, and tosses up chips that creep marvellously close to the hole. The men of Owen's acquaintance in Haskells

Crossing and its environs are to him an array of golf swings, no two alike: staid Morton Burnham a powerful but too-upright lunge with an ineradicable head-bob; loose-jointed Geoffrey Dillingham an exaggerated shoulder-turn, the club flung back way past parallel; stout Quentin Chute a trigger-quick hand-punch, all forearms and grimace; fussy Martin Scofield an agitated, overintellectual set-up, the feet shuffling to widen and narrow, close and open the stance while the club is insecurely gripped and regripped, a mis-hit increasingly certain; serious-minded Gavin Rust a rather comical last-second squat, after a series of solemn waggles with locked knees; careful Caleb Eppes a superslow take-back, like the Tin Man after a night of rain; excitable Corey Cogswell an incorrigible look-up and a subsequent hail of curses upon himself, with an aborted club-toss; and so on. Owen's male friends are ninety percent swings to him; he knows almost nothing of their professional activities, or the religious convictions that frame their sense of well-being, or the erotic adventures that have brought them to their present domestic situations. Most, in fact, are still married to the girls they had married in the 'fifties. Most have a sinusoid New England accent and the playful regional reti-cence, perfected through generations of close dealing, as New England's proportional share of the national wealth dwindled. Owen's ignorance of these natives, however, is partly willful; their seeming blankness is something within him, a lockout of input. He is not interested in them because, as Julia has pointed out, he does not covet their wives. Their wives are twittering biddies, haggard rasping former debutantes, perky, mannerly, and as finely fitted to this society as the parts of a well-milled machine. In Middle Falls, on the outer rim of a greater metropolitan area, none of the women had quite fit; all wanted something different, though it was hard to say what, hard even for them. A widespread discontent had filled the town with an erratic, rueful energy not unlike that of Owen's mother. He had grown up breathing an atmosphere on the edge of blow-up; female revolt, rumbling in the romantic comedies showing at the Scheherazade, threatened the peace of his grandfather's house. While his fiery-haired mother had lacked the resources for striking out toward freedom, the women of the 'sixties and 'seventies were less constrained. Fresh on the Pill, barred by early marriage and motherhood from the wild party—love-beads and bell-bottoms, crash pads and rock concerts, acid and pot—that they could hear on the other side of the generational wall, the women of Middle Falls were restless, wry, and lovable.

In Haskells Crossing, it is Julia who loves the women. She finds reality and comfort in their company—at bridge, on committees, in the seasonal cycle of parties all catered with the same six hors d'oeuvres by the same dignified family firm. Julia fits in, so snugly that Owen feels like a spare part. He is the husband, a figment to be evoked when she deals with male plumbers, carpenters, tree surgeons, lawn caregivers. "They resent dealing with women," she confesses, "so I say *you* say this and that, and they perk right up." In her feminine coffee-klatches, husbands are described as balky appliances, comically absent-minded and inept. Feminism has brought with it a cheerful misandry. Male refusal to ask questions when lost, male blindness to the most glaring facts of decor and dress, male inability to distinguish zinnias from phlox, or the refrigerator from the broom closet, male clumsiness at the simplest home tasks, and even, when the vermouth had been flowing, male sexual demands, so impatient, primitive, and lacking in stamina—these are merrily mocked. The genteel social surface of Haskells Crossing is gender-riven, and Julia likes it that way. That a married couple share a bed as well as a bank account is assumed but made little of. Husbands, who at meaner economic levels generate dependency and fear by rages and beatings, are here tamed by the impossible cost, in an old age rich in jointly owned savings and equities and real estate, of divorce. Husbands are superfluous, dutiful adjuncts to the busy interaction of women. Owen has no trouble accepting such a role, since his own father had struck him as similarly pathetic and unnecessary.

iv. *Village Sex—II*

IT HAD BEEN HIS FATHER who had successfully urged him to get a practical, scientific education. Floyd Mackenzie's experience of the Depression had been that engineers were the last people to be fired; he had seen it happen. "The kid needs to latch on to something practical," he announced. "He's in danger of dreaming his brains away." The boy's brains—demonstrated by stellar high-school marks and his ability, during his years of rural isolation, to entertain himself with books and pencil and paper—could be, he reasoned, best engaged by machinery, if not by the giant knitting machines, as long and heavy as freight cars, whose ill-rewarded servant he himself had been, then by some other kind of construction (bridges, dams, dynamos) whose indispensable utility was more obvious to the world than that of strict, honest accountancy. In a materialist age, matter must be trusted. As events proved, the machines of the future were to be lightweight—rockets leaving earth's gravity and computers quicker than human minds, adjuncts of human subjectivity freeing us into an oxygenless space.

An institution in far-off Massachusetts, a so-called Institute of Technology, offered Owen a scholarship. His being a student from a small rural school system, in a Middle Atlantic state, helped his chances with the bestowers of admissions and student aid. He never saw MIT before he got there. The buildings were set back from an artificially broadened river, the Charles, across from a venerable city, Boston, that held at the summit of a cut-down hill a sallow gold dome from under which the Commonwealth was governed. In the early 'fifties, pre-war shabbiness still ruled Cambridge and Boston, yet they were cities of youth, of students eager to make a future. Sailboats and rowing sculls rippled the river, a glittering sporting site bluer than the Schuylkill, which had been black with coal silt. This Commonwealth seemed toylike and polychrome, compared with the industrial scale of Pennsylvania—its sooty cities built on grids, its row houses climbing the hills like stairs. Boston in its oldest parts was laid out not on a grid but on a pattern, it was said, of ancient cowpaths, widened by Puritan footsteps and then paved in cobblestones.

Back Bay, a filled-in marsh, did form a grid, with a grassy central mall ornamented by elms and bronze statues. A long and windswept bridge misnamed Harvard Bridge connected Back Bay with MIT, its hovering pale dome eerily evoking, from across the river, the flying saucers from which, in those days, extraterrestrial creatures were supposedly spying, with impotent solicitude, upon a benighted planet about to blow itself up with atomic bombs. MIT seemed heroic in the grand and mazy scale of its vast central building: a series of buildings interconnected by passageways, each segment known not by a name but by a number. The main entrance, numbered 77 Massachusetts Avenue, led into Building 7, where six great pillars and a high circumcameral inscription to INDUSTRY, THE ARTS, AGRICULTURE, AND COMMERCE upheld the limestone dome. Fabled Building 20, the "plywood palace" on Vassar Street, had sheltered secret radar researches by which, it was said, the Second World War had been won. Underground infusions of government and corporate wealth continued to enlist scientific intelligence in the Cold War. In the analysis center and the digital computer laboratory—rooms entirely taken up with arrayed cabinets full of wires and vacuum tubes, fed by punched cards—all the radar stations around the United States were linked, undergraduate rumors claimed, and electric circuits calculated missile trajectories that a hundred savants with pencils could not compute in a hundred years.

MIT was a male world, its administrators and instructors all but exclusively male, and a number of them military men. Though the great post-war tide of veterans was receding, uniforms were still common on campus. Of six thousand students, no more than one hundred twenty were women, and half of these were graduate students. Phyllis Goodhue stood out, then, as one of a decided minority, outnumbered fifty to one in the endless corridors—floors of tan terrazzo and doors of frosted glass strictly numbered in black, even the women's lavatory: 3-101-WOMEN. She was yet more noticeable among the springtime sunbathers in the Great Court, a large sheltered lawn, between Buildings 3 and 4, that overlooked the new segment of Memorial Drive, its double row of sycamores, and, in their gaps, the sparkling, playful Charles and the rosy low profile of Back Bay. Most of the female undergraduates were not lovely—driven grinds with neglected figures and complexions, heads down in the hallways as they bucked the tide, trying to blend in with the boys—and Owen had to look twice at Phyllis to verify that she was. Was lovely.

True or false? Was twice necessary? No: from the start, through that river-chilled, sleepless, and miserable first year in which his head was being stuffed with, among other rafts of basic data, introductory circuit theory (Kirchhoff's law and Thévenin's and Norton's theorems, step function and impulse response, resonance phenomena and conjugate impedances), whenever Owen passed Phyllis in one of the thronged corridors, his own electromagnetic field changed, by an amount as subtle but as crucial as the difference between $d\phi$ and dt. There was a numbness only she inflicted. Her presence transformed the odd-shaped cement-paved spaces scattered among the buildings west of the Kendall Square subway stop, where bleary students loitered over gossip and cigarettes; like Ginger Bitting, this apparition had satellites, a few other girls but, inevitably in this environment, mostly boys. Owen's eyes placed her at the center of this set, though in truth she never appeared to dominate. In a boisterous cluster she stood at the edge and appeared diffidently amused; she never laughed the loudest. She had a light but clear, carrying voice—he could overhear her long before seeing her—and careful gestures, restrained by a reluctance to impose herself that moved him and emboldened him. At his watchful distance, her pallor was a beacon, a broadcast resonance.

She held her head, with its slightly outthrust chin, erect on a long neck. Her straight hair, the mixed blond of half-damp sand, was gathered into a pony tail in back with a rubber band. In the front, bangs came down to her pale eyebrows, which blended with her skin; her brows and eyelashes were almost invisible. She wore no makeup, not even lipstick, and smoked poutingly, her cheeks deeply hollowed on the inhale and her exhale delivered with a certain dismissive vehemence, upward from the side of her mouth. In her offhand, underclad (the same dove-gray cloth coat and dirty tennis sneakers all winter) glamour she came to represent Cambridge for him—aloof, stoic, abstracted, pure. And he discovered that indeed she was a professor's daughter; her father was Eustace Goodhue, biographer of the clergyman-poet George Herbert and editor of variorum editions of the Metaphysicals and lecturer in English at that other place, the university up the river, where the humanities, descended from Puritan theological studies, still ruled, leaving science to the world's worker-bees.

Her distinguished daughterly status was part of the effect she made—made deliberately, he felt. She was like him, he sensed: shy, but with the caution of someone guarding a proud ego. Taller than average, she slouched as if to minimize her bosom, the fullness of which her dowdy winter wraps did not quite conceal. It was even less concealed when, on hot fall days, and again in the sunny breaks of April and May, she took off the long gray coat that made her look like a slender doorman or military attaché and lay stretched on a blanket in the middle of the Great Court with her skirt hiked to the middle of her thighs and her sweater and blouse down to (he could not be sure at his distance) a bathing-suit top or a bra.

She looked like no girl from Pennsylvania, not even the fancy ones from the Main Line. Elsie Seidel, his high-school girlfriend, the daughter of a country feed-and-hardware merchant, was always smartly turned out, with polished penny loafers and ribbed knee socks and sweeping skirts and broad belts in the New Look style, and tortoiseshell barrettes gleaming in the bouncy waves of her light-brown hair. And plenty of lipstick, maroon lipstick that looked black in photographs and rubbed off on his mouth so that, afterwards, it stung to wipe it away with spit on a handkerchief. He didn't want his mother to see; his mother didn't want him to go with Elsie at all, though the girl was respectable, more respectable locally than were the Mackenzies, newcomers to this end of the county and to the school district. The district encompassed several valleys and included families whose first language was still Pennsylvania Dutch. Elsie herself spoke with a "Dutchy" care, slower than girls in Willow talked—her voice seemed older than she was.

There was a country simplicity to her, a well-fed glossiness. The first time they kissed, in the intermission of a dance that Owen had attended because his mother urged him to be less scornful of the region's high school even though it wasn't Willow High, Elsie didn't make the anxious pushing mouth that Alice Stottlemeyer had during spin-the-bottle but somehow let her lips melt into his, at this warm moist spot where their bodies joined. She was a short girl, in her sweated-up taffeta dance dress, and he, six feet tall at seventeen, the recent beneficiary of the Mackenzie ranginess. She had to tug down at him to keep his face tight to hers; she wanted to kiss more, there behind a broken Coke machine, where the overhead fluorescent light was flickering. Her eager small body molded itself to his; he remembered hearing how Carol Wisniewski had let herself be fucked by Marty Naftzinger standing up in the narrow space between the Rec Hall and the hosiery mill, and saw that it could be done.

Not that he and Elsie ever—in a word they never used between them—fucked. He was too smart for that, too anxious to avoid wasting his one life. He knew that fucking led to marriage and he was not ready for that. In the heat and urgency of that first kiss he recognized that she had had her eye on him, as the phrase went—he had been an exotic, aloof arrival at the school, and somehow the idea of him had wormed its way excitingly into Elsie's head. So between them there was always this tilt, this unbalance: she had desired him before he knew what was up. Nevertheless, he responded; he loved her, as far as he could shake the embarrassment of her not being a Willow girl. She was only, in her swinging skirts and white bobby socks, an imitation, a feed merchant's daughter.

He would afterwards associate Elsie with the inside of a car—its stale velour, its little dim dashboard lights, its rubber floormats and chill metallic surfaces. Chill to begin with: after an evening of driving around, the heater made a cozy nook in the dark. On dates, they took his parents' stuffy pre-war Chevy, the second-hand car the Mackenzies had bought as part of their move to the country house. His father was generally back from Norristown by six, and Owen was granted the car for the gasoline-powered roaming that is, in common American wisdom, a teen-ager's right.

Before Elsie, he would sometimes drive back to Willow, looking for the action among his old friends and rarely finding it. He saw Willow now, having left at twelve, with an exile's eyes, as a small provincial place where life—the social life of his own classmates, the bunch at the playground half grown-up—went on without him, out of sight: a deserted village. His grandfather's chicken house was losing some of its asbestos shingles, he could see as he cruised by in the alley that bent around their old house. Not that he was certain to have been happy had his family stayed. Adolescence reshuffles the cards. As a child he had been more spectator than actor, valued primarily as a loyal follower, an admirer—of Buddy Rourke, of the girls he scarcely dared imagine naked.

Now, with Elsie in the car, he had real nakedness to deal with. At first, just kissing, on and on, eyes closed to admit behind sealed lids a flood of other sensations, an expansion of consciousness into a salty, perfumed space quite unlike the hushed and headlong vault of masturbation. In the dark seclusion between cool tight sheets, his parents' muttering having died away, he would seem for some seconds to stand on his head, having discovered with his left hand a faithful mechanism impossibly sweet, an astonishing release, a clench that took him back to infancy, its tight knit of new-ness before memories overlaid the bliss of being. Into this private darkness had come another, another seeker, and what was being found, clumsily yet unstoppably, was a core self explored by another consciousness. Elsie was both wit-ness and witnessed. Her eyes were the wet, honey-tinged brown of horehound drops. By the particles of light that entered through the windshield he saw the dark dents of her dimples when she smiled, and the side of one eyeball gleam as she studied him across a gap that closed in a few seconds. Huddled beside him on the front seat, a bench seat in that era, with her back gouged by the knob of the win-dow crank and her calves and ankles roasted by the heater, she seemed cupped to receive him, a nest of growing per-missions. With each date she gave him an inch or two more of herself that he could claim as his henceforth; there was no taking back these small warm territories. Beyond kissing there was so much to touch, so many hooks and tricks among the catches and aromatic coverings, there in the shelter of the car, which sometimes became her car, for, though a year younger than he, she also had a driver's license, and when his poor old family Chevy was under overnight repair or commandeered for some adult evening errand, she would bring a car of her family's, her mother's green Dodge or even her father's new deep-blue Chrysler with its V-8 engine, to pick him up, at the farmhouse where his mother had not without a struggle accepted that Elsie had become his "girl," whatever that meant as the world embarked on a new half-century.

Some of those evenings when Elsie did the driving, pulling up in an impressive machine, she would be invited in, into the little house's front parlor, where the bulky Rausch furniture from the Willow house had suddenly gone shabby and was covered with hairs from the two collies his mother had acquired as part of her vision of rural life. Smartly dressed in this setting of declining gentility, at whose edges Owen's two grandparents made a shuffling, murmuring retreat, Elsie spoke to Owen's mother with a lively courtesy. Her honey-brown eyes flashed; her scarlet lips smiled. Uneasily standing by, in a flannel shirt whose sleeves were too short, in scuffed laced shoes that looked oafish compared with Elsie's polished penny loafers (much on view as she smartly crossed and recrossed her legs), Owen felt like a baton being passed. He felt he was present, as one pleasantry followed another, at a duel. His mother too had once been the smartly turned-out daughter of a successful rural entrepreneur; she knew a certain code, she knew "how to behave." She also knew how people *did* behave, and couldn't do much about it.

When the young people, these social observances discharged, achieved freedom in a car of Elsie's, it seemed perverse, after the movie or the miniature golf was behind them and they had found a parking spot, to have her seated on his left instead of on his right. Come at this way, she felt like a strange girl, with whom he must begin from scratch. Their chins and mouths made angles opposite from the usual, and his hands coped with reversed routes.

"Should we switch?" she asked, when he remarked on this strangeness. Her voice came out breathier, lower in her throat, than the polite, Dutch-flavored voice she used with his mother and the teachers at school. Her lipstick had already begun to smear and flake. Her face was waxily lit by a streetlamp half a block away; they sometimes parked in a hidden place he knew from his childhood walks, at the back of the Dairy Queen lot on Cedar Top. He lived ten miles away, and she four miles more to the south, but Willow was the town whose map he knew and where he felt safest. Other times, they would park up by Shale Hill, near what had been the Victory Gardens, on a dirt road made by recent developers. Always, as the scope of her permissions widened, he searched for even safer spots, where the police would never come up and shine flashlights in their faces, as once had happened, behind the long low sheds of the old farmers' market. As she sat high behind the wheel of her father's expensive car, her mussed hair caught fire in stray loops and strands from the distant streetlamp.

"Let's," he agreed. "If you don't mind my sitting behind your father's wheel."

"I don't mind, Owen. I don't like it poking me in the ribs all the time. I don't see how you can stand it."

"Elsie, when I'm with you, I don't notice such things. Here I go. I'll get out and you slide over."

Thrusting himself into the public space outside the automobile, where adult morality pressed down from the stars, he opened and shut the Chrysler's passenger door (it made that sucky rich rattle-free sound) and scuttled around the broad chrome bumper and white-walled rear tires hunched over, for he already had an erection. Even behind his fly it felt scarily as if it might snag on something, until he settled behind her father's steering wheel, which wore a suede

cover. The tang of new-car smell was warmed into fresh-
ness by the heat of their bodies. As he slid across the front
seat, wide enough for three, into the space where she huddled, the far streetlamp illumined her blurred face and a
small pearl earring and the fuzzy wool of her short-sleeved
angora sweater. She let him slide the sweater up and sneak a
finger into her bra and stroke the silky skin there, the gentle fatty rise of it. Though Elsie was plump her breasts were
small, as if still developing. When he had advanced to taking off her bra and pushing the sweater way up, her chest
seemed hardly different from his own; a breast of hers in
his hand felt as delicate as a tear bulging in his eye. One
night, parked this time up by the Victory Garden wasteland, where the streetlamp was closer than on Cedar Top,
he watched raindrops on the windshield make shadows on
her chest, thin trails that hesitated and fell as his fingertips
traced and tried to stop them, there, and there. She had
dear little nipples like rabbit noses. She let him kiss them,
suck them until she said in her breathy, un-Dutchy voice,
"Ow, Owen. Enough, baby," and touched his head the way
the barber did when he wanted it to move. Sitting up, he
made circles with his finger and his saliva around her nipples, softly round and round, loving the sight of them so
much he felt dizzy, as the parallel shadows of the raindrops
faintly streaked her chest and the backs of his hands.

She never touched his prick. It was too sacred, too potent.
They pretended it wasn't there, even when their bodies
straightened at the angle permitted by the front seat and
its heater-crowded foot space and he held her buttocks
through her rumpled skirt and pressed himself rhythmically
against her, all the time their mouths kissing, until he came,
came in his underpants, where the dried jism made a brittle stain he later picked off with his fingernail, hoping his

mother wouldn't notice it when she did the wash. In the house they had now she did the wash in a dim cobwebby space under the cellar stairs, on a newer machine than the tub-shaped one that had seized his hand in the Willow basement; this machine had a lid that closed, and a spin-dry phase in its cycle instead of a wringer.

His sense of sexual etiquette was primitive, gleaned from the way men and women acted in the movies up to their huge close-up kiss at the end, and from enigmatic dialogue in a few books, like *For Whom the Bell Tolls* and *Forever Amber* and *A Rage to Live* and *The Amboy Dukes*, that he had looked into, and from a pornographic poem that Marty Naftzinger's younger brother, Jerry, a runty curly-haired kid in Owen's class, could recite, if you paid him a dime. But it was developed enough to ask, after one such climax against her compliant body, "What can we do for you?"

This embarrassed her. Elsie liked to pretend that what had just happened hadn't happened at all. "How do you mean?"

This made him shy in turn. "I mean—just holding still for me isn't enough, is it?"

She said, "We can't do more, Owen. There might be consequences you don't want." She never touched his prick and never said "I love you," knowing it would put him to the discomfort of saying the same thing back, when he wasn't ready. Otherwise she could have explained, *I love you, I like exciting you, it excites me, isn't that enough for now?*

Yet there was more, both knew it, and as his senior year ran out they groped to find it without committing sins so dark and final their lives would be forever deformed. Elsie was less afraid of this than he; he refused to test how far she would let him "go." It had become their way in the car for him to bend over and kiss the silky warm inner sides of her thighs and then press his mouth as far up as he could into the warmth, her warmth, its aroma at times like the tang his mother gave off on a summer day and at others of the musky mash bins in the back of her father's store. At first she resisted, pushing at his shoulders, and then came to expect it. In those days even teen-age girls wore girdles: the crotch of her underpants was guarded by edges of stiff elastic, and though she shyly edged her hips forward in the car seat his lips could not quite reach the damp cotton. Not that he knew enough to make her come with his mouth, or how girls came at all. The pleasure was his, in being this close to a secret, in having her yield it up to him, even her fragrance, which was strong enough at times to exert a counterforce, a wish to pull his face away. But he loved it there between her legs, and how hot and sticky his cheeks grew against her thighs, and the graceless awkwardness this maneuver asked of her, still wearing her knee socks and loafers.

The summer before he went off to MIT, their experiments took on a desperate edge. She knew he was slipping away; the baton had not been passed after all. Owen had got a summer job on a surveying crew, tending the target marks and chopping brush out of the sight lines. Elsie had been sent to a Lutheran camp in Ohio, where she was a counsellor, for six weeks. He would get rides with the crew to far corners of the county and have to be fetched from Alton when he could not hitch a ride south; he would come home exhausted and dirty, and tried not to think that college in a foreign region was swooping down upon him and would carry him away—for good, he both hoped and feared. His grandparents were ailing and his parents were no longer the young couple on Mifflin Avenue into whose bed he would climb when a dream scared him.

After Elsie returned from Ohio, it seemed almost too much work to take a bath in the farmhouse's one tub and go out again, into the dark. He and she needed the dark now. With the freedoms they had granted each other they needed such privacy that even a distant streetlight or the remotest chance of a Willow cop with a flashlight and barking voice could not be borne. Where could they go, with their maturing needs and fears of eventual desertion? His summer had not been so distracted that he had missed the implication, in her letters from camp, that she had found companionship with the boy counsellors, or the gossip, when in August she had returned, that while he was cutting brush in future housing developments she was to be seen at the township public pool, lounging in a two-piece bathing suit on a towel on the grass, with another boy, a boy her age, in her class, who would be there with her after September.

"My father owns a hundred acres of woods not that far from Brechstown," she told Owen, after an hour of directionless cruising one evening. "There's an old road in. Nobody ever comes there."

"Sounds perfect," he said, but did it? He let her direct him, turn by turn, on narrow roads he had never driven before. He was frightened at the road entrance, with its No Trespassing sign and rusting remains of barbed-wire fence; there was a sandstone boulder that with his summer muscles he rolled five feet to the side so they could get by. They were in the fragile old black Chevrolet that his father, mocking his own poverty, called "the flivver." As branches raked the creeping car's sides, Owen felt guilt, yet less than if it had been her father's Chrysler, which was kept so shipshape and Simonized. A litter of cans and wrappers in the headlights revealed that others had been here before, also pushing aside the boulder in their strength of desire. The road was rough; the old car rocked. Suppose they broke an axle or got a flat tire? The scandal, the disgrace would stain his charmed life forever.

"Isn't this far enough?" he asked. He felt a trap closing behind him.

"It goes in for a long way but gets worse," Elsie admitted. He turned off the ignition and the headlights. Such darkness! It pounced upon them with an audible crackle; it locked around the windows as if the car had plunged into a black river. As Owen's eyes adjusted, he saw a star or two high in the windshield, in the spaces between the great still trees overhead. Occasional headlights on the dirt road a half-mile away twinkled. Their own headlights must have been equally visible. Elsie's face was a mere glimmer in the cave of velour, rubber, shaped steel, and shatterproof glass. His lips found hers, and they were full and moist, but the old melting, one mouth into another, met impediments, things he couldn't put out of his mind. Suppose the Chevy didn't start when they wanted to go? Suppose he couldn't back it out on this overgrown road, the bushes a solid mass behind them and he without the machete he used on the surveying crew? He felt life, a silent vegetable life, enclosing them, on this her father's land, this man present in every leaf and reaching branch. Owen was still young enough to invest the darkness with spying presences; they distracted him when he should have been purely bent on the treasure at hand, in the deepest privacy he and Elsie would ever know.

It was August; she wore shorts and no girdle. As their embrace gained ardor and flexibility her crotch came into his hand as if rising to it. She lifted her hips on the car seat so he could slide her shorts down; through his clumsiness her white underpants came off with them and Elsie did not try to grab them back. She seemed to stretch, elongating her belly. Even in this darkness he saw wet gleams upon her eyeballs like faraway fireflies and the pallor of her long belly descending to a small soft shadow. Frightened of that shadow, he turned his attention to her breasts; with a touch more practiced than with her underpants, he unhooked her bra and tugged up her short-sleeved jersey. She crossed her arms and pulled the jersey the rest of the way, up over her head, with the bra. Her hair, cut shorter this summer so she could be in and out of the lake at the Lutheran camp, bounced, releasing a scent of shampoo. The bony smooth roundness of her shoulders gave him the shock of her nakedness; he hid his face in the side of her neck, saying, "Oh God. I can't stand this."

Her cheek tensed, smiling. "Now you, Owen," she breathed into his ear. "Your shirt."

Quickly, not wanting to let go of her for a second, he pulled it off, wishing he had bathed more carefully at home, for the smell of his armpits joined that of her shampoo and her skin in the close air of the car. He could see more and more, as if light were leaking from the patches of sky in the gaps between the trees, shedding glimmers into the woods, where faint noises were reviving and becoming less faint. He kissed her breasts, trying to be delicate, trying not to bite as the nipples grew hard, while she pressed into his ear a voice that seemed made up, enlarged and rehearsed, like something in the movies: "Owen, I used to take off my clothes in my room and walk around looking at myself in the mirror, wishing you could see me."

"You're beautiful—amazing," he told her, meaning it, but, as if her voice had swabbed out his ears, he now heard other things, whispers and stirrings around them, on the other side of the glass and metal. From somewhere not too distant there was a hoot, an owl or possibly a signal from a murderous, demented gang that lived here in caves and came out at night. *Suppose the car doesn't start?* he thought again. It often didn't, in rainstorms, or on cold mornings, his father frantic, flooding the engine in his panic, so the wearying starter turned it over uncatching, *cooga cooga*. "Did you hear something?" Owen asked Elsie.

She had left her loafers on the gritty floor of the car and had risen up, bare now even to her feet, to kneel on the seat beside him, stroking his face as he tongued her breasts; even in his state of growing terror he marvelled, holding her tight, at the *give* of a girl's waist, at the semi-liquid space below the ribs and then, behind, the downy hard plate at the base of the spine and the glassy globes of her buttocks, smooth into the cleavage, all of it unified like the silvery body of a fish, all so simple and true, the simple truth of her, alive in his arms. He heard the distant hoot again. Something rustled near the car tires. She felt his mouth losing interest in her nipple, and began to listen with him. Behind the skin between her breasts her heart was beating. "I don't think so," Elsie answered him, her voice losing its movie-screen largeness and becoming small, with a childish quaver.

For reassurance she added, "He says nobody ever comes here except in hunting season." But she too must have seen the cans and wrappers in the headlights, evidence of others. *He:* her father, the owner, all around them, hating Owen, what he was doing to his daughter, striving in every twig and trunk to eject the two of them. They listened and heard a noise so faint it could have just been saliva rattling in their held breath. Owen's hands began to move again, gathering her tender taut nakedness closer to him, his fingertips finding a touch of fuzz in the cleavage behind. He wondered how to get his head down to kiss that soft shadow he had glimpsed; it had seemed shyer, gauzier than what he had seen in dirty photographs and drawings, the few he *had* seen. His prick was aching behind his fly, and her hand dropped and, the first time ever, began fumbling at his belt buckle to release it, its imperious pressure, its closeted sour smell.

But he had spooked her, he had spooked them both, and the desire that dominated him, bare-chested though he was, was the desire to escape, to see if the car could start and he could back it up that narrow road without hitting a tree or deep hole. Her father's land, and her nakedness in it like a shout: Owen was vulnerable, criminal even— trespassing, and she a minor. He must restore her intact to society. The rustling he had imagined near the tires became a sudden thrashing, a distinct lunge of the unknown.

"Elsie," he whispered.

"What?" Perhaps expecting some avowal, some earthy plea.

"Let's get out of here."

She hesitated. He heard her heart beat, her breath whistle. "It's up to you," she decided in the mannerly voice that she had used with his mother. Then, catching his mood, she whispered, "Yes, let's."

Often afterwards he would remember details of this hour (her shorts and underpants in one sweep; her gleaming eye-whites; his sense of her slithering into the space above his head like a silken kite, like an angel crammed into an upper corner of a Sienese Nativity) and regret his lack of the boldness that would have let him linger with her gift of herself, and taste it, and let her continue undoing his pants. But his nerves had poisoned their privacy. Naked or not, she was a person, and now a frightened one. His retreat was cowardly but he felt brave and cool, successfully managing the maneuver. He started the engine—thank God, it started, drowning out all those other sounds—and backed down the overgrown road by the wan glow of the back-up lights while branches scraped metal and Elsie scrambled into her clothes. He would have backed up right onto the paved road, not bothering to roll back the boulder, but she said in a voice whose calmness sounded stern, "Owen. We should put it back the way we found it."

Her father's precious land. This had been her show, he realized. He got out angrily and in the glare of his own headlights heaved the rock back into place, for the next trespassers. "Sorry, sorry, sorry," he said when the Chevy was safely running down the highway, to the village, Brechstown, where she lived. "I chickened out."

Elsie said, after lighting a cigarette (rare for her, but girls in Willow smoked, and he had taught her), "You're more citified than I am. Woods don't frighten me. My father and uncle hunt in the fall. There are no bears or anything, not even bobcats any more. I felt safe."

"You should have told me that while we were in there."

"I *tried* to distract you, to keep you interested."

"You did, you were stunning. I loved it. You."

She was silent, putting his jerky speech together.

He told her, "It's just as well. We might have fucked."

Not a word they used, with others or between themselves: it was a kind of offering. But she held her silence. It occurred to him, his face heating in a blush, that he hadn't been prepared even physically, with one of these rubber things he had seen years ago up by the abandoned Dairy Queen. *Don't touch it!*

She at last spoke: "I wouldn't have let you, Owen. I intend to be a virgin for my husband. It was just, like I said, I wanted you to know me, to see me as I see myself."

"You were beautiful. Are beautiful, Elsie."

Was she crying? "Thank you, Owen," she brought out. "You're a nice person."

Too nice, was the implication. Still, he couldn't blame himself. Her body like that of a slithering cool flexible fish in his arms had been a revelation, but it had been revelation enough for one night.

Were there other nights, to follow? There might have been, but when he looked back, trying to recall each under-lit detail, it didn't seem so. Their futures came upon them fast. Elsie had another boyfriend for her senior year, and married yet another boy she met at the local Penn State extension. Surprisingly, they left the region, settling in the San Francisco area. If Owen wouldn't take her away, another would.

They must have driven around that night, burning up gas, letting their heartbeats slow down, trying to talk into place what they had learned about each other and their own lives, before he drove her home, to Brechstown. It was a village almost in Chester County, an erratically spaced cluster such as Willow must have been before the advent of trolley cars made it a suburb of Alton. Right behind the houses were fields and farm buildings, barns whitewashed white by their Amish owners and silos built of a brown-glazed over-sized brick. Mr. Seidel's feed-and-hardware store, with its loading platform and checkered Purina ads, sat between a gas station and a one-man country barbershop, closed, its striped pole not turning. Elsie waited on store customers on Saturdays, and Owen had more than once shaken her father's hand in there; Mr. Seidel was a muscular man bordering on fat, and even though he lifted eighty-pound feed sacks into the Mennonite trucks and Amish buggies he wore a shirt and a necktie and a gold tieclip. He would take Owen's hand with an expert lunge, flashing a mischievous smile beneath a small, squared-off mustache. His house was a quarter-mile away, up a long crunching driveway, an old farmhouse like Owen's own family's but fussily improved. A new addition held a two-car garage below and a family room above, with a TV and built-in loudspeakers and furniture that all matched; the addition was covered in aluminum siding. The original house was built not of sandstone but of limestone, because that was what the earth yielded here, near the Chester County line.

When he and Elsie kissed good-night, again there was not that melting together, though he took the liberty of stroking a breast as she leaned toward him getting out of the car. Owen felt he had failed but no one could take from him his stolen treasure, how far Elsie had "gone," leaving him with a kind of home movie his mind could run and rerun in a rickety projector, not just in bed but in inward moments of daylight, flickering bits and pieces of her—her shampoo, her heartbeat like a stranger knocking on the other side of a door, the surprising elastic give and stretch of her waist.

So Phyllis Goodhue was not his first love interest, though it must be admitted that even for the innocent 'fifties Owen was an innocent. Having been taken too deep into the woods by Elsie, he saw sex as something to be deferred until he had made space for it and didn't feel squeezed. His freshman year had been squeezed by his efforts not to fail and fall back into the farmland and his disconsolate family. At home, his grandmother, crippled by Parkinson's disease, stayed more and more upstairs in bed; when he would visit her she would hold out her clawlike blue hands to him and say, "Up. Up." Grammy had always been active and didn't want to stop exercising. Owen would gamely pull her up, and then let her down, her head in the wild disorder of its thinned white hair lowering to the pillow, and pull her up again, until he impatiently wearied. Downstairs, his grandfather spent hours sitting at one end of the old caneback sofa reading the Bible. When a car passed on the lonely road outside, he lifted his head as if sniffing, in hopes that it would be the mailman, who never brought him any mail but the Alton morning paper, already out of date, and dues and notices from the Masonic lodge in Willow, of which he had been a member in his prime, a new arrival in town and a significant local investor. Last summer, his daughter had driven him into Willow for the Saturday funeral of his last old friend from those prosperous days; both of them, father and daughter, had come back with tears in their eyes, Owen was startled to see—jewel-like trophies from the world of "for keeps," where shots rang out and panicked horses ran back into their burning stables and the second law of thermodynamics refused all reversals into a condition of lesser disorder.

Back in Cambridge as a sophomore, he found the squeeze slightly lessened; Owen knew the ropes now. In September, he ventured across the river to see the Braves play the Phillies; he rooted for the Phillies but kept it to himself, in the shirtsleeved crowd whose skimpiness foretold the move of the franchise to Milwaukee within a year. The symmetrical eight-team leagues of his boyhood, as immovably fixed, he had thought, as the Ten Commandments, were beginning to shift and slide across the country. On a Friday night in November he and a pack of five other future engineers took the subway at Kendall and walked up Cambridge Street to the Old Howard at Scollay Square, which itself would soon disappear. Before a somewhat sardonic all-male audience of sailors and geezers and college boys, a glittering woman with an implausible cinnamon-red upsweep strutted in fewer and fewer clothes and ended up on her back on a velvet chaise longue kicking her legs in the air in a sufficient pantomime of orgasm, while the drums in the orchestra pit pounded. Under the harsh stage lights, well-used, half-amused women went through routines that did not seem lifeless to Owen; in feathers and breakaway ball gowns and hourglass corsets and ruffled garters and satin heels, these women had the pure life of dreams, dreams sent up from the pit of oneself, fantastic enactments of what was at bottom most real.

A New England daintiness and wit leavened what in Pennsylvania, in the milltown brothels and dives, had a sullen, suety heaviness, slightly rancid. Up here, where the Puritans had left their traces in the white steeples and prim brick architecture, sex was tricked up, if not altogether banned. Boston's highly evolved civic morality prescribed certain limits on costume. Pasties on the nipples, G-string on the pubis, high heels on the feet, tiaras on the head, bright paint on the face—all mitigated the simple glimmering nudity that Elsie in her innocence had offered him one night. Nudity, New England seemed to say, was too serious, too vulnerable, to commodify; only goddesses in marble or Mother Eve in crabbed engravings could flaunt it aboveground. Underground, there were stag films in frat houses, projected to uneasy hooting, starring actors and actresses whose sagging, pouchy, wistful, and impotent humanity roused scorn in the viewers, young and inexperienced as they were.

In his sophomore year, then, after a summer of the surveying crew and a few unsatisfactory dates with Elsie, who was more guarded and sparing of herself now that she was a Penn State freshman, Owen returned in his daydreams to Phyllis, without ever having spoken a word to her. But she turned up in a class that he too was taking, Introduction to Digital Computer Coding and Logic:

> Survey of principles of logical design and of the elements of coding programs for large-scale digital computers, discussed from the user's point of view. Brief descriptions of the logical structure of digital computers operating at M.I.T. and elsewhere. Interpretation of sequences of arithmetical and logical operations into digital computer instructions, with examples chosen from typical engineering, scientific, and business problems and from real-time control applications. Techniques for simplifying and improving the programming and operating of computers by the use of subroutines. Execution on the M.I.T. Whirlwind I computer of examples discussed in class to provide first-hand experience with automatic high-speed machines.

v. *How Phyllis Was Won*

"**Y**OU'RE GETTING all of this?"

It was an awkward, side-of-the-mouth kind of ice-breaker, addressed to the tall sandy-haired girl as, having spotted her momentarily alone in the post-class rush and quickening his steps, Owen drew abreast of her in the long hall.

Her eyes as she darted to him in polite surprise were a blue so mild as to be gray, like her winter coat, which he thought of as the color of a dove in the distance. Her eyebrows and lashes were almost colorless, and her mouth as she spoke had an intriguing frozen quality, a delayed way of moving, her whole face delicate as if outlined in silverpoint, though shot through with living tints of pink. Her eyelids were pink, and the tip of her nose, and the crests of her slanted cheekbones. "Oh," she said cautiously. "I think so. It's all so lovely." Her reply had a certain soft bounce to it, suggesting that she had been waiting for him to approach her, having sensed that he wanted to. They were some weeks into the course; leaves were turning, football was being played at more frivolous universities, and her nose still showed a bit of sunburn, achieved lying on a blanket in the grass, in the Great Court or down by the river. Strange, Owen thought, how sun-worshippers often have unsuitably fair skins.

He went on, in a voice that sounded whiny in his own ears, "I didn't expect all this rather creepy mathematical logic, Frege and Russell and Gödel's paradoxes—all this propositional calculus, my God, what a tempest in a hypothetical teapot! I thought we were going to learn how to program digital computers."

"Oh, we will, I'm sure. But he's"—the assistant professor who taught the course, whose name was Klein, his style murmurous and spasmodic and hard to follow—"leading up to something, a whole new way of looking at numbers, seeing them the way machines do instead of how we do."

"I can hardly wait," Owen said, more sarcastically than he had intended. He was sounding like a malcontent, a surly know-nothing, and after all that watching at a distance might lose this marvellous girl her first minute on the hook. This was a fastidious, almost transparent fish on his line, with surprising, quick leaps to her talk. She made him feel (and always would) dark, a little thick-blooded, slightly slow and heavy.

"You're too practical," she told him. "Mr. Klein wants us to think about how *we* think. Our so-called thinking is messy, with many little determinations, more or less simultaneous, whereas machines have no intuition, no mass of experience. Normal human illogic won't do for them. Nothing is obvious to them that isn't absolutely spelled out."

"They can do only what we know how to order them to perform, like Lady Lovelace said." He was parroting Klein, that silky embodied intelligence, who spoke with a retractive tremor, as if voicing anything loudly would jar his delicate brain. "Wasn't she something, for a woman back then?" Owen added lamely, trying to keep up in the hall, sidestepping and being bumped as Phyllis floated at his side. "She was a number," he added, a joke to dilute, perhaps, the taste of flirtation in his mouth; for by bringing up Ada Lovelace, Byron's daughter and Charles Babbage's handmaiden in the invention of the Analytical Engine, he had hoped to flatter this other mathematically minded female.

"She was," was Phyllis's flat reply. She was drifting away; he had failed to engage her. They had come, in the numbered maze, to Room 7, the ten-pillared entrance hall, where right-angled paths diverged. Seeing they must part, and recognizing that this stranger had made an effort, she took a livelier tone: "Didn't you like, today, the way he diagrammed *inference*? All these 'well-formed' formulas for something so obvious we all know it without thinking twice about it?"

He mustn't lose her; he must try to rise to her with some provocation, something to carry over to their next encounter. "You're *not* practical?" he asked.

The two stood, immobile in the flood of swaddled, pimpled, boisterous bodies hurrying to their next class. "I guess not," she told him, in her gentle, fading voice. "I love what's pure and useless." She shrugged, lightly, apologizing for all of her, the whole length of her pale, pink, diffidently carried body.

"That's beautiful of you," he told her. It just popped out of him, too coarse a compliment; he saw her wince. Owen hurried to patch it up: "Look. Let's have coffee some time— would you like to?"

He saw, there in the enhanced light of this high-domed chamber, that he was adding to her burdens—she was already fending off many suitors, many potential coffee-mates. He tried another joke, taken from the lecture they had just heard, which had touched on the Turing machine. "That's not an if/then," Owen assured Phyllis. "No necessary consequences. It's more an n plus one. You're n, n for 'knows it all,' and I'm a one, meaning 'simpleton.' I'm a simple scholarship hick who is dying to ask you about"—he snatched at another phrase from the lecture, Klein's concluding phrase—" 'primitive recursion.' "

"That's what it's going to be all about, primitive recursion," she prophesied, turning away after an upward glance at the clock. There was a characteristic look, he would learn, a regretful gaiety in the moment of parting, that she would convey over her shoulder; she was never lovelier, with more affection in her smile, than when saying good-bye. "And I *don't* know it all," she added, leaving his direct question unanswered.

But she did, as winter bore down upon the school, share coffee and then more with him. Why? What did she like about him? She was a year older than he, as Elsie had been a year younger, and Owen saw her as a creature above him, in advance of him, moving easily in these realms of enlightenment. In MIT's forest of fact and concept he had at first felt lost, but his marks were all right and got better as he blended in and his interests narrowed. He was tall, thin then, with a thick head of soft hair, darker than his father's wispy brown; he let it grow carelessly long, in that strictly barbered era. Where so many of the high achievers were bespectacled Asian-Americans and pudgy Jews, Phyllis must have liked the big-boned way Owen stood taller than she; they looked good walking together. Though never athletically competitive in the public schools of Pennsylvania, he had a nervous wiriness that, in those daydreaming farmhouse years, he had worked up into minor feats of agility— juggling three tennis balls, hopping over a broom held in both hands before him, taking harmless pratfalls on the steel-edged stairs, thus alarming Phyllis and making her laugh when she saw he was unhurt. He loved seeing the blood of surprise pinken her pale, thin-skinned face. His mock injuries parodied a wish to abase himself before her that was real enough—the clown, the pretender, daring to present himself before the princess.

As winter took away outdoor spaces from the students, they crowded after class and in the evenings into the luncheonettes and cafeterias and cheap Chinese and Indian restaurants of Kendall Square—not yet a high-tech Oz but a pocket of low-end industry darkened by a century's grime—and the southern end of Central Square. Doors swung open to admit sharp drafts of snow-flecked air with fresh arrivals, and mirrors sweated as the heat of the packed bodies interfaced with the cold walls. Wedged around a Formica-topped table with three or four others of Phyllis's set—Anne-Marie Morand from Montreal, Amy Toong from Boston, Jake Lowenthal from Flatbush, Bobby Sprock from Chicopee—Owen admired the way she listened, said so little, just fed cigarettes into those pale, numb lips and exhaled up into her dirty-blond bangs. She had the magnetism of those who make no effort to shine; she held them together, many actors playing to an audience of one. Noisy, fast-talking Jake was mocking the first digital computers: Harvard's Mark I, ENIAC down in Philly, the Lincoln Laboratories Whirlwind housed a few blocks from where they sat. "Mountains that don't produce a mouse," he proclaimed. "Thousands of switches, boxes and boxes of punch cards, miles of wiring, tons of hardware all to do what a slide rule and half a brain can do in thirty seconds."

"Jake, you don't believe that," Phyllis told him, so levelly and quietly Owen felt a jealous pang: a well-established connection was being used.

"Why don't I? Hey, Phyl, why don't I? By the time ENIAC was built, the war was over and the Army couldn't use it. It was a thirty-ton dog. It takes two hundred kilowatts to run it, it gobbles up electricity even when it isn't running, it costs a fortune just to keep the tubes cool—there are eighteen thousand of them. Eighteen *thousand* tubes. Not to mention ten thousand condensers and six thousand switches."

"Yes, and it does math it would take thousands of people to do by hand," Amy Toong said, glancing quickly sideways to check that Phyllis, to whom Jake had spoken, was not replying.

"You're talking obsolete," Bobby Sprock told Jake. "Vacuum tubes are on the way out. Already, Whirlwind's storage unit uses magnetic cores instead of tubes. Punch cards are being replaced by magnetic tapes. Bell Labs has come up with something called a transistor that does the switching with semi-conducting strips of silicon and doped germanium. Circuitry is going to be all thin-film layering soon. Pretty soon we'll have a computer no bigger than a refrigerator."

"Yeah, and we're going to fly to the moon on gossamer wings," Jake scoffed. Owen wondered if their ganging up on Jake amounted to anti-Semitism; but his persistent aggression seemed to invite it, to relish it. He said, "There are molecular limits in thin-film they've reached already. Face it, guys and gals, computers are basically clunky energy-hogs so expensive they'll only ever have one customer, and that's Uncle Sam. Look at UNIVAC. Remington Rand finally got the kinks out, mostly, and now they can't sell them. They run so hot they've got to put dry ice in the ductwork."

"Well," Owen pointed out, as mildly as possible in imitation of Phyllis, "UNIVAC picked Eisenhower over Stevenson right enough. And did it so early nobody believed it; the network had the results and didn't broadcast them!"

"Predicting elections is a stunt," Jake said.

"The first airplanes were stunts. The first horseless carriages," said Bobby Sprock, with the agonized expression and near-stutter of those who feel all the justice of an argument heaped on their side. "The first t-telephone, right here in Boston!"

"Analog computers, I can see," Jake conceded, with a tongue emboldened by his opponent's sputtering. "Amplifiers, differentiators—that's what I call electrical engineering. This digital, binary stuff is a toy—it's one step up from tic-tac-toe."

"Jacob, aren't you funny?" Phyllis said, not smiling. Owen heard the soft familiar tone with which she addressed him, and felt—the jolt that went straight across his chest— certainty that these two were connected as more than friends. She was the passive, negative pole of a number of highly charged connections: this inference, there in the circuit of close-pressed bodies and tousled wool wraps jammed around a small table littered with the soy-scented ruins of a Chinese meal, did not unplug his insulated belief that the course of his life must flow through this particular girl, this woman.

That she had not been born the moment he first set eyes on her, that he found her in the midst of attachments old and new would have dismayed him had he not been numbed into becoming a mere implement in the hand of a designing Nature. Their bodies knew they would make good babies.

In the midst of this student seethe and chatter, they were kindred exotics, sheltered children groping after reality, singular in a pride they couldn't express, gifted but defective, set apart. They promised to each other a fresh genetic start, a beginning of real life. He had no cause for jealousy. As computers know, the past is mere storage, to be called upon only as the present calculation requires. When they were indeed alone together, he asked for no more information than she volunteered, and she was vague. "Oh, I went out a few times with this section man from Projective Geometry, but that was last spring, and I have no idea where he's got the idea that I owe him something. I can't believe it was anything I said."

"How do you know he thinks you owe him something?"

"He keeps sending me unpleasant letters. He's very angry I won't go out with him any more. Now he's angry about *you*."

"Me?" Flattered, scared: Owen's tender stomach registered these incompatibles. "But why me especially? I'm just one of your crowd—why would I stick out?"

"Well," Phyllis said, "to him you do." If she was in his arms, she wriggled a little deeper, as if wanting to shrink away from the entanglements her unassuming beauty had brought upon her and, it seemed, on him, too. "He's right, of course. We're more—serious?"

"We are?" Again, the abdominal chafing of incompatibles. He wanted life but was scared of it. It was easier to roll over and dream on. In her light-handed, abstracted way Phyllis was tenacious. "O.K.," Owen said. "What shall we do about—? What's his name?"

"Ralph."

"Ralph. How can you be worried about somebody called Ralph? Ralphs are roly-poly, beer-belly types."

"Not this one. He's short, and dense. He does boxing to keep fit. One of his letters talked about smashing my face in."

"Oh my God. Your gorgeous face?" Her skin appeared to him thinner than other people's; it sunburned in minutes, and a blush stayed on her cheeks for an hour; his lightest touch, he felt, travelled instantly to nerve centers all over her body.

She blushed; even her lowered eyelids blushed. "That's what he called it, too. Gorgeous. He wrote that he would leave marks on me I would always remember him by."

"Oh, dear. What kind of section man was he? How was his Projective Geometry?"

When Owen tried to remember this conversation, he had trouble locating it. The authorities of MIT discouraged privacy for mixed-sex couples. MIT didn't know where to put its female students; some were housed across the river, at 120 Bay State Road, and then the university opened up a section of Bexley Hall. Phyllis's room in either dormitory was out of bounds, but there were chintz-covered sofas at 120 Bay State Road, and corners of the big reception room where the lights—stately floor lamps with pleated shades and three-way bulbs—could be dimmed to coziness. Students would lounge and lie in the semi-dark with their brush-cuts and perms; the boys then wore white bucks and narrow rep ties, the Ivy look not yet yielded to the blue-jeaned geek look, and the girls wore single-strand pearls and pastel sweaters whose wool seemed to melt in the hand. It wasn't until Phyllis moved in her senior year back to her parents' home off Garden Street that she and Owen could be alone between four walls; but that was later, surely, than the scare from Ralph Finneran.

"Smart enough," she answered, "but he had a pugnacious

way of making students feel stupid. He came from—how can I say this?—very ordinary people, near Worcester. He took me out there for Thanksgiving once, and all anybody cared about was the high-school football game, this sacred rivalry between two old mill towns; we all had to go, though it was bitter cold that year. His nephew was playing and got injured, even. They were tough, I should never have tried to be nice to him. After that Thanksgiving I knew it and tried to pull back." Owen made noises of sympathy but she talked through them, her gray eyes gazing at that past gray day. "They were Roman Catholic, and though he was quite dismissive of what he thought were people's attempts to cling to illusions, he once told me that we of course would be raising our children Catholic. When I expressed surprise, he became very angry. When he was angry, he would go all dark in the face, I don't know how he quite did it, but it frightened me."

She tried to imitate, in her fair and passionless face, Ralph's lethal look, and the effort was like a cheap beer poured into a crystal wineglass. Owen thought for the hundredth time how fortunate he was to be with her, if only for the time being. She was an education. "And me?" he asked her. "Am I tough and ordinary?"

"Owen, don't fish for compliments. You're a Bird."

In her girlhood, she and her girlfriends at Browne & Nichols, in the innocent cruelty of their adolescent clique, had classified people into three types—Birds, Horses, and Muffins. Owen could not quite grasp it, just as he could not grasp the ritual she described, acquired when she was thirteen or so, of lying in bed and, when she could not sleep, resting her eyes, with religious rigor, on each of the ceiling's four corners. It meant more to her than she could say, or would say.

"A cute little bird?" he asked. "Chirp, chirp?"

"Not really," Phyllis said, pursing her lips in a concentrating, solemn way he adored, crinkling the unpainted flesh of them. Making a *moue*, she told him it was called, when he had lovingly described this expression of hers to her. Now she told him, "A big lazy bird that hovers all day, in circles, hardly moving its wings, and then swoops to the kill."

"Oh, dear! I sound frightful."

"No more than anybody else. Kill, kill, kill, kill, kill, kill," she said. She explained, "That's from Shakespeare," adding, "Just using mouthwash—think of all those microbes you kill."

"I'm shocked," he said, "that you could ever see me killing anything. I can't even step on a spider. I have a phobia about them." Yet he was pleased by her description, as granting him some initiative and force, when his inmost sense of himself was of an innocent witness, acted upon but not acting. He snuggled closer into Phyllis's cool warmth and asked, "And you? What are you? I keep forgetting."

She was shy of talking about herself, as if touching too tender or shameful a part of her body, or as if her ego was difficult to locate. "Not a Horse," she said. "I have a Birdy look, but am really a Muffin, inside."

"Surely not."

She was offended. "Muffins aren't a bad thing to be. They're accepting. They're non-disruptive. They don't hurt anybody."

He saw himself swooping in her mind, a dark shape empowered to hurt. "Not even other Muffins?"

"They don't meet other Muffins, Muffins are too rare. Most people are Horses, clumping along."

He laughed at the subtlety of this boast. She valued herself highly enough, but in terms so subtle as to be almost beyond him, like higher math, or the fine points of a foreign grammar.

Impatient with self-exposition, she reverted to an earlier topic: "I showed my father the most unpleasant and threatening of Ralph's letters, and Daddy wrote him one of his own, mentioning legal action."

Owen felt relief; he wouldn't have to handle it, then. Her father was still in charge. "Well, good. And did that shut the creep up?"

"We don't know yet. That was just days ago."

"You poor angel, you're still in the middle of this, aren't you? Uh, did your father have to write to any other boyfriends?"

He was giving her a chance to laugh; he had not expected her to mull it over. "Last year, there was, but this was his idea, not mine. A boy—man, really, he was older than I—I used to see in the summer, who my parents didn't think was at all suitable."

"They didn't, but you did?"

She pursed her lips again, this time keeping silent. She did not like, beyond a point, being probed, and had already taken him in so much deeper than he would have dared hope a mere year ago, when she had been to him just a vision, floating through the halls. "You *did*," he concluded.

She didn't disagree. So: he had rivals lodged in the exterior world, like Jake and Ralph, and rivals lodged in her heart, her secret being, like the tremulously clever Klein and this unnamed man her parents objected to. Owen was learning when to change the subject, encountering a closed door in the corridors of her past. "Was it your parents' idea to have you become a math major?"

"No: they were rather horrified, they're such humanities

snobs. Literature and the arts are all they care about. To them make-believe is life. Science is vulgar. My father's specialty is the English Renaissance—the sixteenth and seventeenth century—"

"Thanks," he interrupted, nettled by their previous conversation and this summer lover she was refusing to talk about. "I know when the English Renaissance was."

"Of course. Some people don't. My father doesn't do just the poets and playwrights, Shakespeare and so on, that everybody knows about, but these prose writers nobody can bear to read any more, Sidney and Bacon and Lyly and Lodge, always writing about Arcadia in this elaborate way—he loves them. That's where my name came from; all those old poems are full of Phyllises—sprightly Phyllises, naughty Phyllises. I turned out to be a dreamy Phyllis, rather disappointing."

"Not to me. Nor to a number of others, it sounds like."

"About ten years ago," she went on, on her preferred topic, "when the man who teaches eighteenth-century prose had his sabbatical, Daddy took that on, too—Dryden and Bunyan, Addison and Steele, Boswell and Johnson— and he *revelled* in it, working it up, *shelves* of this impossibly dry old stuff. He hides in books, my mother says."

"My father hid in numbers."

"So do I; I'd love to meet him some day." Owen shied from trying to imagine it, poor beaten-down Floyd Mackenzie with his tender stomach and penny-ante job, and this cosseted Cambridge princess. It would make a meeting as awkward and painful as the one between his mother and Elsie. Our parents hatch us but cannot partake of our work in the world. Phyllis explained to him, trying to give of her deeper self, "Don't you find it so beautiful, math? Like an endless sheet of gold chains, each link locked into the one before it, the theorems and functions, one thing making the next inevitable. It's music, hanging there in the middle of space, meaning nothing but itself, and so *mov*ing, Owen." Did he need this nudge? Had he been falling asleep beside her long, soothing body? True, he relaxed when with her, as if home at last. "It used to make me *cry*," she said, "when I was a teen-ager, having a problem come apart for me—the way it cracks open at a certain point, goes from being all outside to all inside, if you believe the equations and follow through on them. It's like, at the beach, turning a horseshoe crab upside down, all the little legs wriggling and the tail flipping to turn it all over. No, my parents didn't encourage me. They thought science was for plodders, grubby guys usually from the Midwest. I tried to tell them, math doesn't do useful work, it does *useless* work. Which of course isn't exactly true; physics and technology depend on calculus. And set theory."

"Do you understand," he asked her—and such a question must have demanded a more intimate setting than a corner, however dimly lit, of the visitors' lounge at 120 Bay State Road; it might have been in her Bexley Hall room, against the rules, on one of those weekends when her roommate, Sally Fazio from Providence, was back in Rhode Island or off skiing in New Hampshire—"set theory? I mean, why it's so wonderful?"

"I think I do. It *is* wonderful, so elemental and original. It's one man's invention, you know. Newton and Leibniz invented calculus independently, Lobachevsky and Bolyai did the same for non-Euclidean geometry, and if they hadn't Gauss would have—it was just sitting there waiting to be picked up—but without Cantor set theory might not have ever come into being. Hilbert said nobody will ever expel us from the Paradise Cantor created. Isn't that nice? To create a Paradise nobody will be expelled from?" Talking of mathematics, Phyllis became more animated and precise — quicker-voiced, wider and more reckless in her gestures. Her blood ran faster beneath the thin fair skin.

"It is," he had to agree.

"And he did it, a lot of it, in a mental hospital. His brain snapped, set theory was so powerful."

"What *my* brain doesn't quite get," Owen persisted, elevating himself to Cantor's class of mental fragility, "is why it was such a big deal when Russell and Gödel found these internal contradictions or paradoxes — as Klein points out, the confusion is basically semantic. I don't see what undecidability has to do with the history of the computer."

"You don't?" said Phyllis, unable to quite conceal her disappointed surprise, as if her own clarity of mind had been conferred upon Owen by her regal act of accepting him as her boyfriend. The two of them met before class and rejoined afterwards; they shared mid-morning coffee and a dragged-out late lunch at the Student Center across Mass. Ave.; they went to movies together in Harvard Square or on Washington Street in Boston; sardonic Jake and menacing Ralph had been banished to the rim of the circle at whose quiet center Owen found himself. In the evenings, unable to be away from each other for more than four hours, the two reunited amid the smoke and misted mirrors of the little restaurants where students huddled in overheated symposia.

"I mean," he said, insisting on his own obtuseness, thrusting it upon her, "so *what* if there exists a set of sets that are not members of themselves, which makes it a set that both is and isn't a member of itself?"

"But, Owen dear," Phyllis said, "the antinomies — the paradoxes — undermine classical logic, but the way they have to be phrased brings us to symbolic logic, which brings in Boolean math and the Turing machine and algorithms. Undecidability is like knowing you have a swamp and having to invent methods to build on it anyway. It's like the Back Bay on all its pilings," she said, so pleased with her own analogy that her face for the moment was more a Bird's than a Muffin's.

Phyllis inhabited an attenuated realm where he longed to join her. Her very air of absence pulled him up, led him on; at times he had the sensation that the void which the rigors of post-Aristotelian logic discovered at the very roots of arithmetic existed also in her—a refusal to be obvious, an implacable denial beneath the diffident, compliant surface. "You know I don't love you yet," she said after they had been going together for a year and were already considered a couple by their peers.

Owen was shocked, especially since they were lying stretched out together somewhere, on a bed or floor—it must have been in her senior year, when she moved back to her parents' house, giving them some sneaky privacy. They didn't shed their hot clothes but were, in those inhibited, swaddled times, "making out." Owen had assumed he was lovable, though beneath the regard of the Ginger Bittings of the world. His mother and Elsie had loved him.

He betrayed no feeling, simply hugging Phyllis tighter and saying, "Really? Well, I love you. Maybe you love me but don't know it yet." At the same time he felt his own body drifting away, washed backwards by the thought that he should not be directing his life to flow through this other, alien body.

"Maybe," Phyllis ambiguously agreed, in a voice thickened by regret that she had revealed so much. Her face was inches from his in the shadows of the room, which in his memory of the moment he felt to be on a high floor, perhaps her brother's room in her parents' house. He had been kissing her, those lipstickless numb lips, as if to press blood to their surface, while individual strands of her mussed hair tickled his face with the exasperating persistent delicacy of flies' feet on a muggy day. Sometimes it seemed that she was the one being tickled; more than once, as a spasm of love drove him to a flurrying multiplication of kisses on her lips, and her high blushing cheekbones, and her fadeaway eyebrows, and her lids with their squirming pulse, the whole marvellous silverpoint precision of her, she laughed aloud, disconcertingly, deflatingly. He read these moments of rejection as his clumsy, premature rupture of the delicate barriers she had erected in twenty-one years of being so fine, so solitary. He tried to imagine what motion within her, what minute climate change, would persuade her that she loved him. She had let slip, at moments in their courtship which stuck in his mind as illuminations of her obscure inner life, that she and another girl at Browne & Nichols used to hold hands and that the unspeakable boyfriend that her parents agreed would never do had been, in a way that made her hands fly apart in memorial measurement, "enormous." He had been a creature of summer camp and perhaps had acquired for her the mythic stature of the mountains, the great rough-barked pines, the distant granite outcroppings, the thunderheads on a still summer day blazing white above the dark evergreen ridge. Hank—his name, which she let slip—had been head of maintenance at the camp, captain of the battered pickup truck, master of the trash dump and the pine-needle-covered roadways, and though he had spent a few semesters at the University of New Hampshire, he professed no ambition but to continue in Nature, hewing and hauling and spraying DDT on mosquitoes and black flies. His lack of ambition had included placing no claim on her, though they knew each other through several summers. Perhaps she had been the suitor, the shy aggressor, like Owen setting up the Monopoly board for Buddy Rourke. Phyllis's face, when she thought of Hank, shed its absence, its indolence, and somehow steeled itself, though she tried to hide her feelings behind a pensive *moue*. Owen comforted himself that, if he was less intelligent than she, Hank had not even competed.

They no longer shared Introduction to Digital Computer Coding and Logic. She, a senior, disappeared into the counterintuitive exotica of advanced topology—differential manifolds, invariant Betti groups embedded in Euclidean space, duality theorems. Her senior thesis sounded suspiciously like Projective Geometry: she said it had to do with "the topological classification of manifolds of dimensions greater than two."

"How high can dimensions go?" he asked.

"To *n*, obviously."

"I can't picture it."

"You can't, but numbers can. Calculations can encompass however many. Don't look so disapproving, Owen. Relax. It's elegant, it's *fun*."

"Fun for you, I can almost believe."

"I'm at a point where I'm not sure Riemann was right, in the case of some local curvatures."

"The immortal Riemann of Riemann surfaces? You're going to refute him? Baby, you're too much."

"He wouldn't mind. He was a saint, of sorts. His father was a Lutheran pastor. He himself died at the age of thirty-nine, of tuberculosis. He left behind notebooks and papers full of ideas he hadn't had time to publish. The whole universe, you know, is a kind of Riemann surface, according to general relativity."

Her eyes wore that expression of abstracted steeliness with which she guarded the thought of those she truly, intuitively loved. A set from which Owen was excluded, even as biology and society swept them together. Always Phyllis was to harbor, as she and Owen travelled together in the thorny common world, memories of an Arcadia populated by that rarefied troop of exalted spirits, whether mathematicians or poets, Spenser or Cantor, Hilbert or Keats, to whom Cambridge in its soul was dedicated. Such a dedication does not guarantee the storms of creativity that are posthumously honored, but it curses all tamer weather as second-rate, and makes the real world a rather anticlimactic insubstantial place of exile.

While she rendezvoused with Reimann among curving surfaces unto n dimensions, Owen was grinding away at the practical subjects that went into a degree in electrical engineering—power-system analysis, non-linear impedances as power modulators, wide-band amplifiers, photoelectric transducers, insulators, transistors, microwave triodes, reflex klystrons, power relations in an electron beam under small-signal excitation, and such formulas that render invisible electrons visible, audible, and convertible to useful work. One advanced course took Owen for a week to Raytheon in Waltham, and another on repeated visits to the Harvard Computation Laboratory, where Mark I reigned in its lordly bulk and overheated obsolescence. As the Korean police action bogged down in cold and bloody mud, Owen and his schoolmates maintained exemption from the draft by passing a government test only cretins could fail: in the lecture hall called 10-250, at a signal, they presented aloft their pencils like tiny substitute guns. Brains won wars. IBM was enlisting manpower in a massive push to counter Remington Rand's triumphant UNIVAC; a business market as well as an industrial-military one was dawning for computers. Amid these heady promises of the future, while technical breakthroughs were coming faster than the professors of electrical engineering could teach them, Owen's overprogrammed neurons began to hum with brain-fatigue. It was like a message emerging from a veil of static when Phyllis, the week after she graduated (her honors thesis, questioning a nuance of Riemannian topology, having been cited for its originality and rigor), said to him, at a table for two in the tiny smoky Indian restaurant, just before he was heading south for another summer surveying with the crew and probing Elsie's responses, "My parents kept bugging me about what I was going to do with myself now, so I told them I was engaged to you."

"You did?" His face went hot, abruptly immersed in his life, his only life.

"Well, darling, aren't we? You're always talking about it." Her eyes, with a shade of nervous challenge, sought his.

In trying to persuade her of his devotion he had often imagined aloud their married life together. But he did not remember exactly proposing; he had feared he would be rejected and his hard-won advances into her enchanted terrain negated.

"Well, I guess we *are*," he admitted. "That's thrilling." What would his mother say? What would Elsie? Well, serve them right. Nature is flux and transformation, MIT had taught him.

vi. *Village Sex—III*

IN HIS JUNIOR YEAR Owen had met her parents a number of times. Their house was on a shady Cambridge street, no doubt once quieter than it had become since rush-hour traffic had discovered it as a short-cut between Garden Street and Mass. Avenue. It was a typical big house on a small lot, with an alarming weight of books everywhere, bookcases even climbing the stairs and filling the hallways of the third floor. The rooms on this third floor had been rented out to Harvard students until five years ago, when Phyllis's maturing had made the irruption of young males uncomfortable for her parents. Until her young brother, Colin, went off to Andover, he had appropriated one of the previously rented rooms as his lair, adding to the mattress and bureau and yellow-oak desk already there his own little radio of white plastic, a 45-rpm record player, some glue-it-together models of obsolete war machinery, a scattering of faintly redolent sweatshirts and basketball sneakers, and, in several unpainted pine bookcases, a tumble of Batman and Plastic Man comics, science-fiction magazines, paperbacks of baseball stats, Shady Hill textbooks, and a child's encyclopedia in fifteen volumes whose spines moved through the rainbow from violet to red but were jarringly out of order. Owen's mother had owned a few books and also borrowed them from the Alton Public Library, travelling in from Willow on the trolley car; in this house books were a monstrous growth, a fungus of reading matter encrusting every surface.

Phyllis was taller than both her parents; the sight of her blushingly towering over them, holding her head at an angle that indicated a wish to shrink lower, Owen found erotic. She was slender but ample-breasted, with abundant dirty-blond down at the nape of her long neck and in her moist places—a hormonally replete body sprung from these two dainty, dry people. Their bodies seemed the last things the senior Goodhues thought of. They dressed almost interchangeably in layers of mousy wool. Mrs., named Carolyn, wore nubbly straight skirts and low brown heels and unbuttoned cardigan sweaters of which one half always hung noticeably lower than the other. Her washed-out coloring and air of distraction linked her to her daughter, but there was an impatience, a habit of interrupting utterances she felt were too slow or obvious, which gentle-spoken Phyllis did not share. "This house—" Owen said, looking about him the first time he entered it, marvelling at the wealth of varnished stickwork, knobs, and moldings, the massive double doors, the walnut-dark staircase forcefully thrusting up to a landing where tall leaded windows cast tinted shadows.

"—has too many books. I know. I keep telling Eustace, but he says they're his tools, and he never knows which ones he's going to need. A book can wait untouched for twenty years, and suddenly, in the middle of some dreary scholarly article, he desperately needs it. It's horrible—

think of the dust mites. I try to get the cleaning women to dust them once a year and they quit instead."

"They get frightened, Mother," her daughter softly interposed, glancing apologetically in Owen's direction.

But there was no need to apologize. All parents embarrass their children. Owen's had seemed to him impossibly sad, putting on a quarrelsome show of discontent and maladjustment for all on Mifflin Avenue to see. Phyllis's, in comparison, seemed model residents of Cambridge, as obedient to their grooves as the little interlocked figures that jiggle on the hour out of a Swiss clock. Owen liked this quick small lady of the house, with her clipped gray hair and upper eyelids collapsed upon her lashes. His experience with small women—Grammy, Elsie—had generally been good.

"Phyl tells us you're quite brilliant, over there at the other place."

"Oh, no, I'm just another plodding electrical-engineering major. It's your daughter who—"

"—outsmarts the professors," Carolyn Goodhue finished for him. "We find it so strange, Eustace and I— mathematics, we thought for years it was a phase she was going through, an awkward age. Girls do, of course, and unlike boys they find such devious ways to rebel, all the time with these sweet smiles so you can't fault them. But, seriously, dear"—to her daughter—"your father and I are immensely proud. We boast. We put on brave faces when our friends tease us, asking why would a girl who could have waltzed into Radcliffe, or Wellesley or Bryn Mawr if she didn't like boys, why would she want to go down the river to a place so—"

"Grubby," Owen finished for her.

"Mother," Phyllis intervened. "We're grubby because we

have to stay up all night, memorizing facts, and most of the boys do things with their *hands.*"

"Not too many things, I hope," Mrs. Goodhue snapped, blinking rapidly when Owen laughed: he had never heard an off-color joke from Phyllis, they somehow didn't enter her head.

It was from Professor Goodhue that Phyllis had inherited her shy slouch. His posture, though, was not trying to hide any excess of beauty but was the organic product of a life at a desk or curled in a chair reading. Chin on chest, he had lost all semblance of a neck, and had swollen in the middle like an old-fashioned clay jug, his head tipped forward as if to pour forth a lecture. His voice was reedy and faint, producing its sound on the intake of his breath, with the same pulmonary motion as sucking on a pipe. He was, in Owen's limited view of him, more intake than output, though an occasional chuckle, like the snap of dried glue in an old binding, could be taken as an agreeable signal. He acted bemused by Owen's appearance at his house and dinner table, and even made a point of this bemusement, demonstrating as it did a preoccupation with higher things. Elsie Seidel's father had stridden forward in his feed-and-hardware store with too toothy a smile under his little sharper's mustache and too fierce and friendly a handshake, signalling hostility and a manly knowledge of what Owen desired of his succulent daughter. Eustace Goodhue's approach was much less confrontational, hardly an approach at all—an amiably baffled air like that of a man who works in a greenhouse with a stuffed-up nose and cannot understand why all these bumblebees keep flying in the window. Phyllis had attracted boy visitors before; her father seemed unaware that she, her college career ending and the professional prospects for a female mathematician being exceedingly slight, had arrived at an age of decision and eternal pledge. The age was reached early in Eisenhower's America; women bred as if supplying a frontier, in that era of pioneer consumerism. To set up a household and breed and buy was to strike a blow against our enemy, those dowdy, repressive anti-capitalists behind the Iron Curtain. Owen was ready to serve, believing that he had found the woman for him—the mother of his children, the nurturer of his career, the presiding angel of a home better-equipped than the threadbare shelters the Rausches and Mackenzies had managed to provide in leaner, less electronic times.

Owen rather despised Professor Goodhue for not putting up a stiffer defense of his treasure. In the more than twenty years in which he and the man were members of the same family, the older becoming a grandfather in perfect synchrony as the younger became, repeatedly, a father, the first ten saw little respect tendered by Owen, a son-in-law exposed fully now to the shadowy, pampered role the professor played in his own household. True, in the last analysis its weight of books and eclectic, picturesque furniture rested on his intellectual labors, which had also wrested from the world a summer cottage in Truro and European travel every other year. But he seemed to dwell too much in the world of books, its conceits and fictions, to make much of a dent on this one.

In the second decade of this close acquaintance, Owen, his knowledge of the world deepened, could better appreciate his father-in-law's sly withdrawal from the front line of family life, and the learned passion that had produced so many lectures and carefully pondered little articles, bound first in buff-colored academic quarterlies and then collected in fat, chaste volumes from the same university presses that issued the professor's several anthologies and his critical biography of George Herbert. Those years saw little change in Eustace Goodhue, as he went from mid-life to retirement, and much change in Owen, progressing from naïve youth to experienced mid-life. They became two men roughly equal, with the companionable affection between them of any who have survived a hazardous voyage together. Owen, himself the father of two daughters, at last saw how weakened, by biology and by humanity's village wisdom, the bond becomes: every cell in the aging father's body yearns to pass her to another man, a man of her generation who can without taboo perform those elemental acts the cycle of generation demands.

There was in Professor Goodhue's absent-minded complaisance something as yet dimly glimpsed by its beneficiary—the dubious pleasure taken in the sexual transactions of others, a polymorphous sharing noticeable not only at weddings, where the weeping parents and awestruck flower-girl unite to consign the bride to the connubial mysteries, but at polite adult parties where custom seats husbands and wives not together but beside the spouses of others, tempting potential confusion and exogamous trespass. Copulation, in short, is so powerful and highly prioritized an event that we take pleasure not only in our own but in that of others, even of a daughter or wife as she draws away from us into the sexual seethe. Phyllis in all her aloof beauty was a fruit with a stem more weakened than was apparent; she fell to Owen rather confoundingly, her fall resisted less than he had expected or, at some deep level, hoped.

All this could be glimpsed only in long hindsight. At the time, as her return to her home gave them more opportunities for intimacy than 120 Bay State Road or Bexley Hall had offered, they felt daring and furtive; in their minds it would have shocked their parents to see them and shocked God as well, if He had deigned to watch. Owen, with the furtive religiosity inherited from his pious grandparents, was not sure that He was not watching, much as He had watched over the house in Willow, in its snow globe of safety. Now, like the vibrant green beam of a science-fiction ray-gun, or like the ruby-red lasers that in science-fact would be developed in the next decade, God's gaze perhaps penetrated through the Goodhues' dormered roof into the third-floor room still flavored by her brother's dirty socks and ratty comic books.

Phyllis liked, Owen discovered, having the back of her neck, with its sweaty pale tendrils, stroked; it loosened her up. And the bluish inner sides of her arms, turned submissively uppermost, and the backs of her thighs, his fingers curled to lightly scratch the goosebumped skin with his nails. He tussled her into advanced déshabille, to the goal of pink-faced nakedness, but he clung to her virginity, as something sacred, a threshold he could still retreat from. Not that he wanted to retreat; she was his prize, his captive princess. She was taller and slimmer than Elsie, with that same breathtaking give to her waist and bigger breasts, so big she made motions to disown them, fighting her hands as they fluttered in instinctive cover-up. When his mouth became too busy at her nipples, she pulled back, deflecting his rapturous smothered comments as if they were the asides of a bumbling lecturer. Product of an academic environment, Phyllis could produce an academic frown, a mental sniff of disapproval. She held him against her, however, with a certain skill, gripping his buttocks; she had done this before, let a boy come against her pelvic region, though her hands felt gloved in tentativity. When it came to mopping up, though, Phyllis participated efficiently, their hands intertwining with his handkerchief as it pursued the puddles of semen on her belly and in her pubic hair, curlier and darker than the hair on her head. On the night of their wedding, surveying the moonlit field of flesh of which he had taken legal possession that afternoon, at a ceremony as watered-down yet graceful as the Unitarianism of Cambridge could make it, he knelt between her legs and combed her luxuriant pussy, now his, as if preparing a fleecy lamb for sacrifice, until she irritably took the comb from his hand and tossed it away from the bed; it clattered against a baseboard over beneath the window.

Rejected again. He scarcely dared ask why she had done that—dismissed his currying, his proud adoration. "What was wrong?" he asked. "Did it hurt?"

"It began to feel funny," Phyllis admitted. "Tickly. Theatrical. Like you were showing off for somebody. Let's just do it."

"Do you want to? We don't have to. I can wait until you want to. Maybe tomorrow, when we're not so tired and jazzed up by other people. Weddings are killing, aren't they?" They were in a cottage, the Truro cottage, lent to them for a week by her parents. He had graduated in the top third of his class; she had spent an unhappy year at graduate school desultorily taking advanced courses in number theory and topology and groping for a thesis topic and not getting along with her advisor. They were to go back to Cambridge for the summer, she to pick up a few more credits at summer school and he for an eight-week internship with Whirlwind that the department of electrical engineering had arranged. They could hear from afar surf breaking and withdrawing on the beach at the base of its sand cliffs and smell the stunted pitch pines. The sound and the smell, which would be there whether they were or not, gave the dark outside a vastness their newly joined lives could never fill. "Why is everybody supposed to like champagne?" he asked, timid of her silence. "To me it always tastes sour."

He could not read her expression, only see the lean arabesque of her jaw and the long tendon of her neck as she turned her head toward the window. A three-quarters moon was framed and bisected by the sash; its light picked out the tab of an earlobe in the obscure mass of her hair. What was Phyllis doing, with her motionless gaze? Saying goodbye to the moon? This small bare house, strange to him, to her was full of girlhood summer memories and quaint souvenirs—books, shells, immature watercolors fading in their dime-store frames—of a bygone family life. The cottage's briny, musty odors would be murmuring a language to her brain. Still kneeling, possessed of the privileges of a husband, his brain sapped by the flight of all his blood into his erect prick, he surveyed the glimmering moonlit wealth of her—the crescents of round hard shoulder and the collarbone jutting above its slant pockets of shadow and her breasts flattened on the fragile splay of her ribs. She turned her head back to gaze up at him.

"No, let's do it," her voice came, softer. "Why buck tradition?"

"Did you say fuck tradition?"

"That's not funny, Owen."

His impression grew that he was looking down at someone somehow slain. The weak moon-shadows of window muntins cast a net over her white form. Her sunken eyes seemed unseeing. His poor prick, so hard it ached, emitted an anxious little stink. Then a white hand drifted from her side and lightly grazed his glans and shaft, testing. She lifted her knees, assuming the exact pose of the drawing gouged into the back of the playground shed, and as if idly, with cool fingertips, she guided him in. He met an obstacle, and pushed through it. What he had not expected, it hurt him as well as her. He finished, and it was not clear that she had even begun. Her mucous warmth had seared him. As if back in the bed of his adolescence, he had had a sensation of his inner world somersaulting, the sensation less pure and violent than when produced with his left hand. Phyllis had submitted, and that was a start. All tension had fled his muscles, and he marvelled at how many times ahead of them they would do this together, each time better, the two of them both less clumsy and shy.

In the bathroom, a resiny salt scent pressed against the window screen; trees were growing right here, live breathing things, scrub oak and bayberry bushes as well as the pitch pines. He washed his genitals of blood and semen and called in from the lit bathroom into the dark, "What shall we do about the sheet?"

"Didn't you notice? I put a towel under my hips."

"Oh my God, I didn't," he said, stricken with tenderness, as if this proof of her calm prudence and foresight opened Phyllis to him wider than fucking her had. He rushed to return to her, to see the towel with his eyes, to make some kind of relic of it. Others—Hank, Jake—would have coveted such a relic. She still assumed the position of the drawing on the shed, the obscene M-shape, looking back at the moon. Perhaps herself dazed, she lifted her hips enough for him to ease the stained towel away; he kissed the terrycloth, pressed his face into it, its receding clash of flesh and blood.

"Owen, really," she said. She swung her naked legs past him and set her feet on the floor, taking the white towel with her into the bathroom. "I'll wash everything up," she announced. When she came out she was wearing a dotted wool nightie and he was still naked, kneeling at the bedside, pressing his face into the pocket of leftover heat where she had become his woman, deflowered. She made him feel foolish, theatrical, trying to make something religious of this moment. Under her nightie she was wearing, he discovered, underpants, with a pad at the crotch.

In her brother's room, in the year past, Owen would move away from one of their tussles on the edge of intercourse and look out the dormer window, to the dizzy jut and recession of Cambridge rooftops and the narrow back yards with their rusty barbecue grills on little brick patios or added-on decks, and feel its communal force, its collective pride. He was privileged to have this elevated access to its wooden cityscape — so many barny mansions built on an industry of thoughts and scholarship. Via one of its maidens he had secured himself a place here, a seat at the Goodhues' mahogany dining table with its diet of dry gossip and liberal indignation, in these days of evil Joe McCarthy and lackadaisical Ike. Yet Owen felt less than fully part of it — he was *practical*, Phyllis had sensed from the start, and, compared with her father, coarse. There was an ethos expressed by these dormered rooftops, these innumerable golden windows admitting views of stuffed bookshelves, of faded Oriental rugs, of kitchens adorned with copper-bottomed pots and quilted potholders, of bathrooms papered in *New Yorker* covers, of narrow, unmade student beds: he could admire it, even marry into it, but never make it his own. Tall and wiry, he had a smile quick to expose the crooked, sensitive teeth of a boy reared far from this self-cherishing village.

Their first Cambridge apartment, where they lived for the six months before he was drafted, was not on any top story but in the basement of a brick apartment building on

Concord Avenue, with an eye-level view of a shady patch
of pachysandra and myrtle, barberry and cotoneaster. The
overplanted patch, hidden from the street, was a trysting
place for cats, a feline bedroom and bathroom both. That
summer and into the lingering warmth of fall the young
Mackenzies had to leave, in lieu of air-conditioning, their
screenless windows open; more than once Owen awoke
with a jowly yellow tom, whom they had nicknamed Uncle
Ugly Cat, sitting purring on his chest, his blue lips so close
to Owen's face the smell of rancid fish oil was nauseating.
Phyllis, indecisive and fretful for the first time since he had
known her, drifted through her course in probability (com-
binational analysis, random variables, laws of large numbers, recurrent events, Markov chains, prediction theory)
and still groped after a Ph.D. thesis topic, unable to find,
in the vast tangle of achieved mathematics, an unformu-
lated scrap she could make her own, while Owen, an ill-
paid apprentice at the Harvard Computation Laboratory,
struggled, in this twilight of the ponderous Mark I, with
the primitive programming system called the A–O com-
piler and with the complications of hard-disk data storage, an innovation that would liberate the machines from
programs on cumbersome punched cards or reels of magnetic tape. Already IBM had marketed, to government and
research departments, the first commercial computer, the
701. The visions that these developments opened up, of
ever more intricate workings down in the tiny layered circuits, an abstract processing not only exponentially faster
and smoother than human thought but single-track, a spark
hurtling round and round the algorithmic loops until it
arrived at the programmed decimal margin that determined
practical equivalence—a clean, lightning-fast process the

opposite of many-branched human thinking, that mist of incalculable factors, emotional, egotistical, and sensual.

In their two dark and dank basement rooms, whose little windows looked out on a leafy cat motel, Owen and Phyllis were gingerly immersed in one another. They learned the noises and movements each made while asleep and how each's bowel movements smelled, even though the bathroom door was closed tight and an overhead fan could be switched on. Their bedroom was so small one of them had to sleep against the wall, and because he was the one who had to get up and go to work five mornings a week, she gave him the outside, which meant that if she had to arise in the night—having drunk too much wine at her parents' table, perhaps, or at a spicy Greek restaurant with another young graduate couple—she slithered carefully across him, a constellation of touches passing close overhead. He would fall back asleep, in his dreams explaining to himself that he was married, that the body was that of his wife. She was still shy, and any passerby on the sidewalk could see into their windows with a downward glance, but on the stickiest nights she slept naked. His wife's body never failed to move him. They made love less than he had imagined when a virgin, and the blame, he felt, was as much his as hers; he studied at night, and so did she, while WCRB emitted classical music on the top of the bureau in the corner. Even half-heard, a Beethoven symphony or Schubert sonata is demanding, leaving nothing to say that cannot be expressed with a sigh and the slap of a book at last shutting. When, on the eve of his reporting to Fort Devens for induction into the Army, she announced a missed period, it was as if she had become pregnant by a process of osmosis rather than a distinct instance of intercourse.

It was always he who initiated what contacts there were. Given his overexcited clumsiness once engaged, especially when a condom, hard-squeezing and smelling disgustingly of its rubber, had been utilized, as the alternative to her inserting a slathered diaphragm (she would emerge from the bathroom blushing), he could not blame her. He never could blame Phyllis for anything; perhaps this was a defect, a deformity, in their relationship. She was a year older, and he trusted her to be right; he never got over his first awed sightings of her in the halls of MIT's busy maze of numbered buildings, its set of sets. How unattainable she had seemed! Just the notion of talking to her, of intruding himself into the sphere of her attention, had seemed blasphemous.

In that honeymoon week on the Cape they had walked on the beach toward Provincetown, a beach belonging to her girlhood summers, and, though it was still too cool for bathing suits, at a quiet shallow place she had taken off her shoes and waded in, her tugged-up skirt exposing half of her thighs and all of the swell and taper of her long white calves. Some young male walkers coming south from Provincetown had stopped to stare. They were burly and boisterous, and it did not occur to Owen that they might be homosexual. He was convinced they wanted his wife; they wanted to seize and rape her on the empty beach. With the force of a blow from behind, he awoke to his inability to protect her—his sheltered treasure, his innocent exhibitionist, his ex-virgin by the sea. He was a pathetic groom. The hazed sky was high and merciless. Beyond her sand-colored head of hair, guilelessly bowed in study of the shells and crabholes revealed in the suds of the surf's retreat, there was only icy ocean and Portugal.

vii. *On the Way to Middle Falls*

HIS LAST DREAM before awaking is of a party, a party back in Middle Falls, though it seems to be in a skyscraper and has the gloss and high color of a party in a movie, a 'fifties movie, or a present-day film's retro 'fifties, where the women are *too* dressed up, in powdery colors and wide-skirted, sharply cinched taffeta and rigidly waved hair. In the dream he slowly notices how the two female guests he is talking to, one of them seated beside him and the other standing, are both dressed in painted china, rigid carapaces with shiny sculptural edges, as if they are eighteenth-century figurines. In looking at the paintings of Copley or Gainsborough or Ingres, Owen can lose himself in the folds of silk, the semi-stiff fall and buckle of fabric, the highlights and the crevasses so passionately pursued by the painter's brush at a remove from the rouged, indolent faces; these party clothes are like that, frozen ceramic, though the women's arms appear soft and alive, gesturing playfully, and their voices and expressions animated and gracious, acknowledging no discomfort or impediment to their motions. Envious, Owen, feeling by comparison ill-dressed, finds himself in front of their host's (whoever he is) closet, with its ranks of polished shoes and tweed jackets, looking for a porcelain suit he can put on. He is distracted from his search by noise from the party: an elderly guest has passed out, a halo of sleeping dogs around his head, and there seems to be a fox loose in the house. Eve, Owen's younger daughter, is tearfully protecting the animal. This, then, is *his* house, the big clapboarded one on Partridgeberry Road in Middle Falls, Connecticut. So *he* is the mysterious host, humiliatingly ill-clad without a porcelain suit. He wakes up.

Julia is not in the bed, and the warm depression she leaves behind is cooling. He feels, more heavily each day, the unnaturalness of getting out of bed, of rising for the same drab bran-cereal breakfast with its fistful of vitamins to slug down, the newspaper to face with its fatal car accidents, its tenement fires in the Boston inner suburbs, its never-ending revelations of priestly sexual abuse of now middle-aged and litigious and not very winning child victims, its further revelations of intricate chicanery in the exalted offices of corporations and mutual funds, its obituaries of the deserving obscure, its impending war to face. His left hand frequently possesses the tingling palm that indicates spinal deterioration or a gathering heart attack, with arthritic aches at the base of one fingernail and, less ignorably, in the joints of the thumb, buried deep in his hand's anatomy. These pains relate, he believes, to the golf season; the aching finger is the third one, with which he has gripped the club most tightly, too tightly, all these years, and the same grip mechanics have somehow misused his thumb—put too much weight on it at the top of the backswing. For decades he has been trying to get golf pros to show him what he is doing wrong, but all they have said was, with hardly a glance, that his grip looked fine, before they proceeded to complain about his feet, his shoulders, his excessive hip-turn, his wretched outside-in tendency, his stiff-legged and excessively upright stance with its companion fault, the dreaded "reverse C." But in his heart he knows that your thumb isn't supposed to hurt at the end of every round. Now he has worn the bones down, beyond repair; the damage and its ache will accompany him to the grave. A surge of love for Julia moves through him, in the wake of the warm sensation that had been she, on the sheet, beneath the blanket. She has stayed with him, *will* stay with him even as he becomes a pathetic, noisome, malfunctioning cripple.

Not even bothering to urinate or brush his teeth, Owen goes in search of her. She is not in the upstairs TV room or at her desk in the spare bedroom. Panic begins to flutter and flip in his stomach. Nor is she in the kitchen, which he approaches by the back stairs, silently, barefoot, the new carpeting pressing snugly, springily back against his soles. The television set, where the Weather Channel, her favorite, was wont to sparkle, is blank, a deadly green-gray. The cry "Julia!" is rising in his throat when a rustle of paper reveals her presence downstairs in the library. She perches on the red sofa, eating yogurt from its plastic cup and reading the *New York Times*. Her blue flip-flops rest on the edge of the coffee table, and the undersides of her thighs are exposed by her shortie nightie and open bathrobe. He sits down heavily in the wing chair opposite her, with the relief of a traveller who has found his way across a desert. The panic tickling his stomach eases. Her toes in the flip-flops look from his angle like two chains of pink circles. The muscles in her treadmill-toughened legs chase one another like smoothly sporting dolphins. He marvels at how keenly her beauty still strikes him, as she glances up from beneath her arched black brows with those wide-set aquamarine eyes, her lips slightly gleaming from the yogurt. Her lips never look numb or frozen, but always decisive, trim, sharp at the edges even without lipstick.

"Take off that absurd hat," she says.

It has become his habit, as his hair has thinned, to wear a wool watch cap to bed, well into the spring. His mother in her last dotage did the same. Even on a hot summer night he misses its embrace of his skull, and resorts to it if he has trouble sleeping.

Obediently he removes the offensive item, tucking it under the armpit of his sleep-rumpled pajamas, and, thinking fondly of his wife's feet, reaches toward them with his naked own, resting them on a Chippendale chair this side of the coffee table. A Wethersfield ancestor of Julia's once did the badly faded crewelwork on the cushioned seat.

"And take your dirty feet off my antique chair," she says, with what seems genuine indignation; the same indignation propels her up, off the sofa with her empty yogurt cup, down the hall into the kitchen.

He trails after her, protesting feebly, "They're clean. They're bare."

"And why," she asks in a pent-up voice, without turning around, "have you *never* learned to comb your hair? It was one thing when you had a lot of it and it was brown and fluffy, it passed for cute, but now it's just this ugly little white washrag on the top of your head."

"I just got up," he protests, "and came to look for you. I didn't want to take the time to comb my hair."

In Willow, when he was a child, his hair was combed only before Sunday school or after a haircut, and no one complained. Or did his mother complain? Trying to remember, he has a faint, scratchy memory of a comb raking his scalp, perhaps his mother crossly tending to his hair before sending him off to school with that pack of Second Street girls. Even now, he fears anger in his mother's touch, though she is more than ten years dead.

In the kitchen, Julia turns on the television set, where a weatherman, young, bushily mustached, and excessively lanky—the tall don't do well on television—keeps lunging a bit too far with his white electronic magic pointer, which slides and scribbles over Ohio as he describes a zone of high pressure moving toward New England through New York State.

"Why do you keep watching this junk?" he asks, in cautious counterattack. "The weather will come no matter what you know."

"*Quiet!*" she says, in the fierce tone with which his mother had once commanded, *Don't touch it!* "Now you made me miss about the front!"

"The front will show up however it wants to, don't worry so about it. Not even you can control fronts. What's in the *Times*?"

"Read it for yourself."

"I read the *Globe*."

"How very stupid of you, Owen. There's nothing in it but rapes in Medford and murders in Dorchester."

"Well, unlike the sanctimonious fucking *Times*, the *Globe* doesn't claim to know what news is fit to print." In his nervousness, he goes to the breadbox in its deep drawer and extricates a bag of Newman's Own Traditional Thin Pretzels, which smell more baked than less moral brands, and bites one. The first bite is the best. Paul Newman is white-haired too, posing with his daughter Nell on the cellophane bag. Owen can remember him in *Hud*, as youthful and dangerous and semi-sleepy as the late James Dean.

Julia cries in something close to agony, "Eat over the *sink*! The floor gets filthy and the cleaning ladies were just here!"

These are a pair of freshly immigrant Brazilians, not sisters but identically shaped, with broad, bustling behinds. Sometimes they form a trio, the third being slimmer, with butternut skin and huge chocolate eyes and no English.

"Oh, you're *such* a slob!" his wife exclaims. "Your mother didn't teach you *any*thing!"

Owen might argue this, if Julia were in a better temper. His mother taught him a great deal, though it is hard, now toward the end of his life, to say what. Her wisdom, mostly wordless, was fitted to life in Willow—how to survive there, who to obey and who to avoid, how to generate a confidence, a sense of being precious, that would arm him for a future elsewhere. She imparted little about hair-combing, and manners in general; Owen accordingly takes such niceties lightly. He is a slob, yet squeamish. He does not like eating over the sink; it makes him feel like a dog at his bowl. He wants to eat as he did when a child, wandering through his grandfather's house with a stalk of celery or a bar of peanut brittle in blissful ignorance of any falling crumbs. Mealtimes there tended to be stressful: Grammy, as her Parkinson's worsened, had a way of choking at the table, and his mother could be having a red-faced temper sulk, or his father, his mournful accountant's face looking drained of blood, could be adding up in his head how much these many mouths to feed were costing him. Owen found that food eaten in solitude, on the run, in odd corners, tasted best. He happily remembers faithfully consuming a six-cent

Tastycake while walking back to school after lunch and, when he was older, walking around downtown Alton cracking peanuts from a paper bag still warm from the roasting.

He does not blame his wife for scolding him, for bursting forth. She needs him to be perfect, or else she has made a lifelong mistake. Each has bought the other dearly, in coin not all theirs. Her repugnance, when she expresses it, he accepts as evidence of her wanting him to measure up to the highest standards. She needs him to be a perfect husband, to justify herself. She does not want to hear about his dream-party back in Middle Falls, with the mischievous women dressed up in colorful porcelain carapaces.

His marriage with Phyllis took a wound, perhaps, in the two years when he was in the post–Korean War Army, enjoying the company of the rapidly obsolescing giant computers devoted, with their skimpy memories and miles of telephone-circuitry wiring, to the calculation of missile trajectories and, linked up with radar, the primitive beginnings of air-traffic control. She gave birth without him, in Mt. Auburn Hospital, to eight-pound Gregory while Owen was stationed at Fort Benning in Georgia. Seven-pound Iris came after Phyllis had joined him in Germany, in military housing outside Frankfurt. Unfortunately, that week, toward the end of his tour, Owen was troubleshooting at a secret missile site in Turkey, and again missed her birth travail.

By then the Russians had long-range aircraft capable of bringing a nuclear bomb across the North Pole, and coördinated air defense had achieved high priority and top-secret status. Whirlwind had been brought up to real-time speed with the installation of magnetic-core memory, and its prototype, the basic hardware of his education at MIT, had become the manufactured IBM AN/FSQ-7, installed at Direction Centers across the nation as part of SAGE, the Semi-Automatic Ground Environment. Holding forty-nine thousand vacuum tubes and weighing two hundred fifty tons and housed in four-story concrete eyesores, these electronic dinosaurs were fed data from a global network of sources maintained by the U.S. Armed Forces; Owen, on loan to the Air Force, became one of hundreds of techno-logically trained servicemen stationed at blinking cathode-ray tubes, deciphering blips. Mistaken blips and misfiring input could be catastrophic in the delicately poised surveil-lance game; but he was struck, touched even, by the basic reliability of the machines, unwieldy though they retro-spectively seemed after chip miniaturization had reduced their bulk, and program languages had made them easier conversational partners. There were still many switches to throw, and blinking lights on the consoles. Owen began to take a hand in the refinement and invention of programs—tedious lines of assembly code, which in the event of error had to be examined character by character, in printed memory dumps that strained the eyes and addled the mind. He showed competence enough to be invited to extend his hitch, with officer rank, and thereby to help hold at bay the dogged Soviets, who were lagging far behind in computer science.

But Phyllis hated military life, both the unpacificist idea of it and the khaki-drab daily reality. "The lowest common denominator rules," she said. "And the wives—so vulgar, so obsessed with their little nests, with sex, which is all they have to offer." Owen didn't think this was such a meagre thing to offer, but said nothing. He respected his wife's opinions. When he talked of reupping, it was to tease a reaction out of her; her pale cheeks flushed pink as her arguments became earnest. Without ever seeming to study him, she could dip into his psyche. "*Don't* think like your father and stick to the safe thing," she pleaded. "He thought a safe thing was the knitting mills, and look what happened to *them*. There *is* no safe thing. America's the bastion of capitalism, that's what all this is about, isn't it? If computers are half the wonders you think they are, they're going to make fortunes, and you're in on the ground floor."

He knew she was, as usual, right, but was offended, slightly, to realize that she was not above considering her material position. She wanted him to earn money, if not for herself, then for her children. She wanted to get out of military housing and into an apartment, a place all their own. Childbearing had thickened Phyllis; her face, no less delicate a silverpoint than before, sat atop a broader pillar, her nightgown falling from her milk-stuffed breasts in straight Doric folds.

She was right: what he had learned with SAGE led nicely, in his job at the IBM complex on Madison Avenue in New York City, into work on what came to be called SABRE, the nationwide computerized reservation system being developed with American Airlines. The largest civilian computerization task ever undertaken, it involved a million lines of program code, two hundred technicians, ten thousand miles of leased telecommunication lines, and a thousand agents using desktop terminals connected to two IBM 7090 mainframes north of the city, in Briarcliff Manor. One computer was live and the other was duplexed, waiting in case of breakdown. A tiny fraction of those million lines of code were Owen's creation; because of him the AND and OR gates and the IF . . . THEN forks shuttled flight numbers, abbreviated terminal names, prices, and individual seats into the right electronic slots half a continent away. His inborn Scots thrift became a passion for electronic economy—for reformulations that would bypass an elaborate subroutine or redundant loop and save a sliver of time he could clearly sense as the monitor screen, like a wearying boxer, responded to the tapped keys.

Phyllis, for the free hour of evening when the two babies were at last asleep and the dinner dishes sang in the dishwasher, could follow his explanations, though this was not her kind of math, these electrons flying around and around the algorithmic circuit like horses plodding around a millstone, and she could sometimes suggest, in a weightless leap of insight, a fresh way around some linear difficulty; Owen would be quite dazzled, and fall in love with her anew.

When he had spotted her floating through the crowds at MIT he had not foreseen the growing weight she would bring with her—the soggy diapers, the luggage of cribs and carriages, bibs and jars of Gerber's puree, the clamor of unsleeping need, the cycles of fretful illness as germs ricocheted within the family, the multiplied responsibilities cantilevered far into the future into college and beyond. Bourgeois comfort took on girth in Eisenhower's second term: big-finned cars, tall pastel refrigerators, roaring, dripping air-conditioners greedy for electricity. Phyllis's spirited intelligence had nowhere to go within the sluggish, clogged dailiness of life in their succession of two-bedroom apartments. They moved from noisy East 55th Street between Lex and Third to 63rd, farther east; still they did not escape the metropolitan racket that kept her awake and left her to sleepwalk through her days with the two toddlers. In the intricate realm beneath the midtown streets, into which helmeted men descended and from which puffs of steam escaped, there was endless revision; all-night jack-hammers went on fixing the same thing week after week.

Somehow she was pregnant again. Owen couldn't imagine how it had happened, he was keeping such brutally long hours at the airline project. SABRE was named in 1960, after a kind of Buick, but posing as an acronym: Semi-Automatic Business Research Environment. Before the system was operational, other airlines—Delta, Pan American—signed up with IBM, and the country's banks and accounting offices were waking up to the computerized future. There arose a hungry market in even smaller companies for programs speeding their payrolls, inventories, invoices. In 1960 there were perhaps five thousand computers in the country, most of them in universities and scientific labs, and the programmers worked with paper-tape readers and punches and stayed up all night for computer time. The word "software" had arrived, and "bugs" and "debugging." FORTRAN had been developed at IBM, for mostly scientific work; CO-BOL 60—Common Business Oriented Language 1960—opened the computer to business applications. The world of affordable PCs was two decades away, but a fellow IBM minion in the Madison Avenue hive, Ed Mervine, began to woo Owen, over lunches in the company cafeteria, with its eggshell walls each decorated by a deadpan sign bearing President Watson's famous imperative. Ed, from the Bronx, had an offhand, stabbing way of speaking that was more efficient than it seemed. He confided above their trays, "You know, O., there's a world out there of medium-sized companies that have paid a couple hundred thousand for hardware they don't know how to operate. As the price comes down, there's bound to be more of them. Manufacturers, distributors, these new franchises, lesser airlines, banks, architectural firms. IBM and Sperry Rand can't be bothered with them; they farm them out, to assholes."

Ed was the first adult to take enough interest in Owen to give him a nickname, "O." He reminded Owen of Buddy Rourke—same stiff hair shooting forward so his brow looked low, same big teeth, corrected in Ed's case by boy-hood braces that left him with teeth that looked a little false, not quite what his face had in mind. He was the same inch or two taller than Owen, though unlike Buddy he was younger, just enough younger to be more at home with the idea of machines that help people think, thousands of tiny thoughts, or bit transactions, a second. To Owen it was a marvel; to Ed it was a fact of life.

"So what are you suggesting? We become better ass-holes?"

"You got it. Smart boy. Contract programming and advi-sory services. IBM is sucking our blood, and it's going to go down one of these years. The company's too fucking big. Smaller is better, more agile. The hardware is shrinking exponentially. Low overhead is the only way to keep up, to see the next thing possible. Set up the operation where there's low overhead and see what develops."

"Where's this low overhead?"

"Beyond the commuter belt. Beyond Stamford. Beyond New Haven, even. The Connecticut sticks."

"Ed, who would do this? You and me?"

Ed was unmarried. He gave off that sexless aura of the true computer devotee: stale air, Chinese takeout in paper cartons, Twinkies and Cokes at 2 a.m. His skin was clammy, he was twenty pounds overweight, his button-down shirt collar bunched around the knot of his necktie, which was askew and greasy. His teeth were false-looking choppers he kept cleaning with his finger, tongue, and a retracted upper lip like a chimpanzee's. He said, "Why not? Your wife has another in the oven. You were telling me yesterday how you can't find an apartment that Phyllis likes you can afford."

He was, Owen realized, being proposed to. He had somehow become more desirable since the afternoon when Buddy Rourke had sneered at his loving Monopoly arrangement. "Ed, I'm not a city boy like you. I'm *from* the sticks, I don't want to go back to them. Bugs, dirt; Jesus. You get mindless." He was stalling. He thought of Elsie, the night in her father's woods, her silky yielding body animated by a sexual will, the scrabbling things that hooted and rustled around them. The sticks had their excitements. "Phyllis and I," Owen admitted, "are beginning to think about the 'burbs. Either Westchester or New Jersey north of Paterson."

"Christ, you don't want that. They're just this same crap without the yellow cabs and the jazz in the Village—the same big-city grapple plus a doggy little yard out back and an hour on the train twice a day. Just as expensive, when you add it all up. *More* expensive, if you count the spiritual cost: they suck you into maintaining false pretenses, into being nice *neigh*bors, for Chrissake. Feed the cookie cutter—spare me. Spare us all. Listen, I don't know Phyl all that well, but my impression is she doesn't give a fuck for the standard rat race. She's a free spirit, my judgment is. She needs to hold her head high; she needs to get out of those roachy apartments with those kids. And as to you, ask yourself this: how much do you want to be flow-charting airline reservations for Tommy Watson Junior for the rest of your life?"

"IBM is good to us, Ed. Last year I made three times what my father did in his best year, and that was during the war, with moonlighting."

"O., I guess you *are* from the sticks. You think small."

"You sound like Phyllis." Owen had to laugh, being pressed this hard, this ardently. "But she loves the city. We both do."

Ed smiled, baring his big teeth, sensing the new mood. It was a downhill, tickle-me-harder mood. "Yeah? What do you like about it?"

"The museums. The concerts. The restaurants."

"How often do you get to them?"

"Almost never. Babysitters are a problem. And we're always bushed."

"Well, then. There's millions out there, O. Big bucks for the picking, for those who show a little initiative. A little imagination. Think, isn't that what they keep telling us? Think outside the lines."

"Ed, please. We don't have the millions yet. It costs money to set up a company. How do we program if we can't afford a computer?"

This question pleased Ed; he had given it thought. "You don't need one, you can use the client's machine or rent time from a service bureau. All you really need is a coding pad and a pencil: that's according to a guy I know, who used to be with scientific programming right here at IBM. Now he's with CUC, that's Computer Usage Company, downtown. They began in a guy's apartment with pure zilch five years ago and just went public, for a *net* of a hundred eighty-six grand. They bought their own computer. Electronic data management, that's the name of the game. Who needs sex when you can have software?"

"Ed, you are too much." In his nervous excitement at this vista opening up, Owen had eaten too much, taking for dessert a pecan pie he didn't want. He was twenty-seven years old and what he ate showed up, as a little pot belly.

"I'll mention what you said to Phyllis. You're right about one thing, we have to do something, this new kid will give me three under four. But what's the attraction for you? You're a bachelor, the city is made for you. You're a native."

"Not really. There's a lot more nature in the Bronx than people know. The Botanical Garden, Pelham Bay Park. I like to fish, to take hikes. Manhattan eats you up. It's too fucking full of nervous, ambitious women. My mother wasn't like that. She was just like I imagine yours was, contented, always shelling peas into a yellow bowl, with a blue stripe around it."

This wasn't quite how Owen, looking back, saw his mother; Grammy had done most of the kitchen work until she was bedridden. And, unlike Ed, he had already chosen his wife, who was as different from his mother as she could be, except that both women gave off a little scent of dissatisfaction. He was comfortable with this scent, it confirmed his first thought about life, that he was lucky to have been born a boy. MIT and IBM had done nothing to contradict this insight.

When he described this conversation to Phyllis, she appeared not uninterested. She was in her seventh month of pregnancy, and moved around the apartment, back and forth between the two rooms, with trips to the kitchenette and bathroom, at a stately backward tilt, her lovely long neck holding her head high, as Ed had noticed. When had Ed noticed? They had had him to dinner once or twice, and in return he came up with three tickets for *Camelot*, with Julie Andrews. "He could be right," she said. "You should give your creativity a chance."

"What creativity?"

He had always felt mathematically inferior to her, earthbound, relatively muddy in his thinking, though he had done creditably at MIT and received faithful raises from IBM, even as costs mounted in its huge New Product Line gamble. He was both sorry and in some pocket of his heart relieved that she had relegated her Ph.D. thesis to the dustbin of old Symphony programs and Browne & Nichols report cards; nobody wants a wife smarter than he. "You're artistic," she told him, blushing in the unaccustomed exercise of appraising her husband. "You love wandering through the Met upstairs, and over at the Modern."

Her thin-skinned face, its flesh a delicate mask for her bones, reddened more than usual in the bodily turmoil of pregnancy. Though these chronic bulges of hers cemented him into the role of provider, he loved the look of her distended body—the belly he rubbed with oil to soften the stretch marks, the way her accustomed air of abstraction was absorbed into a hormonal reverie, and the broadening of her, which included her face and breasts and her buttocks. She let him fuck her in the spoon position, as his body on top became too much a weight on her. They drew closer, the two of them, around this hidden third presence, and Gregory and Iris drew closer as well, patting gingerly with their little square hands the glassy bulge of their mother's belly, its everted navel and brown center line. This was reality—biology at work, a beating, burbling process the ear could eavesdrop on. The unknown animal inside her kicked against his palm. It was a few thin layers of Phyllis away. What a pity, Owen felt dimly at the time and more keenly later, that young couples, preoccupied and self-absorbed, let themselves be distracted from this miracle of theirs. These years of their own procreating came before shared birthing classes and elaborate prenatal concern for the fetus; Phyllis smoked an evening cigarette with her hand cocked on the jut of the belly, and balanced a glass of wine on the same convenient resting place. Owen was proud that his wife made such natural and easy work of childbearing; as long as her pregnancies continued, the thought of infidelity was monstrous. Something primitive in him worshipped her in her fertility, though it indentured them both to the next generation. "Ed says," she told him, "you have a genius for visualization, for spatial relations. You see the programs like drawings in your head."

"Doesn't everybody?"

She became pensive, sucking in her cheeks to contract her dry lips. "I think for many people math takes them beyond what they can picture. You're very tied to your senses, Owen."

He hated to hear this, since having children had reawakened in him his childhood premonitions of dying, and one clear thing about the event was the unlikelihood of taking your senses with you. MIT had shown him the universe swept clean not only of Heavenly furniture but of endless energy—of endlessness in any measurable form. Every form of order, even the proton, ended: he preferred in practical life to forget this fatal thermodynamic pinch. Phyllis's words, though, were the seeds that, in Middle Falls, while he and Ed labored to sustain their infant data-processing start-up, eventually bore fruit as DigitEyes, a breakthrough in its brief moment.

"Would you be game, then," he asked her, while Manhattan traffic bleated and roared below them on East 63rd Street, "to leave the city and let me and Ed try this? If it fails, we can pocket our losses and get salaried jobs again."

"Why would you fail?" Phyllis asked, in one of those casual verbal gestures that set the vectors of his life. "I think it sounds like fun. Ed's a slob," she added, "but he's solid. And he knows how the world works."

Meaning that Owen didn't? "You're great," he told his wife. "How would you feel about Connecticut? There's a town Ed knows of, in the middle of nowhere an hour from Hartford, where there's cheap factory space and good public schools. An aunt of his came from there; she used to work in the local light-bulb factory, when it still made light bulbs. Small-town innocence, honey. White-spired Congregational church. Cannonballs and a statue on the village green. Playmates for Gregory and Iris."

"But—how much factory space do you need?"

"We don't know yet, but we have to have an address to put on the letterhead. Ed even has a name for us, using our initials. E-O Data Management."

"It sounds," Phyllis said, feigning or truly feeling enthusiasm, "very impressive."

DigitEyes, it should be explained, was a method of drawing with a light pen on a computer screen. Owen had been impressed by the way that the cathode-ray tubes on Whirlwind could display T, for target, and F, for fighter, and track them; the process had been elaborated to include radar sightings in the SAGE project, on which he had worked in his military interval. His instinct was that the CRT, the speckly basis of television, was the natural real-time interface for the computer operator, bypassing switches, punched tapes, and code-language command lines. In the early 'sixties, there was already enough complexity in the transistorized circuits for the computer games undergraduates were inventing, and for vector graphics to be plotted, enlarged, worked on, and stored. The images, all in straight lines, could be zoomed, to be worked on in detail, and then returned to standard scale, marvellously refined. They could not yet be turned in a virtual third dimension, but Owen could conceive of this coming, as computer power doubled and redoubled. Engineering and architectural firms were the first customers for the program, but mainframe computers were still out of most firms' financial reach, and the huge future that Owen could glimpse for graphics interaction waited for more powerful chips. When he showed Phyllis the first primitive light-pen plotting, she said, giving it a glance, "Some day every pixel could have an address, and serve as a communication point." Even for Owen it was hard to picture such an abyss of calculation, of electronic information—as if every atom in the universe were an individual, with its own private story.

viii. *Village Sex—IV*

MIDDLE FALLS lay equidistant from Hartford and Norwich but not very near anything, with the Rhode Island border an endless drive away, those successive Main Streets with their peeling clapboard houses and the glaring franchise strips falling away under the headlights, the old state highway rising and sinking with the former farmland's hilly roll. The hilltops were blue half the year, naked trees purplish against the snow, and then green. The town had been named after the second of three noisy, turbulent drops in the rocky, fast-running river, the Chunkaunkabaug, which had turned millstones grinding meal of wheat in the eighteenth century and in the nineteenth the power chains of an arms factory supplying revolvers and rifles to the burgeoning West and the Union armies; the rambling brick structure later became a light-bulb factory, in turn abandoned, as Eisenhower gave way to Kennedy, to a swarm of small businesses that, segregating themselves behind partitions of roller-painted plasterboard, rented some fractions of the vast scarred floors, splintered oak perforated by bolt-holes and darkened by the rubber-soled workshoes of men long buried. Ed and Owen's start-up occupied first a few cubicles and eventually the second floor and finally the whole thing. Hartford's insurance companies added themselves to the manufacturers and retailers, banks and investment firms in need of customized computer programming, and E-O gradually prospered. Ed and Owen joined the local middle class.

Most of the people that the Mackenzies came to know were from somewhere else. Some were refugees from New York, half-failed artists licking their wounds and working in their homes; some commuted to Hartford, serving the state government or the insurance industry; a few were professionals, lawyers and contractors and pediatricians, content with the relatively thin local pickings in exchange for the old town's tonic air of freedom, a freedom bred of long neglect, of being bypassed and as yet little spoiled, of being *no place special* and triumphantly American in that. These immigrant citizens all shared the assumption that their village was ineffably special and superior, rakish yet stylish; by comparison, Lower Falls was a virtual ghost town—a gas station, a convenience mart, and a little brick post office amid a scattering of run-down barns and sheds and vegetable stands and rusting mechanical remnants from a viable rural past—and Upper Falls a dreary bedroom community on the far edge of Hartford's sprawl, with flat tracts of 'fifties ranch houses, gimcrack "starter homes" built on a slab. In Middle Falls, Federalist mansions, waiting for a coat of paint, safer wiring, and a new furnace, stood around the triangular green, once a common pasture and still called the Common. Farther out, charmingly Spartan farmhouses from later in the nineteenth century, with acreage for horses or a tennis court, also could be picked up reasonably, in the low five figures. There were a few surviving pre-1725 structures, with massive central chimneys, small windows, and saltbox profiles; they had been turned, by and large, into antique shops or candlelit, low-ceilinged restaurants. There was a minimal country club, with a nine-hole golf course and four clay tennis courts, and a lake, called Heron Pond, with imported sand, a shallow section roped off for toddlers, and a tall white lifeguard-chair occupied, when it was occupied at all, by the seal-shaped, mahogany-brown teenage daughter of the local high-school principal. The key to her chest of medical supplies was worn on a red elastic circlet around her ankle, and her long black hair, as straight and as mat a black as a Native American's, was caught back in another such utilitarian elastic. She had not only a seal's adipose shape but a seal's style of basking as she lazed, with half-closed eyes, above the mothers and children and the adolescent boys whose roughhousing and splashy horseplay over by the rope swing occasionally brought her upright, the whistle shrill in her zinc-oxided lips.

Here on this lightly lapped crescent of trucked-in beach the town's vivid young matrons burnished themselves in bikinis or, as the lakewater autumnally cooled but still kept small children entertained, gossiped at the picnic tables, smoking cigarettes and nibbling bits of the children's lunches they had packed: "I swore I'd never eat Marshmallow Fluff again and yet here I am, an absolute addict! Peanut butter and jelly, don't talk to me about it—it's making me fat! But it's so much easier, when you're throwing sandwiches together for their lunch anyway, to make one extra for Mommy!" This was Alissa Morrissey, talking to, say, Faye Dunham and Imogene Bisbee. Newcomers to motherhood and one another, the women had quickly grown into a familiarity that allowed them to utter what-

ever floated to the tops of their heads. They seemed to
Owen to have a collective loveliness, like that, in his threadbare childhood, of Ginger Bitting and her brown-legged
satellites. But now he was more closely among them, as if
he had moved up from Mifflin Avenue to Second Street.
His wife, with her fondness for sunbathing, and her trio of
small children—the infant, Floyd, had been named after
his paternal grandfather—joined them. She reported back,
"They're like Army wives, but not so coarse and vapid.
They're nice, if a little superficial. All they seem to think
about is other people—their children and their husbands.
And each other. When one of us doesn't show up, she gets
it. In the nicest possible way."

In Middle Falls, all personalities were studied, cherished,
and glamorized. Women reigned; the wives lent fascination
to their husbands. Husbands and wives were biform creatures, semi-transparent so that each could be seen through
the other, imperfectly. This freakishness was part of their
magnetism and the overall comedy in the round of parties, meetings, games, picnics, pickup lunches, gourmet
dinners, amateur theatricals, choral-society rehearsals, bird
walks, canoe trips, ski excursions, and sleepy, gently boozy
Sunday-afternoon get-togethers that compensated for the
town's isolation from metropolitan entertainments. The
children were the ostensible point of much of it—
the skiing, the skating, the April kite-flying, the August
clambakes—and yet much of it was an escape from the
children, even while they were present, jostling and quar-
relling underfoot, sitting blearily on the edge of the lawn
while their parents leaped and dived in the heat, say, of a
volleyball game. The wives played along with the husbands,
and their easily bruised flesh was elbowed and bumped,

yet they continued—barefoot, lightly clad—to take their places, as in a village chain dance. Such rites were strange to Owen and enchanted him.

He was really, he learned in Middle Falls, a remarkably ignorant and incomplete human being. His socialization had scarcely progressed beyond the Willow playground. MIT and IBM had been soldier brotherhoods, each man absorbed by his own survival, his own sheet of paper or computer screen, his log table or slide rule. New York had narrowed him further, crowding him tighter against a woman who was under social constraint to love him but not to *see* him, in the way that his mother had seen him, somehow fiercely, as a treasure of infinite value—herself projected into maleness and wider opportunity. Even Grammy with her dim eyes and cockeyed silver spectacles had seen him and loved him beyond reason. Once, coming up through the back yard in his shorts, he had felt his bowels begin to move and was unable to keep the call of nature back and ran crying toward the house, and it was Grammy who, wordlessly clucking, wiped the yellow diarrhea from his legs. In his dreams, repeatedly, his excrement overflowed the bowl, flooded the floor, caked all over his body, stunk up the room in which others, inches away, were having a dinner party. For all his good grades and test scores, he had been so ignorant of basic processes that in his freshman year at MIT he went for weeks without changing the case on his pillow, stupidly wondering why it was turning gray. Grammy and his mother had done his laundry; he had never thought about how his socks got back to his bureau, clean and balled, from where he had dropped them on the floor. Learning to cook never crossed his mind. He let Phyllis do it all, baby Floyd on her hip and the two toddlers squabbling at her knees. His family hadn't had money for liquor; he didn't understand the appeal of it, or the portions and customs of it. He let Phyllis mix the drinks on the rare occasions when they entertained another couple, in New York or, more stiltedly still, in the military in Germany— people they knew their lives would shed forever.

Now there was constant entertaining, and games all weekend. The only games he knew he had learned at the Willow playground—box hockey, Chinese checkers, and Twenty-one and Horse, games of elimination a few idlers could play around a basketball backboard. In those first years in Middle Falls, as he turned thirty, Owen learned the basics of tennis and golf, of paddle tennis, of skiing, both cross-country and downhill. He learned to swim in water over his head without panicking, and to ride the Berkshires ski lifts calmly even when the chairs bounced a great distance above cliffs of ice and granite. Ice hockey and equestrian sports he willingly forwent, though the men of their new acquaintance had emerged from childhood proficient in the former, and the women the latter. He learned how to play bridge, and up to a point how to dance, though he never felt quite easy with a woman in his arms, having to thrust his feet boldly toward hers. He was rescued from contact dancing by the fashion of the Twist and then the Frug, which suited his loose joints and solitary habits.

Middle Falls was for Owen an institute of middle-class know-how. Chunky, red-faced Jock Dunham, who had a lovely lithe hard-laughing wife, taught him how to make a martini, a brandy stinger, a white-wine spritzer, and an old-fashioned (you dissolve the sugar in a little water *before* the ice and bourbon). Ruminative, pipe-puffing Henry Slade, who shuffled paper in Connecticut's Department of Revenue, was methodically handy at husbandry, and explained to Owen how he stacked fresh-cut wood for a year outdoors and then in a special dry room in his cellar another twelve months to assure a clean blaze in his fireplace. His wife, Vanessa, was plain and civically active, with wide shoulders, thick eyebrows, and a disconcertingly direct, appraising gaze; she instructed the new couple how to vote, locally, and when to set out their trash, and how it should be sorted. Ian Morrissey, a free-lance illustrator, owned an aging Thunderbird convertible and a new green Jaguar and shared automotive expertise; the Mackenzies had never owned a car before acquiring a Studebaker Lark station wagon that handled poorly in the snow and didn't always start in the rain. After the initial two-year rental of the clapboarded semi-detached just off run-down, well-trafficked Common Lane, they felt able to buy a house, less central, out on bucolic Partridgeberry Road, with a big yard for the kids as they grew and a patch of woods beyond a pond choked with water-lilies and adorned with a collapsing wooden bridge. Roscoe Bisbee, once a country boy from Vermont, undertook to lead Owen through the rebuilding of the bridge, and explained about liming a lawn and applying dandelion killer, and where to buy the best riding mower. Riding mower, fertilizer spreader, posthole digger, shovels and rakes—they were acquired one by one. With the woods and yard trees came a chain saw, a pole saw, a Swedish band saw. Home repairs demanded not just hammers and screwdrivers but a table saw, for diagonal cuts that fit perfectly, and an electric drill with a case of bits of which the smallest was thread-thin and the biggest thick as a pencil, and socket wrenches measuring from three-sixteenths to three-quarters of an inch, and a blue staple gun. Owen's basement became as formidably equipped as the ones he used to envy in Willow, with their panelled, linoleum-floored dens and Christmas yards on trestle-supported plywood.

The village seemed to him an educational toy—its gingerbread town hall, its tall flagpole, its downtown of two-story false-fronted shops, the quaint kink in River Street as it left the river and climbed the hill toward the churches and the burial grounds and the fading brick mansions of the old rich, the Yankee mill rich. The downtown had a pre-mall adequacy of supplies and services: two hardware stores, a lumber yard, two banks, three barbershops, a jeweller's, a Woolworth's, a narrow-aisled old-fashioned Acme, a clothing store for rough-and-ready and children's wear, a news store that sold tobacco and candy and magazines and paperback books, even a furniture store, up near the disused railroad station, next to a place that sold bicycles and sports equipment—there was little you had to leave town for, and Owen left it less and less. He would emerge, with smarting eyes and nicotine nausea, from the factory holding E-O Data's bright, buzzing rooms; everything, every brick angle and tilted street-sign shadow, looked like a problem to be reduced to programming code. He felt himself, stepping onto the squares of glinting sidewalk, as youthful and potent, the modest success of Digit-Eyes safely behind him and other, even more triumphant follow-ups certain to come. He turned the corner, walked along River Street, and had lunch in one of three possible eateries, greeting on the way, in summer sunshine or winter slush, more and more familiar faces. On the sidewalks of Middle Falls he enjoyed a buoying sense of being known, of being upheld by watching eyes, as when he was a child in Willow, rattling along on roller skates or a scooter, pulling a wagon full of horse chestnuts, or pedalling his rusty Schwinn to the quarry: not exactly a celebrity but *somebody*, in the way that small enough towns make everybody somebody. When he spotted, on those sidewalks, a woman he and Phyllis knew, a woman of their little set, taking a child to the barbershop or clothing store or the toy-and-trinket nook called Knacks, he felt as if her smile of greeting were a flower she had pinned to his chest. A pressure of happiness from deep in his being added to his height and the fluidity of his movements; he felt *seen*, without knowing by whom, or how seriously he was, indeed, being watched. He had ripened without quite knowing it, though others sensed it. Another step in his education was due.

The Dunhams liked to give a big party in May, to celebrate the demise of winter. The weather was still chancy, but their house—a rambling Queen Anne behind a tall palisade-style fence—could hold, with its long veranda, a hundred if need be; parties were their element. Jock liked to drink, and Faye liked to dress up, in outfits of her own invention. She had a high penetrating laugh, nappy copper-colored hair, and bony red-nailed hands that seemed always in motion. She lit up a room.

That May Saturday turned out as sunny and warm—the tufty lawn a garish virgin green, the oaks overhead not yet fully leafed, the blooming azaleas already shedding a few pink petals. Late in the preceding year, President Kennedy had been shot and Phyllis had produced a fourth child, bright-eyed, sweet-natured Eve; both events left Owen a little shaky, feeling his mortality. Eve had come a week before predicted, and he had been in California, at Fairchild Semiconductor, to keep abreast of what the new integrated circuits might mean for the art of programming, when the contractions came, and Ed had been the one to drive her to the hospital in Hartford. The nurses had kept mistaking him for the father.

Faye Dunham, when the shadows had thickened under the oaks and the drinks had gone to everyone's head, came up to Owen and said, "Owen, you seem rather down lately."

"Down? I do?"

As if to steady her stance on the soft lawn, in her rope-soled espadrilles, Faye rested the fingertips of her right hand on Owen's forearm in its plaid sleeve. The madras jacket was new this spring; in fact he had put it on for the first time to wear to the Dunhams' party. He was still learning about clothes. "You're usually so exuberant," she said. "So glad to be here." She was wearing a sparkly brown bodice, sleeveless, with a long skirt she had made from a piece of pool-table felt. Her frizzy thick hair, its coppery glints sharp in the slanting golden sun, was bundled up loosely and held in place by a high Spanish comb, of tortoiseshell engraved with silver arabesques. She sparkled, Faye did; she was the woman you noticed in a room, with that sudden piercing girlish laugh. Owen had been struck by her from their first weeks in Middle Falls, though she and Jock moved, he felt, in a slightly different orbit, at a superior height of travel, consumption, and self-indulgence.

"Here in Middle Falls, or here *chez* Dunham?"

"Both?"

"That comb," he said, to divert her disconcertingly intent, somewhat glazed stare. "Did you and Jock pick that up in Spain?"

She laughed, a laugh quickly crimped shut as if by a wry second thought, with a look to one side, putting her sharp nose in profile. "Jock hates Spain, he says they're all Gypsies and Fascists. He really only likes England, where they speak his language, though he says the pub hours are ridiculous." As she talked and looked at Owen, her eyes widened as if to say that Jock wasn't really what they wanted to talk about. Her face, bony and narrow, seemed slightly too small for her features—the large hazel eyes, the mobile mouth, the arched brows pencilled darker than the hair on her head. But her hips were wide in the pool-table felt and her upper arms bare and white and dotted with freckles like small pin-pricks; she was real enough, not a dream he was having.

He dared confess, to stop her from walking away, "I *have* been down, I guess. I missed my daughter's birth, and really she *must* be the last child."

Faye nodded. "You and Phyllis," she dryly pointed out, "don't seem to have a fertility problem."

Did she and Jock? They had two pale children, frail-looking and shy compared with their animated, hard-living parents. Owen told her, "It's not as if we screw all the time, either. I hardly know how it happens." This was too much to confide, probably. He felt he was leaning out over a little abyss—the fresh soft grass at his feet, the gleam of his third gin-and-tonic. But Faye, as wide-eyed as infant Eve, took it in gravely, her lips parted in suspense. Owen went on, "And then, when I was out in California, I saw how these new companies are feeding off of one another, swapping people back and forth. They call it Silicon Valley. I came away thinking that that's where Ed and I should be, and wondering if hardware instead of software isn't where it's at, at least until the Japanese move in."

"How fascinating," Faye said, in a tone that seemed to come from another conversation; Phyllis had appeared at his side.

"Baby," his wife said to Owen, "I know you're having a wonderful time talking with our charming hostess, but we promised the babysitter six, and I *need* to see Eve. And she me." Phyllis's breasts embarrassed him, they were so big, stuffed with milk, straining against the top of the oversize cotton dress, plain beige, with which she had covered a body still somewhat distended by childbirth. Yet Phyllis had her princessly air still, and said loftily to Faye, "Such a glorious day, Faye, and such a good idea for May. 'Sumer is icumen in.' "

"Can't you stay, then? Some people will, when most have gone. We have a ham. Please."

"Oh, darling Faye, we just can't, for a dozen good reasons. We have too much going on at home. I can't trust the sitter to feed the children anything but junk. But you're sweet." To Owen she said, in a lower, firmer register, "I'll go say goodbye to Jock for us, he's on the veranda, and see you at the car."

When she was gone, Faye said to him accusingly, "You complain, but you don't see yourself when she's pregnant or topped up with milk; you *preen*. It's lovely."

"I'm sorry we can't stay."

"Of course you can't, baby. You heard your wife. Her tits hurt."

Owen took the first step, past her, to leave, and Faye turned with him, to walk him across her lawn, the sparkling new-mown spring green, down to the driveway. They walked through broad bars of late-afternoon sunlight, beamed between trees and tall-shadowed people standing conversing in the heat and boisterous freedom of a cocktail party two hours old. Her arm, surprisingly, went around his waist, and his, more smoothly than his inner shakiness revealed, around hers. Their hips slithered together as, faces downturned as if alert for treacherous footing, they walked to the edge of the grass, where the driveway pebbles began. Her waist felt solid and flexible under his hand. Faye was a good compliant height for him; Phyllis was a little tall. Through the filter of his inner tremble Owen saw himself and Faye, stepping down the lawn, as a couple in a Hollywood musical, about to complicate their steps as the background music soared, opening their mouths in duet, or, by camera trickery, taking off together up into the sunlight that lay in stripes at their feet like slippery golden stairs.

The summer was to pass before they slept together. There was so much clutter to work around—children on school vacation, spouses with their own holiday plans, still-living parents to placate with a visit. Grammy had died, but Grampy lived on, sitting on his sofa, his head tipped up, waiting for the mail, which came later and later, since the route, once a matter of connecting the widely spaced mailboxes of rural delivery, was filling in with houses, one farm after another gone under to development. Owen and Phyllis visited the farmhouse, with the kids, once a year, but his wife and mother had never meshed, even their silences speaking in a different language, and Floyd Mackenzie, paler and thinner, stared with some dismay at the visitors, as if he had acquired six new dependents. He felt exploited and taken for granted by the old college classmate in Norristown who had rescued him from unemployment. Owen's mother's weight and blood pressure had gone up alarmingly. The first time she had met Phyllis, before the marriage had taken place, some socks and underwear of Owen's that Phyllis, with innocent possessiveness, had washed in her parents' Maytag emerged from her suitcase and gave her future mother-in-law a fit of sullen temper that never quite abated over the years, though grandchildren and Christmas presents and, eventually, faithful financial support came to her out of her son's marriage. Without being especially religious or conventional, she was offended by Phyllis's liberal assumptions, and her confidently casual clothes, and her lofty lack of discipline with the children. The two women made bad electricity in the crammed little house, and the half-welcome intruders sought escape in car rides and backyard games. His mother's resistance to Phyllis, who unlike Elsie had no local instinct for the tussle, made Owen more loyal, during the brief duration of their visits, yet at a deeper level, back in Middle Falls, gave a blessing to his impending betrayal.

With Lyndon Johnson as President, the old decorums and austerities were melting away. Johnson ordered bombing of North Vietnam after a U.S. destroyer was attacked in the Gulf of Tonkin. In Philadelphia, over two hundred were injured in black riots protesting police brutality. Malcolm X called the American dream an American nightmare. Hit singles of the year included Louis Armstrong's "Hello, Dolly!," Roy Orbison's "Oh, Pretty Woman," the Supremes' "Baby Love," the Beatles' "A Hard Day's Night," and Dean Martin's "Everybody Loves Somebody." Owen and Faye met at the town's numerous get-togethers, formal and casual, small and large, packing all their tension into mannerly brief exchanges and light touches which they imagined were unnoticeably discreet. If anyone noticed, that was all right; in this particular social setting it was to be expected that some men and women would like each other especially. Liking each other was what all of them needed, to get through the slog of child-rearing, of homemaking, of earning a living, hour by hour. It was what they had instead of what younger people had—the defiant scarecrow costumes, the drugs, the crash pads, the sleeping where you fell, into whoever arms. Up to a point even Jock and Phyllis approved, what they could see and guess, because to have your spouse desired increased your own desirability; it increased the value of what you brought to the table of general acquaintance.

At a party at the Morrisseys', where the illustrator's cluttered, casually artistic decor encouraged latent recklessness, Faye told Owen, speaking in a clenched way as if her lips might be read, "My psychiatrist wants me to ask you something."

"Really? What?"

"Guess."

His mind obediently flitted about, startled by the news that she saw a psychiatrist, but settled on nothing. "I can't."

"It's so obvious, Owen. He wants me to ask you why you don't want to sleep with me."

He felt his whole body blush, as if plunged into hot water. "I do, of course. But—"

"But there's your lovely wife." Faye's small face with its big features looked feral, drawing her lips back over these last words.

"I was going to say, But how do we arrange it?"

She opened her mouth to laugh but in her tension nothing came out. She too felt the hot water. "And you so clever, they say, arranging the insides of computers. Can you use the telephone, or is that too simple?"

Yet this was not simple: the phone at E-O Data, his desk just separated by a chest-high cubicle wall from Ed's desk, offered no privacy, and if Phyllis was out of the house there were still Gregory and Iris, who were eight and nearly seven, with sharp ears and childhood's guileless curiosity. Phoning Faye was a grave, irrevocable step compared with flirting with her; there was no misconstruing it, or passing it off as part of normal life. He stalled for days, walking through the motions of normal life with a tingling body and a numbed, guilty head — guilty chiefly in regard to Faye, for ignoring her unambiguous overture. When he lay down beside Phyllis to sleep, his head churned with bits of this other woman — the inner curves of the two shy, shallow breasts that a certain low-cut dress revealed; the glazed bold stare of her muddy-green irises when she'd had one drink too many; the nervous dampness of her hand when it touched his; the look her face acquired when excited and amused, of being all eyes and mouth, and then the wry crimp of the lips, clipping shut a smile. He had trouble sleeping, and blamed Phyllis. He felt that if only Faye were beside him he could fall asleep in an instant. It was like wanting to stretch out beside Ginger Bitting on the top of the playground shed.

There were phone booths dotted about Middle Falls; he finally resorted to one on the edge of town toward Upper Falls, in the strip of highway, once orchards and dairy farms, now filling in with fast-food franchises or low cinder-block buildings selling discount carpeting and tiles. Trucks kept roaring by, drowning out the faint scratchy words at the other end of the line and blowing late-summer road dust into Owen's lungs. "Hello?": it was Faye, he was sure; her voice, disembodied, had a contralto timbre he had never noticed, a cello color at an opposite pole from the high bat's cry of her laugh.

"This is Owen Mackenzie," he said, in case there was someone else there listening. If there was, her stiffened voice would tell him, and he would ask if by any chance he had left a pair of reading glasses there the other night, when the four of them, on an impulse after volleyball, had had pizza with their children. *It was a long shot,* his phone call would go on, *but he had tried everywhere else, and it was driving him crazy.* In her silence, he began, "I'm calling to ask if by any chance I left a pair of reading glasses—"

"Owen," she breathed. "Well, at last."

"You told me to call."

"And then you didn't. For a week!"

"I was scared."

"Why? It's all so natural, Owen. It happens all the time. You hurt my feelings, not calling before." Her contralto had a singing, lullaby quality he had not noticed before.

"I'm sorry. Like I said, I—"

While he tried to think of how not to repeat himself, Faye interrupted. "You want to see me?"

"I do. God, I do."

"Can you get away next Tuesday?"

"Next Tuesday! What about right now, now that I've got you? Are you going to be home?"

"I am, but somebody could drop by any minute." She paused, and then her voice hurried, laying down rules. "I want it to happen, but not in my and Jock's house. Not the first time."

"Oh? It, as you call it, doesn't have to happen at all; I just want to hold you a minute. To see you, and make sure you're real."

"I know. That's what they all say."

"Who does?"

"Men. Don't do your naïve act, Owen. Now, listen. I have a sitter coming Tuesday at ten. I'm seeing my shrink in Hartford and then supposedly going shopping at G. Fox and Sage Allen and then looking at what's on at the Wadsworth Atheneum. Could you get away from Ed for a few hours? Say you have a dentist appointment. We'll have a picnic. I know a place. I'll meet you at the new mall, parked in front of Ames. You know the car—a maroon Mercedes. Call me Monday if there's a problem. If somebody else answers, tell them you found your glasses."

"It's all so cold-blooded!" he protested.

This made her laugh. "Owen, you must learn," she said, solemnly, "to be practical. Life isn't some dream you can just wander through." She was being a teacher; he loved that.

The picnic spot was a twenty-acre nature preserve called Whitefield's Rock. The great evangelist was supposed to have preached from there, but scholars now doubted it and thought, from the topography, he must have preached from a similar outcropping of ledge some miles away. The rock itself, worn smooth with footsteps and its crevices littered with cigarette filters and Popsicle sticks, was not their destination; they found an open space, well off the path, sheltered from the September breeze and, they trusted, from any stray walker's sight. The preserve, with its religious taint, was never crowded and after Labor Day virtually deserted. People, over the summer, had found this secret space before them; a beer can glinted beneath a bush, and the grass, soft and yellowish in the way of constantly shaded grass, showed matted patches. She had brought a blanket and their picnic in a well-stocked basket but neither Owen nor Faye had an appetite, even for the Portuguese rosé in a squat round bottle with a twist-off cap. They fell into each other as if to hide from the other's gaze. He could not believe the monstrous miracle of it, a woman not Phyllis kissing him, licking his ear, sighing in his arms, not resisting when he began to unbutton her blouse.

Faye had dressed for Hartford, in a suit of light pimento tweed, over a cream-colored silk shirt, with two-tone high heels that she had changed, in the car, for old loafers, to hike in. She moved the picnic basket off the blanket to give their bodies room. He undid the blouse and, as she lifted up on one arm to let him get at the hooks and eyes, her bra. Her back was bonier than he was used to; to slacken the bra a second her shoulder blades dipped inward, as if in sitting-up exercises. Her shoulders were brown with summer's merged freckles; her flat midriff showed a tan where Phyllis was sallow and stretch-marked. He wanted to cry out as Faye's breasts, smaller and tauter than his wife's, came free, to be touched by his trembling hands, his careful lips. The trees around them formed green walls, twitching and rippling in the breeze, showing leaves' silver undersides, with here and there a maple or beech leaf already turned yellow.

When they were done with her breasts she lifted her hips up from the blanket matter-of-factly. "The skirt, too," she directed. "It's getting rumpled." He tugged the tweed, but her hip bones, wider than her shoulders, didn't let go. "The buttons at the side!" Faye said, in the urgent, ungentle tone in which his mother had once said, *Don't touch it!*

He undid the buttons, the skirt slid down, and then, with the faintest gust of genital scent, the silk underpants, paler than her bra. They slid down, as with Elsie, but that was in the deep dark and this moment was awash in daylight. Revelations were coming too fast to take in, like presents at a speeded-up birthday party. Faye's pubic hair was scanter than Phyllis's; two gauzy waves met in a coppery crest down the middle of her mount. He wanted to see her face, to watch her watching his face as for the first time he saw this essence of her, this crux of her femininity; however long or short their future stretched from this moment, there would never be another such first time. Her face looked sleepy, complacent, her eyes halfway lidded, as if she were drinking in with him the sight of her, the top of her cleft visible through the scant reddish hair; she was drinking in the sight of him drinking her in, her expression proud and skeptical both. He loved her for her innocent lewd vanity. Faye enjoyed, he was discovering, being naked, even here in this precarious open, while his ears strained for a broken twig or a suppressed rustle in the forest around them. Her skin was a blinding pelt, not quite hairless and pricked by stray pink dots and threadlike capillaries. Bare but for her barrettes and loafers and a ring or two, she knelt to unzip him, his wits too slowed by listening for forest sounds to assist. He recovered his manners enough to ease his unbelted corduroys and Jockey shorts around his prick, already thumpingly erect. She gazed down at it as if into a baby's face, touching it with the same fingertips that had gently rested on his wrist at the other end of summer. "Sweet," she said. "Scary."

He was average, he had always supposed, from what he saw in locker rooms and, at MIT, stag movies. There was now a new roominess in his and Faye's relationship, space into which he expanded. His voice had grown husky and murmurous, a seducer's. "You can handle it, I think. But"— in more his own voice, too light and tentative—"do you want to? You don't have to. We've already done a lot, for a first date."

"Owen," she scolded, "I want you to make love to me. I'll be very angry if you don't."

"O.K., wonderful. I brought this for us." He rummaged, so awkwardly he began to blush, in the pocket of the corduroys, still rumpled and caught around his knees. In a square foil packet, brought from the bathroom cabinet at home, where one wouldn't be missed from the box of them.

"Oh, darling. I'm on the Pill, isn't Phyllis? No wonder you two keep making babies."

A flock of crows, six or eight, raucously rasping at one another, thrashed into the top of an oak on the edge of the square of sky. The heavenly invasion made his heart race; he looked down at his prick, silently begging it not to be distracted; his mind fought skidding into crows and woods, babies and Phyllis, and his prick stared back at him with its one eye clouded by a single drop of pure seminal yearning. He felt suspended at the top of an arc. Faye leaned back on the blanket, arranging her legs in an M of receptivity, and he knelt between them like the most abject and craven supplicant who ever exposed his bare ass to the eagle eyes of a bunch of crows.

Faye took him in hand. He slipped in. He became an adulterer. He went for the last inch. She grunted, at her own revelation. His was that her cunt did not feel like Phyllis's. Smoother, somehow simpler, its wetness less thick, less of a sauce, more of a glaze. It was soon over. He could not help himself, he was so excited, proud, and nervous. When he was done, he opened his eyes, and saw this stranger's face an inch from his, seemingly asleep, the closed eyelids showing a thin pulse, her long lips curved self-lullingly. "Sorry, sorry," Owen apologized. "You never had a chance. Next time I'll do better. If you'll give me a next time."

"You were lovely, silly," she said. "So intense."

"I was?" She could compare; she had had other men, he knew from the practiced way she had managed this meeting.

"Yes." Now she was feeling her nakedness as vulnerability; her mouth made its little deprecating crimp, and her eyes moved from side to side, taking in their green, breeze-rippled surroundings.

But he felt in no hurry to get off her. "Tell me about it,"

he idly demanded, in a soft growl that rubbed his throat like a purr. "About my coming."

"It tells me that this is important to you."

"Isn't it to every man?"

Faye frowned, perhaps at his weight still being there, upon her. "No," she said. "To some . . ." She shrugged and didn't finish. Owen guessed that Jock was one of the some.

She told him things. She saw him as living an unnaturally proper and aloof life with Phyllis, and needing instruction. "You should drink more," she once told him, as if his moderation were a diet deficiency. She wanted him to join her on the muddy earth, to be more like Jock. Yet she appreciated that he was not like Jock. She told him, later, of this day, that, after dropping him off on the parking lot in front of Ames, as she drove around in her Mercedes with its uneaten picnic lunch and then home she cried to think that she could never have him, except for a time in this illicit, doomed fashion.

Later still, years later, he would wonder why he had loved her so much, flashy and hard-nosed and shallow as Phyllis explained to him Faye was. For some months he dreamed of marrying her, so as to have her always at his side, and everything touching her—her two skinny, wan children, her rambling Victorian house, her jauntily improvised costumes, her casual mix of furniture (Jock's inherited antiques, her faddish sling chairs and airfoam sofas), the photographs of her in her attic that she showed him, herself as a girl, as a college freshman, as a bride in white lace—everything touching her seemed holy. She tinged the world a new color, an iridescent stain in her vicinity, giving even the gritty parking lots where they met for a tryst a sparkling, poignant glory. Later he would come and stand on the spot where their cars had parked, one driver furtively becoming a passenger, and he would feel a hollowness spreading around him. Like strong sunlight she faded once-important sections of his life—his children, new wrinkles in programming code, E-O Data's growth and struggles, even the news, as freedom marches wracked the South and a distant sliver of Asia took more and more front-page space—so that he moved insensible through these realms of former interest. This tinge, this sweet sickness of love, lingered in his system for years, an imbalance that was precious to him. Faye had dwindled to an inner sore, but that bitter remainder he pressed deeper into his sense of himself. She had given him, at thirty-one, a freedom that others (Marty Naftzinger, say) had long known, a freedom of the body. He was grateful but could not repay her—had ill repaid her. The women, including Phyllis, who advised him told him he was making too much of it. Women took their chances, their gambles, and sometimes lost. Faye had lost.

But what only he could know was that he had failed a kind of child. Naked, Faye showed round white hips and thighs, though she was lean and bony above the waist, with a face her features seemed to be struggling to escape. She was experienced, sexually, more than he, but adultery had left her innocent. Sex with her was straightforward, with none of the elaborations others were to demonstrate. The grip of her vagina had something infantile about it, something heartbreaking, like a child's shy, hopeful question. She persuaded him he had the answer. During the months of the affair his lovemaking with Phyllis became more confident and insistent. He spoke more loudly and warmly to his children, when they materialized to him through his mists of being mentally elsewhere. Photographs from that time show him as mussed and manicky-looking. He felt fonder of the world at large—the old mill town with its services and cheerfully laborious local characters and the winter weather with its scrape of plowing and their cozy circle of friends. He felt especially fond of Jock; he wanted to hug the man, red-faced Jock with his baked-on alcoholic grin, for feeding and sheltering such a marvel of beauty and concupiscence. He could hardly contain the wonder of it— this well-cared-for woman, in such expensive and amusing clothes, taking such risks to perform for him acts that Phyllis performed reluctantly, ironically, looking to one side, in her own safe home, with all society's sanctions backing his thrusts.

Why Faye would behave in such a reckless and adorable way—why any woman would—was still not clear to Owen. He assumed that she had wanted something in return, him as husband, and that he had failed to give it to her; the heat of his failure annealed her image to him. He would show loyalty where he could, in his inner theatre. He would always remember how she looked at certain moments, wistful moments, her generic female beauty married to something specific and complicated happening in her face, an awareness of cross-currents and half-lies and underlying sadness. "Well, I'm glad it was you," she said at the end, trying to make a life-stage of it, a lesson learned.

Toward the end, they were getting careless. Once, trying to find privacy down a dirt road, they got her heavy Mercedes stuck in the March mud and had to phone for a tow truck from the home of the owner of the property they were trespassing upon. Tired of sleazy motels and furtive excursions, they would sneak him into her house, with Jock off and the children at school and no plumber or cleaning woman scheduled to show up. To bring them, after a while, something to eat or drink, she would wander naked through the winter-bright rooms, like a deer at home in the camouflaging forest. Returning to him where he lay languid in the wrecked guest-room bed, she would laugh at something, something utterly marvelling and grateful, she saw in his face. She would laugh, and her mouth would stay open a second longer as the girlish high sound died away. Even now, an elderly resident of Haskells Crossing, looking both ways before judiciously forcing his creaky body to cross the street, he feels his heart skip when he sees a young woman of a certain taut, bony-faced type emerge from the 7-Eleven or wait in front of the new Starbucks, giving someone she suddenly spots on the street a big grin, exposing her gums as well as her teeth, as Faye used to greet him at one of her and Jock's parties. She has come back to him.

ix. *Convalescence*

IT WAS FAYE who ended it, by telling her husband.
She let Owen know over the phone. When he, knocked
nearly breathless by the betrayal, asked her why, she was
vague. "Oh—my shrink thought I was getting confused. It
was too much, Owen. I didn't know what you wanted, and it
was killing me, frankly. I'm sorry. If I hadn't loved you so
much, I could have handled it better."

"But you never told me any of this. You were always so
gay, so—so giving and cheerful. Like this was all you
wanted. Even that time we got stuck, the cool way you
offered to pay the man for repairing the ruts, after using his
phone. You were *won*derful, Faye." Meaning wonderful in
everything, and said very softly. Owen was at his desk, with
Ed in the next cubicle and their employees passing by with
coffee and folders. He murmured into the receiver with his
back turned and his chair, an ergonomic swivel on a five-
roller chrome pedestal, facing the wire-webbed window. If
he stood up he could have seen the Chunkaunkabaug, most
of its rocks concealed beneath the fast-running meltwater,
heading for the falls.

"I was terrified that man would tell Jock," Faye was explaining, a tiny voice caught in the receiver, like an insect under a water tumbler. "Or that somebody would see us in a car together. It could have happened at any time, and then Jock would have had me over a barrel—he can be very tricky, about money. This way at least he found out from me: the errant wife confesses. Owen, I can't talk forever about it; we were awake all night, except for a couple of hours, and he just went out of the house to go buy cigarettes and the *Wall Street Journal*. Watch out for him downtown."

Owen was not sorry to think that the conversation would be short. The workaday world around him had become realer, for the first time in seven months, than that illicit annex into which he was pouring his voice, through this little electronic hole at his lips. "Still," he said, seeking for leverage in the sudden shift, "you should have discussed this with me."

"You would have argued and got me more confused." Faye laughed—a disagreeable yelp, a high-pitched sound a child would make when pinched. She said, as if reading the words from a card, "Men don't think beyond their next piece of ass."

Was she deliberately trying to offend him, to soften this blow? He said, angry anyway, "Is that what Jock tells you?"

"It's what I tell him. You'll get over it, Owen. We all will. People do."

Those showy clothes of hers, that babylike happy nudity, those wide-open hazel eyes, that voice with its stagy range from high to low, all slipping from him, into the abyss of forever. "Thanks a lot for those comforting words," he said, so sarcastically that she hung up.

Ed, visiting Owen's cubicle in the next hour, took a look

at him and said, "You want to go home early? You look like you've been socked in the belly. You look like shit."

"I think I've caught a spring cold. I never know how to dress this time of year." But he did leave the factory early; he couldn't get home fast enough. To their surprise, he dragged Gregory and Iris out into the threadbare, muddy yard to play a little softball. Their puzzled efforts to please him, to find the ball with their wild swings, broke his heart. Without their understanding it they were trying to work an exoneration for the sinner turned back into a father. He would have liked to stay in the yard on and on, enclosed in the bubble of family life, never telling Phyllis and never answering the phone, but the afternoon grew dark and cold, and they all went into the warm house, where Phyllis was making the dinner, putting the meatloaf into the oven and fluttering her nearly invisible pale lashes to rid herself of the tears from, he guessed, having chopped onions. She was not quite herself; there was something stale and studied about her cheerfulness as she chatted at the table with the children and fed little Eve, in the high chair, her applesauce and creamed carrots.

When, that evening, with the four children at last in their beds, he began to confess, she cut him off. "I know. Jock came over this afternoon and told me. Well, do you want a divorce?"

"No." The softball game with the two older children, taking their determined stances at the imaginary plate, imitating the gestures of ballplayers on television, cocking the bat so it pointed straight up at the fleecy, tossing April sky, and then so touchingly striking out, had erased his recurrent dream, a kind of fever dream, of a life with Faye.

"Well, you better tell *them* that, before they go ahead and get one."

Of the subsequent agitated palavers—the four of them at one grim, eventually drunken conference in their house, where he had more than once been an illicit guest, and then in scattered tête-à-têtes, as the increasingly public aftermath unfolded, between Jock and Phyllis, Jock and him, Phyllis and him, Faye and Phyllis, every pairing except the one it was all about—Owen had the defective memory of the severely embarrassed. He didn't want to remember it. Moments continued to stick in his mind as contexts melted into forgetfulness: Jock asking him, across the booth in the old-fashioned aluminum roadside diner toward Lower Falls, "Did she have climaxes with you?"

Owen took the question as rude aggression, some kind of cuckold's gibe, and refused to answer it, but in hindsight imagined a watery earnestness in Jock's eyes, their strained, pickled whites. What would the honest answer have been? It was too embarrassing—Owen wasn't sure. Faye had been so loving, so smiling, and had bestowed upon their trysts (pathetically rare, in retrospect) such a glad aura of excitement and relief, that he had assumed so without any more evidence than his own easily obtained satisfaction. She would lie under him with her eyes closed, a little pulse in the lids, and when she opened them give him her gorgeous big grin and speak in a higher, shyer voice than usual. Phyllis, though he thought of her as cool and not often interested, gave clearer signs of orgasm. But, he reasoned, on this matter where so much of his education was yet to come, female sexuality must have many styles; he pictured it as a kind of harp whose strings, always faintly murmuring, were of widely different lengths and thicknesses. Yet the notion that Faye had been faking climaxes, or unprotestingly feigning contentment without them—that she had been, beneath her flashiness and show of ardor, frigid—wounded his sense of her; she had been deceiving him.

Phyllis, too, in the long aftermath, contrived to diminish his image of Faye and reconcile him to his loss. "Didn't you kids," she asked him, "ever seriously discuss divorce and remarriage?"

He could not exactly remember. He had more than once said how lovely it would be if she were his wife, but this wasn't a proposal, was it? It was a dream, an alternate universe.

"It seems obvious," Phyllis went on mildly, considering the problem like one in topology, "that she wanted it. Jock takes good care of her financially, but as a husband I think he's exhausted her capacity to romanticize him."

"Did she romanticize me?" He had felt, merely, that she had assigned him his true value. Their whole affair, from the first event in the woods by Whitefield's Rock, had taken place under the sign of truth—fresh truth, fresh seeing. A smeared window had been ammoniated and wiped clean. As he plodded through one of E-O's contracted applications programs for an insurance company's records and logarithmized risk margins or a Danbury hat factory's cost accounting, payroll, and stock control, he was aware of a lessened ability to link and combine logic chains, a fuzziness in his neurons brought on, perhaps, by their saturation in memories and anticipations of sex with Faye. But he was confident that eventually a new mental strength would result from this dip into sexual adventure. His marriage to Phyllis, when new—just lying beside her sleeping body, in unconscious partnership with her breathing and her dreams—had brought on brainstorms of which DigitEyes was the final, precocious product. After a few years, however, many rival such programs entered the market, while his vision of a graphic computer-user interface remained frustrated by the limits of the hardware, and the hardware's high cost.

High cost—what it came down to, perhaps, was that Faye had seemed too expensive for him; he could time-share her but not own her.

"Of course, it's what people do," Phyllis told him, wearily, even tenderly, out of that ambient Cantabrigian wisdom she had absorbed as a girl. "Romanticize. Otherwise it all seems gross. Fucking," she clarified. There had been a time when she wouldn't have used the word, but the counterculture had changed that. Phyllis liked the *faux-pauvre* costumes of the young, their lack of makeup, their attachment to radical causes, their theoretical bent and belief in contentious discourse; it felt like home to her, something she had been part of before E-O Data had brought her to middlebrow Middle Falls. "Not that you needed much romanticizing; you're an attractive man, Owen."

"Now you tell me."

"I told you from the start, the best I could. I can't gush the way Faye does. Attractive, and she took you for rich, too."

"If she did, she was wrong. The new version of DigitEyes is selling very slowly. Sketchpad, out of the Lincoln Lab, has taken away market share. Also Ed is worried about this new minicomputer DEC is putting out for only eighteen thousand, the PDP-8. Everybody can own one and the market for standardized programs will take off. Contract programming like we do will become obsolete." With their marriage revealed as an abyss beneath them, he was happy to shift their ground to technology. She was, too, for a few moments.

"Really? That's not what Ed tells *me*. He says the more people own computers the better for the software business all around. And anyway Faye didn't know any of that. She wanted you for a husband, darling, like one of her cute new costumes. It's the tragedy of women, isn't it? The only thing we can trade on is fucking, and with the Pill now the price has gone way down."

"Please, stop talking so tough. It isn't you."

"I thought you liked women tough. Or at least crass. It *is* me, Owen. It's what you've made me, with this sleazy town of exurban misfits and this grotesque infatuation with Faye. First I had to put up with your deceit, and now with all your adolescent post-facto mooning. My mother was right: you weren't for me. You were too much of a boy. My father was the one who liked you, though I never heard the two of you exchange more than six words. After scuttling Hank, I suppose he felt he owed me one."

Color had risen to her cheeks, through her throat; her level eyes, silvery in some lights, flared in rare indignation. He suppressed an admiring snicker: Phyllis had a lonely talent for seeing through things, to their bleak bones. Poor Faye, yes, she had told him to be practical, and had given him what lessons she could, but now her practical value to him was as a conquest, a badge he could wear in their little local society, where sex was less and less a household secret. True, he ached in her absence, but having her day after day would have brought with it daily life and its tedium, and sickly children with half of Jock's genes, and a wife who thought half like Jock. "How could I marry her?" Owen asked his wife, plaintively, anxious to discuss this with somebody impartial. "I have four children, the youngest a year old!"

Phyllis told him, "That wouldn't have stopped some men. She saw you as reckless, Owen, because you're creative, but in fact you're very self-protective, very Pennsylvania-Dutch one-step-at-a-time. She rushed you, and you hate being rushed."

He took these observations for compliments, or at least for knowledgeable attention, and said with pleased sulkiness, "Ed says the trouble with programming is it's been *too* creative. The need now, with the basics in place and all these new chips piling up hardware capability, is to make it less of an art and more of an engineering discipline."

"Does that scare you?" Phyllis asked him, ever a wife. In spite of the domestic horrors of the spring—scandal, possible breakup—she had found time to sunbathe in their big back yard, down by the lily pond with its rebuilt bridge, and the tip of her nose was pink.

"No," he said, relaxed again into being a husband, "E-O has younger people for the nitty-gritty, the coding and debugging, it comes like second nature to them; they don't know there was ever a time before FORTRAN and COBOL. My task is more to dream, to dream big. I have my theories. I think graphics is the way into a *huge* market. If you can find a way around all these line commands that have to be memorized, and use simple intuitive images as the interface, everybody can use them. You can have *games*."

"Do people really need," Phyllis asked, looking over her shoulder as she left the room, "even *more* ways to waste their time?"

The Dunhams had a family lawyer, and Jock for a while talked about suing Owen for alienation of affections, or making the Mackenzies move out of town, but they produced a lawyer of their own, and in the end the most desirable thing seemed to be for the Dunhams to sell that rambling place with its veranda and move closer to the city, to Norwalk or Wilton, where the schools would be better for the children, and Jock would be closer to where the Dunham money was managed over three-martini lunches, and Faye was fifty minutes away from Manhattan's stores and shows and display cases. Owen thought of her striding through the city he had left five years ago, sinking happily into its glitter, and felt a jealous relief. He would always love her, she was his one fling into the dreamland of sexual happiness, but it had not been practical, and it gave him a metallic taste in his mouth, a touch of dread, to know that he had intervened in the lives of others, dislocating them, causing something as serious as a change of address and a change of schools for the two bewildered, delicate Dunham children. Marrying Phyllis had occurred under the supervision of adults; engendering his own children—a blunt intervention in the world's statistics—had occurred under her supervision. But fucking Faye had been his idea, or an idea of hers that he had readily adopted, alone with her beneath the square sky that day, with the crows, and the bed of soft grass behind the holy rock.

At the start of his convalescence he focused with invalid closeness on the workings of his family—the four children nosing ahead like earthworms in the world's substance, encountering pebbles like bad school reports and the deaths of pets, but pushing on, growing, speaking in ever more complete and complex sentences. Gregory turned nine and suddenly was full of sports statistics. Iris at seven and a half was given to undressing her Barbie dolls and then finding she could not put the tight little clothes back on the unyielding plastic bodies. Owen more than Phyllis had the patience to tug the bits of cloth within reach of the fasteners; some of the outfits reminded him of ones Faye used to wear, playfully.

He was a good father, the mothers of their circle told Phyllis, she in turn told him; but he knew he was not. An only child, helplessly self-centered, he could not bring to these four little souls—strangers to the towering cosmos, each a different mix of his and Phyllis's genes and each varyingly susceptible to the surrounding culture—the same morbidly hopeful concentration his parents and mother's parents, stripped of hope for themselves, had brought to him. He had been outnumbered, four adults to one child, and now four children outnumbered him. He felt less their progenitor than their brother, and this fraternal lightness, a love leavened by distraction and pinches of sadism, for good and bad characterized his fatherhood. On the one hand he did not sit heavy on his children; on the other, he did not strive to shape their lives, to inculcate patterns of behavior. There was little in the children's lives like the tiring, tedious, but impressive Sunday walks he took with his own parents. Instead, all was tumble—squawks and shouts and squalling appeals for justice. Television and other children, first from the packed Common Lane neighborhood and then, ferried to and from the Partridgeberry Road place, the children of their friends, filled the little time left over after sibling interaction and school. Phyllis's schooling had been all private, and his all public; they agreed to begin with the latter, which was handiest and most democratic, reserving transition to paid private schools as the child's needs seemed to indicate. He was proud of being able to support these dependents, from above as it were, but in most respects he dwelt among them, sharing in both the entertainments—*Captain Kangaroo, The Sound of Music*—

and the moral bafflement of the era, as a rising political fury shadowed a holiday giddiness. Still, after Faye he was noticeably more of a paternal presence, all summer taking his lunch hour at Heron Pond once or twice a week, there among the dragonflies and peanut-butter sandwiches and gossipping near-naked mothers.

At work, too, he tried to rededicate himself, patiently stringing together those long but finite binary chains, those rickety scaffolds of contingency, that, once debugged, gave companies in an electronic twinkling the information that used to be pieced together from typed or handwritten files. It was like knitting: a single mis-stitch necessitated tearing up dozens of rows of code, yet whole patches of previously perfected subroutines could be crocheted into a fresh customized design. Except for strokes of ingenuity, of logical lumping and short-cutting, which only another programmer could appreciate, his work felt trivial; the kind of data-processing he was making possible on a two-hundred-thousand-dollar mainframe could have been carried forward, in most company systems, on punched cards, more clumsily and slowly yet with no qualitative difference. Number-crunching, it was called, with an affection that yet dramatized its basic drudgery.

"Ed," Owen asked his partner one day at lunch, "doesn't there have to be a next thing?" Once a week they tried to share lunch, just the two of them, since the success of the company, its multiplication of projects and employees, came more and more between them, as if the hyphen in E-O was implacably lengthening. The restaurant was the least crummy of the three eateries left along River Street. The downtown had been struggling for years. Empty stores were rented, newly tricked out as boutiques or arty stationers or educational-toy stores and, after a spurt of customer curiosity, slowly failed, and were empty again, with butcher paper taped across their windows. The Ugly Duckling had a swan on its signboard. Only the two back windows overlooked the river, but the mock-tavern decor—dark-stained oak beams, rough-hewn maple tables, waitresses with frilled aprons over their blue jeans—was cozy and acoustically merciful. The meat-and-potatoes menu was being infiltrated by pasta salads and macrobiotic soups; nevertheless, Ed ordered a Reuben thick with cheese and fatty pastrami, and fries and a Heineken. He had added twenty pounds since his days at IBM. Entrepreneurial success and pricier clothes gave his bulk authority. The front man with their corporate clients, he had taken to wearing suits, with a shirt and tie; Owen remained loyal to the 'fifties student garb of khakis and soft flannel shirt, augmented in winter with a down vest. He had lost five pounds in the affair with Faye and its painful aftermath, and had worked to keep it off, vain of his newly wiry figure. He felt nimbler now, more dangerous. He had taken to black turtlenecks, and joined an indoor tennis club in Upper Falls. As longer hair became permissible for men, his own showed a bounce and a tendency to curl.

"You're talking what?" Ed asked. "Private life? You did the next thing already."

Owen blushed; he wanted to believe that his adventure with Faye, if not secret, was conversationally off-bounds with Ed, who had known him and Phyllis so long he seemed part of the marriage. "Computerwise," he primly clarified. "This OS/360 of IBM's is turning into a fucking disaster. It's costing them tens of millions, and *still* they can't take it to market for all the bugs. They got a thousand programming people on it out there in Poughkeepsie and it's more and more a mess, I hear."

Ed asked, through his chewing, "What are they gonna do? They gotta work it through if they're going to get any of their investment back out. They tried to use multi-programming and that made problems. The larger the program, the greater the tendency to crash. One bug is all it takes."

"It's more than problems, Ed, it's a basic imbalance. The capacity keeps doubling; programming can't keep up. Hardware developmemt is industrial; it's knitting mills. Software is still sitting in the cottage working on an old hand loom. It's piecework."

"It'll catch up. Electrical engineering is everybody's major; it's everybody's toy these days. Remember when metallurgy was the sexy thing? Not to mention nuclear physics. Why sweat it, if what we do is piecework? We're getting paid."

"Yeah, but look who can afford us: banks, insurance companies, airlines, the Pentagon. The world's dreariest mentalities."

Ed stopped chewing, and said across the table with mock solemnity, "It grieves me to hear you talk like this, O. Tell me, what do you want out of life you're not getting?"

Owen pictured Phyllis, because he knew Ed was picturing her too. What more could a man want out of life than Phyllis? That was what Ed's owlish stare, through glasses so thick a tint of skin was refracted into the bevelled edges, was asking. Owen didn't know the answer but knew Ed's estimation of Phyllis was unrealistic. "What I want is a little shelter from the trivial," he answered. "My desk sits right in the thick of traffic; everybody keeps asking me things, to double-check this or that approach, to look over their schematics. We could keep the desk where it is, and I'll be at it most of the time, but couldn't I have another, at the other end of the floor, that would be private? I need to really think about the DigitEyes redo, to make it cutting-edge again."

Ed resumed eating and was having trouble with the Reuben. The greasy pastrami had soaked through the thin rye bread, making it slippery to hold. He was lowering his big head to get his mouth under it, the drooping strings of cheese, and the odd angle emphasized how much his hair had receded from his forehead; it had once looked like Buddy Rourke's, boyishly thrusting forward. When he had taken his bite and swallowed and the Reuben was under control again, down on the plate beside the French fries and the paper cup of coleslaw, Ed said, "So that's your new thing? To cut yourself off from the company mainstream? These kids we hire don't know how to write economical programs. Everything is GO TO, GO TO. They think there's no end to capacity now."

"They're almost right. They may be right."

"Enough big baggy GO TOs hanging out there, logical contradictions begin to show up."

"They'll learn, Ed. We're all learning; it's still a young trade. All I'm asking is a little privacy, and one of the new DEC minis. I'd like a PDP-8 and a graphics CRT screen, as well as the telex assembler reader. Give me six months and cut my crunching to half-time. There's something I'm missing, some fresh approach."

"So that's your new thing. You're pulling out on us."

"Ed, it's how I'll be most valuable to the company—a little detached. I'm just the head ribbon-clerk as it is now. All that socializing up front produces nothing; it's driving me crazy. The brain ages. Time runs out. Look at the breakthroughs—most of them by guys younger than we are. Einstein at twenty-five. Turing the same. Phyllis says she couldn't possibly do her math thesis now, she's gotten too stupid."

"That's sad, that Phyl thinks that," Ed said, touching his loosely knotted necktie with greasy fingers in synchrony with a semi-suppressed burp. He did that chimp thing with his upper lip, bulging it out over his upper teeth, trying to work some bit of pastrami loose. "Hey. You want to know what *my* new thing is?"

"Sure. Didn't know you had one," Owen said, hurrying into his salad of chickpeas and bow-tie pasta, to catch up after talking too much. The little room he had in mind, an old watchmen's locker room with one little metal-framed window too high to look out of and a row of battered green lockers, locks long gone, was at the head of steel-and-cement stairs that descended down to a door that opened onto a disused sidewalk leading toward the permanently locked pedestrian bridge across the river. In the days of the old arms factory, a workforce on foot crossed the river from the region of row houses. The door, sheathed in metal painted red to match the bricks, was never used but was kept unlocked in daytime, as an emergency fire exit. Owen would use it, unseen. The door, the stairs, the private room appeared in his mind in luminous vectorized form, the whole projection turning as if he were passing through it, the geometric shapes transforming as the underlying mathematics determined.

"I'm getting married," Ed announced.

A mass of pulped chickpeas found resistance in Owen's throat. He chased it down with a sip of water and brought out, "That's great. High time. Who to? Do I know her?"

"I hope you don't, you lech," said Ed, for the second time

offending Owen's strict sense of sexual propriety. "She's eight years younger than me, nine years than you—just a kid, O. An innocent kid. Have a heart."

Owen felt a pang. Phyllis was a year older. Maybe that was their trouble, simple biology: the man should dominate. He never had. Ed had a lovely patience, to wait till he could marry so much younger. "We met at a conference," he was explaining, "that thing in Seattle, remember I went last year? On integrated circuits. Stacey's a rep for Texas Instruments."

"Integrated circuits," Owen said, to show he was following. He had never thought of Ed as marriageable, which was silly. Almost everybody is, the way Nature has set it up, with its usual tremendous margin for error.

"Yeah, and what to do with such tiny ICs. Last year TI brought out a hearing aid. Next year they're marketing a desk calculator that weighs less than a chicken. She tells me this as if everybody knows what a chicken weighs."

"Is she a Texan?" *Why do I feel so betrayed?* Owen asked himself. *What do I care if Ed is married?*

He had counted on Ed to remain loyal to the business, so his own attention could wander to higher or lower things. He needed to know about life. "Not so's you'd notice," Ed answered. "Her folks are really from the West Coast; her dad worked for Grumman. She says 'my daddy.' They moved to Dallas when Stacey was nine. She picked up the accent, but, more important, the attitude."

"The Texas attitude."

"Yeah—it's great. She thinks the American dream is still on. I get so fucking tired of wise-ass sourpuss Easterners, who think everything worth doing was done before 1750, always taking cheap shots at America and LBJ."

"Another Texan."

"Damn right. Johnson's done more for blacks in two years than Saint Franklin Roosevelt did in twelve, and still all these knee-jerk liberals keep knocking him, calling him a redneck."

It occurred to Owen that Ed considered himself a redneck, Bronx-style. A girl from Texas would see him as the suited-up electronic empire-builder he was. "When do we all meet her?" Owen asked.

"Soon, O. I'd like you to be my best man."

Owen blushed. "With pleasure, Ed. I'm tickled pink, as they used to say." It smelled a bit as if he was being restored to society's good graces, after his Faye episode. He wasn't sure he wanted to be restored. "When is the, the happy event?"

"We thought soon, May, maybe. Later than that it gets stinking hot down there. Then we come up here and have the Eastern summer before the long winter. She's never experienced a Northern winter. The only snow she's seen has been on mountaintops, on the San Gabriels." Already Ed was sounding pompous, a consumer of geographies and climates.

The waitress came and offered dessert or coffee. Ed thought he'd try the prune-fig brownie, with whipped cream, and a cappuccino. Owen settled for mint tea. He asked Ed, "How did you do all this courting? I never knew about it."

"You haven't been paying much attention," Ed said, for the third time jabbing in the direction of Owen's private life. Owen was still not, the Middle Falls consensus was, "over" Faye. "I've been down there, she's been up here a couple times. Phyllis has met her."

"She *has*?" Mint tea, hot water barely tinted green, was put down before him; Ed's brownie looked as heavy and rich as chocolate cake, wearing a toppling squirt of whipped cream. Saliva sprang from Owen's inner cheeks. Was this to be the rest of his life, self-denial? He said, "She never said anything to me."

"I asked her not to. She liked Stacey a lot," Ed told Owen, squinting as if daring him to object.

Ed had sought Phyllis's approval, and she had given it, all without her husband's knowledge. *We all have inner lives*, Owen thought: secrets to protect. The recognition seemed to click into a segment of his own liberation.

Stacey was a charmer, it turned out. She was skinny but soft-boned, floppy even, in the way she moved and talked. She had a wide soft mouth that seemed to slow her words, like a child's endearing impediment. She was enough younger than they to lack some of their inhibitions. She liked to swim naked in the heated pool that came with the somewhat pretentious house Ed bought for them in the new hillside development on Wilson Drive. "Woodrow, Charlie, or Don?" Owen had asked, but Ed was too besotted with the married state to hear any sarcasm. By the second summer, Owen and Ed had gotten used to her nudity and some nights Phyllis joined her in it. It was no worse, after all, than a hot tub, which is supposed to be good for you. The older woman's figure, breasts and stomach taut now that her spell of childbearing was forever over, had nothing to lose in the comparison with Stacey's, which was, younger though she was, droopier. Ed and Owen kept their bathing suits on.

"Aren't they sweetly shy," Phyllis said to Stacey. The pool as well as being heated had underwater lights that revealed wobbly truncations of the two women's hips and water-treading legs. Their heads looked small, with their hair licked flat against their skulls.

"Oh, aren't men just!" Stacey said back, in her twang. "They're afraid of having their little jimmies chopped off."

"Or laughed at," Phyllis suggested, to make the image less horrific.

"Pretty much the same thang," Stacey said.

The men being teased sat in the shadows, on aluminum chairs, with cans of beer, while the mermaids wobbled in and out of the pool lights. When Stacey decided to emerge from the water, she would thrash to the ladder and stand on the pool edge and, tipping her head way over, wring out her long dark hair towel-style. If light was behind her, Owen would see her pubic triangle dripping from a point like a wet goatee between her skinny thighs. Languidly, her long feet leaving prints on the flagstones that rimmed the pool, she would seek out a beach towel to wrap herself in. With the hand not clasping the towel at her chest she would fiddle a cigarette from the pack on the little white poolside table and, her head still tilted as when she was wringing her hair, manage with wet fingers to get it lit in her mouth. It was in this pose, Owen thought, that she looked most glamorous, squinting and exhaling, and her drying hair backlit like a burning haystack. Stacey brought whiffs of the counterculture into Middle Falls. Somehow she produced pot in little cellophane envelopes, and Zigzag paper, and the four of them would partake, usually on Sunday nights, in the Mervines' living room. Fridays and Saturdays there were dinner parties to give or go to, dances for this or that good cause, and the Mackenzies' house was too inhibiting, with all those children upstairs listening. Ed and Stacey did not intend to have children, at least not immediately. This was somehow shocking to Owen; Phyllis offended him by seeming to agree. "I think it's better not to hurry," she said, making her little frosty *moue* of thoughtfulness. "The kids now have the right idea—have the sex but don't get trapped."

"Trapped?" Owen asked, offended. "Who's doing the trapping?"

"Nobody, sweetie—it just happens. Used to happen. Are you going to pass that joint or just hang on to it in that foolish way?"

"Do you really think Owie is foolish?" Stacey asked in her slowed, sweet Texas voice. "I don't think he's foolish, he's just *stunned*." The last word elongated in Owen's mind like a lasso. When had women started to talk about him as if he were absent? Nearly being sued for alienation of affections had given him a sort of Exhibit A status.

"You mean . . ." Phyllis began, and let the thought trail as she relinquished the joint and passed it to Ed, who held the smoking thing up before his nearsighted eyes and studied it as if it were a distasteful puzzle.

"Drugs," he announced, "eat up your brain cells."

"Yeah," Owen agreed, anxious as always to preserve male solidarity, "but so does aging. Brain cells die all the time, and still the brain has more than it needs, for most purposes." Completing so extended a thought seemed a miracle, like a strand of DNA.

"Listen to them," Stacey said to Phyllis, "worrying about the size of their brains. Isn't that macho?"

"Men," Phyllis offered, "are into quantification. Did you mean," she went on, in her lovely light laid-back style—he had always been drawn by her diffident voice, from the days at MIT, when he had to strain to overhear it—"that Owie, as you call him, is still stunned because of that affair he had *ages* ago with that ridiculous woman? I forget her name."

"Faye Dunham," Ed supplied, taking a very gingerly hit from the joint, which was becoming a roach. In these Sunday nights all the Middle Falls gossip came out, bringing Stacey up-to-date, including Owen's affair, mostly as presented by Phyllis, as a pathetic breach not only of marital vows but of self-respect and enlightened self-interest. Stacey seemed interested, to Ed's discomfort, which he expressed by withdrawal into silence or laconic pronouncements. "Faye was O.K.," he said. "Just easily bored. She was at a restless time of life, married to a lush like that."

Stacey crooned to him, "Don't you ever get to that time of life, honey."

"How could I?" he asked.

Nobody knew the answer. Did he mean he was too fat? Or Stacey was too perfect a wife? The women were in clothes now. Stacey sat on the floor, on a large Navajo rug she had brought as part of her dowry. Its stripes, black, red, green, and clay-color, vibrated around her. She sat in the yoga position, her miniskirt hitched up her thighs and barely hiding the crotch of her underpants. Phyllis was erect on the pale sofa beside a slouching Ed; her long neck stretched as she sucked down the smoke on a deep inhale. Owen sat in the ample, cunningly made Danish teak armchair that was probably Ed's when there was no company. They were drinking watery bourbon-and-sodas, with a beer for Ed. Phyllis passed Stacey what was left of the joint. From the floor Stacey cried, "How'd this poor little thang git so *wet*? Who's been slobbering, honey?"

"Not me," Ed said. "I passed."

"Now I'll need to make another," his wife complained.

"Not for me," Phyllis said. "I feel funny."

After what seemed quite an interval, Ed said, "You need air. Let's go walk around."

"How funny?" Owen asked.

There seemed to Owen to be a curious double quality to time in the room: very slow when people spoke, yet speeded up in the silences, with many hurried pulse beats crowded into seconds.

Phyllis refined her statement: "I feel sick to my stomach," she said, and asked the air, "Who would have thought this country would wind up dropping napalm on a lot of Indochinese peasants and children?"

"That's no worse than what we did to the Indians," Stacey said.

"Is that all they are?" Owen asked Phyllis, as if at home they didn't have time to exchange views, which in a way was true. "Or are they also Viet Cong, who are burying village chiefs, head-down, and trying to force a grotesque style of misgovernment on the South Vietnamese?"

"Good question," Ed admitted.

"Poor Owen," said Stacey; her face seemed to swim in her hair as she sat on the floor at Owen's feet, beside the glass coffee table, through which he could see one of her deeply tanned knees. "He's such a patriot. He reminds me of the true-blue men in Texas."

Phyllis stood, with a tumult of cloth and audible breath that brought back to Owen how sizable she was, what a catch she had been. "I need air, I guess," she said, "and, Owen, we both need to go home and rescue the babysitter."

"Right," he agreed, but with no intention of moving. Life was too good here, with this hopeful new couple, in high bourgeois comfort. He wondered where the joint had gone and hoped it wasn't burning a hole anywhere. He put the glass of weak whiskey to his lips and sucked, the glass's rim making a cool brittle arc in his mind.

Ed had stood, laboriously, in delayed synchrony with Phyllis. There was a discussion among them as opaque and irrelevant to Owen as consultations among his parents overheard when he was three or four. He could have listened and understood, with the half of his mind that was clear and cold, but his attention was turned to the other half, which was experiencing an extraordinary happiness befalling him, permeating him like the fog of neutrinos that pour by the trillions out of the sun, even during, as now, nighttime. This was bliss: the slick texture of teak under his fingertips; the black and red and clay and cactus-green Navajo zigzags of thick wool under his eyes; the very grain of wood in the broad bleached floorboards, testifying to cycles of growth within a distant spruce forest; the clean white plane of the ceiling meeting the white-painted bricks of the Mervines' exposed chimney; the horsey scent of Stacey's damp hair, not far from where he was sitting; the soft, pecking sounds of adult conversation; the very feel of his awareness along the length of his body, as if consciousness were a silken robe tapping his skin wherever he chose to direct his attention; the enclosed air of this room, this parallelepiped clipped from the trillions of cubic feet of domestic space in America, snugly but freely full of human love, his for his wife and for his partner and now his partner's partner, whose deeply tanned knee no longer showed beneath the glass coffee table because she had moved closer to his Danish armchair. These details, animate and inanimate, arrived on his neuronal structure with that lost purity, that flat enumerative wonder, of childhood illness, when one is confined to bed and relieved of every duty but the one to exist, to survive, to continue to be. How could he have so long mislaid so basic a treasure, this dimension of bliss in things?

Parental voices mixed in the hall; the sounds of a door opening and closing were followed by those of a car starting and receding. "What's happening?" he asked Stacey, whose face had come closer to his own knees.

"Phyllis asked Ed to take her home. She felt like she might be sick."

"Couldn't she be sick here?"

Stacey's face looked broader than he had ever noticed, and more intelligent, with kindness molding every molecule of the curving, insouciant lips. They had known each other for going on two years and he had never noticed this encompassing, angelic quality of hers before. She said, "And she's worried about the babysitter."

"Who'll drive the babysitter home if Phyllis is so sick?"

"Ed will."

"What about me?" Owen asked. "Why am I left out of all this?"

"You weren't, you dear baby. She asked you to come home with her and you refused."

"Refused?"

"Well, you didn't say anything. You just sat there stoned, and I guess she felt too funny to stay and argue."

"I was thinking about how lovely everything is, here among the four of us. She has a negative side, Phyllis."

"I know she does, darling Owen. I know she does. I know all about you both. Ed talks about the two of you all the time. Phyllis wouldn't let you have Faye and you've given up inside. May I be frank?"

"You may be frank."

"It makes me *sad*"—"*sayud*"—"to see the way you've given up. Owen, you're jes' gone through the motions."

"Am I truly? How do I know? I mean, I don't feel I'm just going through the motions. It's like everybody asking if computers think. Well, do people? All you can say about people is that they think they think." He was fending; her assertions about him seemed self-serving, his cold half-brain saw, but overall there might be something in them.

"Oh yeass," Stacey said. "You pore, pore beautiful prisoner."

Her warm wide face had moved even closer, to between his thighs as he slouched dreamily in Ed's teak armchair. She leaned her face against the inside of his thigh so that when she smiled he felt the bulge of her cheek press lightly through the khaki cloth. "Prisoner?" he asked, trying to coördinate the word with these surfaces, the walls and furniture that he had felt to be such repositories of bliss not many seconds ago. The clear half of his brain felt like a splinter in the flesh of this bygone revelation. "When is Ed coming back?" he asked. People were in the wrong places and he had to straighten it out.

"Not quite yet, you sweet thang," Stacey said, still smiling, her perfect white California-Texas teeth biting down on the lower lip as if to taste her own smile. "I want to do something, Owen. Now, you'll just have to bear with me." With her middle finger and thumb pinched as if to untie a bow, she pulled the tab of his fly zipper down. "Don't you get nervous, I just want to *see* him, all by myself," she explained soothingly, with a touch of petulance.

The windows were black, Wilson Drive outside was clean of traffic, it was late on Sunday night. They were, in a sense, alone, but, then, Owen half-saw, the world, all those atoms and neutrinos and electrons, is always with us. Her clever hand had found the fly of his boxer shorts and the little limp sleeping thing was in the open and then in her warm soft mouth. He felt himself begin to harden, and said, *"No."*

"No?" she repeated in puzzlement; her mouth, backed up an inch or two, was still shaped, it seemed, by what had been in it, being wetly warmed. She was a different generation, Owen thought from a distance, and this was less of a deal for her. Cocksucking was just friendly. The smell of her damp horsey hair swelled in his nostrils. "Because of old Phyllis?" she asked.

"And Ed," he pleaded. "Think of Ed, we can't do this to him. To Phyllis either. She needs your friendship, Stacey; she really can't talk to these other women around here. The only time I see her relax is when she's over here with the three of us. She likes you a lot."

"Really?" His prick, not listening to him, had woken up and was getting harder. Stacey saw this and said, "Look at that dear friendly jimmy. Faye used to sing his praises to her girlfriends, they do tell me."

He found this hard to picture and stopped trying. "We don't want to make a mess of things," he insisted. "E-O Data and all that."

Rebuffed, sitting back on her bare heels, Stacey began to explain herself: "Owen, I just felt so fond of you, like you were going to waste—it must have been the pot."

He had talked himself out of a pretty good deal, he saw, sickeningly. He was wilting, listing to one side. "You could do a little more if you wanted," he suggested, "it's just that in the long run—"

"Oh, no, darling. You put him right back," she said, and floppily pushed herself to her feet, tugging down the miniskirt to ease out the wrinkles, rocking back and forth for balance on her long brown feet and staring angrily around at her own room, as if the walls had been witnesses to her rejection. Her mouth had shocked him with its warmth; now he felt a chill.

"Listen," he began, "that was terrific but—"

"Owen, you are one hundred percent right, I don't know what I was thinking of."

"You were feeling sorry for me," he reminded her.

"Or something like that. But, honey, you shouldn't tease a girl. We are going to be friends. And whenever I get a tingling in my pussy I am going to tell it, *You shut your big mouth*."

He laughed, working his disheartened penis back into his resistant pants, and zipped. "You're sounding more and more Texan," he told her.

"I try to keep it down, it embarrasses Ed. He's very insecure."

"I never noticed that about Ed."

"Oh yes. He doesn't like being fat but, I tell him, it won't go away by itself."

"Feed him salads," Owen suggested. The half of his head that was not icy and lucid was being squeezed to one side, above his right ear. "And lots of loving." Or did he just think that last phrase? Stacey registered no reaction, moving about the living room clearing glasses and ashtrays. Was he really such a homosexual, Owen asked himself, that he was trying to provide for Ed's sex life? When Stacey came off her high she would see she'd been spurned, and be pissed off. Already she was moving in and out of the room, back and forth into the kitchen, with an excessive, closing-up-shop energy. He could not stop thinking about her loose warm mouth, with regret and a sour sense of righteousness. She was Ed's, Phyllis was his; did things have to be that simple?

Stacey's housekeeping would have soon come down to how to get him out of here, but the other couple pushed at the front door and were back. "What happened?" Owen asked them, looking down to make sure his fly was zipped.

Phyllis followed the direction of his glance but was in her stately mood, above it all. "Ed drove me toward home but then, just being out, with the car windows down, I felt better and thought we should come back. Didn't you two miss us?"

"We did," Owen told her. "We felt abandoned. We had run out of conversation."

"Then let's go home, dear. Are you too stoned to drive? I still feel too detached."

Ed and Stacey were murmuring together, so that Owen felt cruelly excluded from the couple. He rose, hunching a bit in case anything still showed. He had uxoriously extricated himself from his partner's wife's mouth, but her aggression had reopened him to possibilities. Polymorphous life beckoned. The dark gods were in fashion. Everyone was sinning, including the government. He resolved in his heart to become a seducer. He would never treat his poor prick that cruel way again.

It was 1967. Walt Rostow averred, "Victory is just around the corner." Robert McNamara, not sure this was so, resigned the office of Secretary of Defense to become head of the World Bank. H. Rap Brown claimed of the black riots in Newark and Detroit that they were a dress rehearsal for revolution. Stalin's daughter, Svetlana Alliluyeva, defected to the West. Lunar Orbiter V was launched, to obtain a complete mapping of the moon's surface, including the dark side. Heavyweight champion Muhammad Ali announced, "I don't have no personal quarrel with those Viet Congs." In San Francisco, an estimated hundred thousand hippies claimed "Haight Is Love," and Golden Gate Park played host to a giant "Be-In."

x. *Village Sex—V*

IN HIS DREAM, Owen is back in Middle Falls, moving between his house on Partridgeberry Road and his central desk at E-O Data and the little retreat room, with a DEC PDP-8 and a CRT and a desk and telephone and an imitation-leather sofa, that he rigged at one end of the old arms factory on the Chunkaunkabaug. Between these stations of his life lay a network of village streets and vendors—the three restaurants, the two banks, the Woolworth's, the dry cleaner's, the shoe-repair shop, which was beginning to do a nice business in hippie-style leather sandals and clogs. The town, pre-CVS, had multiple drugstores, the oldest of them, Amory's Pharmacy, on the hill, still holding some back shelves of patent medicines with faded Victorian labels and displaying in its window the two traditional oversize vials of emblematic liquid, iodine-red and litmus-blue, that since medieval times have advertised pharmacological healing. On another, more personalized level of the net were the family dentist; the doctor, taciturn and unsympathetic with any but the most dramatic complaint; the pediatrician, for the children's many minor ills; the optician, a tall bald Jew who winced with back pain when he leaned over to administer his pupil-dilating drops twice-yearly; and, at an annual appointment, the tax accountant, a pointy-nosed mole of a man who waved his hands in agitation when Owen threatened to confide information he didn't want to hear. There were the schools— the public schools until Gregory turned thirteen—which involved periodic teacher conferences and recitals, playlets, choral performances, and team-sport events, usually in the rain. And there were committee meetings—the Chamber of Commerce and the School Building Needs Committee for Owen, the Garden Club and the Downtown Betterment Society for Phyllis, along with her madrigal group and yoga classes.

Somewhere in this thick net, he dreams, there is his rapidly burgeoning relationship with Julia, compact, firm, decisive, surprisingly sexy Julia, but he keeps losing her, it is just too hard to keep up the precarious secret connection— the hurried, hard-breathing phone calls, the panicky trysts where the edges of this town merge with the edges of another—and weeks go by, in his dream, without any connection being made, and his love object sinks deeper and deeper beneath the surface of the everyday, the respectable thick weave of citizenship and work and parenthood, and this relationship, forged in such a summer lightning of passion and mutual discovery, is cooling to nothing, like a holiday bond between children dissolved when vacation is over. Julia, uncontacted day after day, is withering smaller and smaller, and is falling through the network, to become forever lost beneath the barren busy-ness of "normal," licit life. Panic wakes him; Owen awakes bereft, bewildered as it slowly dawns upon him, along with the wallpaper and the merciless seaside sunlight already burning in the chink beneath the windowshade, that it is Phyllis who is lost, sunk beneath the surface of things, and that he and Julia, long and lawfully married, have been for over twenty years living together in Haskells Crossing, Massachusetts.

Among the checkpoints of Middle Falls had been the beach of imported sand at Heron Pond. Here in summers the young mothers of Owen's acquaintance, nearing the midpoint of their three score and ten but still lovely in his eyes, took their children for an hour's easy entertainment in the middle of the day, a quick lunch, and then home for a nap, sometimes reappearing in the shadowy afternoon, the slow time sloping toward the children's dinner after five. Gregory, at twelve, and Iris, at ten and a half, had outgrown the tepid brown water, the tetherball on its rickety pole in the center of a circle of dust, the jackknife-initialled picnic benches and tables, the oil drums painted green and labelled TRASH, the corroded aluminum water-slide close to shore, the lifeguard chair still occupied by the principal's straight-haired mahogany daughter, no longer a teen-ager. Her plumpness had become denser, even menacing, with a hint of mustache above the lips white with zinc oxide, and her thick legs conspicuously hairy—a statement presumably political. Among the young, hair had become an emblem; armpits flourished, boys' ears vanished. Gregory became a mophead, a miniature Beatle, protesting haircuts as if they were a form of assault, a vaccination that would hurt. Little Floyd, a second grader, and Eve were still docile visitors to the pond; when Owen would run over there at lunch in the red Corvette Stingray he had decided, as of 1968, that he owed himself, he would come upon them and their mother as if in fresh discovery. He liked seeing his wife in a bathing suit—a white bikini that set off her pale, pinkish tan. So close to nude yet still stately, she seemed the Phyllis he had hoped for, and the whole sleepy, scruffy beach by the pond recalled a lost paradise, with its brown-legged tomboys. The mothers spread blankets on the grass and picnicked with their children, Alissa Morrissey making her usual jokes about the caloric dangers of Marshmallow Fluff. She was short enough that any extra pound showed; but something anxious, nervous, and double-edged about her whittled away and kept her plumpness in check. Her husband, Ian, was getting to be difficult, it was said. Against the trend of the times for long ironed hair, she had hers, snuff-brown with induced highlights, cut short and brushed back as if she were speeding by on a motorcycle. She wore glasses rimmed in flesh-colored plastic, even when lazing at the pond; her eyes—dull blue, abraded like much-washed denim—shifted his way, Owen thought, more than his strict share. Men were a rare sight at Heron Pond. When Alissa smiled at something he said, her smile curved to enclose him; it was as if she read his mind and knew about the murky incident with Stacey, and the clear resolution that had followed. He was available.

One night of too much to drink at the Morrisseys' house, perhaps New Year's Eve, in that messy tail end after midnight, they had accidentally met in the upstairs hall—she was checking on a feverish child and he on his way to urinate, the only downstairs bathroom being attached to Ian's off-limits studio. Ian was quite humorlessly strict about his studio being off limits to company. Veering toward each other like planets out of orbit, Owen and Alissa kissed. She pushed up so hard their teeth touched; he was startled, as he had been years ago by Alice Stottlemeyer. But this was no longer spin-the-bottle. Unhinged by celebratory champagne, roused by her party outfit of see-through blouse and cerise harem pants, he slid his right hand down her side and tucked it a moment into her crotch. She jumped back as if scalded. "Oh no you don't," she said, in the tough voice of a dance-hall hostess, as played by Barbara Stanwyck or Ann Sheridan in a black-and-white movie at the long-lost Scheherazade. There were layers to Alissa; there were layers to all women, he was discovering; the trick was to find the layer where you were welcome.

The Morrisseys entertained a lot, a sure sign of marital distress: they needed others to help them bear each other's company. Ian Morrissey, a decade older than Alissa, was a magazine illustrator. As the world of middle-class magazines needing illustrations shrank, he had grown glum and sarcastic. The years had given him more gray hair than a man not much over forty should have, and trembling fingers stained by ink and nicotine, and a hollow-chested slump. He had acquired the idea that, while his own professional world, of dashingly glamorized women illustrating romantic short stories that always ended well, was yielding to sensational non-fiction and photographs airbrushed to within a few hairs of pornography, Owen and Ed were riding a technological wave steadily upward. He spoke of them derisively as "nerds." Owen tried to explain to him how volatile and chancy the rapidly changing computer world was, and how he and Ed were facing ever younger and more innovative competition, but it had settled into Ian's ego that he embodied a dying fine-arts tradition which was being crassly smothered under an onslaught of rock music, industrial robots, and psychopathic violence. He had grown a stubby goatee that made him look unshaven and sunk in the déshabille of failure.

"What you nerds don't get, utterly don't get," he told Owen one night, "is those hideous machines of yours aren't superhuman, they're *sub*human. Everything that made us human is going by the boards."

"It's just a device," Owen said, determined to be amiable, feeling Alissa's eyes insistently on him. "Like a hundred others — the steam engine, the automobile, the movie camera."

"Yes, and they've all changed our tempo — speeded it up to the point that we don't live at all."

"What is it we do, then, Ian?" Phyllis asked. It was just the two of them to an informal dinner, there in the Morrisseys' 1730 house in the older part of town. Unlike the Mackenzies, who at first had been their neighbors, the Morrisseys had remained loyal to the town center, near the Common. While Owen had been tinkering with the original Digit-Eyes, Ian had been up on his roof pointing the brick chimney; vigorous and optimistic, he had scraped and scorched the old lead housepaint from the clapboards, which then he had stained. Staining was supposedly the more authentic treatment, but it looked dark and ugly, temporary and cheap, to go with the low ceilings, the cracked plaster walls, and the shopworn folk-art oddments — duck decoys, jointed wooden dolls, a tin weathervane of a top-hatted man and bonneted woman — picked up at Connecticut roadside shops back when the couple, having left Manhattan, was freshly, acquisitively countrified. The whole house, even Ian's neatly kept, fluorescent-lit studio, felt dusty; heart had gone out of their house, which made their invitations harder to refuse. The Mackenzie children did not like to come here to play, though the two Morrissey children were close in age to Gregory and Iris.

Phyllis's careless soft voice drew attention to her. A third glass of wine, or a touch of intellectual stimulation, put an unaccustomed flush on her cheeks. Her distant beauty—that pallid head held high above the throngs in life's mazy corridors—diminished the nervous, rounded attractions of Alissa, though Owen felt them curved around her discontent like the feathers of a plump bird nesting. Other people's unhappiness, it occurred to him, had been his element since childhood; sensing it focused and invigorated him.

"We react," Ian answered quickly. "We react to the damn machines, and go dead when they're shut off." The two couples had grown expert at these evenings together—the children upstairs with the mumble of television, the venerable neighborhood quieting down beyond the windows, which leapt into light when a passing car swung through the curve of Common Lane. Phyllis didn't mind Ian; like her father, he had spent his life hunched over a two-dimensional task, and his darkly prophetic mood reminded her, perhaps, of dire adult palaver in Cambridge faculty circles. Sensing this, Ian played to her. "Are you aware," he said, widening his appeal to include Owen and Alissa, "that as recently as our grandparents' generation it was a common ability of people of any means to play a musical instrument, to carry a harmony part in group singing, and to be able to draw—to sketch out of doors and do at least watercolors? All those Victorian travellers could draw, and all the writers, not just Thackeray. Now not even the professional artists can draw. They slap up these huge abstractions that are an insult, a joke. The common man has a Brownie camera. Not even Brownies—that dates me. Brownies would take too much skill, they aren't automatic enough."

In agitation at hearing so much of her husband's voice,

Alissa crossed and recrossed her legs on the old velvet sofa, which had been recovered with sailcloth and decorated with several tattered crocheted shawls. "I remember my father," she volunteered, her washed-out eyes moving from face to face uncertainly, "pacing off the distance with his old Kodak. That was how he photographed me and my brothers. The pictures came out surprisingly sharp. The little triangular viewfinder had broken off, too. He did it by guess. The snapshots fascinated me—there weren't too many of them, the way there are now. He kept them in old candy boxes; when you took off the lids there was still the faint smell of chocolate."

"See," Ian said, "your old man, limited as he was, had mastered his tools. Nobody can use tools any more. They have to have everything done for them, by so-called experts, at twenty-five bucks an hour. And even so it's all done *badly*. One of the few good things about this so-called revolution under way is that middle-class children are taking up the trades, carpentry and so on, in rebellion against their ham-handed white-collar parents."

This tired tirade, Owen was aware, related to Ian's own increasing difficulty getting commissions for his flashy illustrations, full of induced verve and unfinished margins; many framed samples, once reproduced in the *Post* and *Collier's* and *Redbook*, surrounded them on the cracked plaster walls. Owen was enough of an art-lover to take Ian's art lightly, but did not want to reveal, in defending his own field of endeavor, this disregard. "A computer is a tool," he said. "Its moving parts are electronic impulses, but the same identical actions could be worked out mechanically—in fact, that's what Babbage and Pascal before him did do, but the machines got too complex to be machined. Ian, why do you need to imagine some whole new demonic order? Do you feel the same about the pop-up toaster, as opposed to frying bread in a skillet?"

"O., dear, let Ian talk," Phyllis said. "I want to hear more about how we're all becoming subhuman."

"Speaking of more, does anybody want another drink?" Alissa asked. She sounded hopeful of the offer being declined.

Ian sardonically promised, "One more Scotch-on-the-rocks, my dear, will greatly clarify my insight into the pitch-dark future."

"A *very* weak bourbon-and-water, Alissa," Phyllis conceded. "Can I help?"

"Just water for me," said Owen, to reprimand Phyllis and to please Alissa, who was worried about her husband's deterioration. Her glance at Owen suggested that it was they, sober, against the others. Her plump bare legs, as she uncurled and pushed herself up from the sailcloth-covered sofa, excited him to thinking graphically; her convex thighs curved steeply inward where they met and transformed, without violating her fundamental homeomorphism, into a concavity delimiting another sort of space, beyond the sensitive V that he had, in one electric trespass, touched. It was late; cigarette smoke had pasted itself in eddying strips against the low ceiling, subdivided by boxed beams painted that custardy Williamsburg color.

"Capitalism," Ian asserted, "asks only one thing of us: that we consume. The stupider we are, the better consumers we are, not just of that sliced pap called bread and of dishwasher detergents that kill fish in the river, but of canned entertainment. The less friction it makes going in our ears and eyes, the more we can take in and pay for. There is no more art in the old sense of something *made*, by hand, by an artist responsible only to his eye and his sense of beauty. Huddled over his drawing pad trying to get the exact shading for the, let's say, the stones of Venice or a patch of wildflowers, he was processing the external into something human; he was *understanding* it, and we could understand it with him, empathizing with his process of discovery, step by step. Music lays this right out in the dimension of time: we travel with the composer as he solves the problems, the key-changes, the resolution. You don't need to understand anything to watch television; they want you so stupid you keep staring at the commercials."

Phyllis said, "I wonder if that's why the young are so rebellious, because we've become so stupid. If that's why they want to go back to Nature and blow up banks. They're trying to break the shell of everybody's stupidity."

"Thanks, Alissa," Owen said, as their hostess placed a pleasantly tall, heavy-bottomed glass of ice water, its exterior slick with the riveted sweat of the heat differential. Was it an accident that Alissa, bending over to place a coaster beneath his glass, showed him, in the catenary curve of the loose neck of her peasant blouse, her breasts? Their tops were brown but there was white skin, too, deeper in shadow, and a dark cavity between them where he could thrust a finger, or a tongue, or even socket his erect penis. At Heron Pond, Phyllis and Alissa both in two-piece bathing suits, Phyllis's made an effect on her upright body of two bands of white, whereas Alissa's two bikini pieces were all adhesive arcs, little tucked triangles secured with bows of tinted string.

Ian didn't bother to respond to Phyllis, which offended Owen. Sitting in his tattered plaid wing chair, stained on its arms and where his head—greasily long-haired in artistic fashion—habitually leaned back, Ian clutched his fresh drink with his yellow fingers and spoke to Owen without deigning to turn his head; the two women on the sofa might as well not have been there. His goateed profile, stony-pale, snarled as if in a trance. "You nerds. You're squeezing the juice out of life. To you we're all just statistical constructs to be manipulated. I don't blame Ed, he can't help it, poor slob, being a nerd; if he wasn't a nerd he wouldn't be anything, a short-order cook at an all-night diner perhaps. But you, O. old boy, you know *better*. You have a soul, or had one once. Let me put it this way—you know something's missing, and still you've signed up, a good soldier for Moloch. Whatever you call it. Industry. The defense establishment. Defense, death, pollution, and mass-produced crap for the crappy masses."

"Actually," Owen said, enjoying the other man's meltdown into hostility, calculating that he had less and less reason to avoid fucking his wife, "a lot of our present work involves putting insurance records on tapes or, the newer thing, disks, and devising systems for hospitals, cutting down on paperwork. Or are hospitals and insurance companies part of Moloch's armies? Ian, what's missing began to go missing a long time ago, with Copernicus and Martin Luther, and you can't blame technology for not bringing it back. Technology works with what, as Wittgenstein said, is the case. Some would say, incidentally, that the women's magazines you do your illustrations for are good soldiers for Moloch, selling cosmetics and tampons and dishwashers and sexy underwear and whatever else women can be persuaded they want. It's the Devil's bargain, Ian—medicine and electricity and rocket science in exchange for an empty Heaven. We've all signed on to the bargain, and a bunch of kids going up into Vermont and doing without flush toilets isn't going to cancel the deal." He wondered why he had become so heated; he didn't want to believe this. He wanted to have technology and illusions, too: both were the ameliorative fruits of human imagination.

Phyllis loyally said, "Owen isn't anti-art, he's always going to museums. DigitEyes was all about that, sublimated."

Owen flinched at the "was." She was right: the program was becoming obsolete, and he was stuck in updating it, groping for the next thing. Tonight's conversation, dragged out toward midnight by Ian's pompous venting and Phyllis's winsome egging him on, no longer interested him; he had satisfied himself that neither he nor Alissa owed Ian a thing. She, curled up on the sofa as if to melt into its cushions, was fighting sleep behind her flesh-colored glasses. Her lids looked pink and chafed, her thin smile patiently vengeful. In the car going home, Phyllis said, apropos of nothing, "She loathes him."

Was she reading his mind, as it moved like a tracer point over Alissa's remembered curves? He was startled, but believed that his wife was always right—a vault of wisdom he was in danger of totally forgetting the combination to, as he struck out on his own. "Really?" he said. "It's just the same old Ian, rambling on. Why would she loathe him?"

"The same reason he loathes himself. Impotence."

"Really?" The dark space his headlights probed seemed to deepen. It thrilled him to have her mention such things as potency and disaffection, coarse matters she usually disdained to touch.

"Well, figuratively, for sure. He's beating a dead horse and knows it. Nothing is the same, suddenly. The middle-class magazines he fed off of are gone or dying. People watch television, and if they read it's the tabloid at the supermarket checkout. Even *The New Yorker* has changed. It's become strident, about Vietnam."

"Everybody's becoming strident," he said, adding, in his sudden fitful fondness, "except you."

"I'm strident inside," Phyllis said, in a level, resigned tone, as their house, behind its semi-concealing curved driveway off Partridgeberry Road, took their headlights full on its white clapboards, behind which their four children slept.

Alissa, too, was a frustrated artist—at least, she made love to Owen as if each time had to be a masterpiece. In his little locked room at the factory, or the motel or hotel room they once in a while managed to find the time for, or her own bedroom with its sagging low pre-1750 ceiling on the few occasions when Ian was safely away in the city peddling his wares and the children were safely in school, she gave herself to fucking as if to save her soul. And sucking—his prick in her mouth, she would go into a trance, repetitively nodding like one of those drinking birds you fitted to the edge of a water glass. She was oral: sitting impaled on his lap while his tongue played with her nipples, she would put two fingers into her mouth and, eyes shut, begin an inner ascent. Coming was not easy for Alissa; she was an artist in that conditions had to be just right and her concentration undiluted, his parts—tongue, prick, fingers—distributed just as she wanted them. Owen felt like a translator who had to be present so that Alissa could communicate with herself. But, unlike smiling, light-loined Faye, she came unambiguously, with an increasingly rapid succession of high-pitched gasps capped, at a summit both lovers had almost despaired of reaching, by a sharply lower-pitched whimper, as if she had been struck, while the hand of hers not half in her mouth beat on Owen's back like a panicked wing. He was proud that, after a few early misfires bred of guilt and fear, he could go the route with her, holding up his side of it. Her body as he grew to know it had a curious way of emanating heat where she wanted to be touched, so that his hands and mouth went there of their own. He had slowly, timidly realized that, while sitting on his prick having her nipples teased, she wanted his finger in her anus, deep in it at her climax. He became an enabler, an abettor, joined with Alissa in sweet trespasses, crossing a line drawn by their Protestant ancestors, who never wholly shed their Bible-black clothes and made their love in lightless log cabins.

He discovered in himself the capacity to be cool in sex, cold even, watching their sweating bodies from a distance, freezing his own orgasmic curve with deliberately unsexual pictures—a calm Caribbean harbor at sunset, or a smartly executed double play. When Alissa reached her inner divide, and the summit within her was irreversibly attained, he could give her what he had been effortfully holding back; he could steady her ass with two hands and sock it to her upwards without thought of delicacy or mercy. Her whimper, coming from the territory beyond her own climax, renewed itself in the higher register; he wondered, amid his own sullen blood-thump of release, if she might faint. Then her hand on his shoulder blade slowly ceased fluttering and she covered his face with weak kisses.

Her gratitude for his learning to make love to her, in the deep but narrow furrow of stimuli that her nerves accepted, included a license for him to ask of her what he would— but, again, within limits. Rapt fellatrice though she was, Alissa did not want him to come in her mouth, "like men do with prostitutes," and if an impulsive flutter of her tongue brought him too far she took his ejaculation on her chin or chest, where his gob gleamed embarrassingly. But fucking her a second time on days with a few extra minutes to the tryst, as she knelt on the bed or floor, was allowed: an image that lingered long after she was no longer available to him was the gleam of her coccyx, a bit of hard tailbone catching the light just above the creamy spread of her buttocks. From his vantage, at the other end of the spine cleaving her back into two plump and golden halves, her cervical vertebrae peeped touchingly from beneath fluffy tufts of her snuff-brown hair, cut short in her style. *This is the neck*, Owen thought, *the executioner sees.* On the day of this thought the light fell from the single high factory window, sifted through grime and reinforcing wire. His cell at E-O, with its oily scent of former industry and its walled-off hum of many-bodied intellectual activity, excited them both to a breathless, whispering shamelessness, a fascination with their bodies as thorough, perhaps, as that which hospital patients receive and bestow in the days before death.

But he, too, had a squeamish side, a limit. He couldn't suppress his surprise and disgust when, in a stolen half-hour in a parked car, his exploring finger came out from under her skirt bloody, the thin redness of such blood like a medicinal coating and abhorrent to him. He resented her failing to warn him that she was having her period—it seemed a betrayal of decorum even worse than his semen puddled above her breast like an explosion of snot.

He failed, Owen saw in retrospect, to use her compliance, her spells of tranced utter slavery, to the hilt. Though both confessed to being nervous, needy masturbators, they never masturbated for each other, though it would have been easy, it seemed to him in the darkness behind his eyelids, as he lay beside Phyllis missing Alissa. But in actuality their genitals, when the opportunity was there and the love-flush was hot upon their skins, seemed made to be hidden, as it were, one by the other, their warmth and wetness merged.

Though innocent herself, a few years over thirty and never having cuckolded Ian before, Alissa tried to ease Owen away from the certain strangeness he felt in inhabiting a body at all. Once, in a flash of shyness soon after becoming her lover, kneeling between her spread legs, he put his hands over his flaming erection, and she said, slightly offended and gently directive, "Don't hide yourself, Owen." "Yourself"—this sore-looking blue-veined thing was himself. These hair-adorned nether parts, closely fitted into the sites of urination and defecation, were seats of being, ugly and odorous in external contemplation but in sensation exquisite. This high value was altogether inward and had to be taken by others on faith. The daze of sexual excitement bestowed this faith but then left Owen uncertain as to why—the question he had asked himself behind the playground shed—women put up with it. So much risk, so much potential for disgrace and abasement. Abasement was part of the bliss, perhaps: being lowered like a bucket into the black well of biology while knowing that the rope was still attached, the daylight of society waiting above.

He could have talked her, he imagined when it was too late, into swallowing his semen. He could have coaxed her, too, into letting him kiss her between the legs until she came. Elsie had allowed this, that last summer, when both were angry because their love was coming to nothing. So he gave her a treat for a virgin. Hitched forward on the car seat with her skirt around her waist, she came with a snap, an unmistakable inner percussion. His back and shoulders ached from bowing his face into her lap, there on the bench seat of her father's Chrysler. He liked it, being in touch with her another way from watching her face and hearing her voice. Alissa said she had never come that way and never would. He should have insisted. She would have remembered him for it. But sexual events easy to stage in the privacy of his skull encountered obstacles in reality, limits in the psychology of the other.

A sexual transaction was a psychological transaction—one must feel the other, however ideally submissive, *has* a psychology, a mind registering events somewhat in parallel. Otherwise we are stuck with the sordid pathos of the inflatable female bodies, with usable mouths and vaginas, advertised in the back pages of *Hustler.* There must be a who, not a thing—another consciousness. With otherness a political dimension enters the psychological. He could relax into Alissa's blowing him because she had breasts; his joy in a sensation another male could equally well have administered was sanctioned by her vagina, that rosy badge of her authority to service the male. And she, she needed to arrange him strictly, tongue and prick and hands, like a child arranging pillows and stuffed animals around her before she could go to sleep. Her dull blue eyes when she was making love, and a minute after, became as bright and dark as wet ink. Then they faded back, as she allowed him to untangle their arrangement so he perched by her knees and she reposed, like Manet's *Olympia*, semi-reclined the length of the three cushions of his Naugahyde sofa in his E-O aerie. Her breasts, minutes ago tipped with erectile sensitivity, sank against her chest. He lit a cigarette, a Parliament, for her, and they searched their heads for things to talk about.

That was the problem: what do you do with the bodies afterwards? A man and a woman like-minded enough, with physiologies and sexual educations roughly matched, agree to meet and use each other for an hour; then what? After the melodramatic disaster of his breakup with Faye, Owen was determined not to fall in love next time, for everybody's sake. Alissa seemed to accept this emotional prophylaxis, as fitting her own situation. She was loyal to Ian if not faithful, and he to Phyllis. Yet it was a strain; Alissa was so lovable, so much wantonly his in their cozy crimes, his body cried out to possess her forever.

He even felt cozy enough to ask her his question: "Why do women fuck?"

She laughed, her cigarette smoke coughed away before the inhale. "Why do men?"

"It's obvious. Women are so beautiful."

"And not men?"

"Not. As far as I can see."

"How unflattering to me, Owen. I thought I had loved that idea out of you. You're gorgeous."

"Oh, *you*, sure; you make me feel good about myself. But you could do that by flirting at a cocktail party."

"Well," she said, "screw you."

"You know what I mean," he insisted. "You get this thing poked into you and have the risk of making a baby or if you're a hooker or the girlfriend of somebody primitive of getting killed. Every day in the paper you read about some poor girl killed because she fucked some simple-minded guy who couldn't let go."

The word "fuck" and its cousins bore in this era a pleasurable charge of decided intimacy. Also in this era, incredibly, sex was thought of as safe. At worst its consequences were easily reversed, by a shot of antibiotics or a trip to some more enlightened land where abortion was legal. Women were on the Pill or contained an IUD; crabs were something that happened to hippies, as part of their good-humored, anti-bourgeois life-style, and herpes was not yet a proclaimed problem. Itches were passed from vagina to penis to vagina and nobody in polite society mentioned it except to the doctor, who provided an ineffective salve. Sex was then thought to be innocent even if its practitioners weren't. Owen and Alissa were explorers in a terrain, adultery, not totally strange but far from deeply familiar to them. They had been driven into this wilderness by annoying or neglectful traits of their spouses, and the film of guilt that attached to them was, like the secretions of lovemaking, something to be wiped off before they went back out into the street. Like those secretions, it was part of it, part of its defiant health.

"Making a baby mightn't be so bad. But don't kill me, Owen."

"I know how it happens. I get crazy with jealousy sometimes, lying in bed at night picturing you and Ian in bed together probably screwing."

"Do you and Phyllis always not?"

"Not quite always, no."

"Well, then. We're married and this is extra and let's not think too closely about it. You ask why do people do the things they do. People don't know, it's deeper than the brain. It's pheromones and all sorts of programmed behavior, like the nest-building instinct. Haven't you ever watched birds building a nest and wondered how they do it, just the right twigs and so on? They don't know either."

"Welcome to my nest," he said, of the bleak tall brick room around them, feeling uneasy. Ed might be needing him—some little crisis or other, some scramble nobody else could sort out.

"Women need attention," she explained. "They don't

have a lot of a man's ways of getting it. So they do what they can, with what they've got."

"You fuck just to get attention?"

"When you put it like that it sounds silly, but, yes, sort of. For this time with me you *are* paying attention, though I can feel you beginning to wonder how you're going to ease me out of here and get back to work."

"Not at all. I'm crazy about you." A substitute for that poisoned chalice of a phrase *I love you*. He didn't say it to Elsie and now not to Alissa. Faye had believed it and so had he and they had done damage. "Give me twenty minutes and you'll see how much." He pictured her on her knees on the hard floor, or back on the sofa: the curly downy bits at the nape of her neck, the glossy knobs of her spine.

"I appreciate the thought, kind sir," she said, and jack-knifed her flashing legs together around him, so she sat up and her bare feet rested on the floor. "But I must go shopping for Ian's dinner and pick up the cleaning before school gets out." Alissa and Ian had two children—Norman, who was ten, and Neysa, whose entry into the first grade had freed her up yet left her, she had told Owen, at enough loose ends to begin her affair with him. Her lips had trembled, after laughing at this comic connection. Though this was November her body still bore the gold-and-silver disparities of her summer tan. Having made the effort to rise, she slumped back on the squeaky imitation-leather cushion. "I don't think it's good, by the way," she volunteered, "for a woman's health, to screw like mad and then jump up and do errands. We're supposed to harbor the seed, or something."

He would treasure such casual glimpses into what it was like to be a woman, which Phyllis rarely afforded him; she knew she was female but didn't deign to dwell on it, whereas Alissa was something of a village philosopher on the subject. "A woman would rather be hit on the head than ignored," she once told him. He couldn't imagine ever hitting her on the head, but the idea of it fed the brutish tenderness with which he contemplated her back as he pumped away at her on his smarting knees. After their little contretemps with her menstrual blood, she confessed, "When I was just, you know, coming into womanhood as a teen-ager I imagined that would be the time when I would be most attractive to men, when there was the blood."

It was such an intimate illusion for her that she trailed away shyly, and he hardly dared pursue the subject. "What did you think," he asked, "men would do with it?"

His mistress blushed. "Oh, I don't *know*, Owen, don't keep after me; it was just a *feel*ing. It's like giving milk, it feels very feminine. It's exciting."

"Even with the cramps?"

"The cramps aren't so great," Alissa admitted, "but they establish a woman's relation with pain. You have it, and you hide it. Everything, come to think of it, that makes you *you* is hidden. Including," she went on, melancholy overtaking her nudity and with it a need to lighten the mood, "your savage lover," and jabbed him, not just in play but with enough animus to shorten his breath and give him pain, there in that defenseless pocket just under the sternum. Seeing the shock on his face, she looked away and sighed. "There are so many claims on me, or on any woman, Owen, that it's a relief to know that when I'm coming to you it's for one purpose. There's not that awful vagueness there is in marriage—will we or won't we, and if so shouldn't we be getting to bed before we get any sleepier? At least with you I know we will, you've been counting on it, dreaming about it; I feel focused. Sometimes down on River Street, before or after seeing you here, I can't get the smile off my face, and it frightens me that everybody out there in the sunshine will guess, that I've been fucked or soon will be."

"Do you feel that way after Ian?"

"Don't fish for compliments, darling. It's unbecoming. I've already told you, we're sleepy. Sometimes one of us falls asleep before we finish, we're so bored."

"Ian *can* be boring, lately," Owen pointed out, with tentative cruelty.

"He's boring," his wife explained, "because he's trying to explain away in general terms what he really feels is a personal failure, a loss of creativity."

"I know the feeling," Owen said, in a tone that said they were done for the day.

For a year and a half more they carried on furtively, hardly believing their good fortune. Ian and Phyllis didn't appear to know, and although the village knew—not just their set of friends but pedestrians who saw her smiling on River Street and the lady at the desk at the motel on the highway toward Willimantic—it isn't a village's way to tell. A village is woven of secrets, of truths better left unstated, of houses with less window than opaque wall. She and Owen might have gone on longer, meeting never more than once a week and in summers less than that, until the pressure of deceit deformed one of them beyond what the other could love; but Alissa became pregnant. Her wistful talk of naïvely expecting her menstrual flow to be admired had actualized into a panicky wait for the flow to recommence. Many hurried phone calls confirmed that it had not.

"But whose is it?" That was the question, once her period was three weeks late and she was waking up nauseated.

"Who did you make love to at the right time?" He was shouting over the pay phone beside a highway, straining to hear, his finger poked into one ear and clouds of last winter's salt and sand, pulverized by rushing tires to a fine dust, billowing into his face. He said "make love" instead of their usual frank verb as if a telephone operator, that obsolete eavesdropper on village life, were listening.

"Neither of you," came the faint answer.

"Oh my God. You've been seeing somebody else?"

"No, no, you silly. I mean it could be *either* of you, but I don't see how. The Pill was making me feel bloated, so I went back to the rhythm method, but Ian and I used it successfully for years before he let me have Norman. He said he was an artist and children were hostages to fortune."

"It must be me," Owen said gamely, "the great way we fucked."

"Darling, it doesn't take great to make a baby. If it did the population crisis would be no problem."

"I'd rather believe, of course, it was Ian. I thought you said he was impotent." This was a slip: he remembered that it was Phyllis who had said it.

"Did I say that? I may have said he was *discouraged*. But he's only forty-three, he's not *ancient*."

"Don't tell me about it," Owen begged. It was repulsive. Her blood, Ian's semen, his own. His insides were feeling watery; he was on the edge of the doom that waits, bottomless, where the skin of the humdrum tears. "What are you going to do about it?"

"What do you want me to do?" He had to repeat the question; an eighteen-wheeler had been roaring past.

"Can you get an abortion?" he shouted, there by the dirty highway.

"I don't see how," came the faint answer. "How would

I explain it to Ian? He knows about my period already. Where would I go without telling him?" Her faintness was increasing; she was getting smaller, sinking down into the transparent depths, away from him, forever away. "Owen, I'm going to have the baby," she called. "We must never see each other again."

Perhaps these revelations and determinations did not come all at once, in one noisy, dusty conversation over a roadside pay phone, but in repetitious, relentless snippets; her abrupt withdrawal from his life did him so little credit that he repressed the details. By late summer Alissa was visibly pregnant. Why hide it?—that was clothing designers' new thought on this perennial fashion issue. Her snug and unconcealing jerseys and loose-waisted miniskirts and even, at Heron Pond, adjustable bikini curved around a new center. Her plumpness was freshened. With dimpled smiles she received the pleased notice of their friends. Pregnancies among them were thinning out. Owen was horrified by the paternal ambiguity of this growing fetus, yet the tiny complicating creature, whom he would have gladly killed if he could, was ever more securely wrapped in Alissa's body, and in social acknowledgment of its being. A village is a hatchery, cherishing its smallest members. A fresh birth votes for the status quo, validating the present and assuring the future.

The last summer of the 'sixties brought more news than comfort: Nixon and Kissinger trying to bomb their way to an acceptable surrender in Vietnam, Ted Kennedy drowning a starry-eyed young campaign worker at Chappaquiddick, the first man on the moon looking like a Puppetoon. Judy Garland dead, Bishop Pike gone missing, a pregnant Sharon Tate stabbed to death in Los Angeles, everywhere in the United States defiance and hatred of the government. But in Owen's vicinity the news was Alissa Morrissey's pregnancy, and his hidden tie to the event tugged him close to the dreadful, ruinous realm behind the headlines, where people made their bets and met the consequences. It affronted his innermost innocence that his body in experimenting with freedom could have thrown off, once again, a consequence as irrevocable as this, this living being whose cells daily multiplied along the majestic, ramifying routes laid down by DNA. Poor Ian preened, his pompous little goatee waggling as he parried the party jests, for though not ancient he was older than the others, and Alissa's pregnancy, like the Biblical Sarah's, had not been looked for. Owen felt a searing guilt toward Ian, whom he had never liked but who seemed in this biological event totally a victim, blindsided, smugly oblivious. Why so much tender remorse toward Ian, and so little toward the child that he feared to be his own, and even less toward Alissa? Swiftly she had sized up the situation and decided to jettison her lover to keep her baby safe. He thought back to his first triangle, his father and mother and himself. His mother had given him love and guidance and a sense of his life's being a charmed one, but when his parents quarrelled his sympathy went always to his father, his wan, worried, literal-minded, beaten-down father. Men understand men, mechanisms with very few levers—a few earthy appetites, an atavistic warrior pride and stoicism. Women are shining moon-creatures, who hurt us when they withhold themselves, and again when they don't.

xi. *Developments in Hardware*

SEDUCED AND SEDUCING, Owen now bore upon him the scent of love. He had established himself, at the level of pheromones, as a man with a taste for what women can give. Discreetly, by way of murmurs and hand-squeezes, teasing and flattery, they flocked around him. Time was pressing on their generation, though they still considered themselves in their primes, with an infinity of options still open. He slowly got used to the sight of his former mistress, once so privately wanton, publicly pregnant; she complained so all could hear of the pains the child was bringing her, her legs, her back—her beautiful bare back. In the last months she had to spend hours in bed to keep from losing this intricate invader of her body. When the child was born, only three weeks premature, it was a girl, who everybody said looked just like Ian. The little preemie, not quite six pounds, had Ian's sharp shrivelled features and his artist's squint, peering up from the vanilla-colored carrycot where she lay as if into too bright a light. Owen had been sure it was going to be a boy; a weight of seriousness felt lifted from his shoulders.

"A chip off the old block," Ed said in his ear. Ed was leaning on Owen from behind, there among the guests crowding around on the Slades' sunporch to view the infant, now three months old, with her red face and scanty fine hair. It was Easter of the new decade; an unfiltered sun cut through the bare trees onto the wicker porch furniture and off the noontime cocktail glasses and into tiny Nina's squinting eyes. The Morrisseys' willingness to toy alliteratively with their children's names struck Owen as crass and cast a baleful backward light upon the joys of his affair. Alissa still carried her baby weight. Her breasts, which had been just the right size for him—round handfuls—strained with their new burden against the silk underblouse and purple jacket of her Easter outfit. People had dressed up, even though few of them went to church, even on Easter. The Slades, the squarest couple in this set, did go and had fallen into the habit of giving this brunch party; it had come to be expected of them, as part of the set's annual festive cycle. This year, the baby came, as if to replenish the children who were growing too old to engage in the Easter-egg hunt that the Slades dutifully staged. Owen could see nothing of himself in the infant with her florid little face and wide-open steel-blue eyes. There was an annoying heaviness of meaning in the touch of Ed's hand on his back; Owen turned to relieve himself of it, facing his partner.

"Hard to see the goatee," he said.

Ed barely smiled. He too, away from Stacey's salads and sprouts, had put on weight. Stacey had left him and gone back to California. A bachelor again, traipsing from house to house as a dinner guest, Ed presented it as a simple matter of her being too young, and a member of another culture. California wasn't another state, it was another country. Connecticut had never seemed real to her—too green, too quaint, everything too close together—and, with the hours he had to keep at the plant, she was lonely. Thus he reframed what must have felt to him as a shameful failure—a lack of juice, of enough entertainment value to a young woman. If only they had produced a baby, he speculated to Owen, it might have been different. He had wanted one, she hadn't. Owen often thought back to the night they had smoked pot and Stacey had stayed on the floor. He wondered if her offer of a blow job had been unique to him or been repeated more successfully with others around Middle Falls. He was sorry she was gone, because he would accept the offer now. He understood it better now: it had been no big deal. She had had an expansive Western nature and Ed was an emotionally cramped nerd from the Bronx, where a gangster tact and taciturnity ruled the streets. To know more than you say was part of Ed's code, here in Middle Falls, where the game was gossip; he somehow knew about Owen and Alissa and the baby, but would keep the secret.

Phyllis, three glasses of white wine to the good, wanted to hold the baby. She had dressed, showing her contempt for this most Christian of holidays, in tight blue jeans, small pearl earrings, and a man's striped shirt folded back at the cuffs as if to expose the thousand-dollar Swiss watch Owen had given her for their fifteenth wedding anniversary. "It's been so *long*," she explained, bending her tall, slim-hipped body down through the shards of porch sunlight and in her hands quickly gathering up the little blanketed body from the carrycot. Alissa couldn't conceal her alarm—her glasses flashed—and she rose in her chair and almost reached out, but Phyllis gently beamed down upon the mother a gracious smile of reassurance. "I haven't forgotten about the head," she said, and showed how she was supporting it with her left hand. "How hot their little skulls are!" she said, and gazed into the infant's face as if searching out a meaning there, a riddle, in the unfocused wide stare. "Oh, Alissa," Phyllis went on in that soft yet somehow commanding voice that Owen had once strained to overhear, "she's exquisite. Owen," she went on, finding his face in the clustered, hushed group, "we *must* have one more, before it's too late."

"We'll talk about it," he said, bewildered when this stopgap of a reply sprang laughter among their friends.

Phyllis with her eerie dreaming appropriation of the child had created a tension. Only the infant did not feel it. Her blue eyes, darker than her mother's abraded color, had closed. "Dear little Nina," Phyllis told her. "You're perfect. You'll do wonderfully well." She kissed the bulging red forehead, which rumpled with an eddy of a frown, and looked to the women nearest her. "Who wants to be next?" Phyllis asked benignly, and several pairs of hands quickly reached out to treasure little Nina in turn.

In the red Stingray going home, Owen dared tell her, "I'm not sure Alissa was quite ready for you to grab her baby like that."

"She loved it," Phyllis said. "All women want to have their babies admired. Alissa would have been hurt if we hadn't begged her to hold it. Her."

"I missed the begging part. Uh—I assume you were joking about another child. Eve is going to be seven, and she's been the baby all her life. You don't want to go back to diapers and being up at night and all that, do you?"

"Only if it will bring us closer together."

"How could we be closer? My God, we're practically welded together."

She didn't speak for a moment, then said, "Of course I

was joking, Owen. You must be crazy, to think I'd have another baby with you."

This was more absolute than he wanted—on the opposite end of the curve from her betranced party deportment. The real Phyllis was becoming harder and harder for him to locate. He offered, less able than she to tolerate silence in the car, "I thought with Eve off most of the day you could go back somewhere, maybe to Trinity or even Yale, for a course or two. Some kind of refresher, to get you back into your Ph.D. thesis."

"Or I could go back to the ballet lessons I dropped when I was eleven," she said, so serenely he didn't realize for some seconds that she was being ironical.

In Haskells Crossing, in the twenty-first century, Easter shows the rich to good advantage. They attend church then, and at Christmas, if never else, as if keeping up the supernatural contract by which they have prospered. The Episcopal is the church of choice, three and a half centuries after the Puritans established their iron theocratic rule. They were fanatics; the United States is a conservative country built upon radicalism. The white wooden Congregational church in many a New England town has grown seedy—the paint peeling, the steeple nearly toppling with dry rot, the bulletin board outside advertising sermons with jocular sermon titles like I'M O.K., GOD'S O.K., or FORBIDDEN FRUITS CREATE MANY JAMS—compared with the sharply gabled, half-timbered structures devoted to Cranmer's graceful words and Henry the Eighth's regal whim.

Owen, though himself rich enough, thanks to the split-up and sale of E-O Data in the 'seventies, viewed the rich, the hereditary rich, as an exotic tribe. He believed that the mill-owning wealth of Alton had oppressed his father and had defrauded his grandfather. Certain local textile fortunes had had, in Willow, the mythic resonance of the Mellons, Fricks, and Carnegies in Pittsburgh. But, though he strained to see over the spiky sandstone wall of the Pomeroy estate near Cedar Top, and overheard the distant splashing of a swimming pool, he had never encountered any of these fabulous creatures. At the Scheherazade—a windowless, slant-floored hall, with a siding of tin sheets stamped to resemble bricks, an interior decorated by a few Chinese lamps and Art Deco stripes, an outside ticket booth containing the owner's gray-haired wife, and a marquee whose lights attracted masses of moths in the summer—the rich, played by Cary Grant and Fred Astaire, Joan Blondel and Katharine Hepburn, Charles Coburn and Eugene Pallette, were projected in an affectionate silvery light, as stars in a comedy of misunderstanding eventually remedied by sexual attraction and a limitless reserve of lightly taxed money. What a triumph of capitalist art that was, deflecting the poor from hatred of the rich into a chuckling pity for them! With a flick of changed fortune, the poor might be rich themselves, as foolish and happy. For the moguls manufacturing these films it was, of course, no fantasy. They had made it in America. So, in a lesser way, had Owen.

Now he can see in three dimensions and natural color, at the ten o'clock Easter service at Haskells Crossing's Saint Barnabas, the Wainthrop clan, taking up two front pews. The eighty-year-old matriarch, long a widow, is enthroned in a wheelchair that blocks half the aisle; congregants going up to the rail for communion step around it. Before the service begins, one by one her grandsons, each clad in a blazer and rep tie and button-down broadcloth shirt, lean or squeeze past their elders to do this eldest, in her rigid blue hair and black straw sunhat, honor with a kiss smuggled sideways under the hat's broad rim. Not a pasha or Mafia don could more grandly receive dutiful homage. Owen pictures all the money stoppered by the octogenarian's living body, like tons of wheat waiting to pour forth from a prairie grain elevator's unloading chute. In the meantime, enough trickles through: the boys in their blazers sport the honey tans of winter vacations spent in the Bahamas and weekends spent skiing, and the girls, even those at the awkward age, with braces and acne, display costly dresses and animating hopes of good schools and a fair value on the marriage market. Wealth is health.

Their parents, the middle generation, sit through the readings, the prayers of the people, and the sermon *(Yes, He is risen, as He rises up in our lives, on many a personal Easter!)* with the polite, slightly smiling expressions they bring to the myriad board meetings and bibulous social gatherings that maintain their membership in the network of the profitably engaged. Owen especially admires two peculiar traits of the male rich: their ability to grow more and more polite as the object of their courtesy becomes more and more annoying, and their ability to wear shoes, not just moccasins but loafers of fine leather, without socks. Owen, of humbler origins, is unable to conceal annoyance and to endure shoes, sticky and unclean, on his feet without socks, the thicker and woollier the better. Rich men and boys deny themselves the comfort of socks in order, he has decided, to display their thoroughbred ankles. Owen also admires the ability of the rich of both sexes, at cocktail parties, to pop enigmatic hors d'oeuvres into their mouths and, when they discover how fiendishly hot they are, to not spit them out but instead meekly, painfully swallow, giving themselves esophageal cancer miles down the road.

The crammed two pews contain every life-stage from terminal disablement through alcoholic corpulence, deep-lined sun damage, gym-hardened muscularity, spa-enhanced svelteness, teen-age bloom and sudden growth spurt, adolescent squirminess and giggliness, childish pudginess suffocatingly wrapped in boredom, toddler stupefaction and imminent tantrum, on down to the recently baptized infant sleeping in milky bliss on her young mother's lap. The Wainthrops form a synoptic image of life's tragic progress, but it is an image overlaid with graciousness, mannerliness, and tribal consciousness of a value greater than the sum of its parts. Not for the rich the scattered wandering, the flight from the ill-equipped nuclear family into America's wasteland of tawdry entertainments, of shopping-mall parking lots as large as lakes and seedy roadside bars advertising karaoke on Wednesday nights, of deserted downtowns and razed forests, of roving job to job and mate to mate, amid such meagre electronic distractions as heist movies featuring car wrecks and fireballs and television comedies that reflect as in a fuzzy, fizzing mirror the awkward comedy of our desperate daily improvisations beyond the ordering principles of church, village, and family hierarchy. Only the rich—and not all of them, for some turn rebellious and others topple through self-neglect into lower castes—can afford the old structures that carry us from cradle to grave, well-fed, well-clothed, and well-respected. To Owen, an only child most intensely himself when engrossed in coded conversation with the coolly burning face of a cathode-ray tube, the interlocking clans of Haskells Crossing are paradigms of community, a web spun stronger than as of steel. The women are mostly of Anglo-Saxon blood—fair, with forthright warrior jaws—and the men so big-boned they look a touch sheepish in their tailored business suits. However, the web has snared, here and there, brides of Asian or Latin blood, and grooms recruited from swarthier races—the Jewish lawyer, the Italo-American bond salesman—to keep the gene pool fresh.

After church, while Julia, drawing upon her years of experience, is giving a lengthy piece of advice to the rector, Owen finds himself standing on the fringe of the Wainthrop cluster, and especially close to the young mother of the sleeping infant, who is now weakly, crankily awake and being jostled on her mother's twitching hip. The woman is more statuesque than she had appeared in the crammed pew. She has the glossy long free-falling hair of 'sixties flower children and Nordic features slightly larger than lifesize. Her feet are long and strong, in high heels held in place by white thongs wrapping several times around her ankles; her blond hair sets off unplucked dark eyebrows and pouting broad lips lipsticked a luminescent coral tint. She has jumped the season by donning (the Sunday having begun sunny though it is now turning cloudy and cooler) a minidress of broad horizontal stripes the colors of half the rainbow, its fit everywhere tight, as if her body might overpower her clothes at any moment. As Owen furtively watches, other Wainthrops come up to her to admire the new baby and to receive and give the deft little air-kisses of the rich. He has to look away; his gaze could become an indiscretion; here is the kind of raw big beauty, radiant as a naked mother's breadth in the eyes of her speechless son, that bids his male heart, old as he has become, to worship, to drop his body at her knees in pure pagan adoration, on this specifically Christian terrain of Haskells Crossing.

. . .

Who wants to be next? Phyllis had asked, there on the Slades' sunporch, and it was some time before Owen could have answered. He was more and more on the road, as E-O Data struggled to hold its place in an industry ever more tipped to the West Coast. In 1968 he had travelled to a computer conference in San Francisco to see a former radar technician named Douglas Engelbart demonstrate a hand-held invention called an "X-Y position indicator for a monitor system," soon to be called a "mouse." In a ninety-minute lecture Engelbart showed, via a computer twenty-five miles away, how commands could be issued, with no text command, to a monitor screen divided into windows. Owen realized that the hardware of the future was here, and back at E-O he experimented with integrating the X-Y principle with the light pen that was still the tool for computer-aided design. But in the absence of pixel-specific pinpointing, dependent upon sufficient computer capacity to store and resolve the line-scan CRT, he was still stuck, for his second redesign of DigitEyes (DigitEyes 2.2), with the light pen, placed directly on the monitor screen to communicate an X-Y address. Enlargement or rotation of a sketched vector image still required a variety of numerical line commands. The speed and precision of the graphics were dazzling, and enlargements and reductions to the 10^3 order were possible, but the methods were still tied to an alphanumeric machine-language with its cumbersome manual.

It was in 1974, at the Palo Alto Research Center, or PARC, belonging to the Xerox Corporation, a sponsorship that tipped the research toward mass-marketable products rather than military or corporate problem-solving, when Owen saw his first true graphical user interface, on the PARC Alto. His heart sank; the interface, with its mouse-manipulated icons and its schematic imitation of an ordinary desktop, relegated all technical instructions to the hidden program. The operator simply moved an on-screen indicator with his mouse and dropped and dragged icons or blocks of highlighted text. The day of the command-line interface was over. The geometrical increase of chip capacity enabled each pixel on the line-scan monitor to have an address—coördinates that a simple manual motion hurled in silent storms of computation to the next location, along with all the other pixels in its icon or text block. The inventor, a PARC scientist with the suitably elemental name of Alan Kay, had gotten the idea from watching school-children write and run their own small programs using Seymour Papert's programming language, Logo, whose commands were all expressed as objects and movements— "turtle graphics." Children led the way. It would always be the young who had the intuitive connection with this gor-geous toy, this brain in a box, a brain not mired in a messy, bloody animal. Owen was no longer young. He saw, out there on this other coast with its sea cliffs and palm trees and sun-battered, earthquake-resistant, low, glassy research centers and dust-free microelectronic manufacturing units, an alien future, a world of computers as mass-marketable as typewriters, all their elegant mathematics, once the remote province of electrical engineers and Boolean logicians, now buried beneath a cartoon surface as vulgar as a comic book. At MIT and the monitors of the Turkish missile site and in New York at IBM and in the garage behind the clapboarded semi-detached on Common Lane that he and Phyllis had rented their first year in Middle Falls, Owen had felt on the forward edge of a revolution, a new technology's breaking wave; now, though E-O Data could keep exploiting the expanding number of CEOs who knew nothing about computers except that a modern business had to have them, and had to have programs that would make them work, doing work for which people would be no longer needed, Owen and Ed were like farmers hurriedly working their fields before the rising waters of a newly dammed lake inundated them. Soon every company office boy could program a stripped-down mainframe, and the minimalist, add-on approach of Unix, salvaged by Bell Labs from the GE Multics debacle and licensed to universities at nominal cost, further democratized what had been an arcane craft. Owen must henceforth think in terms of niches, special projects, European clients, and passing flings.

There were more women in the computer world than ten years ago. A few were programmers and engineers; more were installers, support staff, and sales reps for the wallowing giants of the industry—Sperry Rand, IBM, GE, Honeywell. These young women, many of them math majors like Phyllis but some of them reborn out of English and psychology departments, showed up at conferences, and from time to time Owen and one of them explored the opportunities of a night far from home. Jacqueline, Antoinette, Mirabella—they tended to have fancy names, trim bodies, short skirts, long hair, and liberated morals. Until Vietnam ended and Nixon resigned, the 'seventies were an extension of the 'sixties, of the rebellious fever inflicted by irritation from above. But the new decade was more shopworn and hard-eyed. Female bodies were hardening, as exercise and diet became a mode of feminist assertion. Drugs and promiscuity had catered to spiritual health; now physical condition's turn had come. Owen could not help admiring, as he kneeled on the San Jose hotel's shag carpet to pull down Jacqueline's pantyhose, the flat tendony knit behind her knee, the calf-bulge modulating upward into the biceps femoris and the gluteus maximus, so firm to his touch; he had to pause to kiss the dear adductor longus on the inside of her thigh, and she, halfway out of her pantyhose, had to clutch the hair on his head to steady herself. She was, fully undressed, a little solemn-bodied, less flexible than her muscular development promised. Her skin and hair had a sour tinge from day-old jet lag and twelve hours on her feet singing the praises of a DEC PDP-11 with its time-sharing software and magnetic-tape units, taller than she even with her impressively "big" hair. Once inside her, he was too tired himself to hold back, and she didn't accept his apologies. Lack of sleep came with these hasty conquests, and lingered as a faint grogginess, for a week, while the sensation of conquest faded, overnight, to nothing.

Antoinette was a severely thin, tough-talking debugger met at a Saint Louis computer fair—acres of pale metal and convex black-green screens, within a walk of the great arch through which Lewis and Clark opened the West. The fair occupied a vast shed recently erected where a black ghetto had been torn down, its residents fleeing to East Saint Louis, and the fair's sponsors seemed not to know at whom its glamour was aimed, big business or the private hobbyist who had the patience and hundreds of hours needed to assemble an Altair 8800. In that dusk before Apple dawned, and the hobby computer became a consumer product, even a Tandy TRS-80, out of Radio Shack, cost more than a new Buick, and the cheapest DEC, the PDP-8, went for "only" eighteen thousand dollars. Owen stood guard at the E-O stall, hawking without much heart a packaged games application Ed had insisted on developing. Trying to cash in on Atari's Pong coup, he had bypassed Owen with a design team of younger employees. But Pong itself was still a matter of a two-hundred-pound box that people in an arcade or a luncheonette put a quarter in to play, like a pinball machine. A home that had a computer in it was one in a hundred thousand. It was hard to believe that video games, requiring sound and color and joysticks, were the future of a device born of a great war and presently hauling numbers for the financial, industrial, and scientific armies of the world. Corporate types in gray and putty suits circulated among the booths with ponytailed computer-heads in old blue jeans and flannel shirts. In another generation, the second uniform would have displaced the former as the height of moneyed fashion, and lawyers and bankers would dress casual to welcome their most valued clients, the electronic superrich.

Owen spotted Antoinette working the booth for Cray Research, a new company for high-performance computers up in Chippewa Falls, Wisconsin. She had black hair that looked hurriedly cut by a child's plastic scissors, and an electric aura of grievance that boded well. He homed in on her at the boozy reception hosted by the city's newly created Association of Electronic Industries. Very quickly, it seemed to him, she was confiding to him a tirade against a fellow employee, slightly her superior, an "asshole" whose "shit" she was tired of putting up with. The words made squeamish Owen wince, but there was a promise of intimacy in them. He curbed his repugnance, telling himself that this was a passionate woman, who lived like him in a small-town Falls, and that they were thrown together in the heart of this great, free country. They went on from the reception to a celebrated steakhouse a cab ride away. Her tale continued: "This absolute, stuck-on-himself shit, Eric by name—and can't you just bet that anybody called Eric is going to be stuck on himself?—kept dumping on me in these subtle ways that nobody could fault him for but that I could certainly sense, saying these bogus-polite things like 'I'll let you' and 'Would you be an angel' and yatata-yatata, when what was involved was literally all night going over the machine code, matching it number by number against a master, twenty-plus pages of dot-matrix with hardly any ink on the ribbon, it's a wonder I didn't go blind. And in the morning, you know what the peckerhead did?"

"No, what?" said Owen, nursing his second beer, which he hoped might dilute two stiff bourbons at the reception, in case he would have eventually to perform. He was learning to pace himself in these matters, on the principle of deferred gratification.

"He said, 'Thanks—thanks, Antoinette'—that was all the scumbag said, taking the printout I'd marked up, number by number, circling the possible bugs, it killed my eyes, I need to get a new prescription and I bet that's the reason. 'Thanks,' he had the nerve to simply say to me, 'you're a dear,' and put it on the other papers on his desk as if it was the merest little five-minute favor in the world, knowing fucking damn well I'd been up all night."

"That does seem rude," Owen said, his brain beginning to feel puffy, lifting him up out of guilt and the worry that Phyllis was telephoning his hotel.

"At the same time he's constantly pulling these chauvinist tricks, he's talking a great game of what a terrific IQ I must have, so much quicker to spot redundancy and garbage than he is, I actually should have his job—can you imagine, he had the crust to admit it, I ought to have his job?—if there was any kind of a level playing field. He's one of these guys who thinks being a great women's libber is an easy way into your pants. What a prick, truly. What a conceited, smarmy, phony prick."

"My wife is brainy," Owen shyly told her. "Or used to be."

Antoinette didn't hear him. She told him more about Eric, how he dressed for work oh-so-casual and boyish and yet pulled out his comb twice every hour, he had this wavy reddish hair he was really vain of, and wore these broad belts and cowboy buckles to show what a flat stomach he had—he ran five miles a day and only drank soda water and white wine to keep his figure, just like a woman. She suspected he was gay, in fact. "When he walks, he seems conscious of his ass, the way a woman is—this skinny little ass of his, and his long lanky legs. Why would any guy but a queer wear such tight jeans, he must use a shoehorn to get them on? And not blue jeans, either, they would be too common, he wears *black* jeans, with the white stitching on the hip pockets. *God*, what a pompous turd."

Even in Owen's hotel room, Antoinette out of her clothes and slithering through the shadows like an agitated white snake—her skin cold against his, the very chill of her hostility exciting, something to overlook and overcome—she continued to express her venom toward her colleague, who thought he was too hot a shit to come to this miserable so-called fair and sent her instead, expecting her to be grateful for this non-existent favor. Even as she was being fucked, her tongue ran on about how some people just get under her skin, she knows she shouldn't let them, it's exactly what they want, mega-pricks like that, her girlfriends tell her to rise above it and not give the creepy bastard the time of day, and even as Owen came in her—she was one of these circus-performer types, bringing her legs way back like she is being shot from a cannon, he didn't see how her clitoris was getting any contact but then she should know—it occurred to him that she was in love with this hateful Eric and felt spurned by him, and was using Owen to make him jealous. She thought that Eric could see her, that he was with her every moment. She was obsessed with him and was angry because, drunk as she was, she could feel Eric not caring; hanging up there like a bat in the corner of the ceiling, he didn't care who she was acting like a circus performer with.

She awoke, finally, as they lay beside each other overheated and disappointed, to the dim reality of him, Owen, as opposed to that of the man tormenting her self-esteem back in Chippewa Falls, Wisconsin. She announced, in a different, sobered voice, "Hey, whatever your name is. You're not so bad. Thanks for listening. My girlfriends think I'm crazy on the subject."

"Well," Owen said, mild and acquiescent as he tended to be, "we *are* crazy. People in general. Eric sounds like an interesting guy."

"He's not. He's a prick, and I should have his job," Antoinette said, as if he hadn't been listening at all. Yet they lay there another hour, side by side, their drying sweat chilling them so they pulled up the flimsy hotel blankets, then tossed them aside for trips to the bathroom. Her hard white buttocks gleamed in the strips of shadow and light that fell through the venetian blinds, at the window overlooking the silent lit courtyard, while Owen drowsily wondered if it was true, as she said, that women are always conscious of their asses. Returning, she nudged up against him, even stroking him where he was limp and silky-soft, as if to demonstrate to herself that he was there, a not-Eric, and that none of the grievances against Eric applied. She made an effort, as the red digits on the bedside clock radio jiggled through the minutes of the wee hours, to give him his due, a man who had stuck with her through all that tipsy tirade, processing Eric's snubs, and who had made love to her, after all, praising her body and flexibility while keeping his reservations about her clitoral management to himself. But it was too late, the Association of Electronic Industries was striking its tent tomorrow, and they would be winging their way back to lives for which this interlude was no lasting solution.

No solution, but an event nonetheless, partaking of sublimity. When they met the next day, under the high metal roof of the exhibition shed, they took a break from their duties to share coffee in Styrofoam cups, in the back room set aside for workers, for exhibition insiders, with free crullers and disgustingly hi-cal Danish. Neither had enough to say, but as they fumbled sheepishly and sleepily for words they were acknowledging that, though they would not meet again, they had made a start, a stab at significance. There was a flavor to this, a taste, amid those of coffee and sugary fried dough, of sluggish animal ease and of mutually achieved knowledge—a swallowed mournfulness which lovers with a future avoid knowing. Two kinds of women existed in the world, Owen perceived: those with whom you have slept and those, a cruelly disproportionate but reducible number, with whom you haven't.

One-night stands had their underside of sorrow, but had he ever been more crazily happy, more triumphantly himself, than when Mirabella was blowing him while he sped at ninety miles an hour into the flat Nevada desert, straight into the rising morning sun? There was just space, in the rented tangerine Camaro, for her head to fit between the steering wheel and his sucked-in abdomen. The honeyed sensations in his prick, hard-used the night before, were mixed up with what he imagined her sensations were in that confined space, as the westward-bound cars materialized in the morning glare and flashed past at a combined speed that made the Camaro shudder and suck toward the middle of the highway. The highway was a thin ribbon beginning to show trembling puddles of mirage as the sun settled to baking the miles of lilac-gray vegetation on either side; distant cattle lowered their heads to graze. He knew a twitch of the wheel would annihilate them both and Mirabella knew it too but kept giving him exceedingly welcome sensations, including, with a twist of her head of bleached and teased hair, warm kisses on his naked abdomen, his button-down shirt rumpled and pulled up. Under his caressing fingers her shell of curls felt stiff and sticky, from too much spray. When he glanced down, he saw slant sunlight piercing her hair so the chalky pink of her skull showed through, the defenseless epidermis of it, skin on bone, and he had to fight losing his erection in the suppressed shock of the sight.

This conference was in Las Vegas, in one of the enormous luxury hotels—was it the Sands? or the Stardust?—that have since been pulled down to make way for yet larger ones. Her hair was dyed to a platinum pallor except for a half-inch of hometown-brown roots. Her ears had been double-pierced for two sets of little earrings, in those days an advanced self-mutilation. He took her, in her chamois-colored hotpants and green net stockings, for one of the hookers of the place, but she surprised him by knowing his name and saying, "You invented DigitEyes. My father was a structural engineer in Fresno and when I'd go to his office he used to let me play with the things on the screen. How they turned in space and still stayed together, the volumes described by these, like, wires, all with a few commands on the keys—it was magical."

"An ingenious artifact of the past, I fear," Owen told her. "Like the apple corer and the treadle-operated sewing machine." He must have had a few drinks already; he had been on a panel, and when there was a reception afterwards girls from the hotel circulated among them with plastic glasses of champagne.

"The future builds on the past, and you can too," she reassured him, Mirabella with her two-tone hair and green fishnets on her legs like a shrunken piece of costume from Sherwood Forest.

He confessed to her, "I'd like to gamble here but I don't know how." She led him to the roulette wheel, but he didn't like it, because it was pure chance and the odds were unashamedly in the house's favor. At the blackjack tables, he won because the game was a problem in mathematics, and most people, stupidly optimistic, tried to improve their hands with one more hit: the house counted on that. He most enjoyed the machines, the impersonal slots, gaudy and solemn both, their melting colors and the silky tug of the handles, the soft leveraging within, and the gush of their occasional jackpot spitting Kennedy half-dollars into the battered trough.

In his room high above the Strip she showed him something else—a line of white powder on the glass coffee table. He knelt on the carpeted floor as he had with Jacqueline in quite another city, in another hotel room. Mirabella, her broad face shining and smiling, guided him in rolling up a twenty-dollar bill and inhaling the powder as best he could. He had never been good at blowing out candles on a birthday cake, either. He disliked the tickly sensation, like loose hair across his lips except that this was deeper into his head. The powder that eluded his nostrils she scraped up quickly, neatly, with a one-edged Treet razor blade, and inhaled herself, making afterwards an ingratiating child's grimace. She was an angel, Mirabella, with something Slavic in the shine and breadth of her face.

Owen distrusted drugs because he needed his brain cells, but this was a slow icicle to the brain that awoke that gray organ to its potential, gave it the precision and speed immortal spirits must know. His body, too: he had never wanted to fuck so much, and been so good at it, so hard and controlled, a man of iron, desire rising in him throughout the night like hydraulic pressure and always being greeted willingly by the marvellous Mirabella, her body as thick and resilient as a peasant woman's, her breasts thoroughly brown and a ghost of non-tan around her trimmed pubes smaller than a doily. She reminded him of Alissa except that she was firmer-bodied and younger and didn't want a baby. Her back viewed from above as he humped her was less touching, less articulate in its muffled spine. Her back was blank. Her cunt became full of him, so soppy he felt less and less friction, and she confessed toward dawn that he was hurting her with his cock. He apologized and kissed her all over tenderly, including the vertebra just above the sallow cleft of her ass, but in fact he was not sorry, he enjoyed the idea of hurting her with just himself.

She said she wanted to show him something beautiful and suggested he rent a car. He said it was six in the morning and no rental agencies would be open.

"They all will," Mirabella said. "This is Vegas."

Las Vegas was her Sherwood Forest, it seemed to his hopped-up head, and it was just as well he forgot to ask her what computer company she worked for. Or if he had, he had forgotten her answer. But she was right: they rented cars right off the main lobby of the hotel—was it the Dunes?—and in his confused, extremely happy state he chose tangerine when it was offered because he figured it wouldn't get lost in a parking lot. He drove east into the sun, and the cars coming toward him with what seemed electronic speed were black silhouettes, shapes without people, dangerous imperfections in the great clean pane of the morning. After they stopped for coffee and eggs, with the inevitable hash browns, at a place she seemed to know, Mirabella, fed and sleepy and playful, went down into his lap and undid his fly and pulled up his shirt and started to suck him off. He was sensitive enough there it felt like a bite; he asked her to stop but she giggled and didn't, and it occurred to him that some women did sex because it was what they could do, just as he could write programs for pay-rolls and pension plans. It was what they were programmed to do, there was no mystery. Why had he ever thought there was a mystery? The sun was getting higher, burning down through her spun-sugar curls, so her scalp felt warm where his free hand lightly massaged it, and the backlit mountains in the distance were giving up more and more of their shadows, and her lips and fingers were doing this sweet tugging number on him, and he came, came upward into the cozy pink darkness beneath all those bobbing shel-lacked curls as a long side-slatted truck roared by in the opposite direction, and she gagged. He loved her gagging. He would drown her in his jism.

In his imperfect memory, the truck had shuddered past with a load of white-faced cattle looking out between the slats. But how could he have seen them? He was concen-trating on keeping the little Camaro on the road; he must have observed the cattle truck at some other point in that glorious, wide-open morning. The vast alkaline sky with its translucent towers of cloud, the purple-tinged pastures stretching on either side of the highway. Mirabella lifted her head from his lap and raucously asked, "Where do you *get* all that stuff? I'd have thought you'd be pumped out by now." Her face was shining with sweat from the close quarters she had been working in. She sat up, and with a thumb and finger wiped the corners of her mouth. Batsy. She settled back, leaning her skull on the padded headrest. She looked tired and not as young as he had thought. Her profile against the hurtling lilac desert showed a double chin, and a ripple of collagen around the cheekbone.

"I don't know," he answered. "You excite me."

"I'll say. You should get a wife."

"I have one, thanks."

He was getting a headache, where the transformative, clarifying icicle had entered. When they came to the beautiful sight Mirabella had promised—a huge blue lake, there in the middle of the desert, created by a federally financed dam—it seemed part of his headache, another unnatural intervention, with speedboats and a tacky marina. Owen later wondered if she in fact was a hooker who had been primed by pals of his at the conference to say she was a childhood fan of DigitEyes. But he couldn't believe it, she seemed too computer-savvy, and she charged nothing for the sexual services, though she did say he owed her six hundred dollars for the cocaine.

xii. *Village Sex—VI*

BACK IN MIDDLE FALLS, in the 'seventies, the
path to illicit sex had grown shorter; the skids were
greased. The scent upon Owen had ripened, the
scent that told women he was in the market for what only
they could provide. Not every man was. Some in Middle
Falls were more interested in the next drink than in the next
woman—Jock Dunham had been like that. Some, like Ed
Mervine, put their passion into their work—the machinery,
the payroll, the bottom line, the buccaneering of chancy
enterprise in a fertile but mined field. Certain husbands, of
whom Henry Slade appeared to be one, were simply too
dry, too stiff, too consumed by the drab business of earning
a living and husbanding his property, to play the love game.
His bureaucratic post in Hartford, in one of those colorless marble boxes that sprawl around the spiky, turreted
basilica of a capitol building, with a gold dome as narrow as
the band at the top of a pencil, defined him and fulfilled
him, so that what he brought to the social life of Middle
Falls was a mere residue, compared with his wife's many
involvements. Not that Henry was absent at weekend get-

togethers; on the contrary, he was, with Vanessa, at every cocktail party and Heron Pond kiddy swim meet and informal picnic and formal benefit dance. He gave no sign, save a dry chuckle, of enjoying social life, or of not enjoying it. He smoked a pipe and nodded as he listened, seldom replying with more than a word or two, knocking out his pipe or pinching his lips together, with shifty sideways motions of his eyes before granting that word. He gave the impression of hesitating between brands or flavors of wisdom within his capacious available store; after over a decade of acquaintanceship Owen decided that Henry instead of silently wise was stupefied by years of meticulous drudgery in the service of Connecticut's most picayune regulations. He was a swarthy man, not tall; he walked as if a board were keeping his back straight, thrusting his pipe and head forward while he plodded along, like a villager under a load of fagots.

Vanessa was a bit younger than he—she had been an underling in his Hartford office—and had a brusque, ageless quality, moving too purposefully to count the years. Her plain, androgynous face, tanned by the sun in every season—for she was a keen skier as well as golfer, tennis player, and gardener—was exceptionally frontal; that is, where Owen thought of Henry as always in profile, preoccupied and heading off somewhere, Vanessa looked people in the eye, as if daring them to blink or smile in nervousness. With the same faintly challenging authority, she ruled the several town committees she served on, as well as her bridge circle and the Garden Club. She was an impressive sight in her own garden, gloved and long-sleeved in protection from rose thorns, up to her trousered hips in delphiniums and phlox and well-staked peonies, a loosely woven straw hat throwing her watchful, unsmiling face into a shade evenly speckled with sunlight. The flowers, it seemed to Owen, softened her, adding a feminine element missing in her confrontational gaze, blunt manner, and husky tenor voice. The Slades were a one-child couple, which made them unusual, and hinted at something foreclosed and firmly settled in their marriage. The child was a solemn, olive-skinned boy, Victor. Amid the many couples the Mackenzies had come to know in Middle Falls, the Slades were not unusual in that the man of the couple was a comic figure but the woman was not. The women had competence, mystery, and at least a hint of beauty. Vanessa was not beautiful—she hardly bothered with makeup, and her upper teeth, like Owen's own, had come in crowded, pushing her eye teeth forward—but she was dignified and matter-of-fact. How matter-of-fact Owen did not realize until she came to sit beside him on an antique two-person sofa covered with striped satin—a love seat, they used to be called—on the fringe of an improvised dance floor at a party given by the couple, Dwight and Patricia Oglethorpe, who had bought the old Dunham place. Vanessa seated herself and said to him, keeping her voice low, "We ought to have lunch some time."

Too startled to stall, Owen asked, "Why?"

She gave a slow, constrained smile at this gaffe. Vanessa's uneven teeth had led to a curious source of power, the rarity of her smile. "There's usually only one why, isn't there? To see if we want to have lunch again."

Stalling now, distracted by the sight, not ten feet away, of his tall, long-necked wife dancing with Vanessa's hunched-over, rhythmless husband, he asked, "Is that the way things are done?" Phyllis was gazing stoically over Henry's head; Heaven knew what she was thinking.

Vanessa expressed impatience with a stab of her cigarette,

an extra-long Pall Mall. "Owen, why do you always play innocent? You're not innocent."

"No? I still feel I am. How do you know I'm not?"

"Everybody knows, you silly." Her mannish voice became gruff. "Don't put me on, or we won't get anywhere."

"You mean Faye?"

"After Faye, more. Faye was a starter. We all need a starter."

"You too?"

Vanessa said nothing, just inhaled smoke and let it cascade from her nostrils, above her slow smile. He began to see her—her small neat cat's nose; her thick dark eyebrows, unplucked, level above her eyes; the crowded mouth tweaked at the moment by a smile in spite of herself. He felt abruptly admitted to a too-large intimacy, in which he was in danger of merely rattling around. He said, to say something and seizing on what lay uppermost in his mind, "I suppose you wonder how could I have ever looked at anybody but Phyllis, who's so lovely."

"We know you think she's lovely, it's rather touching. And I suppose she is, but she's not my type, frankly—too bluestocking. She never left school. But nobody around here wonders about what you mentioned. She doesn't give you shit. Or anybody else, really, except her children, up to a point. She is about the most insulated person I've ever seen."

"Insulated."

"Wrapped up in herself."

This was fascinating to Owen—a road map out of his guilt, being offered by a woman he hardly knew. Other people, seeing by their faces that their conversation had reached a heated depth, avoided approaching them. He said rapidly, "O.K., let's have lunch some time. Way out of town, and not in Hartford. What does Henry think?"

"About what, dear?"

"About Phyllis and me and whatnot."

"Henry and I don't talk about anything. That's the beauty of it."

"I've often wondered," Owen admitted, "what the beauty of it was." He liked his so quickly, dryly saying this; he felt that, in a few furtive minutes, he was learning to dance with this woman.

"Likewise," Vanessa said, tapping the ash from her Pall Mall, as the music stopped and their spouses approached. Henry and Phyllis were laughing in relief that that was over and squinting blindly, out of the flickering strobe lights that the Oglethorpes, overanxious to please, had installed for the evening.

The lesson Owen learned from Vanessa was a surprising one: masculine women give great sex. It was perhaps no accident that it had been the tomboy Doris Shanahan who had let him look up the leg of her shorts. Sex is more up front, so to speak, with them. They go at it straight out, pouncing on orgasms like a hawk on a baby quail. Though Vanessa rarely (unlike giddy Faye, unlike dimpled Alissa) smiled during the process, she often laughed, gruffly, her low husky laugh. In her customary thick-fabricked, wide-shouldered clothes, her ass and chest both looked flat, minimal; undressed, she showed charms enough. Her body, neither fat nor bony, had below her brown face the eggshell smoothness of a plaster cast, an even tone that neither her dusty-red nipples or chestnut-brown pubic hair markedly interrupted. She brought to sex a certain serious playfulness; like a man, she was willing to consider the event basically physical, a meal of sorts, and, like a good cook, was conscious of the need for variety. In a graceful, short-nailed hand she would hold his erection as if it were the stem of an oversize wineglass, her extended little finger resting ticklishly in his curly hair at its base, and study it, the blue-veined stalk and empurpled glans, from inches away, pondering what to do with it. Like a good craftsman she thought about the task while away from the workbench, so she could greet him, at their next tryst, with a fresh idea: "I thought today you could come between my breasts, if you'd bring me off with your mouth first."

"What a divine agenda, Vanessa. But shouldn't I be inside you at some point?"

"Where inside me, dearest? There are choices."

"Oh, God, don't drive me crazy with choices. Just rape me, can't you?"

The feminine side he had suppressed when Buddy Rourke rejected his fancy Monopoly arrangement was coming back to him under Vanessa's tutelage. She said, "That's one of the beauties of being a man—you can't be. You can be aroused against your will, but you can't be raped without your prick's consent." Vanessa was a considerable connoisseuse of the advantages of being a man, and frequently mentioned them.

"Except," Owen pointed out, "by the back entrance."

"Oh. That." She thought a moment. When she thought, her eyes, the amber of a lioness's, darkened a shade, as had Alissa's abraded-looking blue irises when making love. Vanessa didn't afford him Alissa's feeling of an infinitely soft, furry, moist socket to hide himself in, a safe dirty place where a terrible tension was resolved, but she could briskly arrange a buffet of other treats. "Would that turn you on?" Her voice had roughened in her throat.

"I don't think so," he said, and his own voice sounded high and fragile in his ears. "How about you?"

Owen had never had, at the adolescent moment when it would have been useful to his growth, a male friend with whom sex in its mysteries could have been, however ignorantly, discussed. Now, twenty-five years late, Vanessa was that frank friend. She answered, after reflection, "It didn't do terrifically much for me, the few times I tried it. It felt like the wrong way. But that was not unexciting, I suppose. The wrong way as the right way."

He was roused. She knew more than he; he could still catch up. "Let me do it to you, then."

"O.K.," she said. "Just to get it off your list. If I do it to you first."

"With what?" he asked, fearfully.

"My tongue?" Vanessa suggested. "Then a finger, wearing a surgical glove. Then—we'll see."

"This is getting to be," Owen had to admit, "a rather repulsive conversation."

"Yet, dearest, look at how hard you are! You're so hard you're bending backwards, staring into your own navel."

"Suck me," he begged.

"Maybe. Maybe not." Her serious mouth made a pouting little *moue*, as Phyllis used to. "First let's think what you can do for me."

Her cunt, those livid wrinkles looking like lava folds, had become his to contemplate, to finger, opening the petals to their peony-pink inner side and bringing his mouth to breathe on the clitoris, to tongue that gleaming wet nub. *Don't touch it. Don't tell me what to touch.* Between her legs her plaster-pale body took on color and gave up its stately evenness of tone. Her stern face softened as she sat on the edge of the bed and toyed with his hair, the boyishly soft brown hair into which gray was being sifted one strand at a time. Then as if in sudden surfeit she flung herself back on the motel bed, with a violence that jolted into his head an image of what she saw—through the cloudy small window above their bed a glimpse of green leaves flung upside down as in a hurricane. She rested her thighs one on each of his shoulders, her eyes shut against the daylight to be alone with her sensations as Owen knelt there at her service, laboring in his own trance of mounting attention. Vanessa eventually released a throaty grunt and in a spasm clamped his head between her thighs as Elsie had once done; his hot face felt then so imbued with her juices that for twenty-four hours he tried to avoid coming close to Phyllis, even for their courtesy good-night peck. No amount of soap or aftershave quite quenched the smell of one woman in another's nostrils.

She had been with women, Vanessa admitted to Owen. She and her girlfriend in high school did things, and then there were others the year she went to the state university in Storrs before family finances—she had brothers who needed the tuition money more—forced her to switch to what was still called secretarial school, in Hartford. She became an office manager's assistant in the bureau where Henry worked. She learned efficiency. The manager she assisted was a woman, unusual back then, and had tried to talk her out of marrying Henry and into coming to live with her instead. But, no, Vanessa had known she needed men, clumsy and simple as they were. She needed marriage, for a base. She had intuited about Henry that she could always get around him. He was older, he would take her on her own terms. He had never mistaken her for one of the cute clinging girls he could have had. She owed him one child— a son, as it nicely turned out—and after that he gave her her own space. He didn't pry into her day. Weekends, she was his.

"What's it like?" Owen asked her. "Being with a woman."

He saw her amber irises alter, as shuttling interior pictures activated them. "It's like being with a weak man," she said. "Why be with a weak imitation when you can be with a real one? It's all a matter, isn't it," Vanessa went on, perhaps unconsciously echoing that buried Bible never quite scrubbed from our brains, "of being *known*. You want to be known better than you know yourself."

"You kill me," he told her, "so casually mentioning these others you've had. I want you to be all mine."

"No, Owen, you don't. You're like the rest of us. You like the muck and the muddle."

"When was the last woman you slept with?"

"I don't think I'll tell you."

"Then it was recent."

"No comment, dearest."

"Is she around here? She must be. You must tell me about it; could I watch? Could we all do it together?"

She contemplated his still-importunate penis and in a flick of amused indulgence licked the tip of it quickly. Her tongue was grainier than other women's, it seemed to him, and more triangular, coming to a more muscular point. "I think not," she told him. "If you want a threesome, the third is up to you to provide. What a wicked man you turn out to be, you funny dear. You're such a *puppy*."

The Oglethorpes had bought the Dunhams' rambling Victorian, with its spindlework and scalloped shingles, behind its palisade fence and lilac bushes, for themselves and their three children and what seemed, when they came bounding together over the slanting lawn in loose-jointed, crotch-sniffing welcome, a herd of golden retrievers. The

Oglethorpes were both rather comically thin, he with an amiable discombobulation that appeared to seek to disown his embarrassing height (he was six four) with a distracting whirl of hand-flaps and misplaced guffaws, and she with a Twiggyesque knock-kneed winsomeness that chose to set itself off in filmy short shifts and school-uniformish, big-buttoned outfits, as if going shopping with Mommy. Her hair was a shiny, cedar-colored cap sometimes adorned with a big ribbon and bow. The Oglethorpes entertained almost as much as the departed Dunhams had. Perhaps the old house demanded it. Its rooms were scaled for life with servants and its steam heat clanged like a madman trapped in the walls with a hammer. Moving through its familiar rooms, now renovated and refurnished in a less reckless, eclectic style than Faye had favored, Owen frequently found himself pierced by a memory of her. He seemed to see her, flickering gaily through a doorway in one of her bright, improvised costumes, or treading toward him naked, silently barefoot, with a less smiling expression, tentative and imperilled, out of the second-floor back bathroom. He had come to know the brown tearstains on this little room's turn-of-the-century porcelain and its high, industrial-strength showerhead, the size of a sunflower. That particular sentimental plumbing, he noticed, sneaking around upstairs while an Oglethorpe party raged downstairs, had been ruthlessly replaced.

The Oglethorpes fought off alcoholic calories with exercise, from dog-walking to tennis. The sight of them playing tennis was comical, especially when they teamed up together: so many angles of elbow and knee and of feet that in white sneakers projected like those of kangaroos as they hopped here and there with an occasional clash of rackets. Trish was the first woman Owen knew who had made jogging a part of her life, and it was somehow exciting to see her in unexpected parts of town, even along Partridgeberry Road, a good two miles from her house. In rainy weather she wore a short yellow slicker from which her naked legs seemed to dangle over the asphalt like a puppet's, and an extensive rain hat down her back like the little girl's on the Morton's salt box. When Owen suggested her to Vanessa, in playful continuation of a fantasy that turned them both on, as their possible third, his lover said, "Not much meat on those bones, as Spencer Tracy said."

Having seen the movie back at the Scheherazade, he finished the quotation: "But what there is, is choice."

"I don't know, Owen. You're welcome to try, but I never get anything much back from her when we talk. The bounce is too quick. There isn't any depth behind what you see."

"How much depth do you need, Greedy? I like the way the bounce is always a little off, as if she hasn't quite heard you and is desperately trying to imagine what you want her to say. They're both pathetically anxious to 'get with it.' I think she has round heels. There's a sense you get. She's been good all her life and doesn't think what it's gotten her is enough." He spoke a bit rapidly, breathlessly even, like a junior officer reporting to a superior. He wondered if the expression "round heels" was offensive to a woman, as savoring too much of gossip among men—of the brotherhood argot. Vanessa said nothing, nodding curtly and letting him rattle on. "Why have they attached themselves to us," he asked, "when there are plenty of stodgy O.K. couples just their age new in town? What do they call them now? Yuppies. White-flight types who work in Hartford or Norwich. No, the Oglethorpes are looking for action. At least she is. Couldn't you sort of love her?"

" 'Cherce,' " Vanessa said. "That was part of the joke. Tracy said, 'Cherce.' "

There was no lack of meat on Vanessa's bones; she was wide-shouldered and thick-waisted like a man. He had, now and then, an unindulged impulse to twist her wrists, to beat her, knowing she could take it. Like him she had been of the poor and as in an unforgiving mirror showed him the abjectness of his needs. He was learning to resent the hold she had over him. It was possible, he discovered, to accept all the gifts one body can give another and yet dislike the inhabitant of that body. He felt inadequately tender toward Vanessa. For a year, and then another, he was her lover; no doubt not the only one. Her days were long, though she filled them with activities.

He was sorry he had said Trish had round heels. Whenever he came up to her at a party, he was afraid of knocking her over. His discourteous characterization coated the inside of his mouth with a phlegm that made it hard for him to talk to her as he must to win her trust—candidly, amusedly, with no more implication than she was ready for. "So," he said to her at a fall party at Roscoe and Imogene Bisbee's, "how do you like your new President?"

"He seems fine, though I'm not sure he should have pardoned Nixon."

"Oh, we all need to be pardoned, don't we?"

"Do we?" Patricia asked, looking away, as if something were happening beyond the Bisbees' porch rail, down in the darkness where footsteps crunched on the spalled driveway, going back and forth to the cars.

"Maybe not *you*," Owen said. "But seriously, if he hadn't pardoned him the fuss and trial would have consumed all our energy."

"You're right," she said; her agreement felt too quick, a way to get rid of him. He studied her from the side. Her profile showed a chafed pinkness to the nostrils and an underslung jaw that left her plump upper lip protruding as if pensively. He felt in her the crack of some old sorrow, like a teacup's chipped rim on his tongue. Did he imagine, also, a certain impatience, an excess of wanting, expressed, as with Faye, by her clothes?

"I keep seeing you everywhere, jogging," he said. "You look darling."

"Oh, *don't*," Trish quickly cried, twisting there by the porch rail as if in the grip of an unshakable irritation.

She saw him, her reaction told him, as a dangerous man. "In your big sneakers and sweat pants," he hastily explained. "I keep wondering if you're ever afraid of getting hit."

"I try to always wear something white. And the running shoes now have strips that light up in headlights."

And her eyes, with lashes so spaced and starry they might be artificial, flared like headlights. He had alarmed her, been too pushy, too forward. "O.K., good," he said quickly, back-tracking. He had found in his experience that a woman's basic desire to please will hold her to you even after an affront: the way Alissa had jumped back as if scalded, saying *Oh no you don't*, and then come around wonderfully. He said, "Let's talk about something else. How do you feel about that guy in California who had a sex-change operation wanting to compete in women's tennis?"

"Well," Trish cautiously admitted, "it's unusual."

She was not very bright, nor very beautiful. Why was he bothering her, making conversation, risking embarrassment, in the service of some strange dream of bringing this naïve woman to Vanessa like a live doe slung over his shoulders? They could each nibble at opposite ends and meet in the middle. The two women would adore him, vying for him, competing in feats of slavishness. "Speaking of unusual," he pursued, "I was reading where they have a woman prison guard at a maximum security facility in Iowa."

"And why not?" Trish asked, with a spark of pugnacity that brightened the dark of the Bisbees' porch.

He backed off again. "I don't know, and all these sex-change operations. It makes you wonder, what is a woman?"

"Yes," she said. It was as if they were both under a table looking for a lost something—an earring, or a contact lens—and had found it. "Even when you are one," she told him, "you wonder."

The crack in the teacup must have to do with sex, sex and gangly foolish Dwight with his flapping kangaroo feet and ghastly effeminate guffaw. "Sometimes," Owen ventured, "it must make you angry. Women are getting angrier. Look at Patty Hearst, going from Daddy's girl to gun moll."

"She was brainwashed," Trish snapped, with one of her erratic quick bounces. "She was kidnapped and brain-washed and now she's being hunted. And they say women have equal rights." She was just enough younger than Owen to have feminism implanted in her; women Owen's age had had to invent it for themselves, in a range of personal styles.

His appetite for this conquest was waning. He didn't like politically prickly women; he liked them ironical and detached and devoted to the realm of the purely personal, the privilege of the free world. He asked her, "You know what I've really loved so far about this year?" He had in mind the Viking spacecraft landing on Mars, which after a century of talk about canals looked drier than Arizona.

"Evil Knievel not making his jump," Trish replied with

surprising promptness, as though she had given his mental processes some thought. Her hostile edge was hopeful; he was beginning to work within her. He saw from a foot away how her face would look in bed, on a pillow; the realization made him a little tired, with the effort of living on several levels. Her face would be petulant, eager to extract from him payment for her daring, for the risk she had taken.

"Why would I like that?"

"You like flub-ups. Misery loves company," Trish pronounced, tapping him unexpectedly on the chest and drifting off the porch, with its November chill, into the bright, warm, chatter-filled living room.

His private monk's cell at E-O, with its dirty high window and its carefully scheduled visitors from beyond, had been lately invaded from within the factory. A low-level programmer, Karen Jazinski, hired a year or so ago, had delivered a number of papers from Ed's end of the operation—printouts of machine code with problems, contracts Owen had to initial, yellow-highlighted items from *Computing Tomorrow*. Karen had to traverse an unutilized section of upper factory floor (its vacancy a reminder of the company's recent stagnation, of DigitEyes 2.2's relative failure on the increasingly graphics-crowded market) and knock on the gray-painted metal door Owen kept locked from within. Admitted for the first time, Karen was startled by the near-domestic coziness he had created within the small space: the Oriental rug, the corkboard where memos and snapshots of his family had been thumbtacked, bracket-supported shelves of catalogues and computer manuals, the fluorescent overheads seconded by bridge lamps and bulbs enclosed in ribbed rice-paper balls, the molded-plastic, much-adjustable office furniture augmented by a corduroy-covered easy chair and the Naugahyde sofa softened by a striped blanket and several fat pillows, the CRT monitors on separate desks but coupled by a colorful festoon of multi-strand insulated wire. The young woman's eyes took on a glisten; she saw the room for what it was, a chamber for fucking, for binary fantasy. Indeed, she must have sensed it, even without the clues of those instances when he refused to answer her knock, and breaths were held on both sides of the quilted steel door.

She stood there like a spectre; she had been admitted to his dream life. She handed him Ed's sheaf and fled, back across the empty factory floor. But there came a day, as both sensed it might, when, once the thick door had closed with a punky click behind her, she handed him along with the business papers an additional message: a wadded warm handful of nylon underpants. Karen stood there with swarming eyes and lifted up her skirt, showing that her pants were in his hand and not on her. "We don't have much time," she said in a voice doubly fearful—that her absence from her workstation would be noticed and that he would spurn her.

She was small and sharp-featured, with abundant wiry hair and a worried, malnourished look. She was one of the thousands of young people feeding day after day on the sickly light of a cathode-ray tube. She plucked at Owen's heart. "Then let's not waste it," he said gamely.

She took off her gray flannel skirt and little penny loafers but kept on the white peds and pearl-pink silk blouse. If he kissed her, it was afterwards. When she carefully removed her glasses, she squinted, and above her pointed chin her lips thinned with habitual concentration. She said, "Hey, look at you," when she saw how ready he had become for her, his jeans quickly off, but then she was surprisingly slick, without foreplay. She must have carried a rising sexual excitement with her as she hurried across the blackened old floor, with its pattern of bolt scars and gleaming worn nail-heads, her underpants in her hand. Or had she slipped them off right at his door, on an impulse? What a brave generation hers was, that in a mere decade or so had freed itself from centuries of hang-ups.

"Why do you want this?" he asked her in a breathy moment stolen from one of their times together.

Pressed beneath him on the sofa, her thighs spread to embrace his hips, she was not afraid of seeming tactless. "With guys of your own generation," she explained, "there's all this negotiation. There's all this baby stuff and heavy crap about commitment. You feel trapped by your future and what you do with it. With you, there's no future. There's just this. Bim, bam, not even a thank-you-ma'am."

"How wonderful you are," he began.

"None of that, Mr. Mackenzie. I'm not wonderful. I'm functional, and I'm not downright ugly, but that's all. Face it: to you I'm a piece of ass."

"And me, what am I to you?"

Karen was silent. Owen felt time ticking. Phyllis might call. Or Ed. He had promised Ed to plot a revise of an insurance program that needed to combine actuarial probabilities with the sliding interest rate of their annuities, plugged into the Fed's interest rates, with algorithms that included double log functions.

"You, you're a beautiful old guy. I can see you as a kid. I love DigitEyes, what you did back then with those few kilobytes available. I love playing with it, when I start missing you and wishing we had more."

"Then you do miss me. You do want more."

"Of course; that's just biology. Biology is stupid. It wants babies. I don't want babies. Not yet. I just want your cock inside me now and then."

They could talk this way to each other only in the small sealed space, as sealed in by thick old walls as his brain was by his skull; they occupied it like the murmur of thoughts incessant in our heads.

"How often?" he asked. "When are you going to come again? I ought to know, so I'm sure to be here." Vanessa and he might have scheduled something; his four children had their appointments—their sports, their teeth.

"See, that's negotiations," Karen said. "I'll come when I want to, when I can. I'm getting paid to work here, don't forget. Other people watch you. People sense things."

"They do?"

"*I* did, didn't I? You knew, too. You weren't so surprised that time when I first hoisted my skirt."

She was right: even this bit of recapitulation, of purposefully hoarded memory, revealing that she had put some twos and twos together and evolved a plan of action, tainted the relationship. It was weeks before she appeared in his room again, and then shamefaced, as a suppliant; she had caved in to desire, and he didn't entirely like it that he had gained this power over her. He made her, though she said she had only a minute, take off her blouse and played with her little pert breasts, as she had played with DigitEyes. Their impulsive fling was beginning to deviate into sexual politics and a clutter of scrupulously kept old scores.

He had learned to have sex without kindness, without a grandiloquent gratitude. He could dislike Vanessa even as he milked her for revelations and wisdom. He guided her toward discussing the other women of their set, especially those he had known, to revisit them from another angle, in a cooler light. "Faye," she said. "I loved Faye, her giddy spirit, but she hadn't a clue how to dress. Like a ragbag on speed, and those ridiculous long skirts to hide her bow legs."

"I never noticed she had bow legs."

Vanessa laughed her laugh, a growl deep in her throat. "How could you, dearest, you were too focused on what was between them."

"I still feel guilty about her, making that mess of her life."

"Faye was a butterfly—how long do butterflies live? A day or two. She was born to be a victim. Anybody who stays married to an alcoholic likes being a victim. Then *you* victimized her, and you weren't the only one, I'm sure she told you. You're quite naïve to blame yourself."

"Alissa. What do you make of her?"

"What did *you* make of her? Or out of her, you could say."

She meant the baby. He said, "I can't say anything."

"Of course you can't. Nobody can. Hush-hush."

"Except that she's delicious, isn't she?"

"It depends on how much fat you have the stomach for."

He took a handful of the soft flesh at the side of Vanessa's stately waist, above the hip bone, and gave a sharp, cruel squeeze. Her grimace showed her eye teeth. They were in her home—a rare, risky occasion, with his red Stingray in her and Henry's two-car garage like a piece of gleaming meat, if the electronic door were triggered and slid up. The Slades' house, a 'fifties neo-colonial with garage and sunporch, on one of the newer post-war streets in Middle Falls, irritated him with its sanctimonious order, its many evidences of Henry's careful carpentry and groundskeeping and of Vanessa's efficient, traditional homemaking and of Victor's exemplary progress at Choate. The Slades' perversely solid marriage, built on some immovable mute foundation, rubbed him the wrong way. Didn't Henry know what a slut his wife was? Didn't his plodding, complacent obtuseness madden her? No, they seemed to have a perfect arrangement—every silver-framed photo of Victor and Garden Club prize ribbon and matching armchair and footstool in place, like the homes in Willow he had envied, with completely finished cellars.

"Ow," Vanessa said, but without ire, accepting his rebuke as deserved.

"Sorry. I never thought of Alissa as fat."

"Look at her some time. She hasn't managed to lose her pregnancy weight yet, and the child is four years old."

The child, Nina, walked and talked, pretty but somber, the levels of female subtlety in her multiplying, along with her little graces and pertnesses; in Owen's eyes she reminded him more and more of his own first-grade photos, that willingness to please mixed with something skeptical. But people continued to say she looked like Ian: his square frowning brow, his keen-eyed squint. Until she became too big for the stroller the putative father would preeningly push her everywhere, at a run, his face reddening above his goatee. His skinny bare legs grew sinewy. Fatherhood and exercise were Ian's way of coping with approaching fifty. Vanessa's mention of the child frightened Owen, and she knew it. "You sound jealous," he said to her. "Have you ever had a, you know, thing with Alissa?"

"We've had long girly chats, with more white wine than was good for either of our figures. What you don't seem to realize, Owen, is that erotic pleasure comes in all sorts of shades short of fucking. Alissa and I have been *cozy* from time to time."

"Is that why women go to bed with men, to be cozy?"

"You keep asking me that. The answer is, partly."

"When you do it with a woman, really, what happens? You use your mouths, or a dildo, or what? Describe it."

"Oh, darling Owen, I forget. Or let's pretend I do. Do you want to fuck me again before you go, or not? You've shrivelled down to nothing, worrying about what everybody else does."

"Don't forget," he reminded her, this complacent naked woman as thick-waisted and opaque as a plaster Venus, "you want me to deliver Trish Oglethorpe to you."

"*You* want that. Two women serving you."

"Actually, when I fantasize—can I tell you this?"

Vanessa said nothing.

"When I fantasize, it's a woman and two men. I'm not sure a man can really handle two women, but a woman can certainly handle two men."

"And you want to be that woman."

"*Ooh.* That hurts."

"It shouldn't, dearest. It's normal, or normally abnormal. Being your own sex is really rather boring after a while."

"You smug cunt. You're incredible."

"And who's to say," she pleasantly went on, "where one sex ends and the other begins? When we're tiny eggs we're all females, then some lucky ones get that Y chromosome that turns them into tadpoles with a penis. It's all rather mucky, like my cunt right now. But come in, darling, please. Fuck me up to my eyeballs."

"Vanessa, you're incredible. You'll say anything."

"Well, at least I've got you hard again."

Sex was easiest to manage in his head, away from all the furniture, the disgusting marital spoor, the telltale slant of light at the window shades, the village bells tolling the hours, calling the children to school and back again. His favorite sight in Middle Falls came between seven-thirty and eight, the children going off to school, walking in packs or gathered at bus stops with their mothers, their backpacks and colorful synthetic garb at such a festive remove from the dismal knickers and dark cloth coats of 'thirties Willow, children trudging off as if to a blacking factory. At night, lying beside Phyllis in their queen-sized bed, she, to judge from her regular deep breathing, asleep, he could stage-manage himself and Vanessa and Trish Oglethorpe, her skittish runner's body and her upper lip like a flesh-bud evolved to lure men into the chase. His intuition told him that Trish possessed an extra dose of that pliant, chasable quality; it went with the X chromosome. He and Vanessa could tie her up for more exciting access. He pictured mouths, and the orifices below, and vectorized patches of resilient skin, and three pairs of eyes widened in the general stretch and astonishment of it. Muck, Vanessa had said, the muck and the muddle, telling him he loved it, we all do, the mothering muck. Then, his brain losing images and recovering them while his hand kept his grip on his half-asleep prick, teasing and then seizing, Owen would come into a handkerchief spread where his ejaculation could hit. At the crest of sensation, sweat popping from his pores, he recognized that Phyllis's proximate warmth was part of it, the muck, the coziness, as her rhythmic light breathing—light, as her speech was light, not wishing to force itself crassly upon the world—betrayed no sign of awareness of his thumping climax. But she was there, like the finite sum of one of Euler's infinite series.

"Why don't we ever make love any more?" she one day asked.

"Don't we? I feel we do."

"It's been weeks. Am I getting bad breath or something?"

"Not at all. I've never smelled anything on your breath except peppermint and chamomile tea."

"Well, then. Let's go. The children are out of the house from eight to three-thirty. Why don't you come back here at noon for lunch? I don't mention the morning because I know you hate waking up."

"You want this to*day*?" He tried to think if anything was scheduled with Vanessa; there was no telling when Karen might drop by. "What's gotten into you?" he asked, stalling.

Phyllis took no offense at the question, though she blushed—that movement of blood below her slant cheek-bones that he associated with the student princess, offering herself to be carried away. "Nothing," she said. "Just affection. You look so handsome lately."

He saw a welcome opportunity to argue. "Oh, now and not ever before?"

"Before, yes, but, not to sound like Ian, you had a nerdy quality, as though it hurt your eyes to look away from the computer—as if we were all slightly unreal to you. You don't have that so much any more."

"Well, thanks. I guess."

Now she did take offense. "Forget I said anything," she said. "I was just trying to be wifely. I'm human, you know."

"Baby!" He went to her, suddenly stung. An image in two dimensions in his mind had popped into the third; he had forgotten she was human, he admired her so abstractly, as an image from his past, a faded route to his present condition. He hugged her; her face, at near the height of his own, felt hot; both their faces felt on the verge of tears. "You're *super*human," he told her, hoping to break them into laughter. This failing, he said, "Let's make a date. I think there's a problem with today; I have to check my calendar at work."

"You don't want to," Phyllis said, right as always. "I'm *not* superhuman, I'm a failure in every respect except that I bore four healthy children. But even they, I didn't do much of a job. We're letting them grow up like weeds."

There was truth in this, but against it he could have set their myriad usual gestures of parenting: the help with homework, the tucking in at night, the rote prayer to get their anxious small souls through to morning, the family trips to Nantucket and Disney World and Expo 67 in Montreal, the summer rentals in Maine, the countless lessons paid for, the countless evening meals shared in something like hilarity. From the outside, seen through the windows of the warm and expensive house on Partridgeberry Road, judged from the swing sets and hockey skates and dollhouses and golf clubs to be found in the basement, Owen and Phyllis had given all the signs of parenthood, but they had not, like some—like Owen's own parents, perhaps— *lived* through their children, making the leap out of the ego into the DNA chain. Ian and Alissa, for instance, after their rocky patch, had submerged themselves in the needs and deeds of Nina and her two older siblings. Owen and Phyllis were alike in that their pet child was the child within, who still clamored for nurturing. "Tomorrow," he promised her. "I just remembered, today's my day to have lunch with Ed. He's full of gloom these days."

"Tomorrow's my day for tennis at the club with Alissa, Vanessa, and Imogene. Except Imogene can't play and got Trish for a substitute."

"The next day, then," he said, "or at night, after Floyd and Eve are in bed." Gregory was a sophomore at Brown, and Iris in her first year at Smith.

"At night I get dopey," Phyllis said. "By the day after next I'll have forgotten what it's all about."

"What *is* it all about?" he asked her.

"That I love you?" she offered shyly.

He turned her question into a statement: "And I love you." To himself he thought, *I am ruining this woman's life.*

"It's this damn town," she said, petulantly. "Everywhere you turn, it's there, interfering."

"It's just a town," he said.

"No, Owen. It's not. Its people don't have enough to do, except make mischief."

"Well, that's prosperity," he told her. "You'd rather have Communism?"

For some time Owen had been thinking he must break with Vanessa before that affair exploded and repeated the mess after Faye. He couldn't look far into the Slades' strange marriage but believed that, like his own, it would not accommodate open infidelity. This was no hippie commune, no rock-ribbed Republican swap club in the snowbound fastness of the upper Midwest. A tactful skein of attraction and undeclared liaison lay over these Easterners. Owen had lately been attracted to Imogene Bisbee, a significant drinker with a raucous whiskey-cracked voice and graying raven hair pulled back strictly from a central parting, as in a daguerreotype of an ancestor. She had blue blood, and an injured grace. Her family had the money that supported Roscoe's ineffectual little lawyering in town, a matter of friends' wills and a slight grip, won through long-term residence, on Town Hall's business. In the late stages of a party Imogene had begun to bump up against him. Once she had blearily grabbed one of his thumbs and asked, with that affecting crack in her voice, "What don't you like about me, Owen?"

"Nothing," he had answered. "I mean, there's nothing I don't like. How is Roscoe's new snow-blower doing?"

Trish Oglethorpe came up to them, intruding possessively, though he had not slept with her and his visions of enlisting her in a threesome with Vanessa had ebbed. But some afterimage of his flirtation, and some faint resonance from his masturbatory fantasies, carrying across town at night through all the sleeping television aerials, drew her to him, hovering at his side attentively, as if waiting for his next move. Both women looked at him with a kind of vexed expectancy. He said, "I'll let you two talk tennis," and backed away and sought Phyllis in the kitchen, perched high on a beechwood stool, talking with Ed and Henry Slade as in the old MIT days he would find her ensconced in a smoky Chinese eatery with Jake Lowenthal and Bobby Sprock.

If Owen was going to make a serious move on Imogene, he needed to be quits with Vanessa. But would he ever find another woman like her, such a frank sexual friend, so unblinkingly frontal, with such imperturbable matte skin and a clitoris that functioned like a prick, doing the attacking for him? The same effrontery and energy made her locally omnipresent; she was co-chairperson, as they called it, of the fund drive to build an annex—more office space, less for doctors than for the proliferating administrators and bookkeepers of health insurance—on the United Falls Hospital, which was located in town but also served the rude hamlet of Lower Falls and those residents of semi-suburban Upper Falls who did not want to make the drive into Hartford. Most everyone wanted to see the local institution thrive and survive, as medical costs and the efficiencies of greater volume were thinning out small-town hospitals—the same economic trends that were extermi-

nating small-town movie theatres and unaffiliated banks
and independent office-supply stores, toy stores, and book
shops. Shopping had shifted to the areas between towns,
to malls that gobbled up several farms at a time. Even
the gold-lettered Woolworth's, the sundries-packed River
Street outpost of a corporate empire as presumably endur-
ing as the Ford Motor Company and American Tel and Tel,
had become depressing: only a few muttering, demoralized
parakeets and canaries remained in the pet section, which
once had twittered like a jungle, alive with the husky odor
of birdseed and droppings and with the rustle of gerbils in
their squeaky wheels and pungent nests of wood shavings.

The hospital, like the still-unregionalized Middle Falls
High School, held memories for the citizens. The Mackenzies' youngest, wistful, sensitive Eve, had been born there,
and when Phyllis at forty had her cancer scare (a benign
cyst, whose removal barely left a scar) and Gregory at four-
teen his broken ankle and Owen at thirty-four his nearly
burst appendix, the hospital had taken them in and minis-
tered to their pains and fears. The intense mutual involve-
ment of their particular set of friends did not preclude
identification with the larger community. Owen loved the
aging commercial clutter of River Street, and saw his firm
as a chapter in the town's industrial history. He and Phyllis
many times, on the excuse of a child participant, had
cheered at high-school sports events. One cheer, driven
home with many lusty arm-pumps and pom-pom shakes
from the white-socked cheerleaders, went, "Not too lean
and not too fat, Middle Falls is where it's at! Not too big
and not too small, Middle Falls beats one"—index fingers
raised, wagging—"and"—expansive arm gesture, fingers
spread—"*all*!" Since the time when Owen had been a parti-
san teen-ager at Willow High, some slithery dance moves, a

legacy of the 'sixties, had been included amid the exhorta-
tive flailing and spread-eagled leaps of the young maenads
in their pleated skirts and bulky sweaters, but the essential
conservatism of youthful rites struck him—the same dwindled outdoor shouts, the same melancholy scent of torn
earth carrying into the sidelines from the gridiron or soccer
field, the same tribal hope that victory today meant victory
forever, in life's great game.

The fund drive had been successful, subscribed across the
village's social spectrum. There was a triumphant wind-up
mêlée in the hospital's courtyard, in fortunate April sunshine. It had been a gamble to hold the party for workers
and significant contributors outdoors; but there were so
many, and the dusty function room upstairs at the town hall
would have seemed drearily official, and the downstairs
rooms of the three-story Georgian Federal mansion that
housed the historical society too elitist. In the sunstruck
late-afternoon crowd Owen instantly spotted Trish Oglethorpe. Even as he turned to avoid her, she hurried up to
him. "Owen! I never see you any more!"

"I'm around."

"I mean see you to *talk* to."

Apologetically, he said, "I guess we've been hunkered
down for the winter." *We:* he and Phyllis, man and wife,
more and less than a real person.

"Wasn't it awful! All that snow. Dwight says we should
move to the Carolinas. Especially now that the local leash
laws have become so strict." Their rampaging golden
retrievers, everybody knew, had been killing neighbors' cats
and raiding a riding stable a quarter-mile away, gorging on
the horse chow in the manger.

Trish had a new, tousled hairdo; sparks flew from its
cedar-red strands in the sunlight. Her polka-dot dress

was short with an old-fashioned daring; her skinny legs descended into big-buckled duckbill-toed pumps of white patent leather. She looked like an escapee from a comic strip, and Owen had always had a fondness for comic strips. "What brings you here?" he asked.

"Didn't you know? Vanessa got me to sub for someone on her Special Donations Committee who resigned. She's a slavedriver, I can tell you."

"So people say."

"But she's also a mother hen. It really is remarkable, how she does all she does."

"Yes," he agreed, trying to imagine just what she meant. Recalling their conversation at the Bisbees' last fall, which Trish seemed to be resuming with an enthusiasm she had withheld at the time, Owen told her, "Speaking of women prison guards, now we have a woman party head."

"Yes," she said. "Too bad she's such a conservative."

"You're against conservatives, now."

"Only when they're boring grocers' daughters," Trish said, turning her head to show him her profile, underslung and sexy. Her upper lip looked almost prehensile. Her style of talk, at least, had been loosened up.

"Speaking of boring conservatives, poor Ford. It's just about over in Vietnam," Owen said, not quite knowing how to stimulate this new, subtly radicalized Trish.

She ignored this offering. "*Owen*," she said, poking his chest sharply. "You *must* see a movie called *Shampoo*, with Warren Beatty. Dwight and I *loved* it. It's *so* outrageous!"

This was more like the stiff, herky-jerky old Trish. Yet she gave off the natural perfume, the easy animation, the sense of a deftly resumed connection, that a woman you have slept with gives off. Had he slept with her in a dream? Had his fantasies of a naked threesome somehow travelled to her through the village's veins? She seemed in her dolly outfit to explode with self-delight, and to verge, shiny-eyed, on teasing him, like the girls on the walk to elementary school. He had to back off and consider this new factor in his life-complicating sexual equations. Had Vanessa, seeing his feeble initiative fail, seduced this coltish newcomer herself, and were the two of them waiting, glowingly nude yet primly upright, like the de Poitier sisters in Clouet's double portrait, for him to find them? Villages have inglenooks, root cellars, attics where mattresses covered with striped ticking quietly wait for the orgy to begin.

The charitable crowd's clamor rose as it soaked up more cheap champagne beneath the fifteen-foot painted phallic image, displayed for months on the hospital façade, of a thermometer whose red of pledges had finally mounted to the very top. Owen spotted the rueful face of Imogene Bisbee, in her Emily Dickinson hairdo, wistfully searching the crowd for someone who would quicken her life into romantic meaning. She would have to wait, he said to himself, for there was no more room in his life, with Trish apparently still on his hook. He scanned all the donor faces, sallow and giddy in their bath of cool spring sunshine, hoping not to find Karen Jazinski among them. Ed, a big contributor from the company's funds, might have brought her along in an E-O entourage, and if sensitive spying eyes saw Owen and Karen standing together they would spot the magnetic current, the telltale electricity, between their bodies.

But he did not see her. Instead, Ian Morrissey came up to him, his goatee whiter and the hair on his head longer, befitting his recent decision to become an easel "art" painter and reduce magazine illustrating to his spare time—just the really tempting commissions, he bragged, from old buddies in the trade. He announced, "Alissa's stuck at home with Nina, a fever of one hundred one, throwing up half the night."

"How old is she now?" Owen asked, politely.

"Five, for Chrissakes. Makes you feel ancient."

Owen suggested, ironically, "You should have brought her here to the emergency room."

Ian didn't hear irony, unless it was his own. "Naa, basically she's healthy as a horse. Built like a little brick shit-house. The spitting image of my father, it turns out. He was a stonemason, I'm not ashamed of it." Stale champagne flavored his breath, exploded bubbles.

Owen felt a pang, imagining Alissa and the small girl and this flatulent blowhard together, a holy trinity, like his parents and himself on those Sunday walks in Willow. "Well, I hope she feels better," he told Ian.

"She's bound to. Like I say, tough as nails. Both of my grandfathers lived to be ninety."

"Tell Alissa we all missed her." Just Alissa's name, its kissy sibilance, gave a gentle jolt to Owen's mind, and the image of a subcutaneously padded back divided by a spine with tender extremities. He had a feeling of comradeship, of consorting with other veterans of the same campaign, as he moved through this crowd, his fellow townsfolk for fifteen years, a loving and loved feeling that bounced back not just from the women he knew but from the downtown mer-chants in their slippery polyester suits, the jeweller and the liquor-store owner, the surefooted roofer doubling as bar-tender at a white-covered table, and the sturdy nurse, now retired, who eight years ago, when Owen had his appen-dix removed, would bestow upon him the mercy of more Demerol in the dead of the night. Hospital orderlies and receptionists brought some brown and olive faces to this festive throng. He couldn't find Phyllis in it, though her fair head usually floated a few inches above most others. He had loved her, initially, for being tall, tall and female and young. Her curious apparent absence gave him a premonitory stab of guilt; he felt unworthy of his happiness, confused by it. This guilty bliss is life?

Shadows were lengthening. The air was turning chilly. Vanessa, who as co-chairperson had already given an efficient speech of many-sided thanks into a defective, squawking portable sound system, came up to him. She wore a teal-green shot-silk pants suit and had at her side a handsome man in a reversed collar. "Owen *dear*, I'm not sure you've met the Reverend Mister Arthur Larson. He's rather new at Epiphany Episcopal but was a splendid help with the special contributors in his flock. He helped us pin them down."

The clergyman shook Owen's hand. His grip would be, Owen intuited, exquisitely adjusted to the gender and size of the gripped, to his or her economic significance in the town, and to the strength of the presumed friendship with influential Vanessa. Owen received a warm but not fervent squeeze. Reverend Larson's handsomeness seemed something evenly sprayed on, a water-resistant layer of it, from the satin shine on his narrow black shoes to the leathery lustre of his wind-buffed face, that of a weekday outdoorsman. The shirt beneath his collar was not the usual sooty black but a suave dove-gray; the thick hair on his head reminded Owen, in its resilience and tightly matted knit, of some middle-sized, tufty-backed, curly-tailed dog. Larson was still in his thirties, and firm but unassuming in demeanor. This was a man whose way was secure within the Lord's way.

"Owen," he said, repeating the name from Vanessa's introduction, as if fixing it to a roll of remembrance in his mind. His eyes were kindly glints bracketed by the beginnings of creases. Owen liked him; he liked most clergy, for holding off the unthinkable while we dally through life.

Larson moved a half-step to the side, revealing a woman with him, who had tactfully lagged behind, on the other side from Vanessa. She was compact and silken, like Elsie, with a touch of double chin, but also radiated the inscrutable, somewhat humorless vitality Owen had last admired in Ginger Bitting. Her handshake startled him, those fine female fingers coolly sliding into his palm. Her eyes were the sharp aquamarine of, in Willow, the tinted wineglasses and scallop-edged little glass candy dishes that houseproud aunts and elderly female neighbors would set on the locked upper edge of the lower window sash to catch the light. In his schooled and preening baritone, dipping a bit deeper into his chest than mere communication demanded, the other man announced to Owen, "And this is my good wife, Julia."

xiii. *You Don't Want to Know*

I N HASKELLS CROSSING, people die. They show
   you how to do it. They do it out of sight, among professional nurses and faithful retainers usually, though in
rare instances they drop dead without warning while, say,
pushing up the hill on the thirteenth hole, or in the middle
of a nap after a boozy Sunday lunch. Death never loses its
quality of unexpectedness. Life does not expect it; the living
mind cannot conceive of it. Some citizens die soon after
elaborate cosmetic surgery, or a difficult multiple-bypass
operation, or an expensive house renovation, preparing for
the years ahead; they die regardless.

In church, which Owen and Julia attend regularly, though
for her less regularly than when she was a clergyman's wife,
the process can be seen at work. The dying, Sunday after
Sunday, are by increments more hesitant and emaciated as
they totter back from the communion rail with defiant eyes
and munching jaws. Next, they can no longer make it to
the communion rail, or cannot kneel, because of a dropsi-
cal knee or an excruciating hip, and take the wafer into
their lips standing up, like Roman Catholics or Lutherans,

or else—the next stage—the minister and his acolyte bring it to them afterwards in the pews. At this break in the customary ceremony there is no other sound than that of the minister murmuring, no other motion than that of the communicant's shaky white head bobbing and her hand, if she is of the old high-church school, making the sign of the cross after receiving the wafer and wine. The men lose color in their faces, turning a stony gray as their eyes sink in the sockets; the women, who even in life's last stages can draw upon the fleshy tints of makeup, show a glittering gaze above withered but ruddy cheeks. Dying flatters some women, highlighting the austerity and doughtiness that were always theirs. Others, like remarkably rich Florence Sprang, appear as painted, overdressed grotesques hobbling up the aisle between a cane and a retainer to receive their portion of the body and blood of Jesus Christ.

Finally, even the most stoic and determined communicant cannot make it to Sunday service and is present there only as a name in the Prayers of the People, as one of the many—too many, it is whispered—names read in a flat voice by the day's leader, after the formula *For the aged and infirm, for the widowed and orphans, and for the sick and the suffering, let us pray to the Lord.* Or, in Form III, *Have compassion on those who suffer from any grief or trouble.* In the drone of names that follows, "Florence" democratically mingles with a host of ailing and imperilled others, Erin and Jameeka, Shonda and Lara, Dolores and Jade, Bruce and Hamad and Todd, who, though never met by her, are included in Epiphany's outreach program in downtown Cabot City as they suffer, in shelters and subsidized apartments, the ruinous effects of drugs and alcohol, obesity and AIDS, promiscuity and bipolar disorder. Next, Florence's name, its surname restored, figures for a time in the list following the rote words *For those who have died in the hope of the resurrection, and for all the departed, let us pray to the Lord.* The congregation responds, in entreaty to the huge hypothetical entity that hangs over these village proceedings, *Lord, have mercy*, or, of the departed, secure in their coffins and urns, *Let light perpetual shine upon them.*

Light perpetual, in a universe where, the latest scientific reports indicate, expansion, propelled by some unknown factor called the dark force, is accelerating to the point where the stars will eventually be invisible to one another. By other proven laws they will burn out and drift as meaningless ash-heaps of forever inert matter. No one follows the latest turns of empirical cosmology more keenly than the village clergyman, hoping for some peep, around a cryptic equation's corner, of divine mercy. One of the burdens, as Owen sees it, that the modern faithful shoulder is the monstrously enlarged context of time. Saint Paul thought the last trumpet would sound within the lifetime of some living—"Behold, I show you a mystery; we shall not all sleep, but we shall all be changed, in a moment, in the twinkling of an eye, at the last trump"—and medieval men could still picture their intact skeletons clambering up, gumlessly grinning, out of their graves. The next world was around the corner, almost visitable, like the vaults beneath the cathedral floor. Now it must be relegated to another dimension, joining those subatomic strings whose mathematical invention may at last solve the riddle of existence: why did nothingness, the ground note of cosmic reality, the substratum that everlastingly endures, choose so troublesomely to violate itself and give birth to anything at all? The church in strategic retreat abandons the cosmos to physics, and takes refuge in the personal—the cosmos of fragile, evanescent consciousness. In that shadow-world, infinitely prolonged, Florence and Jameeka and Lara and Bruce consort, bathed in God's indiscriminate love, and together mount from strength to strength. *If after the manner of men I have fought with beasts at Ephesus, what advantageth it me, if the dead rise not? let us eat and drink; for to-morrow we die.* In the next verse, Paul ominously adds, *Be not deceived: evil communications corrupt good manners.*

Owen and Julia, as it happened, befriended mostly older people when they moved to Haskells Crossing. Couples their own age, discovering that this polite middle-aged couple did not drink or know any local gossip, tended not to have them back after the first invitation to cocktails. The elderly, though, having arrived by way of illness or AA at their own renunciations, found the new "young" couple fresh and mannerly, and had them to seasonal parties where Owen and Julia were, save for grandchildren underfoot, the youngest guests present. In the cheerful crowd of these elders, jubilantly full of obsolescent lore, the great harvester was already active. Funerals became a familiar occasion—the Episcopal rite, stretched to accommodate informal, sometimes irreverent and hilarious, reminiscences by old friends and aging offspring. There would be a service leaflet, with anodyne verses on the back and in the middle the hymn numbers and prayers and on the front a fascinating photograph of the deceased in the fullness of life, at the tiller of his boat in Maine, or posed by a laden rose trellis, laughing in a sunshine whose neutrinos have reached the star Vega by now, or holding the bridle of a horse, itself deceased, displaying a wild eye and flaring brute nostril. Owen was fascinated by what constituted, for the rich, their happiest, summary moments. Country pleasures: millions of dollars organized into a quest for purity, for aboriginal innocence. Rarely was an indoor photo cho-

sen, or one snapped in the course of a workday or a ceremony, a fortieth anniversary or a sumptuous retirement
party. If the image was taken from the smooth-skinned
youth of the recently dead, it was almost always in a sporting pose—in whites beside a tennis net, or holding a silver
trophy with a smile no less bright. The afterlife, the implication was, would be a country club. After the service, the
widow or widower or oldest child still in this locality would
host a party, at the spacious former home or at the yacht
club or the country club, where remembrance of the
departed yielded to forgetful gaiety and bitter complaint of
how the land-owning, tax-paying residents of Haskells
Crossing were disadvantaged in their struggles with those
corrupt, or just careless, and in any case *petty* politicians
ensconced in the power chambers of Cabot City. The party,
if this was a private home, would have in its view a sparkling
slice of the sea, that omnivorous imperturbable image of
the eternity that awaits each celebrant, each survivor.

One of the earliest acquaintances of the new Mackenzies—Mackenzies II, if marriages were movies, or, if
computer programs, Mackenzies 2.1—had been Bumpy
Wentworth, a small plump woman with thinning blue hair
and a gift for mimicry. She had been called Bumpy in her
girlhood, by an aggrieved younger brother with whom she
was sharing, along with a substantial governess, the back
seat of their father's Peerless. Photographs from 1925, when
she was ten, do attest to a pugnacious sisterly heft. She
became a benign, comfortably proportioned woman, but
the name travelled with her out from the nuclear family
into day school, boarding school, finishing school, and marriage. In the conservative fashion of the region, where a
genial male chauvinism labelled the tribal females like pets,
"Bumpy," with its connotation of "bumptious," stuck. So

did, among her peers in Haskells Crossing, the designations Muffin, Jonesie, Snuggles, and Bunch: these were all dignified women of means in their sixties or seventies.

Now, if Julia had any weakness, it was for light-hearted female friendship. She had been passed from her father, a New Haven banker and high churchman whose three other offspring were boys, straight to her husband, fresh from divinity school, as an exemplary woman: from model daughter and student into perfect helpmeet and homemaker without a break. The one slip of her life had been falling in love with Owen, which she later construed as rescuing him from a desperately immoral life. He was ready to be rescued, but she was not ready to be at the center of a scandal, and to be shunned not only by her husband's horrified parishioners but by, with ostentatious indignation, respectable women of Middle Falls like Vanessa Slade, Imogene Bisbee, Trish Oglethorpe, and Alissa Morrissey. So it was a joyful relief for Julia to fall in, a hundred miles to the northeast, with the likes of dithery, slyly witty Bunch Hapgood, gaunt, gentle Jonesie Wilkins, and kindly, sensible Bumpy Wentworth; over sherry, the younger woman would laugh until tears blinded her at their imitations, with appropriate accents, of Irish maids and Italian gardeners in Father's employ and even of the dear late husband's stuffy, miserly Wasp business partners. Julia was virtually a girl to them, and Mrs. Wentworth saw to it that she, with Owen trailing along, met the right people and, in time, joined the right clubs. As the New England seasons picturesquely lumbered through Haskells Crossing, and the troubles of the Mackenzies' half-dozen children—four of his, two of hers—were confided and then soothed and chuckled away over tea, and funeral after funeral put mutual acquaintances to rest, Bumpy was always there. In her mid-eighties, she visibly began to lose weight and to weaken; alopecia obliged her to wear a wig, about which she was very droll, debating with Julia whether peach or apricot would be the most tasteful shade. Even when taken to the hospital with breathing difficulties, the old woman had been merry; at Julia's last visit, Bumpy got her to giggling unstoppably at the comic side of a tea-pot tempest in the altar guild, which Julia, one of the guild's mainstays, had been taking too seriously. As light faded in the hospital windows, she sank back on her pillow and patted Julia's hand with her withered own. She promised her that she was liking her new medicine and was going to get her strength back in rehab on the other side of Cabot City. She had been depressed but could feel her good spirits returning.

So it was in the aggrieved, incredulous voice of a child who has been tricked that Julia, replacing the receiver after a phone call early the next morning, came back to the bed-room and announced to Owen, "Bumpy died!" Tears stood out in her eyes, making their aquamarine more vivid. Julia was a woman who even in the worst of times didn't cry.

Middle Falls had seen other scandals and breakups, but this was of a novel order, a clergyman's wife and a coolly arranged double split. Owen's second son and third child, fifteen-year-old Floyd, named after his grandfather the accountant, brought home from school the news that Reverend Larson and his wife, of all people, were splitting up. Jennifer Pajasek, a girl in his grade who sometimes babysat for them, said they'd been fighting a lot and the children—a girl and a boy—were very upset.

Floyd could not see, as he relayed this news to his father in a voice of puzzled, titillated innocence, that it was news about himself, the first crack of a doom about to descend on his own head. In a parsonage two miles away, events had been set in motion. Owen had been drawn into that pit of fatality whose rim had been marked so many years ago by the sound of Danny Hoffman pulling the trigger of his father's Army-issue Colt .38 before dawn, two houses up Mifflin Avenue. Now this was at four-thirty in the afternoon, on a bright September day at the kitchen table in the six-bedroom, four-bathroom Mackenzie house on Partridgeberry Road, but the realm was the same, the realm of irrevocable real harm. He was his own child's executioner. The gun was still hidden behind his back but in a few days would have to be taken out and fired. His son would become, like Buddy Rourke, fatherless, his father having strayed. Phyllis already knew. The town would soon know. There was no hiding, no going back. Beyond the kitchen windows, blameless life sounded its songs, as detached from human guilt as a dream—starlings clattering as they gathered in flocks for migration, insects invisibly stridulating as the summer wound up its business.

Julia led the way—the first to spill the beans, the first to separate, the first to divorce. Though Owen desired her, and saw in her his chance to settle safely into married concupiscence and obedience, he might have lagged indefinitely, keeping women in the air like a juggler's gaudy balls, had she not shamed him out of it. Shock at her own fall had galvanized her; the doubt-free momentum acquired when she had been virtuous carried her along. She never looked back, and he weakly followed.

The announcements to his children, the move to an apartment in the slummy row houses across the river from the old mill, the interview with a jaded, non-judgmental Hartford divorce lawyer—these all had an underwater quality. He moved numbly through a thickness of others' pain, scarcely recognizing himself. In this thicker element, he felt oddly light. There was a sensation that, in entering the drastic element—the fatality he confused with the vacant lot next to his first home, where his glasses in their dew-soaked case had been miraculously returned to him, convincing him that his life was charmed—Owen had begun his delayed adulthood. Leaving Phyllis in their mid-forties was the first adult action of his life. To be an adult is to be a killer. Pacifists and non-combatants are just fooling themselves, letting others do the dirty work.

Vanessa, meeting him downtown at noon, outside The Ugly Duckling, said simply, unsmiling, "Good for you, dear," but kept walking. Alissa, crossing Branch Street to the elementary school with little Nina in tow, asked the child, "Want to show Mr. Mackenzie where your tooth came out?" Karen Jazinski had knocked once, that summer, on the door of Owen's cell at E-O; since Julia was with him on the couch, looking with her decisive brunette coloring less like Manet's *Olympia* than Goya's *Naked Maja*, he couldn't open the door, and Karen, perhaps sensing the pair of held breaths within, didn't come knocking again. Trish Oglethorpe, for some odd reason, led the local forces of indignation, and passed by Julia in the supermarket as if she had been a wilting head of lettuce. Roscoe and Imogene Bisbee snubbed the new couple at the Silver Spoon, an overpriced candlelit restaurant in Upper Falls, where Owen and Julia had thought they were safe from recognition, among the faceless tract-dwellers.

This interim of disjunction dragged on for a year, and then there was worse. You don't want to know. The papers and news hours are full of family breakdowns and intra-mural murder. Within the broken marriages there were grieving, backwards-looking interviews, not without their exhilarations of drunken truth-telling and wry hilarity. At a later, more legal stage, there were bitter differences over the division of property—especially bitter for the Mackenzies, who had stumbled into prosperity and been quick to turn it into cultural artifacts. Each Oriental carpet, abstract painting, and fifty-dollar art book had been jointly selected or, in the case of the books, bestowed with loving inscriptions as birthday or Christmas presents. A copy of *Finnegans Wake* from Phyllis to Owen for his twenty-fifth birthday—a tall square-spined volume, the front and back of the jacket identical, with Joyce's fifteen-page list of typographical errors appended to the 1939 text—prompted an especially bitter dispute, though neither of them had made his or her way through more than five pages of it. They had both thought it would be more mathematical than it was, the author being one of the few whose brain could rank with that of the great mathematicians; but the holy text was all music, the music of phonetically misspelled speech, in a broad Irish accent and all of Europe peeping through the puns. In the era of their courtship and marriage, this book had represented the epitome of culture—fanatically wrought, monolithically aloof.

For the Larsons, there was the problem of the parsonage. She and the children needed it, yet the church owned it, and part of Larson's pay was the occupation of it. Christmas, most inconveniently, approached with its spate of holiday entertainments, from youth groups to Golden Agers, at which the minister's wife traditionally presides. Part of a minister's obligation, in those benighted days, was to provide a presentable wife, willing and able to second his social services to the parish. Julia fulfilled her duty so smoothly that not a punch cup was dropped or a single member of the

junior choir cheated of his or her share of eggnog and ginger cookies, even as Owen and his bed in his dishevelled
rooms on Covenant Street awaited her. When at last she
arrived, still in the chaste gray knit dress of the parsonage
hostess, she breezily explained to him, "A woman is used to
living on several levels. Compartmentalizing is part of her
biology. It's not hypocrisy; it's just plain decency not to
show all of yourself at any one time. What a fussy, jealous
boyfriend you are, Owen! It's thrilling for me, to be associated with anyone so innocent."

"After Arthur, you mean?"

"Well—don't let this hurt your feelings, precious, but a
clergyman is hard to shock. He hears the worst sort of
thing, every day of the week. People love telling him, for
some reason."

To this period, perhaps, as Julia continued a show of
cohabitation with her illusionless husband, could be traced
the dreams that afflicted Owen even twenty-five years later,
of her slipping away beneath the social web of the town, of
his simply being misplaced by her as she went through the
familiar motions of being a clergyman's loyal wife.

It was the church itself, in its wisdom, that brought the
awkwardness of the situation to the parson's attention, and
that came up with a solution: the head of the vestry, a
retired and widowed former Providence banker, occupied a
needlessly large mansion facing the Middle Falls Common;
Reverend Larson was most welcome to stay with him until
Mrs. Larson and the children could find suitable housing,
preferably in some other town. When school finally ended,
in June of the bicentennial summer, Julia and little Tommy
and Rachel went to live with Julia's sister in Old Lyme. This
season of separation, during which Owen's plighted mistress managed under her sister's reproachful eye only a few

hurried letters, may also have contributed to his persisting nightmares of losing her, of their connection simply breaking and falling silent as did those first delicate telegraph cables laid on the craggy bottom of the Atlantic Ocean. Her letters, impeccably typed on blue stationery with an electric typewriter, worried him in their sunniness and ease; there were no second thoughts or confessed regrets, no careful ambiguities. She loved being back in sight of the sea. The river and its falls had been put behind her. Rachel was taking riding lessons and loving it; Tommy, always so timid of the water, was now able to swim the full length of the swimming pool at the funky little beach club. Arthur, who often came to visit, wasn't sure, after this, he was going to continue in the ministry. Epiphany, though too polite to say so, was counting the days until he left. Despite Saint Paul's advice against marriage, divorced ministers, at this stage of church custom, were hard to place, even in an inner-city parish. One of the vestrymen, a retired businessman, had told Arthur of wonderful opportunities, if he was willing to move closer to Manhattan, for former clergymen in public relations or company personnel management.

The Mackenzies, adrift on their wrecked marriage, marvelled at the way the sea parted for Julia: she was walking to the other shore on miraculously dry land. Even in separate residences, Owen and Phyllis shared the same mental space, a collegiate kind of space inherited from a big house on a small lot on a Cambridge street used as a short-cut between Garden Street and Mass. Avenue. A genteel-bohemian decency, extending to the end of life the student quest for knowledge, had been the communicated ideal. Colin Goodhue had become a professor of Romance languages at Cornell. He had married a Frenchwoman, and they spent every August in Provence. Phyllis's mother and

father had both died recently—only months apart, as sometimes happens with long-attached couples—and being gentle with Phyllis in her newly orphaned state had been part
of Owen's rationale for not hurrying the divorce process,
with its distasteful facilitators: lawyers, furniture movers,
child psychologists.

A fog of deferred intention had descended upon his
mind. Of the long interim while he shuttled back and forth
between the headless household on Partridgeberry Road
and his unkempt semi-bachelor pad on the other side of
the Chunkaunkabaug, in a four-story firetrap populated by
elderly Polish widowers and overweight single mothers, he
remembered little. With a numbed mind he met the surly
feigned indifference of his two older, collegiate children,
and the eager, round-eyed, yet subtly stilted affability of
his two younger when he descended, in his now distinctly
scuffed and rattling red Stingray, to glance over their homework or carry them off to a movie. Though his upbringing
had been only perfunctorily religious, he could hear the
prayers of his two younger children for his return rustling
above him like the wingbeats of swifts trapped in the old
farmhouse chimney. Phyllis was alternately despondent and
jauntily brave in her abandoned state, sharing his sensation
of an unreal interim. She had never quite fit in in Middle
Falls, disdaining the middlebrow society with the offhand
politesse of a professor's daughter, but some of the local
women now rallied to her, and not all of them the ones he
had slept with, though these were the most companionably
scornful of Julia. "She utterly just doesn't get it, as if she's
from outer space . . . Those eyes of hers, they give me the
absolute shivers . . . Parading around in the Acme as if she
dared me not to look at her . . . That poor husband of hers,
she must be setting him up for sainthood, Roscoe talked to

him the longest time and couldn't get him to say a word against her": Phyllis relayed fragments like this to Owen, as if such cattiness, which had once been a kind of music to him, a murmur of initiation, would bring him back. True, he would awake in his squalid room—the odors of other people's hot plates seeping through the walls, and the squalling of fatherless infants—with the same homesick gnawing in his stomach that he had felt those freshman months at MIT, hung in space by the implacable laws of growth, of aging. But then, as now, he had a mission: then, to survive, to not go back to Pennsylvania, to gain a degree and a career and, as things developed, the willowy girl he glimpsed in the hall. Now, as then, his mission was not purely selfish, and had to do with Phyllis; he wanted to free her of him, as well as himself of her. Their life together, Julia had explained to him, had become a mutual degradation. Staying with her was not doing her any favor. There was sense in this, he supposed, for people who had high standards bred of habitual rectitude; but it left out of account the plea for mercy that goes with human softness. He and Phyllis shared a 'fifties drift, a gliding carelessness. Between them, he felt there had been something off from the start. He had been ambitious and raw, and had used her. Now he wanted to undo his presumption in carrying off this princess; he wanted to give her time to see it his way and to help him divorce her, so it became as much her idea as their marriage had somehow been. At least she had consented to start seeing a lawyer in Hartford, a short dapper rapid talker she was amused by—both Roscoe Bisbee and Henry Slade had recommended him. Named Jerry Halloran, he talked to her in a mathematical language of dollars and cents.

In this delaying period Owen's children invented a mode

of protest, an automotive caricature of adult disorder. Floyd, just turned sixteen and freshly equipped with a driver's license, took his mother's Volvo station wagon out onto Partridgeberry Road and, in his inexperience veering too far to the right to avoid an oncoming pickup truck pulling a horse van, ran into a snow-filled ditch. The Volvo lurched over on its side into a stone wall, at fair speed. The boy was unhurt but the Volvo was totalled. With the insurance money, the Mackenzies settled for a second-hand Ford Falcon station wagon, serviceable although lighter on its wheels than the solid Swedish import.

Gregory, home from Brown for spring break, asked to borrow his father's Corvette Stingray for a date with a girl he intended to impress, which that "tinny old Falcon" would not do. Though he didn't like his son's demanding tone, and regarded even in its old age his lipstick-red convertible as a treasure, Owen felt too guilty to deny the boy. He was wakened at one in the morning by a hysterical call from Phyllis. On the back road leading away from the far side of Heron Pond, where there was a well-known necking-and-make-out spot—one which years ago he and Faye in their innocence had resorted to—the Stingray had somehow veered and taken down four or five aluminum rail posts before coming to a stop. The engine had been moved halfway into the front seat, but neither Gregory nor his passenger was hurt. He manfully took the blame, claiming he had been trying to adjust the unfamiliar radio, but confided to his brother, who confided it to his mother, who told Owen, that in fact the girl, a wild one from Eastern Connecticut State University, had been driving, or at least had her hands on the wheel while pressed against Gregory. No doubt the controlled substance that had enhanced their spooning session at Heron Pond had been still in their systems. Owen, thinking of how not many years before he had sped through the Nevada desert with Mirabella's bleached curls bobbing in his lap, and years before that had hastily backed out of a perilous wood while Elsie hurried into her clothes beside him, could not find it in himself to be indignant. He deserved these assaults on his hardware.

He was more angered, at his distance, by the difficulties Iris was having in Massachusetts with the little cream-colored AMC Pacer coupe he had bought for her to take to Smith: repeated fender-benders while jockeying in the college parking lots, and weekly traffic tickets from the North-hampton police. It began to feel like a taunting, which hurt the more because Iris, the only one of his children with his mother's auburn hair, had been the child whom he felt most himself with, the least unconvincingly paternal. Iris had effortlessly, it seemed, entrusted him with the wry, teasing respect that is a father's due from a daughter.

During this accident-prone interregnum, Ed began to talk to him, at their weekly lunch, about E-O Data designing a PC for a company in New Hampshire to manufacture and market. "PCs are not just the future, they're here," Ed urged him. "There'll be one in every home in ten years. It's television sets all over again. There's *bil*lions to be made. Think Apple."

"Ed, we do software, not hardware."

"What's the big diff? You're talking eggs and chickens. If you can cook one you can cook the other. What the hell was your MIT degree in? Electrical engineering. Well, Christ, let's start engineering. We got a whole empty floor up there, for the prototypes and logic analyzers, once we get past the design stage. Look at Apple. The 141 had to be connected to a television set; a year later the 169 had color and sound and could do games. Thousands of these rigs are out there now, soaking up other people's software."

"Ed, I'm too fucking old for these new tricks you want. Let the smart kids you've hired out of Rensselaer or wherever do it. They're hardwired for it all, it's second nature to them. To me it was adventure, to them it's just appliances."

"You're not fucking old, you're too fucking distracted, is what you are. You can't figure out if you have two wives or no wives. Shape up, O.; your brain will turn to mush."

"It has turned, actually. Sorry about that, Ed. I know you had great hopes for me. I guess I got sidetracked."

Bad conscience, bad memory. But Owen would never forget—he remembered it every day—the sparkling late-October morning when, to deliver an update of his income figures for Phyllis to take to an appointment with her lawyer in Hartford at ten a.m., he drove straight from his Covenant Street pad to his former home on Partridgeberry Road. Halloween was impending; stoops and porchlets sported pumpkins, and some front lawns held straw-stuffed dummies, headless horsemen and sheeted ghosts, arranged in studied tableaux. In Owen's childhood there hadn't been such an elaborate pagan fuss at Halloween, just a little frowned-upon mischief. The holiday, as the major religious holidays lost credibility, had gone from being an excuse for childish mischief and blackmail to being an inoffensive pseudo-Christmas.

There had been rain overnight, giving the roads a shine and the world a washed look. Leaves were coming down, making a wet pulp here and there beneath the wheels. The Stingray had been totalled and the Ford Mustang he had bought with the insurance money never felt right; it didn't like to start on damp days and didn't hug the road like the Corvette had. The seats were covered with some black matte vinyl stamped with a hokey pattern of cattle brands; looking at it made him feel cheesily middle-aged.

Floyd and Eve were off at school. Daisy the yellow Labrador greeted him at the kitchen door with a thumping tail. The two cats rubbed around his ankles purring. Phyllis was up and dressed in a navy-blue suit and a plain white blouse and medium-height heels; she looked uneasy, like a modern nun not used to being out of the bulky old habit. Her color was high. She regarded her fast-talking lawyer as a kind of tutor in the legal facts of life; her face wore a student blush of anticipation, as if before a test. Phyllis was still slender, still erect in posture. She had not attempted to dye the gray that had come into her temples, blending into the sand color like traces of snow at the beach. Except for the animals, and the non-migratory birds chirping outside, they were alone with the house, with its jointly bought furniture, most of it old and showing signs of the economies they had once practiced, a medley of antique and modern now crowded, he could see from the kitchen, by her inheritance from her parents' two homes, the late-Victorian Cambridge one and the lighter-hearted, rickety summer place on the Cape.

"It's horrible," she said, following his eye. "My brother says he doesn't have any space in Ithaca for his share. We know what that means—Francine doesn't want it. You scrimp and save to buy furniture," she generalized, "and then, when you've got your house full, your parents die and dump all *their* stuff on you. Except," she added quickly, as if she had been tactless, "for your mother. She's still alive."

"Overweight, high blood pressure, and all," he comically admitted. "That tough old farming stock." He would lose, he saw, a wife who knew his problematical mother—over twenty years of difficult acquaintance, for better or worse. Julia had of course not yet been to Pennsylvania to meet the prickly old woman. "Most of that stuff she has," he went on, "nobody would want anyway. When we moved from Willow, for some reason, our porch furniture came into the living room and never left." Is this what he was here for, to discuss furniture? "The main trouble with stuff," he volunteered, to consort with her generalizing mood, "is that it outlasts people." These interviews with Phyllis now that they were estranged gave him a pasty, humming sensation, a kind of return to his helpless love-stricken feelings before he got to know her at all—the other side of the bell curve.

She felt his longing to linger in these familiar rooms, amid repairs and readjustments he had once made, and asked, glancing away, "You have time for coffee? In the living room? I guess there's still space to sit down in."

"No, thanks, really, Phyllis. I must run and you must too. Just give Halloran these figures, they're what he asked for. Davis and he can discuss them and come up with a new figure." Davis was his lawyer, a cynic and, it seemed to Owen, a hard bargainer; he had to impress on Owen that, even where the woman was not at fault and did not seek the divorce, the man was the breadwinner and must not be financially crippled. Phyllis would become, as it were, Owen's employee, on a fixed monthly salary, with an annual cost-of-living adjustment. Her duties were to raise their children and stay out of his private life. The house would become hers, but his capital, and the ability to generate more, should be his. Wanting to apologize for this inequity, yet not wanting to give his lawyer's game away, he hung there in the center of his old kitchen, beside the drop-leaf curly-maple table that they had bought in New York, impulsively, on Seventh Avenue in the Village, and that in Middle Falls had been too small when all four children were home, so that they never all sat around it together at breakfast or lunch, taking turns instead, or bolting a sandwich at the kitchen counter. He thought of this regretfully now. For over a year he had not been in this house so early in the day. The rising sun shot a broad ray of light in through the nearly leafless lilacs, blinding the plastic face of the electric clock on the wall. When he moved his head he saw the time to be twenty of nine. Below the clock Phyllis had Scotch-taped new color photographs of Floyd and Eve, portraits taken at school; they looked like those hyper-realistic sculptures sardonically executed in enamelled Fiberglas.

Phyllis laid the numerical printout on the table, adding a little dismissive brushing motion with the back of her hand, as if to shoo it on its way. "Thanks for this," she said, "I guess. He seems awfully hung up on details."

He guessed she meant Halloran. "So does Davis," he admitted.

"I feel as though we're being processed."

"We are, sweetie. They're selling us down the river and want to get the going rate." He felt this didn't come across as a joke, and clarified, "They're auctioneers who have to make way for the next slaves on the block."

"Mine," she said, after thought, "can't quite understand why. Why we're doing it." The way she turned her face from his, gazing down at the corner of the maple table, was familiar to him, as was the accompanying gesture of tucking a strand of hair behind her ear; it was her manner of saying something important. She had agreed to marry him in the same slant style.

"The simplest, oldest reason in the world," he told her

swiftly. "Another woman." He must be blunt. He must cut through this haze of many-layered sentiment, her old smoky allure, projected through diffidence.

"It's hard for me," she haltingly confessed, "to believe in Julia. She seems so fake."

"She's not fake, not in what matters to me."

"In bed, you mean? A minister's wife?"

He said nothing, wondering if it was that simple, and if life accordingly wasn't too simple.

Phyllis went on, having waited for a reply, "Sorry if I let you down there. You seemed to expect alarmingly much. Of something that is, after all, just one of the things people do. I suppose I got stagefright."

"You were and are beautiful," he stated, in attempted farewell. "When you bothered to give it a try."

She took this in silence and resumed speaking of Halloran. "He says we seem so fond of each other. The children say the same thing, and they've lived with us."

"Please," he begged. "Haven't we said all this? For over a year we've been saying it."

"I know, I'm being a bore. And a poor sport. But it bothers me that you, the creator of DigitEyes, can't see what everybody in town can see, that she's a con artist." She laughed one soft syllable, retracted with an intake of breath as if before weeping. "A *con* artist, you tell me," she said.

He had to smile at the pun—he was flattered she gave him credit for enough French to get it—but protested, "Everybody in town, as you call them, has their own stake, their own habits and arrangements to preserve. They like us as we are, we're part of *their* furniture. But *I* don't like us as we are. I don't like what the marriage is doing to *you*."

"Your ladies on the side, you mean? I know Faye wasn't the end. But I took them as punishment for my inadequacies—my refusals, you would call them—and, this is horrible to admit, didn't blame myself that much. I figured some of it was just male nature."

"Quite right," he hurried to assure her, seeing on her gleaming cheeks that there were tears, and hating to have her blame herself for anything, she who had been so above it all. "You're always right."

"No I'm not, that's a copout to say that. But one of your charms, Owen, is that you've never quite grown up. You were so clever you didn't have to. You could remain adolescent and still perform as an adult. Until lately, Ed says."

He ignored the mention of Ed. She had angered him, or he wanted to be angry. "O.K., if you say so, if you're so clear in your mind where an adolescent ends and an adult begins. But I'm *trying* to grow up. I'm trying to get out of this phase we're stuck in. For your sake as well as mine. You can't see it, but my not quite loving you, my loving everybody else instead more or less, is grinding you down, sweetie. You can't figure it out and it's too simple to explain."

"I never," she said, to herself but letting Owen eavesdrop, "should have told you I didn't love you yet."

"Did that ever change, by the way? You never told me if it did."

"I tried to show that it did."

This fetched *his* tears. *"Don't,"* he said, his voice scraping his throat. "Let's just do this. There are the figures Halloran wants. I've told Davis to agree to most anything the other guy suggests. I'll be generous, you know that. The children are mostly raised, and we'll get the younger two through together. Just don't try to talk me out of this any more. I had to have you, and now I have to have her. Then I'll stop wanting; I'll have had my quota."

"Vanessa says Larson keeps offering to take her back. And find another parish, of course."

"Vanessa! I wouldn't trust her. She should have been a man. She wants to manage *every*thing."

"She lives in the real world, in a way you and I never have. If you want to know what I think of Julia, she reminds me of my mother," Phyllis went on, skipping from woman to woman. Her cheekbones burned. "The professor's wife, the minister's wife, everything for show. It offends me intellectually, to be honest, that you can't see it."

"I see plenty," he told her, relieved they had come to combat. "But seeing leads to paralysis, if you let it. Look, Phyllis. It's now or never. You're still young enough, still healthy and gorgeous—"

"Only you ever thought I was gorgeous. Jake Lowenthal thought I was a stiff Wasp stick. He laughed at me—my detachment, my inhibitions."

"Let's not worry at this point about Jake Lowenthal."

"Young enough to catch another husband, is that what you started to say? Who? Who in this claustrophobic town? Ed? He must weigh three hundred pounds by now. He doesn't need a woman. Stacey told me that. He just likes to eat and sit at his machines and make money. The only way she could get him interested in sex—"

"Don't tell me. I don't want to know. O.K., not Ed. Not anybody if you prefer it. I can't live the rest of your life for you. I'm just trying to live mine."

"Your, you, *you*—listen to the only child! There are more people than you in the world. There's me and the children, for starters. No, Owen! I don't want to go through with this, I just *don't*. It doesn't feel *right*. I *won't* let you make such an idiot of yourself with that little con artist, with that cute little double chin you no doubt like to—what did people in the Middle Ages like to do?—chuck. Chuck her under." Her father with his antique erudition was trying to rise from the dead and speak through her. They stood there hip-deep in ghosts.

Owen painfully explained, "Phyllis, I'm trying to reform. Julia wants to save me—"

He stopped himself. He shouldn't have said that. Her eyes flared; her pale lips lost that frozen, immobile quality; she straightened to her full height in her navy-blue lawyer-seeing suit. "*Save* you!"

"She doesn't put it like that," he said hastily. "She says it's as if you're my mother and I'm defying you by—"

"Oh, *spare* me the amateur psychoanalysis; I can hear her voice, that pious little singsong. I'll do the saving today, Owen. I'm going to drive right over to Hartford and tell Halloran to stop coöperating. I'm forty-four years old and sick of being everybody's patsy. I'm not going to give you this divorce. I've invested too much misery in this marriage, too much humiliation."

"You shouldn't feel humiliated, the other women were jealous of *you*, how loyal I was to you, even when I wasn't exactly faithful—"

She screamed, or made a shrilling mindless noise as close to a scream as she could come.

"Like I said," he went on, "you didn't seem that interested—"

"It was your job to *make* it interesting. You didn't."

"Look, Phyllis, O.K., O.K., no argument, all my fault, I'm a stupid klutz, but it takes two to tango—"

"*No!* I won't do it! You and she can go straight to hell! You can tango there and not a minute sooner!"

Her fury was in part a relief for him. Having Julia as his wife—that compact, finely shaped silky body, those clear undoubting eyes, so striking that sometimes she made a gesture of covering them with a hand, like a lush woman trying to minimize her breasts—had always seemed a bit too good to be true. And he was flattered by Phyllis's wanting to fight for him; he couldn't remember a comparable show of passion. But he was in too deep. Julia was already there, on the far side of the Red Sea, high and dry, free, in Old Lyme, where it was getting colder and the children were enrolled in new schools, and he still was thrashing around in his old kitchen under the glassy stares of his photographed children. "It's gone too far," he said weakly, while chill autumn sunshine drenched the world outside, in the wake of last night's rain. He heard a fit of querulous birdsong and the swish of a car passing on the winding road.

Phyllis came gently to his side; her breath was hot, like a crazy woman's. "You don't want to go through with it," she told him. "I can hear it in your voice. You got trapped, Owen. It wasn't your fault, it's just the way you are. You're too nice to people. I'll get you out of it, I promise. Don't worry about her, she'll be fine. You just sit tight. Maybe you should go away for a while."

"No!" it was his turn to cry, his vision of a tidy, orthodox, normally sensual future swallowed up by this tall sandy-haired woman's crazy confidence, not incorrect, that she was uniquely real to him. "I want a divorce. I really do."

"She wants you to want a divorce. That's not the same thing," she said, with the complacence of a Q.E.D. Her light smile, that steady certainty in her level gray eyes—did his memory supply them in retrospect, or were they truly there that fresh morning? He had grown unused to looking at his wife; the same veil had come down that had hidden his mother's nakedness. "I'm off, baby," Phyllis said. "I'm

late, by the time I find a parking space." She forced a wet
kiss on him, a deepening kiss that seemed to come from her
innards, to his innards, the slimy red works we hide from all
but surgeons. Pleased with herself, uncharacteristically efficient, Phyllis backed off and deftly wiped the evidence of
her weeping from below her eyes. She checked her purse
for keys, wallet, Kleenex, lipstick. "You sit tight and don't
worry," she told Owen. "We'll get you out of it. Don't
bother to lock the house. Leave Daisy in, she's been chasing
cars."

She was out the kitchen door and her footsteps pattered
off the side porch before he noticed that she had left his
sheets of financial figures on the table. The Falcon door
slammed; the gravel on the driveway spurted under her
tires. Owen was dazed by the way she seemed to take his
prospects and his troubles out of the house with her. The
terrible metallic soulless taste of fatality, which had entered
his mouth the day at this same table when Floyd had inno-
cently imparted his school gossip, felt diluted. *She'll be fine.
You just sit tight.* The cats sneaked back to rub again against
his ankles. He readjusted the position of the papers on the
table and thought of scribbling a note to go with them but
decided that their insistent presence there said enough.
Instead of leaving at once, he wandered through the pantry,
the living room, and the front hall to see what changes
Phyllis had made lately, as a single woman. He could see
very few—just the extra furniture, and the gaps in the
bookshelves where she had let him have some volumes. He
thought of stealing *Finnegans Wake* but decided against it.
It would be a kind of flirting, misleading her. He tried to
imagine returning to all this and couldn't, quite. Houses
you've left get too small to re-enter: a trick of perspective.
He let himself out by the front door. In Pennsylvania, he

remembered too late, it had been considered bad luck to enter by one door and leave by another. It was a pretty house, he thought, once outside, looking back at its clapboarded white sides, its shingled dormers, its black shutters and sinuous wisteria vine; but he had so long experienced the place as a confinement, a shell back into which he scuttled after a betrayal of its domestic pretense, that he felt the gaze of its windows as reproachful, like that of a forsaken pet.

He drove the Mustang downtown and was at E-O earlier than usual. He let himself into the back stairwell and went directly to his private cell. He needed to meditate. He wondered if he should call Julia in Old Lyme and describe Phyllis's new mood. But, no, it would just distress her, and her efforts to combat this new development might do him more harm than good. There were enough energies at work; things had a way of working out, like his finding his glasses that time in the dew-soaked empty lot, or his discovering, as he was devising the algorithms for Digit-Eyes 2.1, that no matter how many 3D transforms have been nested, one branching from the other, the last coördinate space can be specified in terms of the first, with no more than a displacement vector and three basis vectors—a mere twelve scalars to be crunched. The intermediate steps can be consigned to the void. He was struck less by the possible impediment to the legal proceedings—Phyllis was basically too rational, she would give in, with an improvement in terms that Halloran would wheedle from Davis—than by the passion for him she had belatedly displayed. Or was it a passion merely for her old, carelessly bright and lovely self, of whose memory he had become the curator, now that her parents were no longer alive to bear witness? Not that they, or her kid brother, could have seen what her contemporaries saw—that flashing, loaded impression we make on those with whom we might mate. Her passion had not centered, he felt, on him. Wounded pride, threatened security, fears for the children had activated her. The old question remained unsolved, why do women go along with men? Perhaps it was a simple question of electrical engineering: in a world full of plugs, nature must provide sockets.

His locked door rapped, more loudly than Karen had ever rapped before. Owen called out, "Go away, Karen. It's over."

But a male voice said, "It's Ed, O. You better open. We got trouble."

Ed looked more than startled, he looked frightened when the sticky gray steel door revealed him in a rumpled business suit, his swollen flesh as colorless as a slug's. He was breathing as if poisoned. "A phone call came for you at the company number. The cops. Your house didn't answer and neither did your new digs. I said I doubted you were here but, son of a bitch, here you are. Let's go. We better go together."

"Go where, Ed?"

"Upper Falls. Old County Road. She was headed in the Hartford direction."

"Who's she?" But he knew.

Ed nodded, pushing ahead through the door leading down the stairs to the street, the secret stairs now thundering with Ed's heavy feet.

"What's happened? How bad?" Owen asked, gulping, his palms and arms tingling, his body meeting resistance in this new medium of circumstance. This time he couldn't just close his eyes and roll over and go back to sleep. His mother and father weren't in the next room.

Ed, hurrying ahead, shook his head as if the question were a bee or horsefly buzzing at his ears. "They didn't say. You know how cops are, they hide their stupidity by clamming up. They said an accident, and they wanted you there."

They arrived at Ed's car, a new bronze-colored Mercedes, in its numbered space on the asphalt factory lot. Ed had always been the one to act the role of company head; he had a mental image of the rewards and responsibilities. Owen had tried to shrug it all off, driving a red Corvette like a kid. The inside of the Mercedes, though, smelled of pizza and onion-laden takeout, along with fresh leather and assembly glue.

Owen's face felt hot, as if looking into an oven. He said, "I just saw her, twenty minutes ago. She had an appointment in Hartford; she was late."

"With that Irish lawyer?"

He knew he was Irish. Phyllis told Ed everything, or most everything, and Owen couldn't resent it. "Yes." Ed was loyal, Ed was big. Phyllis's hands had flown apart, describing her lost boyfriend Hank as "enormous." Owen hadn't been quite big enough.

Ed was saying, "She hated that guy. One of these Mick fast talkers, she felt he was trying to con her. Micks're all male chauvinists." He drove with speed, but carefully; the car's sheer weight made it seem a placid ride, four miles in less than ten minutes. The twisting back road, a short-cut to Hartford for those that knew it, was puddled with wet leaves knocked down by last night's rain. The coruscating blue lights of several police cars were visible well ahead; a young cop controlling traffic through the remaining lane waved them through, until Ed talked to him, in words Owen couldn't hear. There was a drumming in his head. He had already spotted the Falcon station wagon next to the woods beyond the shoulder, upside down.

His heartbeat had become so rapid it pushed him across events, missing whole sequences. He wasn't aware of Ed's steering and braking, only that the Mercedes was stopped. For the longest time he couldn't figure out how to open the door: the handle was smaller and higher than in the cars he was used to. He saw that a door of the upside-down Falcon had been pried open and a gray blanket covered something long next to it.

His face hot, his legs watery, Owen struggled away from the Mercedes and across a grassy ditch gouged by something, muddy marks, not deep, left by some passing weight. Another policeman, older and more solid than the one Ed had spoken to, stopped him as he floundered toward the blanket where it lay neatly tucked this side of a low bed of blueberry bushes turned dull scarlet, beyond knee-high stands of white asters.

The older cop told Owen, "It looks like she was speeding, hit a patch of wet leaves, skidded, hit the ditch, and flipped."

It sounded like a reasonable, orderly process, not too violent. "So she's all right?"

"No, son," the policeman said, though he may not have been much older than Owen. "She's not. She wasn't wearing her seat belt and when the car flipped she came down hard and broke her neck. That's the way it looks to us. The coroner will be here to confirm. There's no breath, we tried the mirror. What we need now is definite identification." He touched Owen above the elbow, as if to prevent him from floating away. "Sorry to put you through this, Mr. Mackenzie. Would you rather have Mr. Mervine look?" He knew Ed's name and knew Owen's name, though this was Upper Falls.

"No, I'll do it." He took the remaining steps gratefully, the blanket had seemed so lonely. It was as when you check on small children sleeping at night, so alone in the crib or bed that there is that catch of panic until you hear them breathing.

"Let me lift this here. Tell me when you're ready."

"I'm ready." His shoes and ankles were getting wet. The various grasses, the little shiny blueberry leaves, the gravel and grit of the roadside, with plastic flip-tops and cigarette filters slowly going back to nature: these data pressed on his retina as if to tell him that all was illusion, that the moment would be reversed and redeemed, that he was bending over and picking up his wet glasses case from the dew-soaked weeds.

The cop's hand trembled, pulling back the blanket. Maybe he *was* older than Owen. Pale Phyllis slept, her sand-colored hair barely mussed and her head not noticeably awry. Her eyes were still open, which shocked him, but the face had already begun its transition to the inanimate, all those miraculously interwoven structures intact but lacking the spark, the current that gave them meaning and presence. The responsive skin along her cheekbones had lost its blush. She looked like a statue; but then she had been a statue in his mind for a long time.

A weight was bearing down on Owen: Ed leaning on him, looking over his shoulder as he knelt there in the weeds to view Phyllis. The weight on his back cancelled Owen's impulse to bend down and kiss her lips, which had so lately kissed his, with belated passion. Ed breathed close behind his ear. "You did this, you fuckhead."

"Did I?" Owen asked.

"She was the best woman I ever knew," Ed said, his weight still bearing on Owen's like a wrestler's. "I loved her."

"Me too. Ed, let me up. We're both in shock, let me breathe."

"I'll let you breathe all right," Ed said menacingly, but he backed off to let Owen stand. With space between them, and police listening, he told his partner, "You and I are through, buddy. The sight of you makes me puke. I was going to marry her, you know." His upper lip did that chimp thing, as if to clean his teeth, in sheer aggression.

"No, I didn't know. Did Phyllis know?"

This gave Ed pause. "I didn't want to crowd her, when there was still a chance to patch it up with you. She adored you, you miserable piece of shit."

Owen could have resented the way Ed was trying to steal his grief from him, there in front of the police, but he was thinking of a larger reality: the abyss that had yawned beside his childhood windows, the black lake of awful possibilities, had widened and risen to engulf his life. But he was still functioning, his brain still working, making more connections per split second than he could articulate, re-orienting him in fresh circumstances, his perceptions quick and dry within the lake even as he drowned.

xiv. *Village Wisdom*

VILLAGE WISDOM recommends that a building should not have thirteen stories, nor an *histoire* thirteen chapters. Its dictates tend to caution and conservatism: toss a pinch of spilled salt over your shoulder, and knock wood after claiming good health; keep your opinion under your hat, and don't stick your head above the crowd. Haskells Crossing is a good place for lying low. It is Julia who ventures out, to shop and to join women's groups, to have massages and manicures, while Owen cowers in the house, tinkering with the Internet—a frustrating mass of peremptorily severed connections and blithely illiterate misinformation, offered on what it would be kind to call a junior-high-school level—and with oil painting. He has taken it up. He keeps trying to capture on canvas their view of Massachusetts Bay, his own yew and euonymus bushes in the foreground and in the middle ground scattered islands and tilting sailboats and in the distance a horizon where a few oil tankers ply their viscid, geopolitically critical wares; but the harder he stirs the oils on his palette to get the exact colors, the muddier and more muted they become. The atomic brilliance of reality, its reserved but implacable pop-up quiddity—this effect Nature keeps to itself. With the last of his little Boston consultancies disbanded, he and Julia live comfortably on the proceeds of the sellout of E-O Data that Ed arranged in 1978 with the infant Apple corporation of Cupertino, California. Owen's pioneering work on graphical interfaces was rolled into the Atari-derived visuals of Apple's early microcomputers and into the Alto interface employed in the triumphantly successful Macintosh of 1984. The shares which Ed Mervine had accepted in part payment partook of this triumph, and he presciently unloaded at the right time, and in a curt note advised his old partner to do the same. Owen, ever passive, took this wise advice; Apple's early elegance glimmered out as the chilling shadow of Microsoft overcast the entire computer world. As a program, Windows was kludgy and a chip-power hog, but its hold on IBM and its clones could not be broken, any more than the inefficient, left-hand-favoring early typewriter keyboard could, once lodged in thousands of machines, be changed.

Owen arrived in his new village as a mysteriously comfortable stranger, who had filched a little fortune from the early stages of an increasingly less exotic business. He was superstitiously viewed as a kind of alchemist, but he knew that the alchemy of Babbage and Turing, Eckert and Mauchly and Von Neumann had long since become mere chemistry, a province of dronelike quantifiers and disagreeable smells. For a time he pecked away at his customized, power-boosted iMac, hoping to come upon another next thing, perhaps a form of browser program with a few corners ingeniously cut, while knowing in his heart that he was amusing himself; the room for individual invention had been squeezed from an egregiously "mature" and vulgar-

ized field of exploitation, a practically infinite sprawl of
e-mail, pornography, spam, half-baked data, digital photos
and videos, pirated music—all the importunate demotic
trash that in Owen's youth had been mostly confined to the
print medium, to bales of recyclable newspapers, magazines, catalogues, and flyers. So-called cyberspace was
being stifled by the lowly appetites to which capitalism
must cater. In engineering as in the arts, the dawn time,
before all but a few are still asleep to the possibilities, is the
time for leaps of creation. The computer's engineering
marvels, like those of the automobile earlier in the departed
century, are buried in a landslide of common use: any bank
teller can summon up currency quotations from Hong
Kong, just as any auto driver can push on the pedal for
more gas. And, just as platform countries have stolen the
auto and textile industries from the American worker, so
software is more and more outsourced to India, Russia,
China, the Philippines. It is too sad. But progress is sad,
change is sad, natural selection is very sad. Small wonder
that Owen, in his old age, now that the last of his and Julia's
combined six children are out of the house, has taken up
painting—its silence, its long association with the sacred,
its odor of patiently purified essences and minerals.

The children, as children must, adjusted. Rachel and
Thomas Larson, aged nine and seven at the wedding (a
simple, bare-bones service in the Lower Falls Universalist
Church), deferred to the four Mackenzies chronologically
arrayed above them; they sheltered in their blood mother's
presence even as Julia put the bulk of her maternal effort—
a heroic output of empathy, patience, and affection—into
the traditionally suspect role of stepmother. Owen's children, two of them in college and all four imbued with the
stoic sophistication of a generation to whom family dys-

function is common TV fare, didn't much blame their step-mother for what had befallen them. Only little Eve kept her distance, those first years. Then, as sexuality caught up with the child, she had no mature female to turn to but Julia, and they became, briefly, close, before the girl, at sixteen, drifted away into a woman's necessary secrecy. It is a life-stage, Owen reflected, when one's children become instruc-tors in acceptance and sophistication—in rolling with the punches.

It had been Julia who had known of Haskells Cross-ing. Arthur's first call, fresh from Andover Newton Theo-logical School, had been as assistant minister to a failing Episcopal parish in Cabot City; the more sedate, more prosperous Saint Barnabas in Haskells Crossing had been envied, a kind of rich younger brother. From the perspec-tive of Middle Falls—where the old riverside gun factory again stood empty, though the E-O Data sign stayed up above the loading platform, and a select few of its employ-ees had found employment with Apple—Haskells Cross-ing seemed a fairy-tale abstraction, an ideally remote and obscure site for their new life together. But no village is remote and obscure to itself; its inhabitants occupy the cen-ter of the universe. After twenty-five years, Owen and Julia are woven into that center. Their relationship is loving but haunted. He thinks of Phyllis every day, though her image seldom troubles to invade his dreams; there is instead a generic oneiric wife-figure who, on his awaking, Owen is not certain had been Julia or Phyllis or yet another female. Sometimes she presides over a house whose corners and floorboards and scattered toys and chipped dishes are those of his first house, the home of Isaac and Anna Rausch on Mifflin Avenue in Willow. Everything in that house, every trivial little object and square foot of carpet, was supercharged with significance. His mother had existed in the house as a nexus of need, a wife, child, and mother all at once, hovering between Owen's head and the ceiling, a constant voice in the middle distance, where the view from the window intersected with the dirty wallpaper.

Once, a dream of that house reminded him, his mother bought a wallpaper cleaner that consisted of a pink putty-like substance in a cylindrical container like the Quaker Oats box. He and his father were enlisted in rubbing a ball of this fleshy substance across the dingy pattern of big yellow roses and green thorny stems in his parents' bedroom; when his childish turn came, he found the work strenuous and intimate, with his nose so close to the faintly rough, slightly paling grain of the hopeless immensities of paper. Invisible coal dust, wafted from thousands of chimneys, gradually turned gray the sweet-smelling, adhesive substance in his hands. The chore, whose enlistment seemed to mark, for little Owen, a step up into adult labors, remained in his mind as an instance of his mother's heat— the friction of her resistance to the way things were. To his father and him, the wallpaper had seemed clean enough.

He wonders how suicidal Phyllis's end had been. She had been delayed by her outburst at him and was speeding, to be sure, not even pausing to fasten her seat belt; but to arrange to skid on wet leaves, to achieve a rollover and a broken neck, seemed impossibly precise. And why end her life when she had a new mission, to save him from himself and Julia? No, the accident was just that, an absurd confluence of atoms in space-time, slipped through a flurry of unlikely odds. And yet she had become inconvenient to him, and Owen led, he was early convinced, a life charmed from above. God killed Phyllis, as a favor to him: from this blasphemous thought he seeks to shield himself with the fancy that Phyllis, the beautiful math major, had crossed herself out the way a redundant term is dropped from the denominator and the numerator of a complex fraction.

Julia consigned to a dark cupboard on the third floor photographs and slides containing Phyllis's image, captured before the era of family videos, but his four children were allowed to have their mother's photograph in their rooms. The photos are still there. Owen often studies them, not just colored snapshots but studio portraits of Phyllis's virginal self, in a wasp-waisted, wide-skirted dress of the time, with her bangs sleekly brushed and a certain arch sideways glance invited by the photographer's banter. He blames her ghost, who, unchanging, gathers strength as the living weaken, for his sexual failures with Julia. Five years younger than he, his wife is still needy; there is hardly a night when she doesn't interrupt his going to sleep with a hug or an inquisitive caress. Yet, always a great believer in the health-giving value of sleep, he unchivalrously clings to the approaching oblivion. That oblivion may soon embrace him for good does not deter him. His heart still beats and his prostate gland is still intact, but his receptors for her signals have degraded. Nevertheless, he finds her frustrated attention a comfort and solace, and he hopes, each night as his bedtime book grows heavy and nonsensical in his hands, to do better. Sometimes, he does, and both are greatly gratified. How lovely she is, naked in the dark! How little men deserve the beauty and mercy of women!

Just recently he had a dream in which, in some kind of classroom setting, he was delegated by the teacher to take a pencil or a textbook to Barbara Emerich, who was sitting alone in a corner, at one of those chairs with a broadened arm of yellow oak to write on. As he obediently offered this pencil or textbook to her, she responded by curling more deeply into herself, sitting unresponsive, so that he had to urge himself closer, and sensed, out of the shadowy space between her lap and her downturned face, that she was willing to have him kiss her. She expected it but acted on the expectation only by maintaining a stubborn stillness, her mouth clamped shut on her sunny smile, with its single gray tooth. Barbara Emerich, he happens to know, has grown morbidly fat, and appears at class reunions hobbling with a cane, and her winsome gray tooth has long been replaced with an unconvincing, ivory-white bridge; but in his dream her body was still lissome, in the simple pale-flowered cotton dress, buttoned in the front, such as girls wore to elementary school in the 'thirties. She wore a little girl's dress but was mature, with long white legs and a supple abdomen and an adult capacity to sit still, waiting. The space subtended by her bosom and lap was shadowy with tense expectations; this space was a pool in which he yearned to dip his face, to be greeted by warm lips. He wakes knowing—his erection proves it—that he is still sexually alive, though sex with Julia must compete with his senile desire to sleep.

The dream of Barbara Emerich brought back to him the aura, the *climate* of a woman, the cloud her presence makes as you walk along a street beside her, haunch to haunch, her long hair and skirt symbolizing the primordial difference, a difference concealed by clothes and fig leaves yet advertised by a wealth of external signs, such as her finer skin texture and lighter, quicker voice. At MIT, in their student years, unmarried, he and Phyllis, simultaneously weary of studying, might of an evening decide to go to a movie, in Central Square or on Boston's Washington Street by way of the "T," and there was sex in this, the impromptu joint flight into escapism, an attempt to extend the rapport their genitals timidly sought into the village domain of open entertainment and street life: he loved her then, the atmosphere of her flowing beside him down the sidewalk, hurrying lest they be late, and her consensual silence as she dipped her hand into the shared bucket of popcorn—though much less was made of popcorn in those days, concession profits were not so crucial to cinema houses—and let her attentive face be licked by the electric flashes, like so many short circuits, of *The Caine Mutiny* or *Seven Brides for Seven Brothers* or *Rear Window* or *La Strada* or *Mr. Hulot's Holiday*.

A piece of village wisdom he was slow to grasp is that sex is a holiday, an activity remarkably brief in our body's budget compared with sleeping or food-gathering or constructing battlements for self-defense, such as the Great Wall of China. The unfaithful man and woman meet for a plain purpose, dangerous and scandalous, with the blood pressure up and the pupils enlarged and the love-flush already reddening the skin: is there not a praiseworthy economy in this, as opposed to sex spread thin through the interminable mutual exposure of a marriage?

Phyllis's finding that patch of slick leaves on Old County Road to take flight on, landing upside down there by the buzzing, frothy edge of the woods—this had seemed directed at him, with one of her characteristic sly backward glances, though he knew with the rational fraction of his brain that accidents are accidents and demonstrate only the vacant absurdity of everything that is. Yet we seek to impose patterns of meaning around ourselves, interlocking networks vectored back to the ego, *le point de départ* if not the Archimedean point that lifts this heavy, tangled, cluttered world into a schematic form we can manipulate.

Middle Falls, in the years when he lived there, was mapped by the location of the homes of women in whom

Owen was interested. In that house lived one he had slept with; in another, a woman he fantasized about sleeping with; and in the houses in between them were blank, uninhabited, empty spaces such as used to mark the interior of Africa, and Arabia Deserta, and the South Seas. Driving or walking in Middle Falls, then, gave Owen the happiness of orientation, of his position being plotted on a specific cartography, of being *somewhere*. There are fewer and fewer somewheres in America, and more and more anywheres, strung out along numbered highways. Even those who live along the highway do not always know its number. Though Owen has lived, driving and walking, in Haskells Crossing longer than at any other address, it remains unmapped in his mind, or mapped as vaguely as the Americas were in the sixteenth century, a set of named harbors and approximate coastlines enclosing wild hopes of El Dorado as well as many infidel savages to be exterminated.

There is an enlarging hollow in his life—its approaching end, perhaps. Julia cannot save him, though the sight of her, clothed and unclothed, still lifts his heart. She cannot save him with her silky willing body, her uncanny aquamarine gaze, or her matter-of-fact Christian piety, in which he has joined her in defiance of his scientific instincts and his indifferently churched upbringing. Grampy read the Bible on the caneback sofa; Grammy believed in devils and hexes. His father served the lords of local capitalism with conventional attendance, Christmas and Easter and most other Sundays. It was Owen's mother who was the real cosmic questioner, the uncomforted Job, her face at times smeared with tears while she gave voice to her unhappiness, whose source the boy could never quite see. We do not see our parents well; they are too big, and too close.

In Haskells Crossing and the near section of Cabot City there are public tennis courts, used by those who do not have their own or access to a country club's. The sight of them quickens in Owen a memory that surfaced after long suppression: when he was a boy of nine or ten his auburn-haired mother would put shorts on her pale, growingly plump legs and walk with him and two wood-framed rackets down through the Mifflin Avenue back yard and across the wide high-school grounds past the cinder track and little bleachers for the cinder-circumscribed football field, and open the latch of the four Willow public courts, fenced in by heavy galvanized wire. He and she would attempt to play. Neither had ever had lessons; it was frustrating, so many balls bopped into the net (also of heavy playground fencing, which sang when struck) or blooped into the air where the other could not reach them. He was embarrassed by her bare-legged figure joining him in this lonely game, her face growing redder as her clumsy efforts continued; trolley cars and traffic passed on the Alton Pike close enough for people to stare at this little boy and grown woman trying to pat an uncoöperative ball back and forth. Only now could Owen glimpse her purposes: to combat the weight problem that was overtaking her and to help him gain a skill he might need in life. In fact he went on, in the playful milieu of Middle Falls, to play a lot of tennis, though never with much of a backhand; he gave it up early, in the first years of his marriage to Julia, because of a rotator cuff that hurt when he tried to reach up into the serve. But the game had always been tainted for him by that shameful memory, the public struggle with his mother, while people in the trolley cars stared, to get the ball back and forth; there had been a pathetic impotence to the fuzzy balls—white, back then—as they hit the wire of the net or the fencing with a sad, reverberating thud. Mother and son had seemed so lost, the two of them, there at the far end of the flat school acreage, linked in a common ordeal as they had been at his painful birth.

She had died, finally, some years after his marriage to Julia, having made an impressive, white-haired, broad-bodied presence among the few wedding guests that day in Lower Falls. She didn't have the energy to create with Julia the tensions that had existed with his first daughter-in-law; rather, she let the younger woman roll over her, even submitting to the massages that Julia skillfully applied to the aches in her osteoporotic shoulders and neck. She had never liked being touched; or so she had thought. "Julia," she said to her second daughter-in-law, "you have a healing touch. Owen looks so much better since he took up with you. He had a sneaky, pasty look before, didn't he?"

"To me he always looked very handsome and honorable," Julia said, unanswerably, with a complacent closing of her lips. It was as when Elsie used to come to the house, with a lively courtesy facing his mother down, claiming her share of the son. Women are possessive. The world divides itself into their territories. A smile similar to Elsie's would stretch Alissa's lips when, her face perspiring inches from his, her dull blue eyes turned inky. Though we speak of a man possessing a woman it is she who takes possession.

His mother died neatly, quickly, of heart failure, in her little country house, having exerted herself with an unusual spurt of housework. Her old Hoover burned out its engine as her body lay beside it on the clean carpet. All four of the adults Owen had lived with as a boy died tidily, out of sight, as if to spare him unpleasantness and preserve his charmed, only-child sense of life.

Yet something feels amiss; there is something within him

that needs to be relaxed. His fulfillment with Julia, his arrival at a harbor of safe uxoriousness and well-heeled retirement, is a strain to maintain, as his restless dissatisfaction with Phyllis had not been. Phyllis and he, in mating, had not so stressed the world that they had to be perfect; they had been the age to marry and leave their homes and make another, according to common social usage. He and Julia wrecked two existing households, and caused a death, though no court could convict them for it. Art Larson, as he calls himself now, left the ministry and enjoys well-paid employment as a p.r. interface in New York, but when he shows up, for a child's wedding or the funeral of a dear pre–Middle Falls friend of the former couple, his neck looks vulnerable without the backwards collar. His hair no longer has the wiry health of a dog's tousled, tight coat. His voice, however, is as resonant and gravely melodious as ever, and his manner toward Owen no less benign than at their first meeting. Even vestigial faith arms the believer in fatalism and an energy-conserving disposition to forgive.

There are two evidential arguments, Owen has reasoned, for the truths of the Christian religion: one, our wish to live forever, however tedious the actual experience of eternal consciousness might be, and, two, our sensation that something is amiss—that there has been a lapse or slippage in the world and things are not quite as they should be. We feel made for a better world, and the fault is ours that this is not Eden. The second may be the more solid evidence, since fear and loathing of death can be explained as, like pain, a survival device selected and refined by Darwinian evolution. Because we fear death, we try harder to live. As long as our genes get through, Nature doesn't care how we suffer.

A third supernaturalist argument could be that belief, with a pinch of salt (that is, short of self-mutilation, a martyr's suicide, or murder of one's children as a surefire, low-cost relocation to Heaven), benefits the health; repeated medical studies bear this out. An anxiety-relieving faith conduces to worldly efficiency and success: this argument to Owen seems crassly pragmatic. Optimism tends to succeed, but does this refute the majestic truths of pessimism? The human animal, evolved in trees and then dropped down to run in the grasslands of Kenya, arrived at a highly conscious position awkward beyond any easements of philosophy. At three in the morning, our brains churn within the self, trying to get out of what we know to be a sinking ship. But jumping out of the self is not a Western skill. The walls of the skull stay solid, sealing us in with our fears.

They cling to each other, he and Julia, in what has become their dotage. "I hate it," she tells him, "when you're not in the house, even when you're just off for golf."

"How dear of you, baby. I hate it when you play bridge all afternoon. The house seems so large. When you're here, it seems rather small."

This is not entirely a compliment; Julia laughs at the jab, acknowledging that, yes, when he is in a room she finds an excuse to enter it; when he is closeted with his murmuring CPU, matching wits with the circuitry as it twirls an algorithm, at the rate of two hundred twenty billion cycles a second, through the AND and OR gates toward the conclusory IF . . . THEN . . . ELSE, she enters with a question about their health insurance or the yew and euonymus bushes waiting for him to trim them, as only he can do it, with his artistic eye—the lawn boys hack away, like bad barbers. They don't take enough; they create holes and bald spots that never grow in. Or else she disturbs him on the terrace while he is trying for the hundredth time to render, with flake white, cobalt blue, ivory black, and a touch of Roman ochre, the look of rain clouds approaching above the sea's horizon, their maddening near-colorlessness and their simultaneous elaborate structure and chaotic vapor, a mere brushstroke on wet paper in watercolor but in oils a labored accumulation of minutely three-dimensional touches that will be dry tomorrow. Since early childhood, Owen has sheltered from reality's pressure and misalignments by focusing closely on a paper page, a plywood cutout, a blob of clay, or, under Buddy Rourke's laconic guidance, a copper connection within a braid of color-coded wires. Julia sets up a human clamor against her husband's exclusionary absorption in the inanimate.

He tells her, teasingly, of the house, "Maybe it's too large and we should sell it."

"Don't torture me; you know I love it here. And love you. At times," she tells him, "I look at you when you don't know I'm looking and I get this shiver, a physical shiver."

"After all these years?" he dutifully asks. Their infantile give and take, word by word, forms a music that never palls, scored for a thousand repeats.

"Oh yes," she dutifully answers. "More, even, instead of less. Something about the way you look when you don't think anybody's looking at you."

"So you don't regret . . . us?"

"Oh no. Not really. I'm glad. Aren't you?"

"Oh yes," he says.

Yet she finds, he feels, more and more about him that panics her. "*Don't* eat in the middle of the kitchen floor," she suddenly cries, as if electrically shocked. "Eat over the sink if you *must* eat all the time. I never *saw* anybody eat so constantly; no wonder your teeth are always disgusting."

As a child on Mifflin Avenue he had been afraid the food would give out, and would march through the house nibbling a celery stick or a dirty carrot fresh-pulled from the backyard garden. Phyllis had never appeared to notice his nervous habit of grabbing pretzels, nuts, cookies from the bread drawer, to fill a suddenly felt gap within him. He fights back: "I *hate* eating over the sink, it makes me feel like a dog at his bowl."

"Well, the floor everywhere is full of crumbs and the cleaning ladies were just here." Those bustling Brazilians with their broad bottoms: when they talk together the language is as full of shushing sounds as Russian. Owen suspects that big countries are unhappier than little countries: more responsibilities.

"And don't slurp," Julia will say, of hot soup. She rarely serves soup, as if to teach him a lesson. "You had *such* a terrible upbringing. What was your mother thinking of?"

"She was improvising. She hadn't been a mother before. She was going for the big picture, not table manners."

"Good manners are where it all begins," Julia states, and he accepts the wisdom from her, who looks to be the last of a string of instructresses. "My father used to say, manners are a form of courtesy, and courtesy a form of goodness." She goes on, "And that's what I tell my grandchildren. You observe their manners, Owen, and they'll help you. They don't slurp."

He searches the dump of odd information in his head for a self-defense. "It tastes better," he explains. "In some societies, slurping is considered a compliment to the host and hostess."

"Well, aren't we glad we don't live in such a society? And another thing you do that's truly terrible—I noticed it the other night, at dinner with the Achesons. You don't break your bread into little enough pieces and you dabble at it with your butter knife, pat pat pat. It drove me so crazy I wanted to grab the bread out of your hand."

"Well," he says, "*that* would have been a lesson in manners to edify everybody."

"I'm sorry, but I love you so much, I can't stand it when you eat like an animal."

"Grrr."

"Don't try to be funny, dear. It's not funny. It's your one flaw. And please look at me when I'm talking to you." If he glanced away—say, at the newspaper on the kitchen table with its horrifying headlines of international and domestic tragedy—it was in the constructive spirit of multi-tasking, as mainframe computers used to do in the heyday of time-sharing. It does seem to him, as Julia explains details of their health insurance or their next trip to Europe, that the English language in her mouth has too elaborate a syntax, expanding a simple thought graspable by the mind in a few billionths of a second into a paragraph a number of minutes long. One of the boys older than he back in Willow, probably Marty Naftzinger, who made a study of such matters, confided to him this piece of village wisdom: "The more a girl talks, the more she'll fuck. Their mouths and their cunts," Marty theorized, "are connected by this long nerve down their spines."

Experience bore it out. Phyllis had talked reluctantly, as if the language of numbers had her tongue, or as if the basic imprecision of speech bothered her, whereas Julia in their very first meeting at the hospital fund-drive celebration dazzled him with the excellence of her pronunciation and the glittering completeness of her sentences. Talking for her, as for her husband, was a kind of delight, a public self-pleasuring, and one of Owen's puzzlements concerned why a pair so well-matched had allowed itself to be split up. But ideality becomes by itself, in a couple, a reason for dissatisfaction and rebellion. Americans need to experience room for improvement, for progress.

Looking back, he is touched by how completely his two wives delivered what he asked. Phyllis had hoisted him up into Cambridge and the snob life of the mind, and Julia into Haskells Crossing and the life of bourgeois repose. If both lives were less than complete—less than his mother, who exaggerated his capacities, would have wished for him—then life itself is incomplete, a hasty approximation. It is a rough rehearsal, not a finished production.

The world tends to give us what we want, but what we receive will partake of the world's imperfection.

He remembers his life in Middle Falls nostalgically, as a magical exploration of his male nature, but he forgets the seedy underside—the fear of discovery, the squeezed brevity of the trysts, the guilt that gnawed his innards into gastritis, the messy aftermaths. With Faye there had been legal threats and with Alissa a pregnancy. Once he and Alissa had tried meeting at the Whitefield's Rock preserve, in the woods where he and Faye had gone that wondrous first time, and midsummer mosquitoes feasted on her exposed skin. She stood above him in forest concealment as he tugged down her underpants; her lovely plump legs became quickly hairy with the frantic bloodsucking little creatures. Out of mercy, he said after a minute, "Let's get out of here." He forgets more and more but still remembers trying to brush away the mosquitoes from her thighs as his mistress gazed down at him uncertainly, looking to him for leadership and sexual stimulation, for a sheltered site where they could be themselves.

The children are gone now but Julia and Owen live with another presence in the house, their approaching deaths. And before that, if they are unlucky, Alzheimer's with its idiotic life-in-death. They are both forgetful, she of errands she means to run and he of names, especially of their friends in Haskells Crossing and Haven-by-the-Sea. Names planted early in the brain seem to last; a curling, brittle photo of the Willow second grade awakens names row by row, without a gap, whereas yesterday's golf companion, met on the street, draws a blank, although Owen can picture his swing— a vulturous hunch, a spectacular hook—perfectly. Former President Reagan hangs heavily over the infant millennium: this foggy-voiced actor, this handsome snake-oil salesman who persuaded the poor to vote with the rich, as if indeed they *were* rich, has become a haze of pure existence, unencumbered by any memory of his venturesome life or even by his faithful wife's name, while his own name, thanks to his grateful party, is attached to the capital's airport and a huge downtown building of appropriately vague purpose. He haunts the national village; he warns us of what, even with salubrious amounts of brush-cutting and horseback-riding and plenty of sleep, can happen. In Pennsylvania they used to speak of old people "going back"—reverting, that is, to infancy. Owen and Julia are already turned in that direction, talking in baby syllables, touching each other as if for orientation in the dark, squabbling like mated toucans in a tropical jungle and then flying away in perfect forgetful unison.

Owen's old question—why that anonymous, paradigmatic woman had allowed herself to pose for the obscene depiction on the back of the playground-equipment shed — is still imperfectly answered. The question perhaps belongs to the unscientific order that deserves no answer, such as *Why does anything exist?* and *What is gravity?* Julia takes a jarringly hard-eyed view: women are the world's slaves and in the end must do whatever men demand. As Alissa pointed out, the question *Why do men fuck?* is never asked. The question *Why do women?* perhaps arose in Owen's mind from a childish overestimation of the distance between women and men. He had no sisters; his mother's heat frightened him; the macadam playground surrounding the Willow Elementary School had been gender-segregated by a broad central sidewalk. Decades later, Owen read that, in an experiment on white mice gender-segregated by an electric fence, the males back off at the first severe shock whereas the females continue to charge the fence until all are electrocuted.

Women's natures are very large, he early sensed, to seek sex amid the world's perils, in the face of so many wise societal discouragements. The force that parts their legs overrules modesty and prudence and common sense. Women fuck, his provisional conclusion was, because, like men, they are trapped in a biological universe where the species that do not propagate disappear; the traits the survivors harbor — lustiness, speed, canniness, camouflage — are soaked in these disappearances, these multitudinous deaths. Sex is a programmed delirium that rolls back death with death's own substance; it is the black space between the stars given sweet substance in our veins and crevices. The parts of ourselves conventional decency calls shameful are exalted. We are told that we shine, that we are splendid, and the naked bodies we were given in the bloody moment of birth hold all the answers that another, *the* other, desires, now and forever.

At three in the morning, writing on the wrinkled sheets, unable to find the door to healing self-forgetfulness, as close to his death as Grampy was on Mifflin Avenue but a more skeptical and less frequent reader of the Bible, Owen sees as if looking down into a suddenly illumined well that his charmed life has been a long torment of fear, desire, ambition, and guilt. Picturing himself in Middle Falls, he cannot imagine what drove him into so many hazardous passes and contorted positions: he was a puppet whose strings old age has snipped. Even his attempts at masturbation now fizzle; in his mind's eye he runs the images of those moist, knowing engulfments, those grotesque postures of submission, but, just when he almost has it, has it in hand, the temperature or edge or whatever it is unexpectedly slithers away. The triggering mix of brute mechanics and sentimental illusion dissipates. The secret flees. The system crashes. The workable parameters, once so broad there was ample room for fatigue and ambivalence, draw in. At the far extreme of his pilgrimage, the self-induced orgasms of early adolescence recede. None since have been so intense, so absolute an escape. Similarly, he looks at the contents, the well-made furniture and lustrous crockery, of his present excellent white seaside house and cannot conjure upon them the Christmas gleam, the excited metaphysical urgency, that the shabby homely things in his grandfather's house—the brass candlesticks and embroidered table runners, the paltry few books and toys and vases—had possessed in the pale December windowlight.

What remains to him are moments of tender regard, in nakedness or on the way to it. Vanessa always achieved orgasm, but there was something brisk, even dismissive, in her way of seizing it, as opposed to Alissa's whimpering, finger-sucking dissolution in cascading ripples of sensation that delivered her to what always seemed a fresh surprise. Dear Faye, apparently, flirted on the edge, but with an infectious, innocent gaiety that made her easy to love. Karen had been the least trouble; to her in her generation it had been no big deal, like a coffee break or a spasm of exercise after sitting too long on an airplane. No, this is not fair. She, too, and Jacqueline and Antoinette and Mirabella, especially Mirabella with her spun-sugar hair, brought transcendent value to the act, the supreme interaction. People must be romantic or fail to lift themselves above the deadpan copulation of sheep and squirrels. Phyllis's impatient permission, in that Cape Cod cabin smelling of salt air and pine sap—*Let's just do it*—set an unfortunate grudging tone, perhaps, but did let him enter a realm wherein his own mysterious existence needed no explaining. Things come, for the instant, clear. Owen's past is like a sheet of inky-blue tissue paper held up to a light, so the holes pricked in it shine: these stars are the women who let him fuck them.

It was a celibate villager who wrote, "We know not where we are. Beside, we are sound asleep nearly half our time. Yet we esteem ourselves wise, and have an established order on the surface." Such a surface order makes possible human combinations and moments of tender regard. It is a mad thing, to be alive. Villages exist to moderate this madness— to hide it from children, to bottle it for private use, to smooth its imperatives into habits, to protect us from the darkness without and the darkness within.

PENGUIN ESSENTIALS

AGE OF IRON/J. M. COETZEE

'Care: the true root of charity. I look for him to care, and he does not. Because he is beyond caring. Beyond caring and beyond care . . .'

Capetown, South Africa. Mrs Curren, a dying classics professor, is writing to her daughter in America. Having quietly opposed apartheid all her life, she is suddenly confronted by its true horrors: the burning of a township, the persecution of her servant's son, the murder of an activist who seeks sanctuary in her home. When a homeless man appears on her doorstep, Mrs Curren gradually awakens to her own complicity in a regime of iron in which no soul can survive unblemished . . .

'Remarkable' *Wall Street Journal*

PENGUIN ESSENTIALS

BROOKLYN/COLM TÓIBÍN

'In the United States there would be plenty of work for someone like you and with good pay.'

It is Ireland in the early 1950s and for Eilis Lacey, as for so many young Irish girls, opportunities are scarce. So when Father Flood speaks of a job in New York, Eilis knows she must go.

Living in a crowded lodging house in Brooklyn, Eilis is far from home – and homesick. Yet after taking her first tentative steps towards friendship, and perhaps something more, Eilis thinks she might find happiness. Until bad news sends her back to Ireland, where a terrible dilemma awaits her – a devastating choice between duty and love.

'Unforgettable' *Spectator*

PENGUIN ESSENTIALS

THREE NOVELS/CÉSAR AIRA

Three novels by the cult Argentinian writer

In *Ghosts* a new apartment block is haunted by a collection of spectres, beguiling and threatening the life of the daughter of one family. *An Episode in the Life of a Landscape Painter* follows nineteenth-century German artist Johann Moritz Rugendas on an expedition in Argentina at the behest of his friend, explorer Alexander von Humboldt. Finally, in The Literary Conference, one Cesar Aira is attempting to take over the world using an army of Carlos Fuentes clones.

'Once you've started to read Aira, you don't want to stop'
Roberto Bolaño

PENGUIN ESSENTIALS

LIBRA/DON DELILLO

'Think of two parallel lines. One is the life of Lee H. Oswald. One is the conspiracy to kill the President. What bridges the space between them? What makes a connection inevitable? There is a third line. It comes out of dreams, visions, intuitions, prayers, out of the deepest levels of the self.'

A troubled adolescent endlessly riding New York's subway cars, Lee Harvey Oswald enters adulthood believing himself to be an agent of history. This makes him fair game to a pair of discontented CIA operatives convinced that a failed attempt on the life of the US president will force the nation to tackle the threat of communism head on.

Libra is a gripping, masterful blend of fact and fiction, laying bare the wounded American psyche and the dark events that still torment it.

'An audacious blend of fiction and fact' *The Times*

PENGUIN ESSENTIALS

THE PURSUIT OF LOVE/NANCY MITFORD

**'He was the great love of her life you know.'
'Oh, dulling,' said my mother, sadly, 'One always thinks that.
Every, every time.'**

Longing for love, obsessed with weddings and let's not even mention
the mysteries of sex, Linda and her sisters and cousin Fanny are on the
hunt for the ideal lover. But finding the perfect match is much harder
than any of the sisters had ever dreamed. Linda is first courted by a
Tory MP and then becomes embroiled with a handsome but humourless
communist, before she risks everything on a chance at real, head-over-
heels love in war-torn Paris . . .

'Peerless' Zoë Heller

PENGUIN ESSENTIALS

AUSTERLITZ/W. G. SEBALD

**'The longer I think about it the more it seems to me that we
who are still alive are unreal in the eyes of the dead, that only
occasionally, in certain lights and atmospheric conditions, do we
appear in their field of vision.'**

In 1939, five-year-old Jacques Austerlitz is sent to England on a
Kindertransport and placed with foster parents. This childless couple
promptly erase from the boy all knowledge of his identity and he grows
up ignorant of his past. Later in life, after a career as an architectural
historian, Austerlitz – having avoided all clues that might point to his
origin – finds the past returning to haunt him and is forced to explore
what happened to him fifty years before . . .

'An extraordinary, mesmeric story' *Observer*
